W9-CSF-893

MEARS
Mears, Emmie, author.
Look to the sun :a novel

BOOKS BY EMMIE MEARS

A Hall of Keys and No Doors

EMMIE MEARS

LOOK TO THE SUN

A NOVEL

Livonia, Michigan

Editor: Jamie Rich
Proofreader: Tori Ladd

LOOK TO THE SUN
Copyright © 2021 Emmie Mears

All rights reserved. No part of this publication may be reproduced, distributed, or transmitted in any form or by any means, including photocopying, recording, or other electronic or mechanical methods, without the prior written permission of the publisher, except in the case of brief quotations embodied in critical reviews and certain other noncommercial uses permitted by copyright law. For permission requests, please write to the publisher.

This book is a work of fiction. The characters, incidents, and dialogue are drawn from the author's imagination and are not to be construed as real. Any resemblance to actual events or persons, living or dead, is entirely coincidental.

Published by BHC Press

Library of Congress Control Number: 2016954061

ISBN: 978-1-64397-157-5 (Hardcover)
ISBN: 978-1-64397-158-2 (Softcover)
ISBN: 978-1-64397-159-9 (Ebook)

For information, write:
BHC Press
885 Penniman #5505
Plymouth, MI 48170

Visit the publisher:
www.bhcpress.com

For Tamara Mataya,
a damn fine author and even better friend,
who was kind enough to share her name with Beo.

And for anyone who has ever been told
they don't deserve to exist in dignity and equality,
this is for you too.

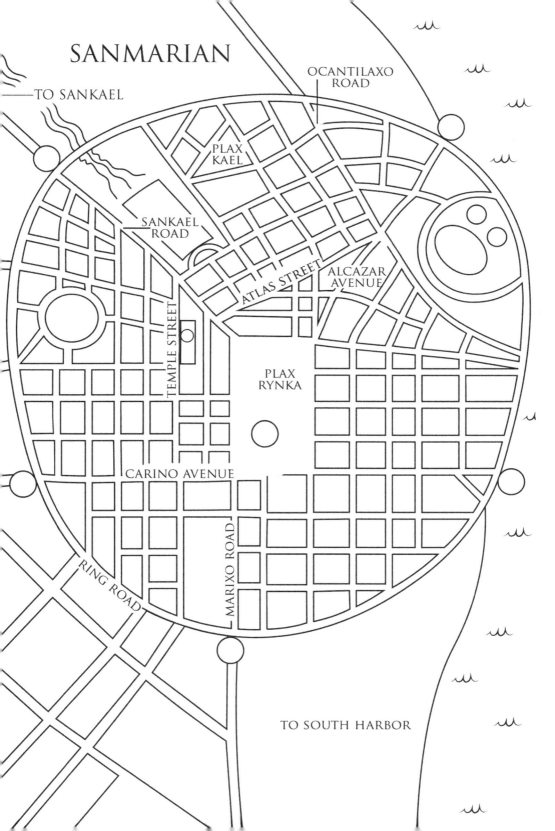

What the gods have sundered
let us at long last make whole
for you and I, Beloveds, you and I?
We share one soul.

Before voices
Before names
Before hands
We knew

All these things that now exist
Began with look, smile, laugh, and handshake
We were love before we kissed.

— From *Red Sunrise* by Mikael Iris —

LOOK TO THE SUN

CHAPTER ONE

S ome days are sneaky.

They wake beside you, stretching in your bed, handing you your house shoes, quietly toasting your bread. While you clean your teeth, they boil the water for your tea. They lull you into that bleary-eyed bliss of the mundane until you believe the day will be like so many others, that you will kick off your shoes at the end of the day much the same way you put them on, as the person you were when the soles of your shoes crossed the threshold of your front door.

But then some small snap occurs. A missed tram. A lost pocketbook. Smoke rising from your office. An egg thrown at your autocar. Getting marooned in the lift just as you're meant to meet with your boss. A bird splat. A bomb. A revolution.

Even more insidiously, sometimes even the winding steps of the mundane troubles only manage to hide within them something bigger, something worse.

Today was a sneaky day.

The sky had a ceiling, and Rosenni Abernethy smelled fire on the wind.

Her small yellow autocar had gotten her through the past fifteen years since Papa had died, and as she pulled the acceleration lever, she willed it with all her might to get her through the final ten minutes of her drive over the bumpy cobbled streets of Sanmarian's city centre.

She was already late for work. Everything had been fine until her toe found the corner of the sofa, and the jolt had sloshed tea onto her chest. Now the hibiscus tea stain was fading to pale pink on the white linen overshirt she hadn't had time to change. The sole of one shoe had inexplicably fallen off, and her only other suitable pair pinched. And then everything else had unraveled like Papa's old grey jumper she couldn't make herself throw away.

A seagull dropped a watery splat on her leather satchel. It took four tries to start the autocar, and one of the ignition buttons stuck on the fourth try, causing the red lights on the dash to flash in panic until she pried it unstuck with a long thumbnail. The streets were packed with traffic, the sound of blaring horns filled the air, and even though the world cooled itself toward the promise of winter, a sheen of sweat took up residence on Rose's upper lip.

The autocar coughed.

"Be reasonable," she told it. "You just got a patch-up last week. Your oils are fine, you've plenty of fuel, and I fixed your button so you didn't die. You owe me."

In response, the autocar's cough became a screeching whine, and the gear exchange suddenly began to vibrate like a hummingbird's wings.

"This is not..." Rose trailed off as the autocar sputtered to a halt on the slope of Carino Avenue and began to roll backward, bumping over each cobblestone. She stomped on the floor brake and yanked the brake lever at once. "...happening."

A horn bawled behind her.

Rose looked at the steering wheel. The shiny round circle at its centre seemed to look back innocently.

"Thanks awfully," she said.

Craning her neck to look over her shoulder, Rose saw her first small flash of luck for the day.

Maybe seagull shit was a reminder that the gods were getting around to her luck after all.

On the edge of the road was a single gap in the usual bumper-to-bumper parked autocars. With a feat of skill even her Aunt Aleis would have to give grudging approval over, Rose shifted the autocar into neutral and, leaning on the horn button with one hand and steering with the other, slid the reverse-rolling vehicle into the gap. The tyre bumped the kerb and scraped along the stones, but she avoided hitting the bumper of the black autocar behind her and squeaked to a halt. Rose engaged the floor brake, put the useless yellow lump of a vehicle into park, and sat back, head lolling against the seat bench.

She gave herself a count of three to pity herself for such an ill start to the day, then gathered her leather satchel (now wiped clean of seagull splat), patted the familiar lump in her trouser pocket where her father's fob watch always dwelled (its ticking was quiet, but no matter how loud her surroundings, Rose could always feel it), and opened her door to step out into the street.

Her toes protested in their too-tight shoes. If she was fortunate, once she got to work she could take them off and nurse her feet to some semblance of health before day's end. She'd need it. Work was now a thirty minute walk across the Plax Rynka, the central square of the city that used to house actual markets more than the now-customary thrice annually.

Outside in the dusty morning air, the sun filtered red-gold through the city haze. Sanmarian's Xaran Tower was just visible over the shops and tenements that lined Carino Avenue, pink-red and glimmering softly. Rose couldn't tell if the fire she smelled on the air was a fault of the car or the exhaust from the others or something else. It prickled at her nose as she rounded the rear of her yellow lumpmobile and stepped up onto the kerb. Normally she took the ring-road around Sanmarian's walls, driving until the fortress towers rose before her and turning southward then into the city's inner centre. Today, though, on foot, she would cut directly across the market square and have to have to walk all the way up the hill toward the fortress.

Sanmarian was called the City of Towers, which Rose had always found grossly unimaginative because there were nine and it was too obvious a derivative name. The city walls and towers—and nearly all its buildings within the walls—were made of sunset stone, a denser sandstone that over the past several centuries had slowly, slowly lost the cracks between its blocks, becoming its own mortar and fusing into the cohesive pink-red, uneven and gritty on the palms but strange and beautiful and glittering in the light.

At least, visitors to Sanmarian said it was strange and beautiful. Rose, who had lived in the city from the time she first had mucous scooped from her newly opened mouth and pierced the air with that first screech of *I'm alive!*, found it beautiful but not at all strange.

Most days, Rose could smell the sea's tang over the dust of the city; always there was the cry of gulls on the wing. Sanmarian wore the jewel-blue Tarenr Sea like a mantle on all sides but one. Only one road ran out of the city to Sankael, the capital of Kael, in the northwest. On maps as a child, Rose had always fancied Sanmarian's dangling peninsula like a dewdrop just about to fall. It was a small city. Not many people came in or out when it came to settling or relocating, though in summers the market square was often crowded with tourists. Strategically superfluous and rather pointlessly defensible, Sanmarian was mostly cut off from the rest of the country (and the continent), and Rose liked it that way. Mostly.

Sanmarian had its own troubles to worry about. Rose sniffed the air again, certain the fire smell was getting stronger. Her feet ached, secondary to the creeping anxiety she felt at the scent on the winter breeze.

She made her way up Carino Avenue toward Xaran Tower. Autocars passed through the tower gates, but pedestrians passed through the foot-gates on either side of the avenue. There were no longer any actual gates—far too impractical with vehicle traffic—but everyone still called them gates anyway. On the other side, the avenue narrowed, the cobbles grew bumpier, and the buildings seemed to inch closer together. Lampposts doused for the day, refuse bins freshly emptied, the rhythmic rumbling of tyres on stones. There was something Rose very much liked about mornings in Sanmarian.

Ahead, she could see Market Tower (another truly creative name—Rose had always called it the Tower of Stories as a child, because it housed the library). Also up ahead, Rose heard shouting. Not just one person shouting.

She passed the last cross street before the Plax Rynka, footsteps slowing warily, louder now that the autocar traffic had given way to the pedestrian zone of the city centre. Rose could hear what sounded like a hundred voices. Sound sometimes ricocheted oddly in the city—something about the nature of the sunset stone, Papa had told her once. Not seeing anything up ahead, Rose quickened her pace again. The cool morning air felt suddenly warmer. Fifty metres before Carino Avenue gave way to the expanse of the plax, Rose saw why she'd smelled fire on the wind.

A mob of protesters poured onto Carino Avenue, holding signs and flaming torches that gave off an acrid bite. Their illuminated faces glowed orange even in the pinkish morning light. Rose didn't have time to get out of the way. One of the protesters slammed into her shoulder, shoving her into the wall of a hat shop. She gritted her teeth, inhaling deeply and striving for a blank face. That was what Papa had taught her, in the years before when Sanmarian often surged with unrest between the progressive magistrate that had governed the city and the fascist party that usurped control from her. Rose had been too young to fully understand it then, but before Papa died, the city had changed hands what felt like once a year.

Rose didn't know who these protesters were or what they wanted. Some of the signs held slogans that said things like *JUSTICE* and some of the signs had photographs of faces. Others simply held a symbol of a scale. That was new. Rose didn't recognise any of the faces on the signs from newspapers, but then, if they were protesting the NPV, the ruling National People's Voice party, she wouldn't. Any faces that vanished from the earth at the hands of the NPV wouldn't show up in a newspaper they controlled.

She edged her way away from the wall, the linen of her overshirt catching on the stone. Her heart had decided to hurry its beat in her chest, and the tips of her fingers felt numb. Her feet, too, though that was the shoes and not the anxiety of being surrounded by an angry mob.

Tightening the strap on her satchel so that the leather sat snug against the small of her back, Rose kept to the edge of the throng, pushing toward the market square as carefully as she dared.

The shouts of the protesters rang loud in her ears. Cries for justice, nothing in unison, just the pulse of anger that wormed its way into Rose's blood and quickened her heart and her feet and her breath.

Someone came pushing directly at her, torch in hand. Rose scrambled to her right ducking her head—and her loose black waves—away from the fire. Her shoulder met another protestor's. Someone's foot found hers. She stumbled. A hand caught her, and for one moment, Rose looked up into a pair of kind eyes the colour of the peat soil Great Aunt Aleis sent away for to tend her plants. Then the grip on her arm vanished, as did the kind eyes, and her hip ran into a fist. The sign grasped by the fist slapped her in the face. Panic gave a harsh leap in Rose's belly. The blows—none seemingly out of malice or intent but blows nonetheless—kept coming. Rose stumbled forward as best she could, the kerosene that fed the torches stinging her eyes and nose. Her face felt at once tight from the passing heat of fire and slack from oozing sweat. Then the crowd shuddered around her, squirting her out onto the wide open plax and into the sun that had only just crested the tops of the sunset stone buildings, peeking around Market Tower as if it were apprehensive about what it might see.

Rose lurched, tripped, then managed to steady herself on a rubbish bin.

In the wake of the mob, the market square of Sanmarian felt still, silent. Even though Rose could still hear their shouts in the distance, they seemed muted as if she had walked through a wall of seawater instead of simply crossing the line between Carino Avenue and the square. Everything grew still, even the breeze. Fluttering pamphlets and bits of singed fabric fell to quiet repose on the cobblestones. Still. Too still.

Rose's hand flew to her left pocket and encountered a dangling metal chain. The watch, that comforting lump of metal that she felt ticking against her hip every day. Her father's watch.

It was gone.

· · · · ·

Papa always smelled of wool and pipe tobacco. Sanmarian lay far closer to the sea than to the nearest sheep, but still Papa's jumpers with their thick wooden buttons wore that ovine scent and the sweet, yet-unburned smell Rose could almost taste. When she pressed her face into the folds of knitted warmth, she heard his heartbeat, always, always with the faint ticking of his fob watch to accompany it. Left pocket. She felt it sometimes when her hug was crooked, and Papa would laugh and pull out the watch to show her.

The watch was crafted in that way that whispers gently that hands made every centimetre of it. Every edge of crystal beveled, every gear coaxed into order, every curve of brass celebrated. It felt like magic to Rose's young fingers, smelled of brass and glass. Such things indeed have a smell, and forever to Rose, brass and glass together would smell of magic. The watch was in the book, in *her* book, in *Red Sunrise*, and when Rose would muster the courage some sleepy nights to ask after the why of it, her father would mould a mystery from the sly smile of his lips.

"Believe," Andreas Abernethy would say, and it was all he would say, and Rose's eyes would drift toward closing and she would try. And before sleep blanketed her view with the ticking of her father's watch close beside her, she would *try* to believe if only to erase that always-accompanying ripple of pain from Papa's eyes.

And always, always, before the ticking faded with his footsteps, she would fall to sleep before she could see if it worked.

Rose stood on the market square of Sanmarian, twenty years beyond the sharpest memories of those sleepy moments and fifteen past the day she had returned home from walking out with her best mate Amelie for ices and fizzy drinks to find Great Aunt Aleis with tears dripping down the wrinkles in her face and horror hiding behind her guarded eyes. Their errand had been thwarted by the shop closing early, and when Rose arrived home, she would wonder only for a moment at the plumes of smoke arising in the city outside the window before looking at Aunt Aleis's face. Aunt Aleis had said nothing at first, only pressed the pocket watch into Rose's trembling hand—it smelled of rubbing alcohol, something Rose would never forget—and grabbed her into a hug so tight it nearly made the front and back of her ribcage meet. When finally Aunt Aleis could make words with her grief-weighted tongue, all she could say was, "There has been an accident, child."

Rose had fallen to her knees, gravity increasing so quickly she could not stand under the sudden weight. Her hand clasped the watch hard enough that the imprint of it would remain late into the night, the brass design of an exquisitely detailed rising sun branded on her palm, slightly askew.

That night, Sanmarian burned.

The next morning, the city still coughed smoke and damp ash, and it seemed the whole of the population fell silent with some overbearing grief that, while separate from her own, Rose would never stop feeling was the city her father loved wailing for his loss. Fifteen-year-old Rose had clasped the watch's chain to the belt loop on her trousers and tucked the watch into her left pocket, and there it had remained. Every day. For fifteen years.

And now it was gone.

Rose felt the sweat begin to chill on her brow as the breeze again picked up. She forgot about being late for work, forgot about the autocar parked five streets down the hill on Carino Avenue, and forgot about the state of her swiftly numbing feet. She turned round and darted away from the square, past the still-recovering passers-by whose faces were a series of blanks, not stopping until she reached the hat shop where the first of the protesters had run into her.

The distance between the hat shop and the square now seemed frightfully short. How had the distance been so stretched only moments before? Rose scoured the pavements and the cobbles of Carino Avenue, tracing and retracing and re-retracing her jagged path through the crowd. The ground wore litter like after a festival where only minutes before the streets had been swept clean and fresh for the dawning day. No matter how many crumpled papers Rose unfolded and gathered in a stack in her hand, no matter how she peered into cracks between the cobbles, no matter how many times she turned and backtracked only to go forward again, Rose could find no trace of the watch nor its remaining length of chain.

The bit of chain that dangled from the fob on her belt loop snapped against her hip with each step, an unfamiliar blip of sensation that made Rose feel as though the chain were electrified. Her breath lived high in her chest, close to the surface, never delving deep enough into her lungs to calm her. She felt lightheaded, feverish. The sun made its way past the tops of the buildings, rising alongside the tower. When the tower clock tolled out a heavy announcement of ninth bell—marking a full hour lateness for Rosenni Abernethy—she couldn't make her feet leave the mouth of Carino Avenue.

When finally she stutter-stepped onto the square again, Rose looked around as if she'd never seen the city before. The buzz of the square's hurried commuters was nonexistent; perhaps due to the protesters. She felt as if her hearing had taken leave of her, for the silence that fell. However it had come to be, Rose didn't know or care.

She found a bench halfway between the avenue and the tower that housed Sanmarian's library, her presence chasing a seagull from its perch on the end, where it squawked and winged into the air. Rose sat down and tried to remember how to breathe.

To an observer, the woman with perspiration-dampened waves and grey eyes reddened from smoke would look very sad indeed. But sadness was not uncommon in Sanmarian, not with the tensions so many in the city had simply grown accustomed to. To an astute observer, though, the sight of Rose Abernethy on that bench would show something else.

The ragged movement of her stomach and chest were very nearly a hiccough. The reddened eyes brightened the grey of her irises until they almost appeared silver with the sheen of yet-unshed tears. But it was the curve of her shoulders that really gave it away. They hunched inward as if maybe, just maybe, they could close the gap in her chest where grief had made its hole so long ago. An astute observer would likely recognise that look, the look of a body collapsing inward on itself. The look of a body that has lived so long with grief that it thinks the hole's just part of the landscaping until one day the owner falls right in again.

Rose had fallen in that hole.

Papa used to say that time was not a line, for a line was only one dimension, and people existed in four. To a young Rose, his proclamation had sounded like pure magic. Papa said that people exist in all of the time they touch, past, present, and future. Perhaps that was why Rose froze just then.

As she sat, she felt the open air of Plax Rynka around her, the knowledge of the citizens whose faces so seldom left their public stoic masks. Rose warred with the weight inside her and the knowledge that she was stranded here, in the city centre, far from anywhere it would be acceptable to feel what she felt. She was fifteen again, a hole suddenly reft in the fabric of her life. She pushed at the edges of the thing that came shoving, pushing, wrestling up from the deepest well in her chest.

And it did no good.

A moment later, any observer, astute or not, could see what Rose felt, for without moving her clawed hands from her knees or the satchel from where it sat lodged between her back and the bench, her chest heaved with a violent sob, and she cried.

CHAPTER TWO

Beomir Mataya's day was not at all sneaky. It woke him with that gasping bit of near-apoplexy when his head popped off the pillow to discover his alarm had not jangled, for he had set it for the wrong time altogether. His heart clanged round his ribcage instead. It wasn't as though he normally had somewhere to be early in the morning, but today he had an appointment.

He slapped the black curls atop his head with icy water from the faucet, grabbed a waistcoat a size too large (he kept meaning to take it to the tailor), threw his camera bag and portfolio over one shoulder, and hopped out the door on one foot, shoving his other foot into its shoe as he went. If he ran, he'd only be acceptably late, if unacceptably sweaty. Since the alternative was unforgivably tardy and an almost certain loss of income, Beo ran.

Beo hated being late.

The rest of the city seemed to feel his urgency, or rather, its own. Every passer-by stepped into his path. Autocars that would have certainly at least slowed in his home village of Viyarenyo today grabbed their acceleration levers in unison to thwart his crossings, and when the fortress towers came into view, one of them with its faithful clock face showing ten minutes past eighth bell already, Beo bid the last of his care over the dampness of his shirt goodbye and ran. Thankfully, he did so in a downhill direction, his feet enough used to the cobblestones not to send him sprawling.

Beo was not a runner.

He heard the shouting just as he burst onto the market square and saw the crowd of people closing in on him. They marched, of course, directly in his path to the coffee shop diagonal across the square to which he was late arriving. There were a lot of them. Hundreds. The sight of the scale on some of the protesters' signs first made Beo's neck tingle with excitement, quickly doused by the more rational anxiety of coming face-to-face with a very angry mob of protesters just this side of being rioters.

An involuntary glance back up the hill at the fortress from where he had come dried the saliva on his tongue and set his mouth to grimness. He wasn't sure if seeing the Liberation Front showing face in Sanmarian's city centre was a good sign or an ill one, but his sense said ill.

The only way to the café where his prospective buyer waited was through the crowd. He couldn't tell which way they were headed. With a chill in his shoulders and the sharpness of burning fuel in his nostrils, Beo realised the last time he'd heard tell of protests in Sanmarian was the year that took his two remaining parents from him. Of course, he had his aunt Irena, but she had been aloof at first when she arrived in Viyarenyo, her eyes digging through the words in the newspapers as if they could unearth some truth about Sanmarian burning, some way to make the ink swirl into new sentences that would reveal to her what the terse print would not. And Beo had been young and distraught at the loss of his fathers, the widening chasm of grief unfilled by the strange, sad woman who had sworn to care for him as his father lay dying.

Those thoughts in his mind, Beo pushed himself into the crowd, falling into step and edging as he could farther and farther toward the centre of the square. They would either go for Sankael Avenue at the northeast corner of the square or veer southward, and either way Beo reckoned if he were quick, he may just be able to skip round the edge of them and get ahead. The single convenient fact about marchers is that they tend to have a plan as to where they're going, rather than running willy-nilly about without warning.

Beo sidestepped to avoid the oily smoke of a torch, his eyes watering. Bodies pressed around him, hot and coiled tight like the springs his father used to use in his work. He felt a brief moment of triumph, and then a cry rose behind him. A surge of bodies like a parting sea shoved him roughly to one side, and in his confusion Beo turned toward the tumult instead of away. A pole made hard contact with his shoulder. Beo reeled away in pain, the initial impact unleashing a hot epicentre of jagged spasms.

A breath later, a foot found his, stomping down hard. He couldn't see where the edge of the mass lay now. Struggling to get back into the flow of the protesters and fighting the rising panic and irritation at his idea to go through instead of waiting for them to pass, Beo tried to let the crowd push him with them.

Finally, an opening appeared. Beo slithered through the bodies as if he were liquid, darting between shoulders and signs, clutching his bag close to his stomach. He burst out of the human din and into the centre of the square, aiming himself at Xaran Tower to the south to orient himself again. One quick glance to catch the direction of the mob, and Beo darted off toward Carino Avenue and the café that awaited him. He hoped for coffee.

His shoulder throbbed.

That was going to leave a mark.

· · · · ·

Café Maya was a small, cramped place (indeed, much of Sanmarian's many cafés and bars and dining places boasted the same, often in old buildings or below them, always smelling of sunset stone, whatever wares they sold, and sweat as often as not). The imported cypress tables were well-polished and well-used, and it was lit by warm brass lights that cast a yellow glow across the small dining area. Coffee and tea and small baked items sprang into being behind a wide, curved bar just as well-polished and well-used as any of the tables. Most of the places to sit sat only two or three comfortably. Only one window seat was available, and it was at that small table Beo's acquaintance sat, his espresso cup empty and crumbs and bits of rosemary from what appeared to have once been an egg tart littering a small plate like shrapnel.

Tarn Susette looked up as Beo approached, his face full of vague disapprobation. His iron hair was as thick as an adolescent's, drawn back from his face with pomade that left it in waves. His eyebrows remained as black as Beo's, though, with Tarn's carefully kept moustache somewhere in the middle, having not yet made up its mind of how far to age.

"I beg your pardon, Mister Susette," Beo said, reaching out his hand to shake Tarn's. An involuntary wince came along with the handshake. "There is a protest in the square, and I'm afraid they caught me up."

"Literally, it appears," Susette said, noticing Beo's wince. He motioned to the seat across from him. "Do sit down. I apologise for not waiting for you to order something; it took quite a long time to get into the city today, and I was rather famished."

Beo sat, smiled, and settled his camera bag and portfolio on his lap. Small talk Susette wanted, so small talk Susette would get. Beo rolled up the sleeves on his linen shirt, fastening them with their toggles. His arms welcomed the small movements of air on his damp skin as he saw Susette take momentary note of the tattoo that covered the expanse of his left forearm.

"The weather is quite fine today, though I imagine I would have found it a bit cold if I hadn't run into such a crowd." Beo gave Susette his most winning grin.

He'd let the protest be the reason for the lateness. It was as good an excuse as any.

A young server came to take his order, and Beo ordered a strong coffee over sweet milk and a Sanmarian specialty he'd grown quite fond of, a crescent bread stuffed with smoked oysters and sharp cheese with a sunny-side up egg served atop it.

Susette watched the retreating server with disinterest, then turned back to Beo, face neutral. "A protest, you say. Did you happen to note who they were?"

Beo chose his words carefully. "They had signs, but they didn't look familiar." He shrugged, the gesture as practiced as the lie. Never let your politics show in business, Irena had warned him when he'd been preparing to move to Sanmarian. She had been frantic at first, when he'd told her his plans. Still, she refused to tell him why. She had retreated to her room—she'd insisted on the smallest guest room even after Beo's father's death, something that had endeared her to Beo even when she showed him no particular inclination of care or love in those early days—and after several days of barely speaking to him at meal times, she seemed to resign herself to his choice. A few days after that, she began dispensing advice. This was after years of them living together. By then Beo could read affection in her fear and apprehension in the way she said she trusted he would do well.

When he asked why she felt so much anxiety at his moving to the city, she'd simply said, "Sanmarian makes meals of the unwary. And the wary." And that was the end of the matter.

Beo gave Tarn Susette a calculated smile and inquired about his show space at the gallery, listening as the man grew animated in response and passing his portfolio across the table, watching as the man paged through it and made small scribbles in a notebook, indicating page numbers of various prints.

Always make sure you let someone know your partnership isn't them doing you a favour, Irena had said. Make them bring something to the table.

Beo may not have fully understood why Irena heaped lessons upon him, but he had by then learned to take careful note of her words. Whatever it was that kept her awake long nights, sitting in the bay window on the wide purple cushion with tea that grew cold in the mug in her hands, Beo reckoned she'd earned that much, as well as whatever wisdom she deigned to share.

So he sat across from Tarn Susette and sipped his hot coffee and let the thick yolk of the egg run over the smoked oysters and yeasty bread, and he didn't let on just how much he needed this show, how much it would mean for his photography to show it in the Overlook Galleria, how much he needed to prove that he'd done what he set out to do in moving to Sanmarian.

At least until the shouting overtook the conversation from outside the window on Carino Avenue.

• • • • •

Beo, who faced the window and had already come close enough to the protesters for one day, lost immediate taste for his crescent bread. Suddenly, the sweet milk of the coffee stuck his tongue to the roof of his mouth, and from the way the rest of the café patrons went quite silent, Beo didn't think he was alone.

Susette turned in his seat, looking out over the rapidly filling street with intense brown eyes and a wholly unreadable expression. He muttered something under his breath that Beo couldn't quite make out, then, seeming to realise he was in full view of both protesters and gawking diners, Susette's already-thin lips became still thinner as he pressed them against one another.

The sounds of shouting filled the street outside and somehow burst through the glass without shattering it. Again Beo saw the signs and felt that odd mixture of nerves and hope. The Liberation Front had no proper name that he knew of beyond that name whispers gave them, but he did know they had been gathering followers for some time and that the fascists in charge hated them. The fascists hated everyone who wasn't an NPV flunky, so that in and of itself was nothing new, but watching the surging tide of people funnel through the avenue toward the ring-road or the Xaran Gate, Beo couldn't decide if seeing them organised en masse was brave or foolish. It was probably both.

The egg and oysters he'd eaten seemed to congeal in the pit of his stomach. The protesters continued to march as time plodded onward, and finally Maya herself, matriarch of the café and keeper of its recipes, exited the kitchen on light feet—Maya was a titan in both stature and presence—and politely bade Tarn Susette move that she might close the blind. The wooden slats descended with a rattle and a thwap. Maya said quietly that Susette's and Beo's breakfasts were on the house, and with that, she vanished back into the kitchen, arms loaded with empty crockery from the tables she'd passed on her way, and a clatter arose from the back of the café. Slowly, the sound of conversation indoors resumed, though hesitantly, with the air of ears still tuned to the shouts out of doors.

Beo and Susette made more small talk then. Neither desired to speak of the interruption, and instead discussed art. Susette favoured realism; Beo preferred the abstract. Susette found that surprising, given Beo's photographic focus on portraiture. Beo inquired after Susette's favourite painters and nodded politely at the answers, though in truth he found the names utterly boring. Beo sipped his coffee. He didn't much want it anymore. It mixed poorly with egg and oyster and anxiety in his belly.

When the sounds of the protesters faded, Susette passed Beo his business card, which Beo already had. On it, though, he had written a wire number to reach him in a week's time.

"Ring there next week," Susette said, wiping a stray crumb from his lapel and standing. He passed Beo's portfolio back to him, leaving small oil marks on the leather from his fingertips. "I shall have an answer for you then. Your work came on especially high recommendation from one of my colleagues, but I will need to verify our show schedule." Susette waited for Beo to nod, and he adjusted his waistcoat. Susette's waistcoat was not a size too large, and there was no hint of running-induced sweat to be found in his visage or attire.

Beo stood with him and shook his hand once more, managing to keep from wincing. He would have to examine his shoulder when he returned home; from the feel of it, he'd have turned purple-red by then.

"Thank you for meeting with me," Beo said. "I apologise again for my tardiness. Please pass on my thanks to your colleague for the recommendation."

"Think nothing of it," said Susette, and Beo couldn't tell from his tone if he meant it.

Susette left the café, and Beo decided to stay. The sweat on his back had cooled him to the point of cold, and he gave a small shiver, wiping away the grease marks left by Susette's fingers on his portfolio with a linen napkin. If this partnership worked out, Beo's portraits would be seen by the most influential art buyers in the city. The type that outfitted homes for the wealthy, chose what pieces could be displayed in the museum, made names for the artists. He had long since taught himself not to hope—hope was the luxury of those without much to lose or of those with little to gain—but at that moment he felt a not-unwelcome glimmer of maybe.

His nerves calmed enough for him to finish his coffee. He heard the clock toll in the square and decided to set out, leaving a five mark note on the table for the server even though she hadn't been seen since the protesters came through. He couldn't say he blamed her.

Outside, Beo blinked into the dusty sunlight. Carino Avenue was covered in rubbish. The air still stank of the torches. The sun's beams reached down over the rooftops, lighting the avenue at a diagonal with an obtuse triangle of light. Something shone in the beam, motes of the city's dust sparkling above it. Beo stepped down off the footpath and onto the street. That was most certainly metallic. He strode toward it, bending to nudge aside a crumpled bit of paper.

The watch lay on its face, fob snapped and dangling in a tail behind it. Beo picked it up, smoothing his thumb over the brass of its back. The pad of his thumb brushed the maker's mark, which he didn't recognise (a stylised R and V, which meant nothing; Beo Mataya was no great knower of watches). The mark was, like many others, two letters squished to become one symbol. Beo couldn't be sure what it stood for. He turned the watch over to get a good look at its face and promptly started.

The brass that made it was slightly scratched from the cobblestones, but the workmanship was clear in each line. It wasn't the craft that drew his surprise, however. The design was a rising sun, meticulous rays stretching from the horizon line two thirds of the way down from the top. The rays themselves were of varying lengths but interspersed with a rhythm that made the watch feel alive in his hand. He could feel a gentle ticking from the watch, and for some reason the knowledge that it had not broken in its fall filled him with relief. He depressed the release button on the top, and the sun sprang away from the clock face inside. Each numeral was still perfect black and lined in gold. The hands resembled aligned stars on delicate strings, and a small window at the bottom between the mechanism and the six showed the current phase of the moon, waxing gibbous, in blue and gold.

Beo knew this watch.

He couldn't help it; he had to make sure. With the single-mindedness of someone quite possessed by an impossibility, Beo hurried toward the square, not looking back or around him. He knew precisely where he wanted to be when he checked the thought that had burst into being in his mind the moment he'd turned that watch over in his palm.

Market Tower was not the most striking of Sanmarian's nine towers, but to Beo it was the best of them all. Squat and completed somewhat half-heartedly it seemed, the tower housed the city library. Though the shelves were emptier than they used to be—according to the librarians who, in occasional fits of pique, would blurt such things out in a whisper only to then fall silent—it was Beo's favourite place in the city outside his darkroom. It was there Irena had made sure he explored upon his arrival. He had written her a quite effusive letter of thanks after his first visit.

Now, he crossed the threshold without caring that the librarians at the desk were gathered in a huddle, foreheads creased like dog-eared pages and fingers worrying at the hems of their shirts or the edges of books to be shelved. Beo went straight for his usual reading place, on the third floor up the spiral staircase at the tower's centre. It was in a nook between the histories and the nature tomes, a plush chair that was probably red velvet once upon a time and now wasn't quite sure if it was brown or burgundy. But it was comfortable, and it was where he read. Only today he needed to read something very specific.

Beo opened his camera bag, wherein was tucked the obvious lenses, camera body, leather-lined brass canisters of film, a few crumpled notes about subjects, and fastidiously folded cloths to clean the glass. It was also home to the other item he was never without, a book so hungrily and copiously read that it was almost digested. Its spine was cracked in so many places the cover wouldn't stay on (Beo kept a leather thong looped around the red leather to keep its innards where they were and the outtards from flapping away in the wind). A few pages near the beginning were quite gone. However, the pages Beo needed were where they ought to be, a little over a chapter into the book. Beo knew the book so well he perhaps could have recited those missing pages from memory, and he found the passage he sought after unwinding the leather and thumbing around for only a few seconds.

...It was quite unbeknownst to Yosif how the watch had come into Vitar's possession, only that Vitar had known he had to keep it. He felt certain it had found him for a reason, indeed that it had found him and not the other way round. And he had given it to Yosif, a token of love. The rising sun that covered the numbers on its face was like the sun over the Tarenr Sea on a clear but hazy day, its beams reaching out in all directions, waving across the moisture in the air under the sky's blue canopy and reaching outward as if they knew they would encounter all things at once. The moon's shifting journey through her forms, the stars in hand—Yosif found that to be a treasurable thing, the hands that held stars as they danced through time—it all struck him as something truly...unique.

And it was his, this immeasurable gift.

Beo looked again at the watch. There was no doubt in his mind that this was the watch from the book. He'd never so much as met another person who had read it. He only had one copy of his own and had never seen another—the librarians had never heard of it, nor had the other centres they'd contacted—and yet here was something clearly designed directly out of it.

For the first time in a very long time, Beo Mataya felt small. Not in a belittled way, but in a gazing-into-the-starry-expanse sort of way that left him strangely affected and elated at once. He closed the book and wound the leather round it once again, tucking it back into his camera bag. His portfolio he now slid into the back pocket of the bag (it stuck out a fair amount and hit him in the side when he walked, but he was used to it). Rising from the chair and suddenly restless, he decided he would walk the city. Beo felt he had done the precise right thing by coming to the library to match watch with book, and now he felt the next right thing was to be mobile. He had to see this city, which existed both in and out of the book.

The librarians at the front desk noticed him this time as he left, two out of the three of them familiar to him. The two nodded in greeting, though they still looked preoccupied. Beo gave a small wave as he left.

Rounding the tower, Beo stopped short. There was a woman sitting on the nearby bench, and she was crying.

Her face was delicate and fine-featured, except for her chin, which was strong and just this side of being square. Her hair fell in loose black waves to her breasts, and a pinkish stain marred her overshirt, prominent enough that he could see it from where he stood. The same sort of pink stained her face in blotches. Her eyes—he couldn't tell their colour—were puffy. Her shoulders trembled.

Beo couldn't look away.

There was something complete about the woman's weeping, something vastly intimate and vulnerable about coming across someone in such a state. What could make someone's pain overwhelm them so as to lose their personal walls in so public a place? Beo knew what it had been for him, something he tried to keep out of his mental periphery as much as possible. But for this woman, he didn't know. Later, Beo would curse himself for the wrongness of his next instinct, but as he stood frozen on the cobblestones of Sanmarian's market square, the tower at his back, his hands searched out and found his camera.

His fingers assembled the necessary lenses without thought, and indeed his mind was engaged elsewhere as his hands worked. When finally he raised the camera to his eye, he was struck by the root of his impulse.

He needed to capture this moment of grief because he understood it. He needed to see, through the lens of someone else, a reflection of something he

She nodded, and Grenye herself— to Rose's surprise—set the kettle to boil on the small gas stove in the office kitchenette. Rose decided she must truly look a mess if Grenye wasn't making Roban do it.

"What do we have today?" Rose asked as the kettle began to heat, blue flame dancing beneath the metal.

"Mostly moving mints," Grenye said. "But if you're not feeling up to it—"

"I am." Rose interrupted, waving a hand. She needed a distraction. One thing she could always count on with Grenye: the older woman would take her at her word. Aunt Aleis or her other partner Helyne would fuss, coddle her, insist upon her resting. If Rose rested, it would mean sitting still (at least in Aleis's and Helyne's eyes), and sitting still would mean having to feel the empty pocket. Having to relive the morning's strangeness. Having to wonder who that stranger with the camera was. Having to guess at why here, in front of Grenye and Roban who she saw every day, Rose suddenly felt like she was cloudy and hazed when for one eternal moment in the square, she'd felt she was in perfect focus.

Rose needed to keep moving.

• • • • •

By the time Rose got home, her linen overshirt was stained with dust from her autocar as well as the morning's hibiscus, she smelled of four different types of mint, and she both dreaded and yearned for the removing of her shoes. She had met a mechanic on Carino Avenue to see about getting the autocar towed, and in helping him rig the tow chain had brushed her right shoulder across the length of the rear fender. It would be past the longest night before the autocar was repaired, and the sinking knowledge that she would spend midwinter walking to and from work drained the remaining energy Rose had to spare. Arriving home felt like an achievement.

Her flat was small and sparsely decorated, a secondhand grey sofa against one wall, an antique mahogany radio plugged in nearby that she seldom used because doing so required a high tolerance for horrid static even Helyne couldn't fix (but the radio had been Papa's and thus it stayed), and a few brass lamps with blue glass covers that cast a green-blue light over the room when she turned them on. She had a large shelf of books against the wall directly across from her, most of them from secondhand shops. Rose had run out of space and had begun stacking books horizontally on top of the upright spines until Helyne could get round to building her a new shelf. The kitchen was small, with hardly enough worktop space for cooking, which suited Rose well as cooking wasn't her strong point. The refrigerator had convinced her that it was the first on the planet by its age, but it still kept her milk and cheese cold enough not to spoil. The water taps were finicky enough that the water was either nearly boiling or nearly ice, and the wood floor bowed in several places. Rose—or rather, Aunt Aleis—had paid for the flat with the sale of the house Rose had shared with Papa and rented it to tenants until Rose was old enough to live there alone. Money wasn't tight, but it wasn't loose either. Her bank account creaked when she turned round too quickly, and she had to save up for the repairs the flat inevitably needed. New radiators. New windows. Once a broken set of pipes in the bath. Eventually new floorboards. But the flat was hers.

Her aunts had ensured it was outfitted with the necessities. A bookcase made by Aleis's partner Helyne, carefully applied wallpaper of dark green vines on a cream-coloured background Grenye had chosen, a very special wardrobe upon which Aleis insisted.

Rose sat down on the sofa, which gave easily under her weight. She shrugged out of her leather satchel's strap and let the bag fall to the cushion. She looked at her feet. Her ankles felt large. She hadn't had the nerve to remove her shoes at work, and several hours of moving crates of bundled mint—spearmint, peppermint, star mint, cacao mint—had left her arms sore and the skin of her ankles swelling at the leather tops of her shoes.

Slowly, she unbuckled the leather strap across the top of her foot. A sensation too painful to qualify as relief spread out over her foot with the sudden looseness. Gritting her teeth, Rose unbuckled the left shoe as well. Her skin expanded with zigzags of electric intensity as blood rushed into her feet. Her eyes prickled as she reached down to pull them off. She would need to get a new pair tomorrow; hopefully one of the shops would be open on the way in to work. Rose doubted Grenye would fuss if she wore her wool-lined leather clogs, but occasionally Rose did have to meet with clients, and she didn't want one of Aunt Aleis's favourite buyers dropping by to see Rose in shoes that looked better suited to a farm than Sanmarian's business centres.

Though if the swelling didn't go down, she may have to go barefoot.

Her stomach made a sound like the pipes in the kitchen did in early spring. Rose hadn't thought to consider supper. Just as she thought it, someone knocked at the door, a quick rap followed by a harder knock.

Aunt Aleis. She knew that knock. Rose pushed herself onto her swollen feet, cringing. Her skin felt full and stretched over her toes and ankles as if putting weight on her feet would make them pop. Hobbling to the door, Rose peered through the peep hole, more out of habit than anything. She unbolted the heavy lock and turned back the other two, tugging the door open and sliding out of the way.

Her pain must have shown on her face, because when Great Aunt Aleis bustled herself over the threshold smelling like curried fish stew—that was the sack in her hands, really, and not the woman herself—and pulling a gauzy scarf down from where it concealed the bottom half of her face, she looked Rose up and down.

"My gods, child, what did you do to your feet?"

"The sole fell off one of my shoes this morning. Had to wear an old pair. They pinch."

"Sit, sit," Aunt Aleis said. She was a tall woman, still Rose's height even at seventy-six and she had been taller. Aleis liked to tell people that she was slowly but surely donating bits of her height to the less fortunate, since she didn't need it anymore with her age.

Rose obeyed, sitting back onto the still-warm sofa cushion. Aunt Aleis locked the door behind her and took the sack of food into the kitchen, calling over her shoulder.

"I thought you might be hungry. Grenye told me about the autocar, and last I was over, you didn't have enough food to feed a rat."

A clatter from the kitchen cupboard suggested Aleis was hunting for dishes. The faucet turned on a moment later with a gurgle and a gush—and a grunt from Aleis, who didn't approve of the building's plumbing.

"I'm not sure anyone has enough food to feed a Sanmarian rat," Rose said. Her face felt warm, almost feverish. Now that she was sitting, the whole day felt heavy, weighing her down until she thought she might sink all the way into the sofa and end up in her downstairs neighbour's flat with bits of cushion fluff in her hair.

"You know what I mean." Aleis emerged from the kitchen with a large ceramic bowl of fish stew, spoon pressed between her thumb and the bowl's rim. She handed the dish to Rose, then knelt on the rug in front of the sofa. "You did work a dockworker's day on these, didn't you?"

The touch of her aunt's cold fingers on Rose's hot feet made her twitch, sloshing broth almost over the lip of the bowl.

"I need new shoes."

"I don't know why you've only had one pair this whole time." Aleis looked up at Rose, gently massaging Rose's left foot. Her eyes were dark brown, wide, and earnest. She almost always wore green. Her brown skin wore deep creases, but her hair had stayed mostly black into her sixties except the front, which was fully grey the colour of steel. The back had begun to change now, like the front bits were sending out rays bit by bit. Aleis's nose was straight and firm, like it had decided exactly how to be and intended to stay that way. Papa had had the same nose.

Rose ate quietly for a moment while Aleis massaged some feeling back into her feet. Her great aunt didn't make a habit of rubbing her feet, but Aleis was always good at caring for people, regardless of what they needed. Even if it involved rubbing the feet of someone who'd been hauling boxes for most of the day in too-tight shoes.

Getting back to her feet with a brusque pat on the tops of Rose's knees, Aleis went back to the kitchen. The faucet turned on again, and Rose could tell it was the hot water this time by the way Aleis cursed at having been splashed. The cupboards opened and banged shut.

Rose shut her eyes, the bowl of stew balanced now on her legs. Her right thumb worried at the moonstone ring on her middle finger. The ring was one of the three things she always kept with her. It had been Aunt Aleis's ring, and Aleis had given it to Rose when she was sixteen, a year after Papa died when Rose kept waking up screaming in the middle of the night.

"Moonstones bring good dreams," Aunt Aleis had told her then.

Rose was never sure if the ring really helped or if just believing in it made it work, but the nightmares stopped after that. It never really seemed to bring good dreams, anyway. Especially when she ate curry.

The ring, the book, and the watch. Three things Rose was never without. Her pocket felt as large as the sea and as empty as a ruin. At least she still had the book, and more than one should she need to replace that. Rose would have rather lost either ring or book. The former owner of the ring was still quite well and clanking around her kitchen. Rose had an entire crate of the same book— why, she didn't know, since she had inherited it from her father—so if that had been lost, she could have replaced it. As it stood, the copy in her satchel was her sixth, having worn out five others until their covers sighed and gave up and their spines split and their pages fell out like teeth.

Thinking of the book made Rose think of the man with the camera, and of his tattoo.

A sloshing sound made her open her eyes again. Aunt Aleis was coming toward her with a copper basin of steaming water. She set it at Rose's feet. It smelled like mint. Star mint, if Rose's nose didn't lead her astray. More mint. She wanted to laugh (or perhaps cry) but managed a wan smile.

"In," Aleis said.

Rose set her bowl on the coffee table and rolled up her trousers. She lowered her feet into the basin, biting the inside of her cheek at the temperature. The star mint in its mesh bag turned the water a pale yellow-green like a giant cup of tea. It made her feet tingle, and her blisters stung so much she winced. Star mint was one of the more potent mints.

There was a long pause where all Rose could hear was her and her aunt's breathing and the small ripples of the water in the basin when she moved.

"Grenye said you lost Andreas's watch today," Aleis said finally.

The top of Rose's mouth tightened, and she couldn't swallow for a moment. "I got swept up in a protest. Something must have caught the fob and ripped it from my pocket."

"The watch wasn't him," Aunt Aleis said.

"It feels like it was," Rose replied.

Aleis's mouth pinched in an expression of pity, but behind it was the same haunted look Rose always saw when anyone brought up Papa. Aleis had raised him, she and Grenye and Helyne. He was more a son than a nephew.

A loud boom echoed through the city. Rose jumped, her feet splashing water over the edge of the basin and onto the rug. Miraculously, her stew didn't spill onto her trousers. She lifted the bowl, looking to the window where the drapes were drawn almost all the way, exposing only a sliver of night sky lit by golden lamps against the deep blue. Rose's chest shrunk in on itself, and suddenly the heat of the water and the cool of the tingling mint on her feet made her feel hot and cold and claustrophobic all at once.

"That came from the Sea Tower," Aleis said, eyes also on the window. Then she looked back at Rose and snapped her mouth shut.

Rose couldn't remember the last time a cannon had been fired in the city, but it seemed Aleis did. Her great aunt's face grew dark and troubled.

"Are you all right, Auntie?" Rose asked.

Aleis patted Rose's leg, then walked to the window where she drew the drapes the rest of the way, obscuring any view of the city. "Quite all right, my dear."

And then she changed the subject to the week's orders and the tea room and Helyne's new dining table she built for a wealthy couple that lived on the sea cliffs outside the city, but Rose couldn't feel relieved.

When Aleis stood to leave, Rose padded to the door to let her out, her feet feeling as sensitive as a newborn's, chilled by the menthol and tingling.

"I'll tell Grenye you'll be in at ten bells tomorrow so you can get some new shoes." Aleis pressed a thousand-note into Rose's hand and kissed her cheek. "Get two pairs, dear."

"Aunt Aleis," Rose looked at the money, which was nearly a week's wages. Aleis hadn't handed her money in years. "This is too much."

"Then use the rest to fix the damned faucet," said Aunt Aleis. She gave Rose a small smile, patted her on the shoulder, and started to close the door behind her. She paused. "Promise me something, Rose."

"What?"

"If you find yourself near another protest, leave. Get away however you can. Promise me."

Bewildered, Rose nodded. "I promise."

Aunt Aleis gave Rose a none-too-comforting look in response to Rose's puzzlement. "You'd be too young to remember the tumult. Your Papa..."

Rose waited for Aleis to finish the sentence, but the old woman stopped and shook her head.

"Have a care you stay far away from any of that is all," Aleis said. "Things have been quiet for most of your life, but an old woman's memory is long."

"I'll be careful."

"Chances are, you've no need to be too cautious." Although Aleis chuckled, Rose didn't believe her levity for a second. Rose had eyes; she'd seen the defaced NPV propaganda posters around the city. She had ears to hear the whispers. And her body too-well remembered the unintentional blows of the passing throng on Carino Avenue.

Some time later, lying in her bed, Rose thought her mind would never give way to her body's exhaustion and let her sleep. Her thoughts spun through her promise, the protest, the cannon, the throbbing of her feet, the car that needed fixing, the loss of the watch.

And the man. She'd only seen him for a bare moment. The barest of moments. That tattoo was from *Red Sunrise*, she knew it was. Rose had never met another soul outside her family who had read the book. Rose knew its characters as well as she knew her own kin. Like Yosif Milabr, Rose had had and lost the watch. And like Remir Roxa, the man with the camera had the same tattoo. Rose didn't want to meet the same fate as Yosif and Remir, but something tugged at her, deeper than she'd felt anything reach in several turnings of the calendar wheel. She felt like Remir and Yosif during their first haunting waltz, could almost hear the strains of the dulcimer's ghosting chords, so vivid that she could have lived the moment instead of simply having read it.

Rose couldn't shake the compulsion she felt. Hours came and went before sleep finally took her, but when it did, she had already decided to find him.

CHAPTER FOUR

B eo usually loved the metallic sting of developer in his darkroom. Today, it washed over him and prickled pain at his temples. Stress, he surmised.

His shoulder hurt.

When he'd returned home finally after a long day at the gallery, he'd examined it in the mirror of his small washroom. A near-perfect rosette of red-purple stood out on his brown skin, small shock lines radiating out from the impact. Today, the red had faded to just plum, but Beo felt it every time he moved.

He agitated the tray of developer with the print in it. For once, he couldn't make himself look at the picture as clouds of black and grey began to form on the surface of the paper. He'd already developed the other negatives; the room's lines were full of drying prints. Beo kept this one for last, but even so, trusting to the test strip and the dull ticking of the timer, he didn't want to see the image emerging.

The timer pinged, and Beo pulled out the print, washing it in water. He submerged it in the stop bath without looking at it. If the image didn't turn out or was poorly exposed, he'd just print it again and look at it then.

His nose was full of the acid tang of the darkroom, and Beo ignored the blossoming headache behind his eyes. Ping. Rinse. Fixer. Rinse. Clear-all. Rinse, rinse, rinse.

Minutes clicked by with the small brass timer. When it pinged for the end of the final rinse, he pinned up the print on the scarce remaining line space and left the room.

Leaving the darkroom didn't much help. The first thing he saw was the pocket watch on his rickety dining table that sat in the centre of his very small three room flat. Beo didn't like that he'd left it there. He picked it up, feeling the walls closing in on him.

The prints would take a while to dry, and Beo tucked the watch into his left pocket. The chain dangled out of the pocket; he would have liked to see it with its proper fob. He pulled on a pair of loose leather boots, tossed his waistcoat on the sofa where he never sat, and shrugged into his thick winter coat, wool-lined black tweed with tails to his knees. The day had dawned colder than those before it, late autumn hinting at the coming winter.

A gust of wind whistled through the corridor of his building when he opened his front door. Bolting the door, he pulled his jacket tighter around him. Beo trotted down the three flights of stairs and out into the street.

The wind was louder outside, the narrow, crooked Altas Street forming a near-perfect wind tunnel. The wind almost always came in from the south, from the open sea, and Altas Street ran from the city walls. Wind coming up from the south seemed to flow over the sunset stone and whip northward. The bronze sign fixes for the few shops on the street caught the wind and flapped and clanked and wailed.

Beo turned north, the wind at his back. A few autocars drove on the single-direction street, their exhaust billowing up behind them like clouds. The Lionfish pub stood at the merging of Altas and Alcazar, and Beo liked it for the way it seemed to provide a bulwark for the housing buildings that lined both streets. The sunset stone looked red-brown in the dusky air, the clouds above skirting the city as if they were in a hurry.

The pub door was heavy cedar, and at one point the designs carved into it may have had significance. Now they simply looked knobbly and worn, and Beo liked things like that.

The barman inside looked up when Beo entered, giving a quick wave. The pub hadn't quite filled for the evening yet, and whenever Beo came in this early, he felt like an egg rolling around in a basket.

He sat down at the bar. Yoan came over a moment later with a mug of spiced wine that wasn't for Beo. It smelled good, though, so Beo asked for one of his own.

When Yoan returned with it, a burgundy drip slipping down the side of the terra-cotta tankard, Beo took it to warm his hands.

"You're in early," Yoan said. He nodded over Beo's shoulder to a passing regular, then looked back at Beo.

"Needed to get out of the house."

Yoan didn't respond to that, though Beo knew he understood.

Seventeen months ago, Beo had arrived at the pub at a full sprint, sweat dripping from his face from heat and terror, barely able to string together a sentence. Yoan had been the one to catch him just before he collapsed on the floor and, unable to get a coherent answer out of him, had sent someone to Beo's flat, where they'd found Zara, Beo's ex-lover, hanging from an exposed pipe in the tiny kitchen.

Since then, Beo didn't have to explain anything to Yoan. It was nice having a friend he didn't need to explain to; Beo had put himself back together mostly, though he couldn't afford to move out of the flat where he'd found Zara dead after her suicide.

Some days being within those walls got to be too much. It'd been a while since Beo had a day like that, and the bulge of the watch in his pocket and the drying print in his darkroom were certainly the reason behind it. His emotions were at full tilt. It made sense. He just didn't have to enjoy it.

Beo sipped the wine and asked Yoan about his day, grateful for the distraction.

Yoan talked about one of the other regulars getting full-bottled at half past midday and how he'd passed out with his forehead almost glued to a table. Beo laughed where he was supposed to laugh and Yoan pretended not to notice that it was fake.

After taking care of a few other patrons, Yoan paused in front of Beo. "Maro wanted to go to another meeting tonight. I can't, but if you want to go, I'll tell you where."

That got Beo's attention. Maro was a member of Liberation Front—or at least Beo suspected he was. Beo shifted his still-sore shoulder. "You're going with him now?"

Yoan shrugged, swiping a drip of rice liqueur from the wooden bar with a cloth. "You heard about the protest this morning?"

"Sounds familiar," Beo said drily.

"Things are tense," Yoan said. His tone closed the matter as he looked up when a new patron entered.

Tense. That was a way to put it. The uncertainty gathered in the city like tiny bubbles on the bottom of a cook pot. But it would pass. In spite of Irena's warnings, it always did. The NPV had Sanmarian in their grip, and no one else—no other party nor person—would change that. They ran the city and the country in relative peace, which was to say they left people alone. Mostly. Beo thought.

They just kill people who disagree. Beo remembered the members of Liberation Front who had recently died or vanished. He couldn't help but swallow. There had been other whispers of disappearances, and if there had been a rash of bad fish in the city, such things did happen.

"When are you off?" Beo preferred to change the subject. He'd left the house to escape that claustrophobic discomfort, and with talk of Liberation Front and secret meetings—because the meeting was undoubtedly secret—it had only shifted the feeling to a different area.

"Last bells."

"I think I'll stay here if that's okay."

Yoan gestured to the rest of the pub, which still hadn't filled up. "It's not like you're stealing seats from paying customers."

Beo raised his tankard to Yoan at that. Yoan asked how his meeting with Susette had gone, and for the next few hours, Beo was able to forget. He told Yoan about the woman in the square and how he felt as if he'd invaded her privacy. Yoan said he probably had, but didn't say it with judgment, and when he asked what the woman looked like and who Beo thought she was, Beo couldn't answer. He didn't tell Yoan about the watch. The wine helped, though the more he drank, the more he fancied he could feel the gentle ticking of the pocket watch through the linen of his trousers. It didn't help the headache, though. By the time last bell tolled out from the nearby tower, Beo's head pounded, and he'd drunk enough wine that it would be worse in the morning.

He stumbled home and kicked his bedroom door shut on the way to his bed. When he slept, all he could see was the face of the crying woman in his photograph, moving upon the page as she turned to look at him, over and over again.

The wine didn't help that either.

• • • • •

Beo woke with something pressing into his thigh. He fumbled under the duvet that lay half on and half off his bed. His hand found his pocket, where the watch was a warm lump of metal. Pulling it out, Beo looked at it. The watch still felt impossible, this piece of fantasy he'd stumbled across on a city street.

He plunked it on the bedside table, face down. He could still hear the ticking.

Lying face up on his bed, Beo stared at the ceiling. Five more days until he could ring the wire number Tarn Susette had left him. Until then, he had work at the gallery to keep him occupied, but only a few hours a day. It had been a long while since Beo felt so adrift.

The watch, which had seemed like a miracle when he found it, now felt unreal. He looked at it on his bedside table, the chain dangling with two tiny brass links trickling over the edge of the wood.

If he hadn't found the watch, he wouldn't have rushed to the library to look it up in *Red Sunrise*. And if he hadn't done that, he wouldn't have walked out to see the crying woman on the bench.

Beo shut his eyes. His head throbbed, and his shoulder felt tight, as if he'd slept on the bruise wrong. Which he probably had.

His chest felt almost as tight as his shoulder, but not for the same reason.

Prying himself off the bed, he half-lurched into the sitting room where his bag was still slung across the edge of the sofa. He pulled out the book again, thumbing through pages at random. He knew the story by heart. Beo wasn't looking for anything in particular, but every so often he'd page through the chapters when he felt lost.

He stopped around page twenty.

Yosif Milabr wore layers like the petals of a rose. On the outside, the petals that peeled back and splayed themselves to the rays of the sun, the petals wore a pale and bitter colour like brittle pages yellowed from exposure to light. Such was his outside, brittle and bitter and base. Those petals surrounded others, and inward they were stronger and present. Their colour knew itself, stalwart and stubborn. It knew it had not the brightness of those at the centre, nor did its colours fade to dust as did those at the edges. Milabr wore petals of shrewdness, of stealth, of sly movements in the snake-like streets of Sanmarian. He built those petals against one another, knowing most of those whose eyes fell upon the layers of those petals would see only the brittle bitterness outwith.

He knew this.

He counted on it.

Those outer layers were his armour. They concealed the most precious petals that remained tucked close together at the centre, guarding Yosif Milabr's most personal truth. And that truth was that at his core was love.

Beo set the book down carefully on the arm of the sofa, unexpected tears needling his eyes.

What was at his own core? Beo wasn't sure. Sometimes he thought he was Yosif Milabr's opposite, wearing love like the fabric petals of his clothing to disguise something rotting within, a worm-eaten hollow of a heart. If he had had love at his centre, perhaps Zara would still be alive.

He walked to the door of his darkroom and opened it, pushing back the heavy black curtain that shrouded the door against any accidental light when it was unwanted. The developed prints shuddered in the breeze he created.

Stepping directly to the one he wanted, he didn't let his eyes linger on it as he returned to the main room. Pulling back the drapes, he stood in front of his only large window, the sunlight stabbing at his hungover headache and his shoulder giving a small sympathy spasm for his head.

He looked down at the print.

It was developed perfectly, the exposure immaculate, the focus clear. Beo's gaze spiralled around the edge of the photograph, admiring the blur of the background cobbles and the slow directionality that led directly to her.

He made himself look at her face.

There it was again, that look of exquisite and complete grief. Her eyes, clear grey in the black-and-white photograph, seemed to look out through the developed image and directly through every defence Beo possessed.

That he had captured that look felt at once powerful and obscene. This was, indeed, the kind of shot every photographer yearned for, the kind of shot that transformed an amateur into an artist. The kind Tarn Susette would be begging to feature in the Overlook Galleria, where people would offer thousands of marks to own it.

The kind that would allow Beo to finally move out of this grief-soaked flat and into a new one, with new furniture, no memories, and stocked with automatic respect for his art.

And yet looking at it filled Beo with absolute and total mortification. Who was he to have preserved this moment of pain? What if, seventeen months ago, when he had collapsed on his knees at the pub in complete and total incoherent hysteria with Zara's swollen, purple face the only thing he could see, someone had photographed him there? How would he feel?

Beo's face heated with rushing blood, and he almost tore the photograph in half.

For the first time in his existence as a photographer, he felt as if he'd stolen something instead of displayed it.

A kind of fever overtook Beo as he set the photograph down on the sofa cushion. He went into the darkroom where his most recent negatives were hung, set, and prepped. He gathered them to bundle them off to Irena later in the day, after he decided if he needed to reprint any of the other photographs for his portfolio, but for now he only wanted the one. Beo picked up the negative, its size too small to show what its fully developed image did, but it still filled Beo with that sense of unease.

He carried it out of the darkroom, its edges between his fingers so as not to smudge it, and he pressed it between the pages of *Red Sunrise* that he'd just read. The photograph itself he placed in his portfolio between a portrait of a red-faced child mid-footstamp and a laughing old man with no teeth and an Honour Medal on his frayed lapel.

Beo's stomach churned, and though he knew he ought to eat something—preferably something made of bread and slathered in cheese—he ignored it. He gathered his bag and bundled himself in his jacket and scarf and set out for San-marian's market square, stopping only at the postal kiosk to send his negatives to Irena.

He knew it was probably futile, but he had to try and find her. To apologise for his imposition and...Beo didn't know what else. It was nearly the same time he'd last seen her in the square; perhaps he could find her there again.

· · · · ·

After two hours of wandering the market square unsuccessfully, Beo slumped onto the same bench where the woman had been sitting, displacing a gaggle of pigeons that cooed and bobbed their flustered little walks to escape. The square still seemed to have a hush over it. From the protest or something else, Beo didn't know.

Absently, he took out his camera. His style was portraits, but today he couldn't even think about photographing faces close up. Instead, Beo opened up his lens on the square itself.

He shot pigeons squabbling over scraps of twisted bread from the city centre's many stalls. A seagull scattering the pigeons. He caught the sun's rays through the clouds as they sent golden fingers out over the square's cobbles, but that was too like the watch, and it unnerved him. He photographed the clock just as it struck tenth bell. A hat mid-tumble in a gust of wind. A balloon in a child's hand. A group of people in uniform, pointing at a building across from the clock tower. Another seagull balanced atop a rubbish bin with its head through the hole.

Beo slowly felt his tension fade, though his head felt like it had been hurting for a month instead of a day. His stomach still sloshed with the after-drinking bile. He ignored it, finding crumbs of pleasure in shooting the mundane moments of Sanmarian's morning.

He had several hours before he had to be at the gallery, and as the sun rose higher in the sky, Beo decided to go home and nap to see if his head could recover in time. He didn't think hammering frames together would suit his headache any more than the tiny nails he used, and his stomach reminded him continually now that he hadn't eaten anything since the previous evening. Possibly midday; he couldn't recall.

Turning northeast toward the fortress, Beo almost tripped over a cobblestone.

Alcazar Avenue had sprouted fluttering fliers on every other building. *NPV IS SANMARIAN'S VOICE.*

They all said the same thing, and the sight of the fliers made Beo's stomach turn with renewed queasiness.

NPV, the National People's Voice. They were already in control of the city; no one doubted that. They had controlled Sanmarian and the rest of Kael for fifteen years, and sporadically before that. Even so, this was the first Beo remembered really looking at propaganda posters of any kind in Sanmarian. When he reached the sharp right turn at the Lionfish pub where his street, Altas Street, met Alcazar, Beo stopped short just before he turned. On the opposite side of Altas was a defaced flier with only a heavy black scale at its centre, blotting out every word except the last. What remained was only the silhouette of a scale and the word *VOICE.*

Beo thought of the protest and the sudden appearance of the fliers. They had to be connected, but there was no way the NPV could be that threatened by a single protest. At least, Beo didn't think so.

He remembered Irena's advice about never letting his politics show and quickly turned away from the defaced flier, an unfamiliar paranoia making him look around to see if anyone had noticed him staring. He couldn't tell; the other people walking the streets all seemed to be going about their own business, and the autocars on Alcazar Avenue were all moving too quickly to pay attention to a man on the footpath looking across a street.

Beo shook off the anxiety as much as he could, quickening his pace to close the distance to his flat.

He hadn't found her today, but he would try again. Beo pulled his camera bag closer to his side, the knowledge of the negative tucked within the pages of *Red Sunrise* a small comfort as he hurried home.

CHAPTER FIVE

Several days passed in similar fashion.

Rose woke early, dressed, and made her way to Plax Rynka, where she would buy a twist-bread and small warm egg frittata from a street vendor and sit on a bench to look for the man. Not finding him, she would turn toward work, spend the day dealing with ordering forms or reconciling the books for Grenye or meeting with clients. At midday, she would return to the square, buy a spicy seafood stuffed pastry—Sanmarian's residents called them clamshells for the shape—and continue to look.

On the third day, the last of the working week, Rose had the horrid thought that perhaps she wouldn't even recognise the man if she saw him. Still, she was determined to try.

That evening, she got home and spent her time rereading *Red Sunrise*. More than ever, she clung to Yosif and Remir's story, and even though she knew it was coming, felt a small jolt when Yosif's pocket watch disappeared. It wasn't the same; Yosif's watch was stolen when his flat was ransacked, and Rose had simply lost hers. But still, she read the passage with more solemnity than she ever had before.

Rose loved that even after almost two decades of reading the book, she still found new ways to see it, though this was a bittersweet instance of that novelty. The words of the story pulled over her like a soft blanket, and for a short time, she felt as if Papa were near again. She remembered the first time she had, at age nine, crept into Papa's library and found the book on the shelf. Its dust jacket had been removed or had never existed, and the red leather of the hand-bound cover was embossed by a rising sun in gold leaf. When Rose looked at it, she knew she had to read it, even if it was too difficult at first. Her fingers itched to touch it, and when she held it in her hands it felt as if it had been written just for her.

She sat down in Papa's large wingback chair and curled her feet under her, and there she began to read. She fell in love with Yosif and Remir, could feel them surround her with every sentence. Her heart broke for their third lover, Vitar, consumed by his fear. Her heart yearned for their love. Having only seen a broken kind of romance—Mama had left them when Rose was very young—Rose read in fascination as Remir and Yosif (and even Vitar at first) loved one another with a kind of desperation she had never witnessed.

Forever I will find you.

She made it halfway through the book that night before she fell asleep with a crick in her neck and a paper cut on one thumb, a small ball on the chair with tear tracks on her cheeks. Papa found her thus the next morning, a hot cup of coffee in his hands and an unreadable expression on his face as he brushed Rose's curls back from her forehead and one thumb wiped away dried salt. Rainbows from the prisms in his window danced across the floor. He hadn't told her the book was too much, simply asked her how far she'd read and what she thought.

"Is it possible," she had asked, her question hesitating in the middle like she wasn't quite sure it would end where she meant it to, "that a book could be written just for one person?"

"Why do you ask?" Papa's face held no amusement, only a wisp of sadness as his gaze flickered briefly from Rose's eyes to the book she still clutched tight in her hands.

"Because I think this one is for me." Rose was surprised at the ferocity in her voice, which made her sound much older than nine years.

Papa's fingers had paused in Rose's hair, and he looked deep into her eyes. "Then it is, my love."

And then he had set about his work, showing her maths and figures for his engineering contract, all the while glancing every so often at the way she held the book tight against her heart.

When Papa had died six years later and Rose had discovered an entire crate of *Red Sunrises*, she wondered at it, for she had never before found so much as another copy herself, only knew that when she'd worn out the first after so many reads in its first year, Papa had given her another, as meticulously hand-bound as the first. And later another. And somehow, miraculously, he had made sure after his death that she would always have it, though the crate contained copies that looked as if they had been printed and bound at a press and not a crafter's shop. It was evidence of being *believed* in a way Rose wasn't sure she ever would be believed again. When she had said the book was for her, Papa took her at her word.

Rose finished her countless reread as the sun set on Sanmarian, and she lay on her sofa, the book held tight to her breasts.

This wouldn't do at all. Papa had been gone fifteen years, and Rose was curled up as if it had been instead fifteen days. The absurd thought that she ought to be over it by now intruded into her mind.

She would call on a friend. It wasn't so very late. Amelie and Tomas were always happy when she dropped by.

Rose tucked the book back into her satchel, put on her coat and a new pair of lamb's wool lined leather boots bought with Aunt Aleis's gift, and left her flat.

• • • • •

Tomas and Amelie were Rose's oldest friends. Truth be told, they were rather her only friends, the rest of her circle of people being relegated over the years to acquaintances. But Amelie had been her first school friend, and Tomas had been the second, and the three of them had spent their early days getting covered in mud and their later days frequenting coffee shops where they would attempt to solve Sanmarian's problems. They'd all eventually given up on the latter— and the former, as none of them had been mud-covered in decades—but being around them was a lot like that first sip of cool water from a sweating glass when the sun beat down on the stone of the city at midsummer.

Amelie opened the door at Rose's knock. They lived in a sunset stone row house just inside the city walls, and the warm orange glow of the lamp next to their door flickered and glinted on the tiny sparkles in the stone.

"Rose!" Amelie pulled Rose through the door into a warm embrace, kissing both her cheeks. Her lips smelled of the hibiscus balm she crafted in her cellar and sold in the small boutique she and Tomas owned together.

"I thought it might be nice to stop by," Rose said.

"Of course, of course!" Closing the heavy cedar door behind her, Amelie helped Rose out of her jacket.

Tomas came in from the kitchen, a large earthenware mug of steaming coffee in his hands. He always drank the stuff in the evenings, though how he could manage to sleep at a decent time remained a mystery to Rose. Mug held away to the side, he kissed Rose's cheeks as well. Both he and Amelie were rather short, with straight black hair and skin nearly the same shade of gold-brown. If that was the beginning of the similarities, they would have looked like siblings, but there the common appearance ended. Where Tomas was thin and spritely, Amelie was curvy and voluptuous. Her breasts had been the marvel of their school days, appearing like coconut shells when Amelie was barely ten years old. Rose had been jealous for years, and hers had never caught up, but when they finally became about enough to fill her own hands, Amelie had jokingly bought her a bustier. Tomas had stayed young-looking, to much torment at the hands of their peers, but when he and Amelie became intimate, Amelie had quietly begun the rumour that his small size hid something quite prodigious, and the bullying rather suddenly stopped.

Amelie liked order and meticulous attention to detail—Rose very carefully removed her shoes and set them in a line by the door—and Tomas was often erratic. Perhaps it was all the coffee, which Amelie seldom drank. (Though she did have a penchant for any and all teas Aunt Aleis concocted.) And yet, in spite of the differences in personality between the two partners, they'd always been of one mind. Like now, as both Amelie and Tomas ushered Rose into their dining room, which was all dark wood and deep blue cushions on the benches. They sat down as if their knee joints had counted out the timing. Rose sat across from them, declining an offer for tea.

"Did you hear about the protest?" Tomas asked.

"I saw it myself," Rose said. There it was already. She supposed she shouldn't be surprised. It was news.

"Oh, my gods." Amelie looked over Rose's face with concern. "Are you all right?"

"I lost Papa's watch, and my foot got a bit stomped on, but other than that I'm fit to breathe another day."

Tomas and Amelie both knew the significance of the watch, of course, and Tomas reached out to take Rose's hand and squeeze it. Rose thought she saw a shine of tears in his eyes and wouldn't be surprised if she were right. Every emotion Tomas felt, from joy to rage, came in extremes. Once he'd smashed his own autocar window after getting ill news, back before they sold the vehicle.

"Well," Amelie said, looking to her right at Tomas. "If you're in need of a distraction, we have some news."

Rose immediately sat up straighter on the bench, a button on the cushion poking into her bum. "By all means," she said.

Tomas looked back at Amelie, and Rose couldn't quite understand what passed between them. Finally, he looked to Rose again.

"We're having a baby!" Tomas beamed at Rose, then at Amelie, then at Rose again.

Amelie smiled widely and placed her hand over her belly. "We just found out. We were going to call on you this week and tell you, but you beat us to it."

Rose opened her mouth and tried to speak. A silly grin seemed to flop about her lips. "You're pregnant?"

Amelie nodded. "You're taking this about the same way Tomas did. Our physician had to repeat himself four times."

With a sheepish look, Tomas put his arm around his wife and kissed her cheek noisily. She cringed and pretended to wipe it away when he pulled back.

"Congratulations," Rose said. She got up from where she sat and walked round the table, awkwardly trying to hug the both of them while they still sat on the bench. She sat down next to Amelie, who looped her arm through Rose's, her grip tight enough that Rose thought she just might lose her arm at the elbow. "Wow! Are you excited?"

"Terrified," said Amelie at the same time Tomas said, "Yes!"

Then they both said, "That too" in unison.

"You both make me ill," Rose said, shaking her head. She tried to wrap her mind around it; she hadn't even known they wanted to try for children. Pushing that train of thought off the tracks in her mind, Rose looked at how happy they were, with Tomas snuggled against Amelie's shoulder and the sheen of tears in Amelie's eyes saying more than anything else.

Rose kissed Amelie's cheek and gave her a wide smile. "I'm so happy for you. That baby is going to be the most spoilt creature in all of Sanmarian."

"That's the plan," said Tomas.

"The baby's due in midsummer," Amelie said, her voice heavy with disgust. "Which means I won't be leaving the house, and Tomas is going to have to bring in blocks of ice by the crate to cool me, since I'll be huge and miserable."

"This is a very important plan." Rose nodded with as much seriousness as she could muster.

And then they talked of baby names and nursery plans and how unnerving it was for Amelie to know she would soon feel the brand new tiny kicks in her womb, and Rose gave herself over to feeling absolute and total happiness for her friends, even though a tiny part of her squirmed and wondered how much longer she'd get to have them this closely when their lives were taking such a different path than hers. She thought of the posters she'd seen around town for the past few months, the NPV's pro-family posters depicting a happy woman holding a chubby baby while a beatific man looked on. Never any other type of family, although families with two mamas or two papas or sometimes triads or larger webs of lovers weren't uncommon in Sanmarian. The NPV never showed them, though.

Rose pushed thoughts of the NPV out of her mind, searching again for happiness for her friends.

If nothing else, she could be Exciting Auntie Rose. Rose thought that idea held some charm.

Rose hadn't the first idea about babies. She'd never wanted them.

She rather doubted a book would be a good first gift. Perhaps a very small hat.

• • • • •

When Rose left the house after finally relenting and allowing Tomas to ply her with cinnamon cakes, she turned toward the market square. Some shops were still open, and one might even have a hat small enough for a baby.

She supposed there were shops specifically for children's clothing, but as she knew exactly zero children, Rose hadn't the foggiest idea of where she might find one.

Most of the shops on the main market square were posh shoe shops and jewellery, blown glassworks and art galleries. Gold and green amber often washed up on the shores outside the city, and the sands of the peninsula Sanmarian rested on made beautiful glass sculptures and decorative bowls Rose would never afford. Aunt Aleis had a piece or two.

The square was lit with flickering lamps that cast a golden haze over all the buildings, making them look orange in the evening dark. Rose always loved that, the way it contrasted to the deep blue of the sky above. But tonight, the sky was shrouded in heavy clouds that promised rain, or at least gave it a solid chance. In spite of it being nearly midwinter, it seldom snowed in Sanmarian, the Tarenr Sea close enough to warm the skies.

She had just decided to go back home when she looked over and saw *him*.

He was talking with another man outside a small café at the corner of the square. Rose often visited that café.

It was dark, and she couldn't see his tattoo, but somehow just from the way he moved and his silhouette against the backdrop of the café's entry lamps Rose knew it was him.

He was tall and lanky, with broad shoulders and a serious face that looked as though humour had once dwelt there but had deserted him. His hair was black and tightly curly, the type of curls that, if tugged, would spring back with alacrity. His jaw was rather angled and straight, and his lips held such solemnity between them that Rose had the wild and errant thought that if she did nothing else ever, it would be the greatest pleasure to see him smile at her.

The man spoke to his friend—they stood close enough to one another that they had to be friends or possibly new and uncertain lovers—and paused for a response.

Rose didn't know what to do. She watched.

How did one approach another person in this situation? Rose was seldom in a position to approach anyone. She'd dated other girls and some boys while she was at school, but nothing really stuck. She had had exactly one serious relationship, which had lasted three years and devolved at the end into such suffocating resentment and bitterness that Rose sometimes thought she still wore the stink of it. She hadn't seen him in three years, and good riddance. And why was she even thinking about this romantically?

Because look at him. Her mind whispered it so insistently that Rose swallowed hard.

It wasn't just that he was attractive. He was, but more what it was that she felt was an attraction. Again, like the moment she had looked up to see his camera lens pointed directly at her tear-sodden face, Rose felt as though there were a tunnel between them, something she could see straight down where he stood at the other end. The more rational part of Rose's mind said that it was the tattoo, this mark from her favourite book which was so fresh in her mind having only just reread it.

No matter what happened, if he looked right back at her or if he scoffed and dismissed her, she had to speak with him. He had read *Red Sunrise*. No one else she knew ever had outside her close friends she forced it on, and of them no one felt it like she did. Not enough to permanently mark their skin with its symbols.

She could almost feel the heat of the lamps around her, swirling around the market. When the man and his friend moved to let someone pass by, Rose jumped. He was right there. She couldn't miss her chance to speak with him.

But a second later, they paused a few metres away and resumed their conversation, and cowardice caught her again. She didn't know how to do this. Or even what *this* was. Walk up to a stranger and say, "Hello, you photographed me whilst I was in a state of extreme grief, and I really wanted to talk to you. No, I'm not angry. I think. May I please see your tattoo?"

She couldn't look away from him. His friend was almost as tall as he was, a kind-looking man with long hair pulled back in a knot at the back of his head. He had a short beard and a strong physique. His clothes were well-cut and neat, and his hands were tucked into the pockets of his trousers as he spoke to the photographer, who reached out once to clap him on the shoulder.

Around her, the whole world seemed to recede except for the wavelike rushing of her blood in her ears.

Nervous didn't come near to covering how she felt. Rose thought that any moment, she might vibrate apart into tiny bits and never be seen again. Tomas and Amelie would be short one auntie for little Baby Prysbos.

For the life of her, Rose had no idea why she was so jangled. He was a person. She was a person.

But she did know. It was the intimacy they had shared in that one endless moment. In a public place where Rose had sat and walked and eaten and stumbled through drunk countless times in younger years, she had looked over and someone had been staring directly into her core.

The photographer and his friend embraced, kissed cheeks, and the friend hurried away. The photographer turned southward, toward Alcazar Street where Rose worked.

This was it. If she didn't move now, she might never get another chance. Panic almost sent her fleeing in the other direction, but through sheer force of will, Rosenni Abernethy made her feet move toward the photographer.

She closed the distance between them, and he didn't seem to notice the tread of her feet on the cobblestones.

"Excuse me," Rose said. Her voice sounded real, but he didn't turn. Colour flamed into her cheeks. He must not have heard her.

"Excuse me," she said again, and this time he stopped. And turned.

CHAPTER SIX

Later, Beo would have liked to say he expected anyone else to have been the source of the soft *excuse me* that made him turn. The normal reaction would have been to expect that he had dropped something and that some kind passer-by was simply alerting him to that fact. But the truth was that those two words were exactly what he thought they were the moment they reached his ears. It was her, and he knew it even before he turned.

She stood in front of him, not crying now, and indeed looking kind and strangely hopeful and not at all angry.

"I'm...you took a photograph of me the other day," she said, and her voice was rich and deep.

Beo felt his face turn hot. He felt like a raccoon caught in the light of an electric torch in an alleyway. "I did. I never should have intruded. I'm very sorry—"

To his utter shock, she cut him off with a sharp wave of a hand. "No, please. No apologies. I'm not cross about it."

"Oh," said Beo, unsure what to say to that. He looked around, not wanting to keep standing on a corner of the square to speak with her. There was, of course, the bench. Beo motioned to it. "Would you like to sit?"

The woman nodded, ducked her head with a small smile, and moved across the square. Beo followed, his chest full of the racket of his heart and his head full of thoughts that he couldn't keep up with.

They sat, a small distance apart. Beo set his bag next to him with his portfolio sticking out the side. The silence that followed didn't feel as awkward as Beo thought it ought to under the circumstances.

"Would you like to see the photograph?" Beo asked the question carefully.

"I would." If anything, the woman sounded even more tentative then. Not fragile, though—fragile was a word Beo did not think applied to her.

As he rummaged in his portfolio, he reconstructed her outfit in his mind's eye. Nice clothing. Linen trousers, linen shirt and overshirt, well-cut wool coat that probably had cost a lot when it was new, but it probably had not been new in some time. Her shoes were, though—well-made leather boots. Timeless and sturdy, nowhere near the lifts Zara used to wear. Or even those from one of his mates when he had first arrived in Sanmarian, a man who followed every fashion and trend and wore startlingly red lip paint more often than not. The shoes the woman wore were shoes Beo himself would choose. Beo found the photograph and marked the page with his thumb, reaching into his camera bag to pull out the copy of *Red Sunrise*.

Beo turned, ready to tell the woman that he'd brought the negative and meant her to have it if she wanted, but she didn't give him a chance. Her eyes were glued to the book.

She wore a leather satchel over her shoulder, and she reached into it and pulled out a copy of *Red Sunrise*.

Beo couldn't disguise his shock. Flummoxed, and more out of a need to make his hands do *something* than anything else, he pulled the photograph from where his thumb was wedged in the pages of his portfolio and held it in his hands, staring at the two books. His was much more worn, with its leather thong holding it shut and the cracked spine.

"This is the sixth copy I've read," she said softly. Her fingers twitched on the cover of her own book, as if itching for something. "May I?"

Unable to form an answer, Beo handed her his copy and watched as the woman unwound the leather and opened it with gentle care. Her fingers moved over the leaf-like pages, the hand-stitched spine, and a smile hinted of wonder on her lips.

"I've never met anyone who has read this," she murmured.

"Sixth?" The question was delayed, and Beo flushed, embarrassed.

"My Papa left me an entire crate of them when he passed. I'd already gone through three or four at that point. I was a child. I take better care of them now." Her eyes and fingertips roamed the book as if getting to know it. "How long have you—"

"Since I was sixteen," Beo said. "It's missing pages."

"I see that," she said. The woman seemed to hesitate, a quiet lassitude thickening the air between them. Her face changed, and she wetted her lips, drumming two fingers on the cover of Beo's book. "I saw your tattoo, the day you photographed me. I wanted to find out if it—"

"It is," said Beo. He set the photograph on his lap, image down, and rolled up the sleeve of his coat to reveal the tattoo. "My—" Beo never knew what to call Irena to others. "My guardian gave me the book when I was sixteen. My fathers died. I mean, my father and my stepfather. My mother died when I was a child."

He was babbling. He never talked this much about his family.

"My mother ran off when I was a child," the woman told him. "Papa died in an autocar crash when I was fifteen."

Beo, unsure of what to do next, turned the photograph over to show it to her. "You can keep this. I had no right to take it. The negative is in the book if you want that too."

She took the photograph, her touch as light on the edges of the paper as they had been on the tattered spine of his book. "I can have this?"

"Of course. I meant what I said. I never should have presumed to photograph you like that without your permission."

"Please," she said. "It may sound absurd, but I've never met anyone who knew this book before. I've tried to foist it on friends, but no one ever really cared about it. Not like I did. I'm not angry about you photographing me. I mean that. Maybe I should be, but I don't think you meant it maliciously."

"I didn't," Beo said, any other explanation eluding him.

To Beo's surprise, she took his hand. It sent a shiver of warmth up his arm, and when he met her eyes, he felt that same shock again that he had felt when she first looked at him. For the space of two or three heartbeats, Beo felt a tug in his chest, like some bright cord had pulled taut between them and if he reached up to touch it, he might feel it thrum. Her hand fell away after a moment, and the ghost of her touch remained.

"I'm happy to meet you," the woman said.

"I'm Beo," said Beo.

"Rose," said the woman.

They shook hands, and they looked at each other, and Beo felt the strangest sensation overtake him.

He didn't want to let go.

• • • • •

Beo and Rose spoke for a short time longer, skirting the edges of their lives. She mentioned that she worked for her aunt's tea company; he told her about his work at the gallery. She offered up stories of travels to Coret, the country that neighboured Kael to the north; he gave tales of summers among the olive groves in Sanrien with his fathers. They talked in a way Beo hadn't felt in ages, with words filling all spaces but those needed for breath, with smiles that met stories and bright excitement at each discovered commonality. They talked through ninth and tenth bell until a commotion drew their attention at Market Tower not far from where they sat. A number of NPV-uniformed guards marched up to the library entrance, their footsteps loud on the cobblestones. Around the square, the people leaving cafés and shops hurried in the opposite direction, scattering away from the guards. Though it was still early, across the square, Beo saw several shop owners close their doors and shutter their windows.

Though the library had closed an hour before, a librarian opened the door at the pounding of a guard's fist, and Beo saw her frightened face as she held it open for the guards to pass. A rustle beside him made Beo turn to see Rose surreptitiously slipping both their books between them on the bench and covering them with the wool of her coat. Rose looked at him, worry writ clear in the creases of her forehead.

The square had gone silent.

"We should go," Beo said.

"Everyone else has already gone." Rose looked around. "My aunt said...I promised her if there were another protest, I would leave. This isn't the same, but..."

"You saw the protest?"

Rose bit her lip and looked down at the photograph of herself in her lap. "I got caught up in it. My autocar broke down and I was trying to get through the square to work. I lost something in the chaos. A watch. It was Papa's. That's why I was so upset that day."

"You lost a watch." Beo forgot the guards that had just went into the library. "It was the watch from the book, wasn't it?"

"What?" Rose looked at him, and her worried eyes turned quizzical. "How did you know?"

"I found it. It's at home. I set it on my bedside table—" For a moment, her eyes widened, joy and wonder entwining to form something glowing that barely had time to take root before the sound of a banging door dashed it away. The library door, made of heavy wood almost as thick as Beo's forearm, crashed into the stone of the tower. The guards reemerged from the library, each carrying a crate of books.

"Beo," Rose said, her voice low and urgent, "we ought to leave. Now."

Too late. The guards moved directly toward them. Beo thought of Irena's many, many warnings, and he tried to swallow the ballooning fear in his throat.

Rose's hand found Beo's again, and she squeezed it, tight.

"Laugh," said Beo. "Pretend I've just said something funny."

Rose obliged with a fake giggle that sounded high and panicked to his ears, and Beo leaned in, brushing her cheek with his. The footsteps grew louder.

"It's late," one of the guards barked at them. "Go canoodle at home."

Beo pretended to jump in surprise and met the guard's eyes. The man was medium height with sharp features and an annoyed expression. He hefted the box of books, waiting to see if he'd be obeyed.

A year ago, no one would have batted an eye at people on the market square on the eve of the weekend at high dark, let alone just after ten bells. Suddenly, Beo couldn't quite remember when it had changed.

"Of course, sir," said Beo. "We were just leaving."

Rose nodded as if about to stand and upended her satchel, the contents spilling to the cobblestones. "Oh, bother."

The guard, his face awash in *I don't have time for this*, rolled his eyes and turned away. "Be gone when we come back through," he said.

"Yes, sir," said Beo. He dropped to his knees in front of Rose, obscuring where the books made her coat bulge.

Beo had never thought he'd have the impulse to hide a book from a city guard, but with them carting boxes away from the library, his instincts were the same as Rose's had been: don't let them see.

When the guards left the square, Beo stood, handing Rose's satchel to her. "Will you get home safely?"

"I don't live far outside the city walls. I'll be okay."

"I'm down Altas, off Alcazar," Beo said. "We could walk together—"

"I'm the opposite direction." Rose's face fell momentarily. She hesitated, pulling her satchel against her stomach. "Could we perhaps meet again? I'd very much like to talk with you more."

"I have your watch," Beo said. "Now that I know it's yours, I wouldn't dream of keeping it any longer."

That was partly a lie. Beo would have loved to keep the watch, its mere presence a more magical occurrence than anything else in his life, but in truth he wouldn't dream of keeping it from Rose. Something about her made the magic of the watch's appearance pale and lacklustre in comparison.

"Tomorrow is the weekend," Rose said, getting to her feet. "Would you like to have lunch?"

"Of course." Beo stood as well, straightening his shoulders with the influx of excitement that rose up the length of his spine. "We could meet here in the city centre—"

"I don't want to be a bother," said Rose. "I have to go by the office in the morning, which is near where you live. I could stop by at noon bell and we can find somewhere to eat near where you live?"

Beo found himself nodding, and he couldn't decide whether to offer his hand for her to shake. "Let's meet at the corner of Altas and Alcazar. There's a pub I like called the Lionfish."

The woman's chin ducked as she nodded, and for a moment her eyes turned downcast. Then, to Beo's complete surprise, she closed the distance between them with the quickness of a darting mink and kissed both of his cheeks.

His skin burned where her lips had touched, and Beo couldn't help but stare at her.

"Thank you," said Rose. "I thought the watch was lost forever. I cannot imagine someone I would have rather had picked it up."

"It is an absolute pleasure to meet you," Beo said, and he meant it perhaps more than he had ever meant anything before.

Rose's lips flashed into a smile, and then she turned. Beo watched her retreating figure with a strange fog in his mind. As a young lad, he had read stories of strange meetings, of powerful love, of magic that bound souls to meet. When Rose's silhouette vanished down Carino Avenue, Beo turned round, shoulders slumping.

Whatever he felt, he didn't think he could trust. His life wasn't a storybook—or if it was, it was a tragedy. He hated that little maudlin voice, but he had watched all three of his parents die. He had seen Irena's arrival, known that something had left her hollow even as she promised to care for him once he was well and fully orphaned. And of course, there was Zara.

But part of him whispered words of hope deep in his mind, uncaring about the past and his memories of Zara's death alike. That part felt warmed by Rose's existence, as if she somehow justified every hope, every dream, every wish for something more.

Beo walked down Alcazar, the buildings lining his path still papered with NPV fliers.

He didn't know what would come next, but he knew he wanted to know this woman called Rose.

CHAPTER SEVEN

A s Rose walked away from Sanmarian's market square, the tips of her fingers hummed with heat. She felt warmed to her core. She felt backlit.

In the days to come, Rose would look back on that evening with a blurred sort of reverence, never fully able to explain or articulate what precisely she had felt during those first few hours with Beo, but she would remember that glow. That, she would take with her until her last breath.

The watch, which had been one of the primary occupants of her mind for days, suddenly felt instead like a piece in a larger puzzle. Rose entered her flat with a burgeoning sense of strangeness and certainty. Whoever Beo was, she felt like she had reached out and found a bit of herself. Her flat was the same as it ever was, but to Rose's eyes it took on a new hue. Her world seemed to have moved again, to a brighter place where lines seemed clearer and the night felt more welcoming. Rose sat down on the sofa after kicking off her shoes and wrapped that newfound feeling around her shoulders like a blanket.

Remembering the guards shattered her comfort.

Rose pulled out her book and the photograph Beo had given her, her fingers meeting the paper and leather with nervous reverence. The photograph was striking. Rose wasn't certain she had ever seen herself so clearly in an image as she did in that photograph. Grief, yes, but also love. She had loved Papa more than anything. Once he was gone, it was as if that love had nowhere to go and swam circles inside her, searching for its outlet and never finding it.

She found herself rereading the passage in *Red Sunrise* in which Yosif and Remir met for the first time. Remir's thoughts were shrouded, as this bit of the book was from Yosif's point of view, but Rose felt the echoes in the pages of what she had experienced that night herself. An instinctual twitch of fingers. The brush of skin.

It was absurd. She knew it. Rose knew that the book was a book, and yet she could not shake whatever magnetism made her read and reread the passage, mirroring and not mirroring her memories of Beo Mataya.

• • • • •

The morning dawned cloudy and cold. Rose made her way up Carino Avenue, her fingers tucked into woolen gloves and a scarf wound about her neck. Her satchel swung a bit heavier than usual on her shoulder, because she had added to it a small surprise for Beo. When she reached Café Maya, she meant to go in, to buy a coffee to warm her hands further for the rest of the walk down Alcazar. Reaching the café, however, Rose was surprised to see a *CLOSED* sign on the door.

Even though it was the weekend, Café Maya was always open for the days of rest. For several minutes, Rose stared into the doorway, wondering if perhaps the café was just opening late. The hours were not posted. No aroma of cooking food came from the door, only the scent of fog-touched sunset stone and a swiftly strengthening winter.

Disconcerted, Rose continued on, her belly rumbling. A food cart on the market square rolled into place as she stepped onto the cobbles of the square, and she waited for the operator to get his wares ready, buying a hot breakfast clamshell stuffed with spicy sausage and egg.

"Café Maya is closed," Rose said as she took the clamshell from the man's hand. "You ought to be busy this morning."

The cart owner, a man who looked around the same age as Aunt Aleis, peered at Rose through thick spectacles and the steam that rose from the cart.

"Closed?"

"Yes, sir," Rose said. She could still see down Carino Avenue from where she stood, and a pair of passers-by were stopped in front of the café door, looking at each other with perplexed expressions.

The man's face turned pensive, and he looked over his shoulder at the shuttered store front half a block away. If Rose had thought he would be cheered by the prospect of extra business, he wasn't. Instead, he pursed his lips and turned back to Rose, pressing her five mark note back into her hand.

"On the house," he said.

Rose started to protest, but the man shook his head sharply once.

"Get on with you, child. Listen in to the radio, if you've got one." He glanced at the façade nearest the cart, where an NPV flier fluttered against the sunset stone. On it, a burly man with short black hair stood with chiseled arms on his hips.

NPV SPEAKS FOR ME! the flier proclaimed proudly.

Rose turned toward Alcazar, the NPV fliers lining the street suddenly all she could see.

Her clamshell grew cold in her hand.

• • • • •

The office was nearly as cold as the outdoors, and Rose spent the first while getting the steam heat working and stoking a small fire in the fireplace in the client waiting area. She brought the office books in and laid them out on the small table near the fire, pulling the table closer so she could work and be warm at the same time. The clanking of the pipes that ran along the inside of the walls made a familiar staccato as the steam slowly heated the office.

Ninth bell rang out when Rose finished balancing the books for the month, and she gathered the ledgers in a pile to return to their places in the back. With the office warmer and her meeting with Beo still a few hours away, Rose settled at her desk. Tenth and eleventh bells came and went as she worked, catching up with a busy week of papers and order settlements. She was cross-referencing a bulk sale when Amelie's name caught her eye.

Amelie frequented Aunt Aleis's tea shop, but she didn't often order anything through the catalogue, which was mostly bulk teas and medicinal items. Rose followed the line of the ledger across to see what Amelie had ordered, and her fingernail stopped on the smooth paper.

Tincture of Pennyroyal.

It wasn't only pennyroyal in the tincture, Rose knew, but extra concentrated rose hip extract, mallow root, and several other ingredients, but the pennyroyal was the active ingredient. What made Rose's skin feel cold in spite of the now-heady heat of the office was that the tincture was only issued for one use: to end a pregnancy.

Confused, Rose read and reread the line on the ledger. It was Grenye's script, even and neat. There was no mistaking it, and the date on the order was only a few days ago. Rose had just seen Amelie and Tomas the day before.

Mostly the tincture was issued to people whose pregnancy came as an unwelcome surprise, whose prophylactic administrants (Aunt Aleis also sold those for both men and women, of course) had failed, or who could not care for an infant themselves for any other reason. But Amelie and Tomas were happily married—and Rose thought, excited. She'd thought this was planned.

It was half noon, and though Rose tried to pass the remaining minutes before she had to leave to meet Beo in some semblance of productivity, her discovery had left her troubled. Amelie was her oldest friend. Why, Rose wondered as she tidied the papers on her desk and prepared to leave, had Amelie not come to her with this?

The thoughts did nothing to settle her nerves about seeing Beo Mataya again, and Rose gave herself over to fretting as she doused the fire and closed the vents on the steam heat so not to waste it on Popaxel when it was unlikely Aleis or Grenye or Helyne would be into the office to work tomorrow.

A knock at the door startled Rose as she began to gather her belongings.

Who could be calling now? She stepped toward the door, glad there was a peephole. Her stomach turned over, sloshing the bits of clamshell she had warmed over the fire and the valerian and mint tea she had drunk to calm her nerves.

Rose closed one eye and nudged the brass cover aside from the peephole. On the other side was Samuel Carixo, a chirurgeon who often referred patients to Aunt Aleis for medicinal herbs. His lined face was made bulbous by the curved glass of the peephole, but that didn't change the air of nervousness he exuded. He looked this way and that as if afraid someone would emerge from the solid walls on either side of him. Even through the glass, Rose could see a sheen of perspiration on his upper lip.

She opened the door. "Doctor Carixo," she said, and he hurried past her without answering, shutting the door behind him and locking it.

"I shouldn't be here," he said. "Is Aleis or Grenye here?"

"Just me," said Rose, perplexed. "Are you all right? Would you like some tea?"

Carixo looked at Rose as if she'd asked him to stand on his head in the corner. "Aleis isn't here," he said flatly.

Rose's heart gave a small thump, and she edged away, toward the wire-connector where she could ring Aunt Aleis's flat. Very few people had such luxuries, but Aleis was among the very few in more ways than one.

"I can ring her for you," Rose offered.

"No need, child." Carixo's voice implied that his words were as hollow as they sounded and tinged with new panic. He wiped his upper lip with the back of his hand, leaving a sheen that flickered in the lamplight. "Please pass on a message for me, if you'd be so kind."

"Of course." Rose's bewilderment grew.

"No doubt you're aware of the unrest in the city," Carixo said, and he didn't pause to elaborate. "It has come to my attention that certain types of business owners—and certain types of businesses—may be...at risk."

"At risk," Rose echoed. She'd no doubt he meant Aunt Aleis, or he wouldn't be here. "Doctor Carixo, please—"

He cut her off. "Tell her and Grenye and Helyne that they need to get their things in order."

"What things?" Rose's tendril of apprehension took root.

"They'll understand." Carixo didn't seem to care that he was being cryptic. He looked a bit closer at Rose, then. After a moment of his dark brown eyes staring hard at her, he muttered, "Gods, they have kept you under that many layers of blankets?"

Rose felt she ought to resent that, but she was too alarmed. "Please, what are you afraid of?"

Carixo let out a breath that sounded like steam released from a pressure cooker. "It's not for me to explain such things, if they have not already done so. Ask your Aunt Aleis, child. Or simply open your ears and turn on a radio."

Rose did resent that.

Certain types of business owners—did he mean women? Or families of women, like Aleis and Helyne and Grenye? Rose didn't know what had Carixo so worried.

With a sigh, Samuel Carixo gave her a last long look. When he spoke, it was slowly, as if he were trying to give himself time to change his mind before uttering each successive word. "You would be well to consider disposing of certain records, in a manner that they may not be recovered."

His eyes left Rose's face. His gaze alit on the now-doused fireplace for a fleeting moment, and then, so quickly that Rose couldn't be sure his look at the hearth was deliberate at all, turned back to her. He kissed both her cheeks and though he didn't hug her, his hands squeezed her shoulders.

"Your father would be unhappy to know that so much has been kept hidden from you, and that you are so alone. He was a great man. I think that despite matters being as they are, you may yet make him proud."

The words were unkind and harsh, and Rose's skin felt hot where they seemed to buffet her cheeks. She had no time to form any response, because Samuel Carixo went straight to the door, his shoulders slumped and some of the strength gone out of his spine.

"Perhaps I am being too harsh with you. Even if Aleis had told you every-thing, all of the history of this city and this place, your lifetime has been quiet, and you would not have been trained to see the restlessness. Nor are you party to…" He trailed off, brushing his hands on the knees of his woolen trousers. His back hunched as though he were suddenly very, very tired.

"Bolt the door behind me," Carixo said, and was gone.

Rose obeyed.

For a time she stood in the small foyer, waiting for her cheeks to cool and for her breathing to return to normal.

The clock tower at the fortress tolled a quarter of noon.

"Damn," Rose said. Beo.

She didn't have time to restoke the dampened fireplace and burn anything, and she certainly couldn't do so without Aleis's permission. Nonetheless, Car-ixo's entire demeanour had frightened her. Rose went to the records room where the ledgers sat, meticulously shelved in chronological order. They weren't every transaction the tea shop or the warehouse handled, but they were the most im-portant, the bulk orders and private clients, dating back three decades.

Rose piled them into crates, aware that she would likely arrive sweaty to meet Beo. Taking two crates at a time and thankful for her hard-won strength, Rose car-ried them down to the cellar where, behind the pallets of bundled herbs and the straps used to haul them was a hollowed wall Aunt Aleis used to let Rose hide in as a child. Rose yanked aside a rack of burlap bags and found the panel after a few fumbles. It opened with a click, and Rose stacked the crates behind it. She hurried back up the stairs and brought down the rest, and by the time she closed the wall again and beat a bit of burlap dust over where her fingers had pulled it open, she felt fully silly. Her arms ached, and her mind was no less troubled.

Aleis would probably close her eyes and sigh when she found out what Rose had done, but after Carixo's words, Rose didn't think her aunt could blame her for only heeding some of his warnings.

She made it back upstairs at five minutes to noon and bundled herself into her coat with her satchel. The perspiration from exertion made the coat uncom-fortable, but she ignored it. Rose picked up the wire receiver to ring Aunt Aleis, her finger on the dial to spin it from the three marker. She stopped, the pad of her finger warming the glass beneath it.

Carixo had sounded even more panicked when she suggested ringing Aunt Aleis.

Rose might be ignorant of what was going on, but she wasn't stupid, and she'd read enough mystery novels to know it was possible to splice wires into the communication network and overhear conversations. She replaced the earpiece and let her finger fall from the glass.

After meeting Beo, she would go straight to Aunt Aleis.

Rose had no way of knowing at that moment that the next time she saw Samuel Carixo's face, it would be on a spike. His words had been quite correct: Rose's adolescent and adult life had lacked the sharp breaths of fear, the huddled nights in rickety closets, the distrust of all but the closest neighbours and friends. Rose could not have known the bile that ran through Sanmarian's sunset-gilded veins. But then again, much as he tried, neither did Carixo.

· · · · ·

Rose felt her nerves calm when the sight of Beo Mataya's curly hair entered her field of vision. He stood in front of a pub at the juncture of Alcazar and Altas, and his honey-coloured eyes lit like the golden hour sun when he saw her.

She couldn't help the smile that tugged at her lips. In spite of the cold of the day, Rose felt suddenly warm, warmer than she had been in the office with the piping steam heat and the roaring fire.

"Rose," Beo said. He stepped forward and kissed both her cheeks lightly.

Her skin echoed with the touch of his lips, and the weight of Carixo's visit slowly lifted off her shoulders.

"It's good to see you, Beo," Rose said, and meant it.

"Likewise," said Beo. He gestured to the pub door. "I left the watch at home to avoid catastrophe. I can fetch it after we eat if you like."

Rose nodded, pulling the door open and feeling a gust of warm air greet her. Bashfulness rushed over her as Beo followed her inside, unabated when he waved at the bartender, who gave him a familiar wave and grin. Rose recognised the man as the friend Beo had been with on the square the night before. Slightly shorter than Beo, the bartender wore his dark hair pulled back in a knot and a black beard covering most of his face. His white linen shirt was starched, the slit down the chest buttonless and exposing a tuft of curls over his breastbone. The sleeves were rolled to his elbows with perfectly paralleled bands held in place by strips of fabric that buttoned to the outside of the bartender's arms, which were well-muscled and had the look of someone who began the day with one hundred or so press-ups. The shirt fit well enough that it had the look of being tailored, something that struck Rose as being a bit out of place behind a bar in a Sanmarian pub.

The pub itself was warm and worn, with gaslight fixtures made of brass along the walls that held electric lights in lieu of kerosene. Rose liked the touch. The filaments in the bulbs burned a hearty orange, and it made her feel at home.

Leading her to a corner table toward the back of the pub, Beo motioned at his friend behind the bar as they sat down.

"I come here a lot," he said, his voice as bashful as Rose felt.

"Beo, Beo, Beo," said the bartender as he approached. He gave Beo's shoulder a squeeze and looked Rose over with a gaze that was far more assessing than intrigued.

"Yoan, this is Rose," said Beo.

Rose saw Yoan look at her more closely, felt his gaze like the permeating heat of a summer's sunbeam that lit to expose rather than to warm. He then gave Beo a momentary questioning look. She blushed, wondering if Beo had shown the photograph to his friend, but after a moment of consideration decided he wouldn't have.

Yoan bent and kissed one of Rose's cheeks, and she returned the greeting. "It's very nice to meet you, Rose."

"And you, Yoan," she said.

"There's a good fish curry today," Yoan said, back to bartender veneer. "Bread's just done as well, the hazelnut one you like."

Beo nodded and looked at Rose. She smiled at him. "That sounds good," she said.

Yoan gave them a tight grin and sauntered away. His entire body was as muscular as his arms, and he moved like he had control over every single one. Rose wouldn't want to be on the wrong side of Yoan's fist.

Rose turned back to Beo. He wore a simple white shirt like Yoan's, but softer, less starch-stiff. Where Yoan bulged, Beo was slender, but wiry.

"I brought my portfolio," Beo said, pulling the leather folio from his bag. "I wanted to share it with you."

"I brought something for you too," said Rose.

They looked through Beo's photographs while waiting for Yoan to bring their food, and in those minutes, Rose forgot about her distressed stomach, Carixo's warning, the protest, the watch, everything that lay outside that worn-but-polished table and the photographs contained in sturdy binding of leather.

She had never given much thought to the art of photography. Cameras were beginning to make their ways into the hands of a wider range of people, but until that moment Rose had never understood what possibility lay inherent in that lens. She had thought the image of herself to be a fluke, some moment of magic caught in the glass and clicking shutter. In Beo's portfolio, however, she saw that he collected bits of magic, captured a child's love for his mother or the moment of disappointment in the eyes of a little one when a sweetie fell on gull-splatted cobbles. In Beo's photographs, Sanmarian was a living thing, a breathing city that ran on emotion.

And yet still in the background of the photographs, the spectre of the NPV was visible. The corner of a flier in a shot that Rose could identify without even seeing the whole of it. A guard standing against a wall, cleaning his fingernails with a pocketknife. A pair of guards casually smoking behind two children captured spinning with joy.

In that, Rose could not help but feel the tremor of apprehension return.

When Yoan brought their curries, Rose felt something akin to relief when Beo closed the portfolio and set it down on the empty chair on the other side of their table.

"You're a master with the camera," she said truthfully. Shock made her look down as she found she had to speak around an uncharacteristic lump in her throat. "I've seen magic in words before, but not in images such as those. You have a very great gift, Beo."

Though Rose didn't think Beo Mataya one to lack for words, he opened his mouth and closed it again, a flush covering his cheeks more an answer than any *thank you* could have conveyed.

"My mother died when I was young. When my father remarried a man he knew from work only a few months later, for a long time I didn't know how to make sense of anything. At first I was angry, and I escaped the house to photograph life wherever I could find it. Animals, mostly, because the villagers hold to the old gods and were wary of the camera's stare. My Paxpa found my prints one day when he was cleaning. I was furious with him, even though they weren't in my private space, just in a box in the hearth-room. He greeted my anger with patience and wonder, complimented my work. His love shamed me, and my anger faded like an overexposed image. I grew to love my new father as much as I had grown to love anything. I had loved taking photographs even before then, but he helped me nurture any talent I had thus far squandered. When my Papa died and my new Paxpa not long behind, I lost myself. The photographs became a way to remember them in action, not just their faces on paper." Beo still held a spoonful of curry halfway to his mouth, and he quickly put it to his lips even though Rose knew it must have grown cool during his unexpected speech. He wiped his mouth with a napkin and met Rose's eyes. "I'm glad you like them."

Rose felt a falling sensation, like the forces of gravity had vanished, and she couldn't make herself look away.

CHAPTER EIGHT

Beo had the sudden need to swallow, to do something, but he couldn't stop looking at the pair of grey eyes that were trained so intently on his. Again he had said more than he meant to, but for the first time in a very long while, he felt like the personal history he divulged found a safe home in Rose Abernethy.

Safe. That was the word. It was as if the two of them inhabited a small bubble, outside of which there was danger, but inside of which they were sheltered from whatever the world might think.

The strangest feeling overtook him as Beo sat there, the length of the look surpassing what most would find appropriate. Looking into Rose's eyes, Beo felt as if a cord in his chest were somehow connected to one in hers, the threads plying together until they were indistinguishable from one another. The cord hummed and stretched back into infinity and forward into the same, and it felt like forever.

A crash made them both jump. A server had dropped an entire tray of glasses. At her feet was a thick book on anatomy—anyone would have tripped over something like that, but how had it ended up on the floor?—and no one apologised, only stared in pitying shock. Someone from the table next to them leaped up to help her, knocking into the empty chair at Beo and Rose's table. Before Beo could look back at Rose, one of the patrons at the bar near the door pulled back his fist and slammed it into the man next to him, who reeled backward off his stool and fell to the floor with a crack.

"You think you can grab me? You think you got some right to do that?" The puncher slid from his stool and stalked toward the dazed man on the floor.

"I...I didn't—"

Yoan emerged from the kitchen just in time to grab the furious patron by the scruff of his neck with one meaty hand before the man could grab hold of the other man, whose cheek was already blossoming into a prodigious red welt. Beo's friend spent a large amount of time lifting kegs for exercise as well as for work, and Yoan had the muscles to show for it. However strong the angry patron might have been, he was no match for Yoan's hold.

"He fucking grabbed me! Put his hands on my ass!"

"I didn't!"

"Liar!"

"Easy now. Peace," Yoan said, then turned to the man on the floor, who had his hand raised to the swiftly swelling mark from the blow. "You. Your tab's on me, and I didn't see, so I don't know who you grabbed or didn't grab. Be on your way. You walk in here again and get accused a second time, and you're banned for life. And you," he said to the man he held at arm's length by the back of the neck, "You sit down, finish your meal, and then leave. And after that, don't come back. I don't stand for violence in my pub."

The man on the floor nodded and scurried out the door, clearly wanting as much a lead as possible. The other glared at Yoan but didn't make a move when Yoan released him.

There were several moments of awkward silence, with only the sound of the server clinking shards of glass. Yoan gave Beo a grim, exasperated look and came to help the server with a dustpan and hand broom.

Rose was still staring at the man at the bar, who had returned to his food with a glower. When she met Beo's eyes, she gave a small laugh Beo was sure came more from anxiety than mirth. "Are fights a common occurrence here?"

"Not at all. You saw how Yoan handled it." Beo frowned, then shrugged. "Something in the air lately, I suppose."

"I reckon I'd punch someone who grabbed me," Rose said, and Beo was surprised at the steel in her voice that said she meant it. Then she considered a moment. "Though I'd likely tell them to stop first."

Beo nodded. "The man seems a bit on edge in general."

He did, sitting there at the bar, eyes darting in every direction.

"It's possible the server grazed him as she walked by with that tray," Rose muttered. "Or that the other bloke really did grab him and was playing coy."

Beo nodded again, sopping up the last bit of his curry with a piece of the hazelnut bread.

"This ended up being more of a strange meeting than I had hoped," Beo said, hoping Rose wasn't formulating a plan to never see him again.

"Not the bad sort of strange," she replied softly, and again she smiled in his direction. "And before I forget, I really did bring something for you as well."

Rose reached into her leather satchel and pulled out a brand new copy of *Red Sunrise*. "It's not as love-worn as yours, but it has all its pages in case you'd like to read them again."

Beo took the book with careful hands, his fingers tracing the uncracked spine, the gold leaf of a rising sun above the title, the deep burgundy leather that on his own had faded to brown like the chair in the Market Tower library. Even his copy hadn't been new when he got it.

"This is...I can't take this," Beo said.

"I've got heaps. Papa made sure of that before he passed. I want you to have it." Rose's eyes met Beo's, then her lashes drooped and she looked down. "Open it."

Beo opened the book, pulling back the stiff leathered cover. On the flyleaf, a careful hand had inscribed with a fountain pen, *To Beo, for inadvertently showing me myself.*

It was a very personal note, and from anyone else Beo might have felt alarm. But from this woman, in the context of everything he felt stirring that he had not felt in a very long time, the only emotion that the words triggered was hope. A strange emotion, and one Beo was quite unused to.

"Beo," Rose said, and her voice was low and urgent.

"Thank you," he said, eyes still stuck to the book and its inscription.

"Beo," said Rose again, reaching out and tapping his hand with her fingers. "Your portfolio."

"What?" Beo's gaze snapped to the unoccupied chair where he had placed the portfolio. The chair was empty.

• • • • •

It took the space of several heartbeats for Beo to make sense of the empty chair. Rose was already up, scouring the floor around their table, her eyebrows knitted together in consternation.

"It's not here," she said after Beo made himself get up to look as well.

"Someone must have taken it during the confusion," Beo said. His head felt light and sparky, like his hand had felt the time he accidentally brushed it on a live electric wire for the barest instant. His portfolio. It contained years of work. Even though he had the negatives to all of the prints somewhere, and a catalogue of what he included, the whole thing was a carefully curated and personal piece of art.

He tried to stamp down the sense of loss. *It's just paper and leather and adhesive*, he reminded himself.

Rose's face crumpled in pity, and she stepped forward to touch his shoulder. She dug in her satchel and pulled out a few notes and coins, making eye contact with Yoan as she placed them under her empty bowl.

"There's no need for you to pay for both of us," Beo protested.

"I insist," said Rose.

"Let me just ask Yoan if he's seen anything," said Beo. "If he hasn't, we can pop over to my flat and I'll fetch your watch for you."

Rose nodded and perched on a chair to wait.

Making his way to the bar, Beo avoided stepping on the still-wet floor where the tray of beers had fallen. Yoan saw him coming and motioned at a patron to wait.

"Sorry the mess got in the way of your little date," Yoan said, raising an eyebrow in Rose's direction.

"Did you see anyone over by our table during all that? I know you were a bit busy with the overeager lad there, but my portfolio went missing." Beo leaned on the bar. The wood smelled of the lemon and oil mixture Yoan used to polish it.

Yoan frowned. "I'm sorry. I didn't see anyone." He heaved a sigh that came out raspy; Yoan had had his nose broken in a fight years before and it left its mark on his breathing. On more than one occasion of a drunken night, Beo had been kept awake by the man's snoring when he'd foregone the trek back to his own flat. The nose coupled with his asthma made for a prodigious roar.

"Thanks anyway," said Beo.

"Good luck on the rest of your date. I'll keep one eye toward your portfolio, in case something comes up or someone returns it."

"Thanks."

Beo returned to Rose, giving her a regretful shake of his head at her questioning look.

Outside, the wind had picked up, and it bit through them as they walked to Beo's building. A flier took wing off the side of a house and flew down the street until it encountered the windscreen of an autocar. Rose's face took on an unreadable bleakness at the sight of it, but when she caught Beo looking, she gave him a tight smile. The door to Beo's building was sandwiched between a launderer and news shop that had gone out of business a month before and remained empty. The door stuck, and Beo jiggled the latch with one hand as he turned the key with the other. It had taken him months to learn the trick of it when he'd moved in. Zara used to laugh at him; she'd learned within a day.

Beo couldn't help but steal a look at Rose, who looked down Altas Street to the the south, though there wasn't much to be seen there.

She pushed a curl out of her face, but the wind blew it back immediately. The door opened, and Beo motioned her to go inside.

"I'm on the third floor," Beo said apologetically. "It's a bit of a climb."

"My flat's on the fourth," she said. "I'm used to it."

Beo started up the stairs, thinking again of Rose's face when he first saw her and thought how glad he would be to return her watch to her. "Mind the step there," he said, just before the second floor landing.

Rose sidestepped the sagging wood, following after him as Beo climbed.

At his door, he looked over his shoulder, turning the key in the much-less-finicky latch on his door. "If you don't want to come in, you're welcome to wait here. However you prefer."

Beo pushed the door open, wondering why it met no resistance on the jamb, and all thoughts of where Rose might choose to stand flew out of his head.

• • • • •

The table in the kitchen where Beo had found Zara hanging nearly two years before was smashed into chunks of wood. The sofa where Beo never sat was overturned, the cushions slashed.

"Beo," Rose breathed, stepping over the threshold into the flat.

He couldn't answer. The door, now that he saw it, bore a smashed catch. His tongue felt as if the moisture had been sucked from it. He turned slowly to his right as he stepped into the salon, not wanting to look but unable to keep himself. His darkroom door was splintered. Unnecessarily so. He kept it unlocked; all someone would have had to do was turn the knob. Beo moved into the doorway where a chunk of wood hung from a single remaining hinge at eye level.

Beo held back the bile that rose in his throat.

The developing chemicals' bins had all been opened, and his instruments and trays had been dumped inside the bins. Hundreds of marks worth of equipment, destroyed. The chemicals were unusable now; they'd react with the brass instruments, and the chemical makeup would change. Beo was no chemist, but he knew that much.

"Who could have done this?" The catch in Rose's voice made an ache take hold in Beo's chest.

"I don't know," he murmured.

He was afraid to keep looking around the flat, but he had to find out if they'd left his bedroom in order. He expected not.

Almost every bit of furniture was broken, lying on the floor in chunks. The single rug in front of the sofa had been thrown to the side—for what reason, Beo didn't know. His cheeks felt cold, and after walking up four flights of stairs to his flat, that was never the case.

Rose caught his arm. "You don't have to look all at once," she said gently. "If it's too much, just stop a moment."

"I have to see."

She looked at him and nodded. "I'll be right here with you."

She couldn't have known what that meant to him, but he appreciated her words as much as he did the strong grip she had on his arm.

Like the rest of the flat, his bedroom sat in shambles. The mattress lay askew, half on the bed frame and half off, and the wool stuffing bubbled out. Beo's clothes—what he had, anyway—were thrown on the floor, on what was left of the bed, everywhere. The bedside table was on its side, the only piece of furniture Beo had seen that wasn't destroyed.

Beo knew what to expect anyway, but still looking and pawing about on the floor through mounds of fluff from the mattress and piles of feathers from his pillows made his stomach sink like a paperweight dropped into the sea.

The watch was gone.

· · · · ·

Gone.

From the stricken look on Rose's face, Beo thought he might never see her again after she walked out the door of his flat. Around him, his furniture lay strewn like corpses on a battlefield, except it was a fight Beo hadn't known he was in.

Rose stared around at the debris, bending to pick up a small ball of wool stuffing from the mattress. She pulled it apart in her hands, working the wool as if she were about to start spinning it into thread.

"They were looking for something," she said, fingers worrying at the wool. "They opened every cushion, every bit of wood wide enough to conceal a hidden cache."

"The watch was sitting right out on the bedside table," Beo said dully. "They couldn't have been looking for that."

It crept up on him like a shadow at dusk, the feeling that took root at the base of his spine and seemed to climb its way up every rung of his vertebrae, leaving a trail of raised gooseflesh in its wake. This was familiar, this scene. Familiar like a classmate you don't know intimately but who you see every day at the village school until one day you pass them in a new city and don't quite recognise their face.

Beo recognised it now.

When Rose looked up at him from the wool in her hands, her face said she'd been grasped by the same unshakeable feeling.

"The book," she said before he could. "This is exactly what happened in the book."

It was; down to the placement of the watch and the cushions that gaped at him, the images in Beo's mind from *Red Sunrise* were one and the same as the stark, grim reality of his decimated flat.

"When the Man in Red came for the watch, he was looking for something else," Rose said. "He was looking for the revolutionaries Yosif led, for lists of names he thought Yosif had."

The thrumming of Beo's heartbeat dulled his hearing to a wavelike whisper. He took a breath, the way the Priest of Solace had taught him when he had gone to the city temple after Zara took her own life. Beo imagined the starting in his toes, the air he needed filling him from bottom to top, steadying him. When he breathed out, Rose was watching him, and all thoughts of her fleeing washed away. She was still there. That ineffable certainty that her life and his were irrevocably entwined returned, fleetingly, and then Beo pushed it away.

"I don't have any lists of names, just my photographs. Which they took." He still had his camera bag; that had been between him and Rose at the pub. Only the portfolio had been in easy reach of a thief.

"Whoever took your portfolio knew something about you," said Rose slowly. The pitch of her voice sounded ever-so-slightly higher than usual, and the movement of her chest with her breathing seemed faster. "Can you think of any reason someone might target you?"

Beo shook his head. "I'm just a photographer."

"Maybe not knew. Suspected, then, for some reason." Rose closed her eyes, and Beo could see the flitting back-and-forth moment behind the paler brown skin of her eyelids. "The table closest to us was behind the half-wall that blocked off the keg room. I don't recall someone sitting there, but there must have been. They would have been only an arm span from the chair where you put the portfolio."

She opened her eyes. "Is there any possible reason you can think of that someone would do this?"

It wasn't a robbery; Beo had few things of worth, and what he did have for extra money, he sent home to Irena along with all his negatives. His equipment was the only objectively valuable possession he had, and whoever had done this had destroyed it, not taken it.

"Whoever did it, they did it fast," he said. "Which suggests they knew what they were doing. And arrived here by autocar, from not far away. We couldn't have been more than twenty minutes after the portfolio was stolen."

"Was your name or address on your portfolio?" Rose asked, then nodded. "Your name was, on the inside of the front cover."

"Just the name." The sick feeling returned, the curry sitting in the hollow of Beo's belly as if crouching in preparation to come back out.

"They found your address in minutes." Rose's hand went to her face, where she covered her mouth, fingers tightening on her cheeks. Her grey eyes wore the worry of an oncoming storm.

"This place is ill luck," muttered Beo. Rose looked at him questioningly, but she didn't pry.

"When I lost the watch," she said, "I couldn't help but think of *Red Sunrise*. I even thought how it was different, how it didn't fit the scene in the book. And now this happens."

"I don't know what to do." What remained of his bed was the cheap iron frame and the slats the mattress sat on. He sat on the edge, the metal cutting into the backs of his thighs. Here he was with someone who was nearly a stranger. He couldn't break down.

Yet when Rose sat beside him and placed one hand on his shoulder, filling his awareness with her warmth and the slight scent of mint that floated around her, Beo felt the sting of tears in his eyes. This flat wasn't anywhere near luxury, but it was all he had, and his photography was how he made his living. Or was trying to, anyway.

"I'm not sure you're safe here," Rose said, her voice quiet.

That was putting it mildly. "I'll pack some things. Yoan won't turn me away."

Rose nodded. She leaned back, her hand leaving his shoulder for the slats of the bed. Her fingers found the cracks between the planks, and she appeared to consider something. "I'd like to see you again," she said, her pitch no longer higher with anxiety, but a warm contralto once more. "Tomorrow, perhaps? My aunt has a tea shop just off the Market Square on Sankael. Hearthstone, it's called."

"Your aunt owns Hearthstone? That's my favourite tea shop in town. Whoever makes the cakes is a genius." Flattering as Beo's words were, he knew they sounded simply flat. As Rose sat up straighter, he met her gaze, trying to inject his words with warmth. "I would like that."

"First bell after noon?"

He nodded, standing when she did. A troubled look had made its home on her face, and her eyes searched the room once more.

"Take care, Beo," she said, kissing both his cheeks. This time he managed to kiss hers at the same time instead of standing still like an oaf.

And then, like the watch, she was gone.

CHAPTER NINE

The walk back through the city was a heavy one, and Rose knew she wouldn't sit well until she spoke with Aunt Aleis about Carixo's visit. As she tramped up Altas Street into the relentless early winter wind, she considered asking Aunt Aleis about what had happened to Beo's flat, then promptly decided against it. She barely knew this man, and for all she knew, he had feigned ignorance at her question of whether he could think of a reason someone might have marked his back with a target.

In spite of the cautioning bit of her brain, Rose didn't think so. She had seen his face when he caught sight of the rubble that had been his furniture. She only hoped he'd be safe at Yoan's.

The city grew colder with the wind, and when the lamps flickered into glow as the sun dipped below the rooftops, it felt as though the temperature dropped more than it ought to with the oncoming dusk. The sky above was clear except for some thin feathers of clouds that meant rain or snow was likely within days. The first few stars appeared in the blue-green expanse—or, as Rose had learned from Papa, planets, rather—and they shimmered brightly in the cold.

Aunt Aleis lived with Grenye and Helyne on Sankael above the tea shop. Rose had a key to the shop, which had only just closed for the evening. The aroma of tea leaves and sugary cakes still filled the air. Aunt Aleis served cold sandwiches and occasionally a cold cucumber and mint soup in the warmer months, but most of the menu was tea and small cakes, everything from smoky black lasuox that paired well with lemon-zested biscuits to Aleis's legendary hibiscus that she served only with a complimentary sweet white scone and clotted cream. There was a reason Aleis was well-off and could afford to live above the shop in the very centre of the city: the passion she put into her work showed in every crumb of every cake and every dreg of tea leaves patrons would surreptitiously swipe out of their ceramic mugs with a finger when they thought no one would notice. The shop itself was kept in pristine order. Helyne made all the furniture by hand in the office warehouse's workshop, her expert craftership evident in chairs and tables that never wobbled. Walking through the café, Rose saw not even a speck of dust in a corner, nor a singular finger smudge on the glass urns of tea leaves or the glass case that held pastries during opening hours.

Rose visited the shop often enough, but it always left her with the odd feeling that she could only hope one day to have something of her own she felt as proud of as Aunt Aleis and her wives did of this tea shop.

The alcove between the washrooms and the tea storage held a door to the stairway. Like everything else in the shop, the stairs were kept pristine and free of grime. The handrail gleamed in the dim light from the brass fixtures, and as Rose climbed, she wondered what she was possibly going to say.

The staircase flattened into a landing that hooked to the left where the door to Aleis's flat was. Rose knocked at the door, feeling at once embarrassed and resolute. The memory of Beo's flat with cushions slashed and tables overturned washed away the embarrassment after a pause with her knuckles still hovering at the door, and when she knocked again, Rose felt only that tenuous feathered nervousness one feels when a listener believing one's tale is not a certainty.

Her nervousness tasted like damp feathers at the back of her throat and felt like she'd swallowed a live bird.

Later, Rose would look back on that day with the sharp, unforgiving edge of hindsight, but just then all she fretted about as the breaths stacked up between progressively louder knocks was the possibility that all three of the flat's inhabitants were out to supper.

She knocked one last time, her knuckles now sore from banging against the hardwood.

And at last, footsteps.

Hurried ones, patting out a rhythm of *Oh, bother, didn't hear the door*.

Helyne opened the door, clearly breathless, dressed in her work attire of simple wool slacks with braces holding them up over a beige linen shirt that bore a few bits of sawdust here and a smudge of varnish there. Helyne was from the north of Kael, near the border with Coret, and her features showed the commingling of blood of the citizens who lived in the highlands where the country lines sometimes changed with the seasons. Her hair was a soft gold brightening to silver in her middle age, and her skin was closer to the colour of lightly baked bread than to the darker bronze of southern Kael's people. Her eyes, warm and brown, were just then tight with her flustered demeanour.

She embraced Rose warmly, though, and in spite of her hard muscles from her carpentry work, her touches always felt softer than Grenye's, which felt more like getting pecked at by a hesitant bird.

"Come in, child. Your aunt and Grenye are out, but I can make you some tea." Helyne motioned at Rose to come in, shutting the door behind her.

Rose didn't move too much forward. "Aunt Aleis isn't here?"

"She'll return later this evening," Helyne said, waving a hand. "Errands. They planned to ring me from the office this evening so that I might meet them for supper."

"The office? I was just there."

"They may have stopped off somewhere along the way. If Aleis stops only once for every street she crosses in town, it's a miracle. Come in, my sweet. Don't stand in the doorway."

"I can't stay long. I really only stopped by because Doctor Carixo came to call at the office today."

"And what did that old squid have to say?" Helyne stopped in the entry corridor as if perplexed that Rose wasn't following her into the salon.

Rose decided not to tell about the less flattering things Carixo had said regarding her own probable ignorance. "He said that he ought not be there to call at all, and that because of the unrest, certain business owners were at risk."

Helyne's body went quite still for the barest instant, then she gave up on trying to tug Rose to the more comfortable sofas and leaned on the wall, shoulders relaxing in nonchalance. "Was that all he said?"

"He said Aunt Aleis and you and Grenye ought to get your things in order. And I think he implied I ought to burn the records." At that, Helyne's eyebrow arched and Rose thought she saw a shadow pass over her face, but the older woman's features smoothed once more, and she motioned Rose on. Rose shifted her weight, her new shoes squeaking on the floorboards. "I didn't," she went on hurriedly. "But I did move them down to the cellar, to the nook behind the pallets."

A long silence followed. "Well," Helyne said, straightening again and plucking a curl of wood from the crook of her elbow where it clung to the linen, "I will most certainly pass on his message."

Rose started. "That's it? Are you not concerned?" Again Beo's face pervaded her mind, the stricken expression, the way his body went rigid like every joint had suddenly fused.

"To the contrary, I think there must be cause for concern," Helyne said a bit too lightly. "Old Carixo seems to need his own physician to tell him to drink less espresso. He sounds a bit over jittery."

"Helyne," Rose said, her voice flat. "He did not sound over-caffeinated. And a friend of mine had his flat broken into today."

At that, Helyne gave her a pitying look, the shadow flickering once more across her features. "Is he okay?"

"We were down the pub when it happened. But he seemed very shaken."

"I'd be concerned if he didn't," murmured Helyne. "Rose, I'll tell the others what Carixo said. Rest yourself. It's very likely nothing."

Rose met Helyne's brown eyes. "Ought I worry about this?"

Helyne stepped forward and gently touched Rose's cheek with a calloused hand. "No, my sweet."

For a moment, she was a girl again and remembered the countless times Helyne had comforted her with just that gesture. The scent of honey cakes rose from her memory, and the warmth of Aunt Aleis's knitting-in-progress across Rose's lap, and Grenye telling jokes to Papa back when she did such a thing. Then it was gone, and Helyne was chattering something about a small carving she'd meant to give her for some time and that Rose should wait where she was if she couldn't stay, and before much more time passed, Helyne bustled back with a neat bundle of muslin containing Aleis's lemon zesters, a new tea infusion of Grenye's own devising, and Helyne's wood carving in the shape of a leaping fish.

When the door closed behind her and Rose made her way back down the pristine stairs through the exquisitely kept shop and out into the ill-blowing winter wind that tasted of salt—Maru the sea god's tears, the older folks would say—Rose wasn't quite sure what she should do next.

· · · · ·

It came to her as she walked home, now more aware of the NPV guards that patrolled the city than she had ever been. Above the city was a hushed cloud that rolled in from the sea and took up post over the towers of Sanmarian, sending a dim mist that couldn't quite sparkle in the orange glow of the streetlamps as they flickered into light for the evening.

For the second time in a week, Rose knocked on Amelie's door. Her friend answered after a short moment, unlike Helyne, and Amelie immediately pulled Rose into an embrace. Her hair smelled of honey and beeswax.

"Hand cream season?" Rose asked. Winters near the sea could dry out a person's skin enough that it cracked and bled. Amelie's boutique sold a gorgeous cream made of beeswax that was the perfect remedy.

"What? Yes." Amelie sniffed her hand, but there was little humour in her face. "Come in, let me take your coat."

Rose obliged, watching Amelie hang the coat on a wrought iron stand. If she remembered correctly, one of Grenye's blacksmith friends had made the stand on commission.

Amelie's straight black hair was plaited back from her face, hanging halfway down her back and tied with a red ribbon. Rose sat in the salon next to a guttering fire in the hearth, sinking into a large armchair. When Amelie returned with two cups of warm hibiscus—from her own stores, not Aleis's, Rose was sure—she sat down in the opposite armchair and sipped her tea with a smile that didn't reach further than the corners of her lips.

Of many things, Rose was certain. She had known Amelie and Tomas her entire life. She knew how Amelie used to get scolded for having her finger up her nose all the time and how Tomas wore a straw hat to school every day until they made him stop. But Rose didn't know how to ask her friend about the line in the warehouse ledger, about the tincture of pennyroyal.

Finally, when neither had spoken and a draught licked down the chimney and belched ashes into the air, Amelie got up to stoke the fire and get it properly warm again.

"Are you okay?" Rose asked, and her voice sounded too loud in the quiet bustle of the poker and tinder Amelie prodded the hearth with.

Flames danced from the smouldering log, and Amelie didn't answer.

She instead glanced over her shoulder, at the archway that led to the corridor. Amelie turned back to Rose, sitting back on her heels, and her chest quivered. The false smile was now well and truly gone, and Amelie's lips pressed together as if she were trying to force words to stay behind them, unspoken.

"Please, Amelie," Rose said. Her heart felt as cold as that ashy winter draught, and something even colder and fearful took hold in her chest beside it. "I saw Aunt Aleis's ledger."

A door banged down the corridor, and Amelie's head turned so quickly to face it that Rose thought she heard her friend's plait whip through the air. "Rose is here, Tomas!" she called out cheerfully.

Perplexed, Rose looked at the back of Amelie's head.

"I'll be right there!" Tomas must have been in his office, and a loud clatter of dishes rose in the kitchen. Rose jumped at the sound.

Amelie looked back at Rose, her eyes so pleading that understanding passed between the two women as if Amelie had spoken.

Tomas didn't know.

The pleading on Amelie's face turned to panic, her eyebrows tightening and raising upward and a sheen of tears filling the crest of her lower eyelids.

I won't tell, Rose mouthed, and Amelie's entire body slumped as the tension relaxed. Most of it, anyway. Beneath it, Rose saw more, hidden and taut, and Rose's lungs felt brittle as she tried to draw a breath. Tomas's footsteps sounded in the corridor.

Amelie stood, beaming at him, and he kissed her cheek.

"Rose! Such a surprise to see you twice in less than a week!" He embraced Rose tightly, and she gave him an awkward pat on the back. He didn't seem to notice the charge in the air.

"I called on Aunt Aleis just now, but she wasn't home, so I thought I would stop here on my way. To see if perhaps I could take a pot of hand cream off your shelves," she said on sudden inspiration. "I've been out in the wind a lot."

"Of course, of course," Tomas said. "Darling, you've got some handy, right?"

Amelie smiled at Rose, and this time there was genuine relief in it. "I'll fetch it. Won't take a minute."

She left, and Tomas came into the salon, moving toward the hearth where he warmed his hands.

"Bloody cold in the office," he said. "I thought my fingers would freeze around the pen."

"That wouldn't do at all," Rose agreed.

"How is Aleis?" Tomas asked.

"She was well last I saw her. It was just Helyne at the flat today, though, and she seemed just fine. Grenye and Aleis were out to run errands." Rose abhorred small talk, but it seemed safe for the present. She couldn't shake the image of Amelie's face tight with panic. "How's business?"

"Good, good. It always is this time of year. A lot of paperwork and taxes, but I won't bore you with that."

Fine enough that Tomas wouldn't bore her; Rose did much of the book-work for Aleis anyway and was quite capable of boring herself with figures and ink splotches.

"I got you some of the new batch," Amelie said brightly, rounding the corner. She pressed the ceramic pot into Rose's hand. A tag tied round the groove of the lid with twine poked Rose in the palm.

"What's new about it?" Rose asked.

"Vanilla and hyssop," she said. "I'm also working on one with chamomile your aunt gave me this week."

She said the last so pointedly that Rose nearly lost face. Confused and concerned, Rose nodded. "Let me know how it works out, and I'll tell Aunt Aleis."

"Please tell me if you like the vanilla," Amelie said.

"She's been pestering everyone for reviews," Tomas said fondly.

"I will, of course."

Rose stayed another few minutes, the heat of the rekindled fire the only small comfort in the room, and she made some excuse to go.

When she got home, she removed her boots and turned up the steam heat. She had no wood for her small stove, and besides the steam did well enough. Her eyes fell on the radio, and Rose couldn't help but think of Doctor Carixo's words. Static or not, perhaps he was right. She turned it on.

A harsh crackle popped from the speaker, and Rose fiddled with the dial until she found Sanmarian's primary news station. It was run by the NPV—of course it was—but it wasn't like there were any others.

Rose sat down on her sofa and pulled the cream out of her satchel. She may well use it while she waited for the fuzzy words to say something of note. Rose tugged off the tag that had poked her in the palm, and a glimpse of Amelie's script caught her eye. They used labels in the shop printed with custom stamps, not handwritten.

I'll call tomorrow first thing. Please be home.

Rose held the tiny note in trembling fingers.

Amelie seldom called on her alone; this would be the first time in how many months? Perhaps a year gone by, even. For a moment, Rose couldn't distinguish the crackling static on the radio from the rushing of blood through the vessels in her ears.

And then those ears caught a voice on the radio, the unmistakable timbre of Rico Samson, NPV party leader and Sanmarian's ruler.

"...It is not for Sanmarian to fill slowly with water, to watch her citizens drown. No. This may be the way elsewhere. The people of Sanmarian deserve to be heard. Our businesses suffer because our families suffer. Who cares for the children when the parents toil from sunup until sundown? We must not allow it. We must cling to the power of Kael's families. A mother's body is made for care, to nurture her baby until he is ready to breathe. A father's strength is made for protection."

What if the babe were not male? Rose wondered. Samson's words cut through the static, and though she had to strain to listen, somehow they at once burrowed deep in her mind. She had grown without a mother. Papa had cared for her and protected her both, and Rose knew plenty of folk whose families were the other way besides.

"Too long have we lived, departed from the natural way. No more. The National People's Voice is the voice of Sanmarian, and we will speak for you, for those who have not been heard. We see you! There shall be change, and there shall be prosperity, and we shall all share in it. Kael, our beloved homeland, shall be rich once more on the strength of our families."

A cheer went up, and Rose started at the sound. She had not realised that the broadcast had been recorded live. A boom shook the air once more. The cannon. After a second's delay, it sounded through the radio as well. *Natural way.* What did that mean?

The address wasn't recorded; it was live now. This was now.

A live political address at near dusk on Paxel, the day of rest.

Rose thought of Beo, of Amelie, of Carixo, and of her own family.

Of whom was Samson speaking and thinking? To whom did he speak?

She knew full well that it was for Sanmarian that the NPV purported to speak, and as the sky grew dark outside her windows, Rose sat without turning on a lamp, fingering the scrap of paper tag from Amelie, certain of very little.

One thing she felt sprout somewhere deep within, however, was that for whomever the NPV spoke, Rose did not think they spoke for her.

CHAPTER TEN

It took Beo very little time to bundle up some of his belongings in a bedsheet. Without his darkroom equipment, all he really owned was his clothing and his camera itself. He carefully wrapped his old copy of *Red Sunrise* in a shirt that had been his Papa's, tying it with a lone shoelace and placing it at the centre of the bundle. The new copy, the one from Rose, he slid into his camera bag in place of the old. With no missing pages, it fit snugly, filled out the gap between the padded woolen dividers of his camera bag.

Yoan was no longer at work, and Beo made his way north to the building where Yoan lived, in Plax Kael. It was a small square with an overgrown fountain at its centre that was full of moss, dried out for winter. The cobbles of the square were old, and many were loose like teeth. Years and years before, Plax Kael had been the home of the Roa people, a group that had been driven into diaspora when the empire of Maref had annexed their tiny country to the east and put nearly all of them to death by firing squads. Those who escaped did so as refugees, and while many had formed enclaves in Kael and in Coret to the north, poverty and the turmoil of Sanmarian's past few decades had caused the Roa to quietly vanish from Sanmarian's city centre.

Still, Plax Kael bore the marks of a culture that was not Kaeli, the sunset stone chiseled with square-edged lines that turned inward on themselves like an angular version of Kaeli luck spirals, doors painted brilliant reds and yellows. Some of the exacting designs carved into the stone had worn away in bits, and by now the paint was chipping or sanded away on many of the doors in the square. The colours clashed horribly with the pink-red of the sunset stone, but Beo liked it. It felt like being able to touch history.

By the time he got there, though, his fingers were near-frozen into a claw around the knot of his bundle of clothes, and he regretted his procrastination on the buying of gloves. His breath made tendrils of silver mist in the twilit square, and as he passed the fountain heading toward the yellow door of Yoan's building, the lamps came on and turned the tendrils to gold. Yoan's flat was on the ground floor of the building, but far at the back. It overlooked a tiny courtyard that was home to a single blood maple. The tree had weeks since deposited its leaves on the ground, but a few crimson remnants crunched under Beo's feet as he made his way to Yoan's door, blown in with the early winter winds.

He knocked once, then again, and no one answered. Beo knocked a third time after a few minutes, then sighed and sat down atop his bundle of clothes, leaning on the doorframe. He pulled *Red Sunrise* from his camera bag. He stared for quite a while at the inscription Rose had inked onto the flyleaf—*To Beo, for inadvertently showing me myself*—and then opened the first chapter. He had read and reread the book so many times he had thought he had the missing pages of his own copy memorised, but now having those pages crisp and new beneath the skin of his fingertips, he found himself to have been mistaken. His memory of the words was akin to relating someone else's dream to a stranger; the story felt new again with the pages restored, as if Beo had instead stepped into that dream once more.

Remir Roxa wore her ink like she wore the rest of her skin, as if she had been born to it. Though some gave startled glances to the lines of the rising sun that sent its beams from elbow to wrist, and others still started at the silhouetted birds that flew from her shoulder into the line of her hair, she gave no heed. Remir had long since sloughed off the care of what others thought of her, and everyone who passed the radius of her presence well felt it in their depths.

What they did not know and could not know was that in her very skin lay secrets. Secrets that could save Sanmarian—or send the city to its doom.

Beo read, turning pages with renewed reverence. He read so long that his backside grew numb and stiff from balancing atop his bundle of now-surely-rumpled clothing, and he read so intently that he didn't hear Yoan coming until the man nudged Beo's foot with his own.

"What in bloody hell are you doing here?" Yoan asked when Beo looked up with a start that nearly wrenched the muscles in his back with shock.

Beo closed the book and tucked it away, standing and stretching as his Sanmarian, far from Remir Roxa's and Yosif Milabr's Sanmarian, tumbled back down round his ears. "I'll tell you inside," he said quietly. "Can I stay with you tonight?"

"Of course," said Yoan. He smelled of sweat and spilled beer and the aromatic herb oil he preferred—an herbaceous scent with hints of spring flowers—and to Beo's eyes, he looked tired.

Beo had no watch and had been too lost in his reading to hear the tones of the city bells, so when he entered Yoan's flat to see that his wall clock had passed tenth bell and neared eleventh, he felt surprise.

"How long were you sitting there?" Yoan latched the door behind them and bent to unlace his knee-high leather boots.

Beo removed his own shoes. "About half a book," he said dryly. He set his bundle of clothes down on a puffy green chair, then perched on the edge of the same chair himself, leaning his aching back against the heap behind him. It cracked.

"What happened?"

"Someone raided my flat," said Beo.

Yoan's body froze. He listened as Beo related what he and Rose had found at home, of the missing portfolio and Beo's destroyed darkroom. He left out the missing fob watch. When he finished, Yoan took a shaky breath that whistled in his nose.

"You can stay here as long as you need," Yoan said. "But Beo, I think this is my fault."

It was Beo's turn to freeze. "What?"

His stomach growled, breaking the tension of the moment.

"You're hungry. Let me bring you some food, and I'll explain."

A few minutes passed while Yoan moved about in the kitchen, returning with a deep ceramic plate of lentils and spongy sourbread with a smoked fish on the side. The lentils steamed, but the fish still sat in gel from being crammed next to its fellows in a tin in the icebox. Beo took the plate, his hunger warring for a moment with his anxiety before the rumbling of his belly won out and he tucked in.

Yoan took a sip of water from a mug and sat on a green sofa that matched Beo's chair.

"The reason I was out so late tonight is because I was at a Liberation Front meeting," Yoan said quietly. "I've been going with Maro for a few months, ever since Reyn Halto was killed."

Reyn Halto. Beo had heard the name, but that was it. "What does that have to do with me?"

"I think the NPV has started watching the pub."

Beo's lips felt numb, and it wasn't from the spice of the lentils. "Why would you think that?"

"A guard followed Maro and me after the last meeting. We didn't think we were seen leaving the venue, but it's possible the guard followed us all the way to the Lionfish. I'd left some things there."

A little of the unease lessened. "That doesn't explain why they would do something so violent. They were hunting for something specific, and I don't think they found it."

"I don't think it's a coincidence that they destroyed your darkroom right after stealing your portfolio."

"You think they were after my negatives?" It might explain why they had slashed open the cushions and the mattress, if they thought he was hiding something that small in them.

Yoan set his mug of water down on the coffee table and put his head in his hands, running his fingers through the stray hairs that escaped the knot of his hair at the nape of his neck. "Things are getting very bad," he said. "Our sources say the NPV is planning to escalate their control, but they don't know exactly how."

"Your sources."

Yoan gave Beo a bitter nod. "One of the few remaining. The NPV's caught all but a handful."

"Reyn Halto."

"Reyn Halto." Yoan looked at his water as if he wished it were liquor. "And seven others."

"Why are you telling me this?" Beo wasn't sure he wanted to know. He'd avoided Yoan's invitations to go to Liberation Front meetings with Maro, mostly on Irena's advice. Not that she had given specific advice about Liberation Front—she hadn't—but she had warned him to mind how far his head stuck up over those of others around him.

Beo could not have been aware of the tautly stretched threads that crisscrossed the city of Sanmarian any more than he could guess what had made Yoan and Maro choose to get involved. Later he would look back and see his own ignorance for foolishness, but then as he sopped up lentils and smoked fish with the sourbread, he felt only as if he were standing on the shore of the sea with his feet dug too deep into wet sand to move, and watching the tide come in.

His friend, though seemingly more aware, was in truth nigh as ignorant as Beo himself. He possessed information without context—a combination that is often just enough to truly endanger.

"I want you to come to Lib Front meetings with me," Yoan said. "It's important. Besides, by now you may as well."

"May as well? Because they've already destroyed my flat and my livelihood, so I might as well offer up my neck too?" Beo's food bittered on his tongue. The ache from sitting on his bundle of clothing grew suddenly more noticeable, and he set the bowl down on the table to shift his tight shoulders.

"That's not how I meant it." Yoan's face turned downcast, and he scratched at his beard. "Things are changing," he went on softly. "This time Lib Front is going to do it. We're going to take down the NPV once and for all."

Beo felt as if his blood had turned to the same gel that coated the smoked fish. This was precisely what Irena had warned him of. "Sure, with a few protests when they're taking out your people already."

Once again, Beo remembered the guards in the city centre, taking crates of books from the library.

"You don't know what they're planning," Yoan said.

"Do you?"

Silence slipped over the room, broken only after a moment by the ticking of the valves on the steam heat.

"Think, Beo." Yoan reached under the table and pulled out a book of surrealist art. Sandwiched between the pages were single sheets of paper. Fliers. NPV fliers. "You've seen the posters."

Yoan slapped one down on the table, making the ceramic bowl clatter against the wood.

"It's a family," Beo said.

"It's only ever one *kind* of family." Yoan topped the one flier with others. "Look."

Muscular man. Willowy woman. Their hands clasped one another as their faces beamed out from the poster. In the next they had a child between them, wearing the same style of clothing as the father. Another poster, with a slightly different pose. All with the same message: *A Stronger Sanmarian.*

"And these." Yoan slapped another poster down. This one showed an exhausted woman working in a shop. Patrons held up notes, wanting to pay. Sweat beaded on her forehead, her hair fell out of its bun, and the crate she carried tipped precariously in her arms. The next showed a pristine home, a smiling, radiant woman. She held a baby in her arms.

Beo wasn't stupid. He knew the definition of propaganda, and some of these posters, he hadn't seen. He stuck to the city centre, and that often only the square, the gallery, and his flat.

"What do you think they're going to do?" Beo asked.

"These have gone up all over Sanmarian, but mostly in the poorer districts." Yoan paused to check if Beo followed. At his look of puzzlement, Yoan went on. "Those who cannot afford to live in the city centre are more likely to be in families of three or more parents. More hands to feed small mouths, more support."

Beo nodded. In his own village, it was more common than not for families to exist in that manner. His had been somewhat of an oddity, but never odd enough to elicit comment. He pawed through the posters, selecting the one with the exhausted shopworker. "Clear enough they want to make a point about how women ought to spend their time."

Yoan snorted. "Reyn suspected that the NPV have been slowly gathering enough power to enact sweeping social changes."

"And now Reyn is dead."

"Reyn is indeed dead." Yoan looked very tired. "You don't have to risk yourself if you do not want to, Beo. You are welcome to stay here as long as you want, regardless of what you choose."

"Thank you—" Beo started to say, but Yoan cut him off.

"But," Yoan said, "there will come a time very soon when you will have to make a choice."

Neither of them knew exactly how right Yoan's statement was.

• • • • •

Beo lay awake for a long time that night, mostly listening to Yoan snore in the other room. His brain had not yet spun through the myriad threads of the day. Not meeting Rose again, not her gift, not sharing his work with her, not the disappearance of his work, not the invasion of his home, and not the idea that perhaps his mere proximity to Liberation Front members had made him a marked target.

Though the curtains were drawn and no streetlamps were in a direct line of sight to the windows, golden light danced across the darkened ceiling above the sofa where Beo lay, moving and rippling like waves in sunlight.

He thought of Zara, of the nights like this when their minds were troubled by the day-to-day woes that kept them from fading off to sleep. In the early days, before it got bad, they would lie awake together and tell each other stories. One would listen and then find a tiny seed of humour in whatever the woe may be, and they would go back and forth until they wound up laughing until their stomachs hurt and the bedsprings creaked. Sometimes after that they would make love, and they would drift off to sleep together as the sweat dried on their skin. There were times he missed those days and nights. Before she became withdrawn, before she began stinging him with barbed words no matter what he did, before her grip occasionally left bruises on his arms. Before she first drew blood with her nails when he prepared supper too late. He never raised a hand to her to stop her, and he would not have dreamed of doing so. Those moments had come on so slowly. One comment so acidic he thought he must have misheard it. And then she was back to normal.

Only it kept happening, and eventually the comments became shouts and the feeling of her hand tight on his arm. He could still feel its ghost, like her ghost, as he lay on Yoan's sofa and watched the reflected light from the streetlamps dance across the ceiling. He thought that if he looked down, he would still see the bruises there, dark beneath his skin.

It's not your fault, Yoan had told him, as they sat in the deserted pub after the guard had come and taken Zara's body from where it hung in Beo's kitchen.

In his mind, Beo thought that could be right. Zara had been sick. When he had said he needed to end their relationship, she had threatened to hurt herself. She had threatened to kill herself. And Beo had stayed, for a while, until he could take it no longer because his skin crawled each time she entered a room and because her touch felt like it was made of spider legs.

But finding Zara had hanged herself in his kitchen the day after he ended things for good—he didn't think his heart would ever let go of the blame.

It had been a long while since he had allowed himself to think on the whole of it, but today was no ordinary day. He missed her some days, and he hated himself for it, and he hated himself for hating himself when she had caused him so much pain.

The bad days had poisoned all the good, in the end. Made him afraid, made him feel small.

In that moment, Beo's thoughts turned to Rose, how she had spoken about his work and how she had brought him something that she knew he would prize. He couldn't imagine Zara ever doing any such thing; she had treated his photography like an irritating gnat that buzzed round her head when she preferred he pay attention to her interests. When he had lent her *Red Sunrise* to read, it had languished for months on her bedside table, and when she had read it at long last, her dismissive summary of the book had dashed Beo's eager hopes that she might love it like he did. That she might understand.

It did no good to dwell on the past, Beo knew, except perhaps to learn from it what he could.

He tried to imagine Rose bitter and angry, and he could not. Instead, he heard again her gentle *"Excuse me"* and felt the soft touch of her lips on his cheeks. There was steel in her, he knew. But it was not barbed, nor was it meant to cut.

That didn't mean it wouldn't.

Beo tried to hush the voice, and succeeded after a time, though his heart still raced with remembered adrenaline.

Sleep came, reluctant, and his mind found no relief in dreams.

CHAPTER ELEVEN

A sudden pounding of thuds jolted Rose awake. Her heart in her throat, she jerked in her bed, whole body tight with the flash of tin that flooded her blood.

It had to be someone else's door. No one would slam a fist on hers that hard. *Amelie.*

Rose remembered that her friend was due to visit and shoved the blankets back from her chest, grabbing a soft woolen dressing gown from where it hung from a hook on the side of her wardrobe. She wrapped the dressing gown around her, pulling the ties tight as she hurried to the front door.

Her fingers fumbled on the locks, and Rose flung open the door.

It was not Amelie on the other side.

Three NPV guards stood outside her door, faces like stone and revolvers holstered at their sides. Rose felt the wind in her mouth, sucking away any moisture there.

"Rosenni Abernethy?" The first guard used her full name, and Rose started at the fact that he left out her middle name as much as at the sound of the length of her given name.

Rose tried to voice an affirmative, but her breath caught in her throat with an audible hitch, and she could only nod.

"Child of Andreas and Miko Abernethy, niece to Aleis Nicaro, is that correct?" They knew her mother's name. The guard stepped forward toward the threshold, and Rose felt her body involuntarily give way as she moved aside.

All three guards stepped into her flat, and one of them closed the door behind himself.

Rose found her voice, at long last. "That's correct. Has something—" She swallowed, her throat sticky and tight. "Has something happened?"

Two of the guards strode through the salon and into the kitchen, but the first stayed with her in the entry. Helplessly, Rose watched as one guard opened the cupboards in her kitchen and the other rifled through her bookcase.

The first guard, a blocky man of medium height with greying hair over his temples, watched Rose with shrewd eyes. "You have heard nothing?"

"I heard cannon fire last night while I was listening to the address on the radio. Please, sir, is something wrong?"

Instead of answering, the first guard walked directly to the radio and turned it on. It was on the same frequency as it had been the previous night, and Rose jumped to hear the same words of Rico Samson's address booming through the salon, complete with requisite static.

"The radio always sounds like that," Rose said faintly. "I've tried to have it fixed."

The guard turned it off.

"There's nothing here," one of the guards said from her bedroom. "No one else."

"I live alone," Rose said. Her heart vibrated in her chest like a hummingbird's wings.

"You ought to find yourself a husband," the first guard told her.

Rose didn't know what to say to that.

"Please," she said. "Can you tell me why you're here?"

Were they looking for Beo? The sudden memory of his ransacked flat pervaded, and Rose struggled to keep her face calm—or at least at the same level of fright it had been since she opened the door.

"Tell me, Rosenni," the guard said, "when was the last time you saw your aunt?"

Aunt Aleis.

"I...it must have been Anpax, two days ago. I went to the office yesterday, but she doesn't work on the weekend." Rose took a step backward at the sudden gleam in the eyes of the guard.

"You are responsible for the accountancy of your aunt's business, are you not?"

"Some," Rose said. "I meet with clients from Sanmarian and from other cities and villages who wish to purchase goods from my aunt. I also help with inventory."

"Then you would know where the ledgers are kept." The guard stepped toward her, close enough that Rose could feel the warmth of his body through his grey woolen uniform.

"In the records room at the main office," Rose said automatically. Except they weren't. She'd moved them.

The guard exchanged a look with the other two, who returned from their seemingly fruitless search with sour expressions and perfunctory shakes of their heads.

"If you happen to hear word of your aunt, Rosenni, please make certain you inform us." The first guard handed her a small card. Asuel Saraya was his name.

Rose took the card with numb fingers. "My aunt is gone?" Her voice sounded hollow and stupid to her ears, and the guard didn't answer.

"We will be in touch," Asuel Saraya said as he left the flat.

Rose followed them to the door. She jumped again when the door closed hard behind them and leaned her back against the wall of the entryway.

Carixo had said she was ignorant; just how ignorant had they kept her? Rose slowly breathed deep, her fingers finding the edge of Asuel Saraya's card and tearing it down the centre. She had lied to the NPV. By omission, but it was as good as a lie, even though Saraya had not asked where the ledgers currently were, only where they were kept.

Tearing the card into tiny pieces, Rose forced her spine to straighten. Aunt Aleis. Her breath returned, and she swallowed, wetting her lips.

There was one small thing in which Rose had not been left ignorant. Rose moved through her flat, feeling a vague sense of violation. The books on her shelf were askew, the spines now jagged instead of pulled flush with the shelf's edge. In her kitchen, Guard Three had left some of the cupboards open. She closed them.

Her bedroom was mostly as she had left it, but the wardrobe doors hung open, and the drawers on the bedside table besides. Rose threw the bits of cardstock into the rubbish bin beside her bed and pulled the blankets up. The bedsheets were still warm.

They had opened the wardrobe and pushed some of her clothing aside, but they had missed what it hid. They had missed what made this very special wardrobe indeed very special. It was not lost on Rose that the wardrobe had been constructed thusly at Aleis's insistence. She felt it like the whistle of wind heard but not yet felt, something just out of grasp that she knew would eventually touch her. Rose carefully reached up and moved the clothes bar from where it hung, backing up to lay it on the bed. The catch that released the wardrobe's false back lay in the metal where the bar had hung. Ingenious, really. Helyne had made it.

The back of the wardrobe opened into the wall, the space for the hiding place skimmed from both the wall between bedroom and kitchen and the pantry next to the worktop. It was large enough to hold a person sitting—uncomfortably—but it currently held only Rose's crate of books and a few small valuables.

She didn't know why she'd opened it. Perhaps simply to prove to herself they hadn't found it, since they certainly would have questioned her had they realised she had a secret hiding place.

A knock sounded at the door, this time not pounding, but still insistent.

Rose quickly closed the false back of the wardrobe and replaced the clothing bar, shutting the doors. She didn't know whether to expect her best friend this time or the NPV again. Peering through the peephole as she wished she had done the first go-round, Rose's heart lurched again unexpectedly at the sight of Amelie.

She opened the door, fingers fumbling on the latches. Rose kissed Amelie's cheeks quickly, pulling her into an embrace.

"I am truly glad to see you," she said, tugging her friend through the door and closing it behind her.

Rose wanted to tell her immediately about the NPV, but something stopped her. Instead, she motioned her into the salon.

"I can't stay long," Amelie said, and her eyes still bore the haunted look she had worn the previous night. "You saw my note?"

Rose nodded. "Can you at least share a cup of tea with me?"

"If it's quick." Amelie sat with her knees together, smoothing her skirt over them. In spite of her full figure, she looked stretched thin, like a gourd someone had scraped the seeds out of to let a light shine through. Except there was no candle flickering in Amelie's centre, just a wary hollow and a silence that touched the edges of Rose's awareness.

Unnerved, Rose went to the kitchen and put the kettle on to boil, taking out two ceramic mugs and filling two mesh bags with Amelie's favourite tea, rose hip and hibiscus with a touch of chili. When the kettle boiled on the gas stove, Rose poured the water over the bags, stirring in a large dollop of honey for Amelie and a smaller amount for herself. She brought both mugs into the salon and set them down on the table, sitting beside the other woman.

The mugs steamed, and Rose looked at her friend, the NPV momentarily forgotten.

"I don't know where to start," Amelie said quietly.

Rose was silent, watching the white vapour curl away from the red surface of the tea. Somewhere in the past months or more, she had missed something. Rose knew this woman, had grown from a child into an adult with her. They had shared pillows and the occasional tears, laughter and warm cuddles, walks by the Tarenr Sea and soups during times of illness. There used to be a connection, an easy understanding. Until Rose had seen that note, she thought that perhaps that ease was still there.

Or perhaps only hoped for it. Rose recalled the dissonance she felt when Amelie and Tomas had told her of the pregnancy, the distance. Like walking beside someone for so long in silence that one doesn't notice the quiet has turned from companionship to contemplation to consternation. To look up and see that the person one began walking with is no longer nearby and that one has been moving forward alone, having left them behind.

Rose wondered how far behind she had left Amelie.

"I couldn't do it, Rose," Amelie said, shattering the silence and confused fear in the air. Her eyes were full, and she didn't bother to dab at them with the sleeve of her shirt like she used to when they'd go to the moving pictures together and see an especially sad story.

"Do what?" Rose asked, careful to keep her voice gentle. Had she not taken the tincture?

"I couldn't have his baby."

Oh. Rose looked at her friend, but Amelie did not look back. Though they sat close on the sofa, Rose felt a chasm between them, deep and cold. When had the ground opened up? She could not help but notice the words Amelie had chosen.

"Because you do not love him?" Rose ventured the question with the same careful gentleness.

"Because he hurts me."

The simple sentence fell down into that chasm between them and vanished. Rose felt her body still, felt the echo of the words even after the sound they made disappeared into the air like the steam from the mugs.

Tomas, who was Rose's second oldest friend besides Amelie. Tomas, who had wooed Amelie from the time they finished primary school. Tomas, who had only last night joked about the cold in his office freezing his fingers to his pen.

And Rose saw again the night they had told her about the baby, the way Amelie had hugged her so tight when she'd appeared at their door and the vice grip of Amelie's arm in hers. Rose remembered the sheen of tears in Amelie's eyes and the way she'd said, *"Terrified"* when Tomas had simply agreed to being excited.

Again she felt air filling her open mouth.

"It started when we were in school," Amelie said, and the next bit came out in a tumbling rush. "At first it was just a word here and there. He remarked on the untidiness of my room or that my curls were in disarray."

Rose felt a jolt. She was so used to Amelie championing order and cleanliness that she had forgotten it hadn't always been so. The change had been gradual, not sudden, and Rose felt hot shame heat her face for not having noticed.

"I thought it was my imagination," Amelie went on. She still refused to meet Rose's eyes, staring instead across the salon at the doorway to the kitchen as if she half-expected Tomas to materialise there. "It happened like the lightning flashes, Rose. When the words faded, he would be kind again. Warm."

Rose reached out her hand and lay it on Amelie's knee, and her friend trembled.

Amelie swallowed. "The words got harsher. He struck me for the first time last year, when I broke a dish. Just a dish, like any other."

"Amelie," Rose began, but her friend shook her head and Rose fell silent.

"I was so shocked I only held my hand to my face and stared at him. I didn't realise I was crying until he began to weep himself. And I found myself with my arms round his shoulders, comforting him. I wore the bruise for a week. He ran the shop and told everyone I had the stomach upsets."

Rose remembered that week. She had stopped by the shop and suggested calling on Amelie, but Tomas had informed her regretfully that his wife was too ill for callers. A sick horror took root in Rose's belly.

"I couldn't have his baby," Amelie said, turning finally to face Rose. The tears that had filled her eyes spilled over. "I couldn't."

With a shuddering breath, Rose threw her arms around Amelie's shoulders. "It's okay," she said. The words were empty, meaningless. Of course nothing was okay, but Rose did not know what else to say.

"There's more," Amelie whispered into Rose's shoulder.

"Tell me."

"Two days ago, NPV guards came to the shop when I was working. They asked to see the owner, and I told them I was the owner. They laughed."

Rose thought her blood might turn to ice. She thought of Carixo's warning. *Where is Aunt Aleis?*

"They asked where my husband was, and I told them he was at home. When I arrived home, I asked Tomas what they had wanted, and he said no one came. But there were three mugs in the sink, and when I had gone to work in the morning, there had been no dishes at all. Tomas went to an appointment yesterday. I went down to his office. I've never risked going through his things before. I never even set foot in his office, and he knows it. The papers for our business were right there, Rose. Right on his desk." Amelie gulped a breath, and her chest heaved against Rose's body. Rose held her tighter, unsure of what to do. "He took the shop from me. The seals on the papers were new. He took it. I'm no longer listed as an owner."

For a moment the only sound was Amelie's jagged breathing and sniffles. Rose herself could not let out her breath. Her chest felt full to bursting with the air she held inside.

"He is going to notice when my belly does not swell," Amelie said, her voice stricken. "Rose, please help me. I don't know what to do."

"You can come live with me," said Rose, but the thought of Asuel Saraya's words burned in her mind. *We will be in touch.*

And Amelie was shaking her head no. "This is the first place he will look. I have some little time. A month, perhaps."

"You cannot go back to him!"

"I must." Amelie pulled away, her eyes searching out the clock on Rose's wall. "I've stayed too long already, and he will know I've been weeping." At that, her lips curled in a hopeless smile. "One thing I can blame on pregnancy, is it not?"

"Amelie—"

"I'm sorry I brought this to you."

"Amelie—"

"I shouldn't have burdened you with my problems."

"Amelie, stop it!" Rose burst out as Amelie rose from the sofa. She took Amelie's face between her hands and wiped the tears from her cheeks with her thumbs. "What he has done to you is not love. It is not your fault. Go back to him now if you must, but believe me when I say I will find a way to get you out and make you safe."

The fury that smoldered in her own words surprised Rose, and she gently wound one of Amelie's curls round her finger the way she always used to.

Amelie watched her with eyes that looked as though they wanted to believe but could not. Defeat read clear in every line of her body.

And yet Rose knew that if that defeat had taken root deep enough within Amelie so as to chase out all hope, she never would have told Rose her story.

Amelie leaned forward and kissed Rose's cheek. "You are my only true friend," she said.

Then she pulled away and walked straight to the door without looking back. "You ought to lock this behind me," she called.

Rose knew she was right, but she couldn't quite make herself do it. Instead, she sat down on the sofa where the cushions were still warm and watched the last swirls of steam rise from the untouched mugs.

• • • • •

Rose's mind felt stretched to near-breaking by the time she left her flat to meet Beo. She made her way down Carino Avenue to Plax Rynka, and the cobbles beneath her feet seemed to wobble as she walked. Café Maya was still closed. The wind bit at her face. Rose had no idea what she might find. If Aleis was gone, what of the tea shop?

She soon found out.

Beo stood in front of the shop, peering through the window. "Rose, it's closed."

She joined him next to the door. Sure enough, the café was darkened inside.

When Beo's eyes met hers, Rose felt her chin shake once, and she steeled herself. She would not weep.

"You do not look surprised," said Beo. He closed the distance between them and kissed both her cheeks in belated greeting. "Are you all right?"

Rose looked about. Up and down the street, passers-by ignored them, except one woman who stopped, saw that the shop was closed, and frowned in disappointment before continuing on.

"I have a key," she said without answering his question. "Follow me."

The door opened easily, as always. Nothing in the shop seemed to have been disturbed since the night before. Rose latched the door behind them and motioned to Beo to follow her through the dining room and up to Aleis's flat.

She didn't expect anyone to answer when she knocked, and no one did. Rose didn't have a key to the flat, but she tried the knob just in case. Sometimes the aunts left it open. Not today.

Rose jiggled the knob once more, then closed her eyes, leaned back against the door, and sank down slowly to the floor. "The NPV came to my flat this morning," she said.

"What?"

"They wanted to know where my aunt was."

"Your aunt who owns this shop?"

Rose nodded, looking up through her eyelashes at Beo. After a pause, he joined her on the floor, sitting close enough to be a comfort but not so close as to be an invasion.

"They asked about the records she kept." Rose hadn't told Beo about what she had done to hide them. "First that and now this. Aleis and her two partners are gone."

A moment of indecision passed with quiet lassitude. Rose made up her mind.

She told Beo of Carixo's visit, how she had hidden the records (but not where). She told him of being woken by the pounding of the guard's fist on her door and how they had searched her flat. She told him how she had called upon Aunt Aleis the previous night and instead found Helyne, of the odd trio of gifts given to her and Helyne's entire air that now seemed far too nonchalant. And Rose told him of Amelie's visit and the reason for it.

Beo's face grew darker and darker with every passing sentence, but he did not interrupt or venture any words.

"Doctor Carixo told me that I was kept in ignorance," Rose said. "I heard Rico Samson's address last night. I feel I have been a fool, to not realise what bubbled beneath the surface of my city. I do not even know that I understand it now. But to find first Café Maya closed and now this shop—"

A thought stopped her mid-sentence.

"What is it?" Beo asked.

"Amelie's business. She said the NPV sent guards to her business and asked to see the owner, then laughed when she said it was she who owned it along with her husband. Her business has not been closed, but she no longer owns it. Only Tomas." The same sick horror roiled in Rose's belly. "Their business remains open. Café Maya and Aunt Aleis's do not."

"Maya is unmarried," Beo said slowly.

"Aleis has two women partners." Rose swallowed. "Carixo was right. He came to warn them."

Rose suddenly felt as if she knew nothing of her own city. Her satchel dug into her side. Unthinking, she pulled *Red Sunrise* from it. Beo watched her movements, curiosity behind his gaze.

"This feels like the Sanmarian in the book," said Rose. "But the book is not real."

Beo sat, stroking one fingernail with the pad of his thumb as he thought. "I was warned when I moved here," he said at last. "That wariness is wisdom in Sanmarian."

"Who warned you?"

"My...aunt," he said after a moment of hesitation. "She came to live with us just before my father died. She was my mother's sister. My father was twice married and twice widowed. Her name is Irena."

"Irena is my middle name," Rose said without thinking. It was a very common name, but the way Beo looked at her, Rose felt the cord between them tighten when he gave her a small, sad smile.

"She came from Sanmarian. She never told me why she left, only that the city was dangerous no matter how quiet it seemed."

Dangerous.

Rose did not know what to do. Her family, her friends—in the space of a week all things familiar had been turned inside out.

"The NPV will destroy this city," she said, her voice so quiet she wasn't certain Beo had heard her. In *Red Sunrise*, the party taking over the city was not explicitly the NPV, nor were they named at all other than the Man in Red, though in every deed and word she now knew the parallel to be true.

As softly as she had spoken, Beo had indeed heard her. He nodded, and he reached out to gently squeeze her hand. Rose squeezed it back.

She felt dimly that the book she held in her free hand was exactly what she had always believed it to be as a child.

It was hers.

CHAPTER TWELVE

It was Beo's idea to go to the library. After sitting in the corridor outside Aleis's silent flat for the better part of an hour, Beo and Rose made their way back out onto the street. A pair of nonplussed passers-by greeted them, peering through the window.

"Closed?" one of them asked as Rose locked the door.

"Indefinitely," Rose said, her mouth forming the word as if it tasted bitter to her.

Beo had no blame for her on that. The pair of passers-by, one in her forties and the other, likely her father, exchanged a look.

As they walked up the street, Beo couldn't help but notice that Rose walked close enough to him that their shoulders bumped every few steps.

It was a strange comfort from someone who ought to be a stranger for all the barely a week they'd known each other. Yet some of the tension left him just being in her presence, and somewhere deep within him, Beo wanted to believe the unshakeable sense that she felt the same. They were both quiet as they picked out a path through the Popaxel crowds of shoppers and coffee-seekers, all in a feverish bustle to stave off the Niepax morning alarm that would wake them the next day for another week of work.

Niepax. "No peace," named for the day the gods had created human beings.

Larsi, the trickster, had seen her siblings' work and been excluded from it, and she had taken her revenge by adding somewhat to their creation. It was said she had given humanity a curious mind and the first question asked by the humans who opened their eyes after being formed by the gods as tangles of many limbs and heads was *why*.

The gods split those first gargantuan beings into their now-human forms, that they would wander the earth in search of themselves, finding only glimmers in one another to guide them. The gods thought such a distraction would bring quiet to the earth, but the humans searched and searched and asked the gods why they could not find themselves. From then the gods knew their own folly, and from then they truly knew no peace.

Beo had always felt as if that story were true, for no matter how he wandered, he felt he could not find himself. Rose's shoulder bumped his, and he looked over at her. She gazed straight ahead, her eyes trained on the market square they approached, but he felt her awareness of him.

No peace indeed. Also the first day of the work week, which seemed the more mundane explanation for the day's name.

He liked the second day of the week, Torek, which was named so for the bulls the gods loosed in their fury at Larsi for tricking them. Larsi, being only delighted by their anger, fled the stampede. The remaining gods thought her trampled until they saw her, leaping agilely from bull back to bull back. Each year at midwinter for the longest night that heralded the coming of the new year, the cities of Kael loosed a herd of bulls through the city, with those hoping to gain favour with Larsi for the coming year volunteering to run among them.

It wouldn't be long before that longest night, Beo thought.

The sun had crested the height of the buildings at Sanmarian's centre, turning the square to red-gold. The morning mist had long since dissipated, and as they walked toward the tower that housed the library, Rose broke the silence.

"It feels colder," she murmured.

Beo didn't think she meant the temperature.

Though she had only briefly spoken of it, her forehead was still creased with worry for her aunts. If the NPV was still looking for them, it seemed likely at least that they had escaped the city or found a hiding place, but Rose thought (and Beo agreed) that having no information was worrisome. Sensing she was in need of a distraction, Beo had suggested they go to the library.

It wasn't wholly a distraction; after having seen the NPV guards removing crates of books, Beo wanted to ask the librarians if they could share any information.

The last vestige of hope for any sort of distraction evaporated as Rose held the library door open for him to pass through. One of the librarians had her head bowed over the information desk, shoulders shaking. Another had her arm around the weeping woman, looking around as if she expected to turn her face directly into the barrel of a gun. Stray papers fluttered over the floor in the gust of wind from the door, and behind him, Beo heard Rose's footsteps stop.

"Oh, my gods." Her voice sounded like a shout in the quiet, and the door's loud thud as it closed made all four of them jump.

The librarian who was comforting her colleague murmured something, and the other woman—Beo now recognised her as Veran, who had helped him before—looked up and hurriedly wiped her eyes on the sleeve of her shirt.

"Are you all right?" Beo asked, stepping forward with Rose. He dug in his camera bag, but his usual small stack of handkerchiefs was gone.

Rose had one, however. She reached out with a small scrap of muslin and handed it to Veran, who took it, looking abashed.

Veran and the other librarian looked at one another, and Beo thought he saw the second woman shake her head almost imperceptibly.

"I'm quite all right," Veran said. "It's Beomir, no?"

"Beo," said Beo.

He met the second librarian's eyes with a look he knew said he didn't believe that anyone was all right, and Beo and Rose moved away. Rose bent to retrieve a few stray papers and set them on the information desk.

"The shelves," Rose said.

The gaps between books had grown. Though the library still smelled as it ever had, of leather and paper and the dust of worlds, it felt hollow. The shelves looked like a game Beo had played as a child, a game of stacked wooden blocks and a small tapper in which the object was to poke holes in the wall without making it fall. How many more books, he wondered, would it take to make Sanmarian's library fall?

"They must have come back again," said Beo, and Rose did not have to ask who he meant.

Together, they climbed the stairs to the top of the library. The tower extended some way above even that, but at its top was a circular window of heavy glass that cast light from the noon sky down into the dusty cavern below. Motes sparkled in the light, almost beautiful. Far below—for the centre of the tower was open, ringed by floors of books and staircases—Beo could see the papers scattered on the floor.

"I wish I knew what was missing," Rose said quietly. "If there were some pattern."

"There is," came an equally quiet voice from behind them.

Beo turned to see Veran standing there, her eyes puffy. With her, she carried a small pile of books. Second from the top was a book of verse by a poet Beo had read. His fathers had a copy though he had later discovered the book was rare to find—or had it belonged to his mother? It was by Sanna, often called Honey-tongue, for her verse was as much about the many uses of her tongue as her use of words. She was a great lover of women, and it was said even men had come by the dozen to seek her attentions, dreaming of being immortalised in her words but mostly desirous of the experience of lying with her. Sanna turned them all away with a wink and a sprig of honeysuckle, for she knew well her own nickname and had no need or want for the company of men.

"Alyn doesn't know I'm here," Veran said. "I told her to go on her rest break."

Her face held an urgency Beo recognised, and he thought Rose did as well. He thought he had worn that look as they had hurried from the pub to his flat, and he had seen the same on Rose's face as they moved through the café to the relative safety of the stairwell to her aunts' home.

"I have been hiding these works," Veran said, holding out the pile. "I have seen you here before. You are a great reader, are you not?"

"I am a reader," Beo said, confused. "I'm not certain that is to be equated with greatness."

"You asked me once about a book called *Red Sunrise*, did you not?"

Rose jumped at the title, and Veran marked it, he saw.

"I did," Beo said, caution staying his words.

Some of the tension went out of Veran's shoulders. To Beo's surprise, she held out the small pile of books in her arms. "I want you to take these. Keep them safe."

"I haven't a safe place—" Beo began, but Rose held up a hand.

"I have," she said, reaching to take the books.

Veran hesitated, as if unsure she could trust Rose.

A moment of consternation passed over Rose's face, and she opened her satchel, pulling out her copy of *Red Sunrise*. "You are only the third person other than myself I have ever heard mention this book," Rose said.

The librarian's eyes widened. "Where did you get that?"

"My Papa gave it to me," said Rose. "What do you know of this book?"

Still gripping the small pile of books in her arms, Veran shot a look over her shoulder as if expecting her colleague to return.

"That book is somewhat of a legend. Collectors cannot find it, and every library has been asked of it by two sorts of people. The first is those who value it in some way, as an oddity or a rarity or somewhat more. Those are the rarer people themselves." Veran watched Rose, had to see the way Rose's hands cradled the book as if it were precious. Her voice fell to a hoarse whisper. "The second is the NPV."

Beo happened to be watching Rose's face when Veran finished her sentence, and he saw the flash of absolute panic, which settled into a resolute kind of implacability. Rose met Beo's eyes, and he pulled his own copies from his bag.

Veran's eyes widened as if she could not control them. "You have three copies." A burning curiosity and eagerness filled her face and spread through her body. Her fingers twitched on the pile of books she held. "How?"

"My Papa," Rose said simply. "Accounts for two of them, at least."

"Who was your Papa?"

"Andreas Abernethy," Rose said, the name as warm as a stoked hearth on a bitter winter night.

Veran's expression shifted to blank confusion, and she shrugged. "I suppose it matters not. You say you have a place you can keep these books safe?"

"I have indeed." Rose slipped *Red Sunrise* back into her satchel and took the books from Veran's hands. There were four of them, and Rose managed to fit them in beside the other.

"Veran," Beo said, "why are the NPV taking books from the library?"

"They aren't much for explaining their motives," Veran said, but her eyes darkened. "But when I was a child, a contingent of NPV guards came through my village, on the eve of their rise to power throughout Kael. They were on their way to Sankael, but they paused in my home village to rest and drink and spread their pamphlets. The tavern was also home to the small village library. The guards rifled through it and took a number of books. At first, we thought they meant only to read them that night; the books were there to be borrowed. I was there that evening, on some errand with my Mama. They took the books out to the square, and their leader gave a speech about the responsibility of the people to maintain purity of mind. They doused the books with rum and set them alight."

Rose and Beo stood silent, and Beo wanted to take her hand. He was not sure if the desire was for her comfort or his own.

Veran went on, her voice soft. "They were drunk, and I thought not much of it. I was a child, and I knew nothing of politicking. But Mama was frightened and pulled us away. We went home, and she sent me directly to my bed. I sneaked out, because my heart would not stop its pounding enough for me to sleep. I heard Mama tell Papa and Grand-papa what we had seen. Papa was silent, but Grand-papa said, 'Books are mere kindling for fires intended to burn people.'"

• • • • •

Keep them safe had been Veran's admonition to Beo and Rose as they left the library, and Beo followed Rose across the square to Carino Avenue, twice pausing to pretend to window-shop when NPV guards came walking past.

Paranoia was a new emotion for Beomir Mataya, and it unsettled him how naturally it seemed to settle into his marrow.

Rose led the way to her flat, neither of them speaking as they walked, quickly enough to appear to others as if they wanted to truncate their existence in the winter cold but slowly enough not to elicit undue notice. She pushed open the door when they arrived, motioning Beo through it and then turning every latch.

"Please, make yourself comfortable," she said.

Two ceramic mugs of tea sat on the table in the salon, a strange sight until he remembered that she had mentioned a friend's visit just after the guards burst in on her morning. Beo unslung his camera bag from his shoulder and sat on the sofa, which, unlike his, appeared to be oft-used.

Rose picked up one of the mugs and sipped from it. "If you want some cold tea, no one touched the other. I can make more if you'd like."

"Thanks, but I'm all right."

Beo looked around the flat. The bookcase was in disorder, and when Rose saw where he was looking, she went to it and began to straighten the books.

"They searched it," she said simply. Rose perfunctorily lay a hand along the line of the shelves one by one, sliding the books until they sat even against it.

"Where do you keep the copies of *Red Sunrise*?" Beo wondered if Larsi's blind luck had favoured Rose enough to keep hidden a crate of books the NPV clearly intended to keep out of the public's hands.

"I'll show you."

Beo followed Rose to her bedroom, where she placed the library books on the bed and opened her wardrobe. He had heard of Sanmarian's homes having hiding spaces, but he would never have expected such an ingenious design as the wardrobe. Inside the cubby behind it was the crate of copies of *Red Sunrise*, and propped up on the crate was an envelope with Rose's name on it.

She reached out a hand to take it, and Beo couldn't help but notice that her fingers shook, the movement almost more a vibration than a quiver.

Rose ran her fingers over the rough paper of the envelope. "Helyne makes her own paper," she murmured. "From the sawdust of her carpentry. She doesn't believe in wasting things."

Beo, whose breath was growing hot in his chest from unknowingly holding it, breathed out slowly through his nose. "They are okay," he said. "They must be, if they left that."

Rose met his eyes, but her expression was unreadable.

About the length and width of a book itself, the envelope seemed to hold a large sheaf of papers. Rose slid her finger under the seal on the back.

She pulled out a folder, a note clipped to the front.

"It's from Aunt Aleis," she said.

CHAPTER THIRTEEN

Dearest Rose,

They came.

We hid beneath the floors, felt the wood shake with their steps. When they had gone, we moved. I will not tell you where. Roban has left the city as well with his wife. It is best you keep on as normally as you can for now.

Enclosed is what you need to know about the NPV. Your parents stood against them once. I will not think less of you if you put your feet to a different path.

We knew this day would come. What you do not know keeps you safe, Rose. Ignorance is not blissful, but it can be a shield of sorts. This is why we kept things from you, knowing a day would come when we'd have to let you make your own choices. Ignorance is at best a shield, but knowledge is the truest blade. Often it cuts through the tangles, cuts a path for those the opposing powers seek to silence.

Burn the accounts, and burn this note. You now have everything you need, whatever you may do with it.

Grenye, Helyne, and I love you very much. We trust that giving you choice now was the best course. If not, we hope we will someday earn your forgiveness.

That was all the note said. Rose held it a moment in tight fingers that wanted to shake and drop it. Behind the note was a bundle of papers, typewritten and yellowed with age. The date upon them was twenty years past, and the title, in boldface, was

A TREATISE AND MANIFEST OF THE GOALS AND PROCEDURES OF THE NATIONAL PEOPLE'S VOICE

CONFIDENTIAL: STAGE FIVE

Rose knew Beo could see it over her shoulder—she felt his warmth against the wool of her jumper and heard the slow intake of his breath—but she did not know how to react. Where had Aleis gotten such a thing? Had her father somehow taken hold of it? Rose had no way of knowing.

She read through the papers with a slowly sickening stomach, finding phrases like "Kaeli purity" and words like "sociosexology" that were each given a parenthetical instructing the reader that they were not to be utilised outside NPV circles, that softer words were to be used until someone's loyalties were clear.

The National People's Voice will admit women, but only in the capacity of observer. Women are not to hold office or position within the Party, for their social space is the home, at the hearth, and with their husbands. Those women minded to be of service to the Party shall do so by sharing the Party's wisdom with their children, that the next generation may outstrip the current in adhering to these roles.

All children raised by NPV members are expected to maintain themselves in accordance to sociosexological roles and the biological imperative of gender purity. Those seeking to eschew the biological imperative of gender purity will be reconditioned.

Rose read the paragraphs twice, her breath coming faster. From the context of what she had already read, the final sentence meant that people like Grenye, who did not fit the NPV's biological imperative of "gender purity" were not welcome. Grenye was a woman. Rose had never considered her anything else, and only knew she did not fit the NPV's imperative because Grenye had told Rose herself.

"I was a little boy who grew up to be a woman," Grenye had said perfunctorily one day. "Some people like me would not phrase it so, but for me, I can hold those two things in my mind at once."

That was the end of it, for Rose had been little more than a child, and she knew others like Grenye and those who were neither boy nor girl but instead neither or both, and such was the world Rose knew. Aunt Aleis had come into the room just as Grenye said it and smiled fondly, kissing Grenye on the cheek, and Rose had run along to finish her chores.

Rose reread the paragraphs again, her eyes sticking on the word "reconditioned."

"What do they mean by reconditioned?" Rose asked. Something in her chest felt jagged and frightening. She could not bridge the gap in her mind between the public face of the NPV and the contents of this missive.

The warmth of Beo's body moved away, leaving a cooler void as he stepped quietly around the foot of her bed to face her. Before he could answer, Rose straightened the stack of papers in her hands.

"Never mind. I don't think I want to know."

"This is why your aunts left."

"How did they know all this? How did Doctor Carixo know?" Rose wanted to sit down. Her head felt full of information, heavy and light at once, like it might float away or crash through the floor and she wasn't sure which.

"I don't know," said Beo. "But I think I might know someone who can help."

· · · · ·

To Rose, Beo's face looked as though he weren't certain *help* was the correct word to use.

The city was dark and mostly quiet as they made their way through Sanmarian's winding streets to the old Roa quarter. As a child, Rose had devoured more books than just *Red Sunrise*; among her many favourites were a series of chapter books about the hidden worlds beneath Sanmarian's cobblestones, of spirits that rose up between the rocks and took form in the twisting closes and darkened plax corners where the world had moved on. Those books had whispered that the reason Sanmarian was made of sunset stone was because it became its own mortar over time, and nothing could get through cracks where there were none.

Tonight, whatever sinister spirits slunk through the city, Rose did not think they were made of the dead.

Beo led her to Yoan's flat, where Yoan greeted them with no small amount of surprise that quickly turned to dread on his face. Rose showed him the NPV manifesto and watched his face grow bleaker and bleaker.

"Stay here," he said. He tucked a strand of hair behind his ear and scratched his bearded cheek. "I'll be back in an hour, no more. If I'm not back in an hour and a quarter, go back to Rose's flat and wait till morning."

Rose's stomach dipped with a squirming feeling. She swallowed, and her tongue stuck to the roof of her mouth. She nodded at Yoan.

Beo sat quietly on Yoan's sofa, where a small pile of pillows and blankets was stacked. He leaned one arm on the pile and gestured to Rose to sit next to him.

For a moment she thought if she sat she'd go mad, but a cold wind rattled the windows of the flat, and she no longer wanted to pace.

Rose sat next to Beo, feeling the welcome warmth of his body as the sofa's cushions dipped beneath their weight, making a divot where gravity pulled them together. Their shoulders touched, and neither moved away.

"Do you know where he's going?" Rose's voice sounded hollow against the backdrop of the whistling wind outside.

"I think to someone from Liberation Front, but I don't know for sure."

"You trust him." It wasn't a question.

"I do," said Beo, but there was uncertainty in his voice. "I've never had to think much about what that means before now."

Neither spoke then, only listened to the wind outside the windows and the way the sofa creaked with each shift of their weight.

"Did you hear Rico Samson's address the other night?" Rose asked. It now felt a world away, the boom of the cannon, the words crackling through her radio.

Beo shook his head. "Why do you ask?"

"Because I don't think it's something we can turn away from."

"My Aunt Irena did not think so. I think she knew."

"I think you're right." Rose pushed her feet together and folded her hands on her knees. "I feel like a fool."

"You're not one."

"Am I not? Aunt Aleis said my parents fought against the NPV. It does not sound like they did so with strongly worded pamphlets. How could I not have known?"

"How could you have known when they actively kept it from you?" Beo reached out and took Rose's hand. The contact of his skin sent heat sparking through her. He squeezed it tight. "I ignored Irena's warnings and came to this city, though I think what is happening here goes beyond simply Sanmarian. The NPV is not only a local party."

"Do you think this will lead to war?" War. Rose had not yet been born when the last war ended. Kael had recovered slowly, technically victorious though historians disagreed on the degree of success. Rose had always thought their victory one only of keeping the border in the same place it had been before.

"A divided Kael could be at risk of civil war." Beo had not yet released Rose's hand.

"And that could put the country at risk of invasion," Rose said softly. She was afraid to move, afraid if she did he would take his hand away. Any longer and it would go beyond a momentary comfort, into territory she was not certain of, only that she didn't want to lose the warmth of his palm against the back of her hand.

The lights flickered, and Beo started, his hand jumping away from Rose's.

"How long has it been?" His voice came out in a hoarse near-whisper.

"Twenty-five minutes."

Rose's fingers twined together on her knee, and her thoughts grew dark. The NPV had been in place for some fifteen years; ousting them would be no mean feat, and they had supporters. Some, she assumed, had to genuinely believe the NPV would make Kael a prosperous place once more. Years of uncertainty had lowered living standards for the working classes, but most folks got by. What unsettled her was the way the NPV spoke of families; there could be no mistaking what they considered a family even to a mildly astute listener, and the papers Aleis had left pushed any doubt into oblivion. The NPV had subtly been sending social messages for years. It was that Rose felt most foolish for missing; her own family was so prominent in her life that she did not stop to think what might happen were they to become the scapegoats of society. She had existed in her cushioned job, in an office that was warm in winter and cooled in summer and with her flat paid for from the sale of Papa's house. She had escaped many trials simply due to her family's established comfort.

Rose could not tell where Beo's thoughts had wandered as the minutes ticked by. Twice she heard footsteps, but both times the sound turned up the stairs and the passer-by stomped upward. The clock passed the hour mark since Yoan had left, then the city bells tolled out eight.

"He said to leave after an hour and a quarter passed." Rose's words broke the silence after the eighth bell, and Beo looked at her, face grave.

"Five more minutes," he said.

Rose nodded.

Footsteps sounded in the corridor, more noise than one set could make. Thinking quickly, Rose unlatched the window closest to the sofa.

"If it is not Yoan, jump out and run," Rose whispered. "Go straight to my flat and wait in the close behind the building."

She pulled her scarf up to cover the bottom of her face, instinctively sensing that if it were NPV guards to come through the door, being recognised would make even her own flat unsafe.

Beo did the same, and they both edged toward the window.

A key entered the lock and rattled.

Rose looked at Beo, and her skin tingled. She tried to steady her breathing, tried to prepare her body on how to react whoever might come through the door.

The door opened, and Yoan's face peered through. He gave a relieved sigh and hurriedly entered the flat, motioning a tall woman through and latching the door behind him.

Her face was sun-darkened to a deeper shade of brown, and her hair she wore cropped close to her scalp. She moved brusquely into the room, and Rose felt certain when the woman's dark eyes fell on her that they took in everything about her in one glance. The woman's hands were bare of gloves or mittens in spite of the cold, and they had known hard labour, judging from the callouses and and close-clipped nails. She had broad shoulders but a wiry build, and her eyes slid from Rose to Beo in one smooth motion.

"This is Taran Marpaxan," Yoan said, nodding at the tall woman. She stood an inch or two above his own height, and he gave no further introduction. "She can be trusted."

Rose thought again of Beo's words from before. What did it mean to trust? Trust that words spoken would be truth, at least to the best of the speaker's knowledge and belief? Trust that their lives were safe in her hands?

"Rosenni Irena Abernethy," said Rose, using her full name for once in her life. Taran Marpaxan's face shifted expression at the sound of Rose's name, but she said nothing, only looked to Beo.

"Beomir Lukas Mataya," he said. Marpaxan's face did not give the same shift at his.

Rose found out why a moment later.

"You are Andreas and Miko's child," the woman said. "Your father was a dear friend of mine, and I was sorry to hear of his death."

This time Rose started. "Thank you. I miss him." A thought came to her, and Rose couldn't help herself but to speak. "If you knew my father, have you had word of my aunts? Aleis, Grenye, and Helyne Nicaro? The NPV raided their flat, and they left a message for me, but I've no idea where they went."

Marpaxan glanced toward the window but said nothing for a moment. "I have never met Aleis or Helyne, but I knew Grenye long ago. Last I saw her was before Andreas died." After a pause, she went on. "If I hear word of them, I will let you know unless they ask me not to."

Rose wasn't sure if she felt settled or unsettled by that answer. That the woman standing in front of her had some form of connection to her family—to Papa, no less—was a small comfort, but Andreas had died fifteen years back and many things could change far more quickly than that.

"Beo has been a close friend of mine for some years," said Yoan. "I will vouch for him."

"So you've said," Taran Marpaxan said. She straightened her shoulders and folded her hands in front of her, like a soldier standing at ease. "Yoan tells me you are in possession of an actual insider NPV manifesto. May I see it?"

Rose looked at Beo, whose eyes were unreadable. Rose pulled out the manifesto from her satchel and handed it to Marpaxan.

There was silence except for the rustling of papers while Marpaxan read, stone-faced.

When she finished, she hesitated before passing the sheaf back to Rose. "Thank you for sharing that, Rosenni."

"Rose, please," said Rose. "You don't look surprised."

"We have seen bits and pieces of what you have in the past. Would you permit me to make copies of this?"

Rose froze with her hand on the papers, awareness seeming to creep through the inks and pages themselves into her skin. So far, her involvement had been peripheral. She could burn the manifest along with Aleis's note and go about her life, finding a new job or putting Beo in charge of her aunts' business and running it through him, an avenue through the shadowy machinations of the NPV restricting women in the workplace. But how long would it last before she lost the ability to even work? Would that dampen suspicion or arouse more of it? She may have felt a fool for not seeing it sooner, but as she stood holding twenty-year-old documents that sought to reshape the entire social structure of her world, Rose realised she would become a fool in truth if she tried to rebury her head in the sand.

The world felt colder, sharper, uncomfortable.

Rose took a calming breath and put the papers away, then looked at Taran Marpaxan and committed her first true act of sedition against the ruling party of Sanmarian.

"You may make copies," she said, "after I have a chance to make some myself."

Taran Marpaxan gave a satisfied nod, and Rose did not think it was only because she had gotten what she wanted. Beside her, Beo seemed to relax a small bit.

The lights flickered once more in the salon. Marpaxan ignored them, looking once to Yoan, then to Beo. "What is it you do?"

"I'm a photographer."

"Ah." Marpaxan seemed to connect something. "Your flat was raided. Yoan mentioned it. Do you have any idea why the NPV would target you?"

"None," Beo said. "Yoan thinks it's because of my proximity to him, but I don't think so."

"If the NPV suspected that Yoan was directly involved in Liberation Front activities, they would have taken him already."

Beo nodded his agreement. "It must be something else. Rose and I were at the pub, and I showed her my work at the table. It's possible they saw something in those photographs that led them to steal the portfolio."

"That sounds likely," Marpaxan said.

"They seemed to be looking for your negatives, too," Rose added. "They searched the flat top to bottom."

"Did they find them?" Marpaxan's eyes narrowed, looking approvingly at Rose once more.

"I send them to my aunt in my home village," Beo said. "I seldom reprint photographs unless it's for a show. Which," he said ruefully, "I may have to do shortly. I'm meant to speak with Tarn Susette of the Overlook Galleria; he and I met the day Lib Front marched."

"Do it," Marpaxan said. "I know little of Susette, only that he prides the Galleria on art without censorship. He has danced close to NPV flames more than once, but never close enough to elicit real speculation about his loyalties. If you have an appointment with him, keep it. Whatever you do, do not show that you are ruffled by things as they are. It is best to go on as if nothing is wrong."

Yoan, still standing by the door, smoothed his hands over his hair, pressing down flyaways from his bun.

Rose felt strangely calm. "I will return to my aunts' offices tomorrow and carry out some of the things they told me to do. If the NPV come by, I will tell them I'll search for new employment as soon as I make sure the office is in order for my aunts' return. Let them think I truly believe the aunts will come back as if nothing has happened."

"Yes," Marpaxan said. "Stay in your home. Be inside before dark if you can. Yoan or I will contact you by week's end."

"What happens at week's end?" Rose asked.

"The next meeting," Marpaxan said. "That is, if you would like to join us."

Rose thought of her father, and though she had no way of knowing what went through Beo's mind beside her, she could almost feel his decision made at the same time as her own.

"We'll be there," said Rose.

Taran Marpaxan looked over them one more time as Yoan unlatched the door to let her out. "Your father was a good man," she said. "He deserved a better end than he got."

She left before Rose could work through what she'd said and ask what she meant.

CHAPTER FOURTEEN

Both Beo and Yoan walked Rose home that night. She was quiet as she walked beside them, though more than once before they left her at her flat, she offered to let them both stay there so as not to have to wander the city more than necessary after dark.

"Taran said we ought to keep to as normal a routine as possible," Yoan said. "We'll be quite all right."

Still, Beo didn't like leaving her there. It wasn't, as one might suppose, leaving her alone that made him disquieted. He thought of her hand warm beneath his own earlier that evening and found that the truth of the matter was that he did not have any desire to leave her side at all.

The following days passed with a strange return to the mundane. Beo went to his job, framed paintings, and returned to Yoan's. On Torek, he checked in on his flat and made a half-hearted attempt at tidying some things up but gave up when he found that a family of mice had found the tear in his mattress to be a serendipitous new home, and he didn't think he could stomach the idea of turning the mattress over onto the bed and possibly squashing mouse babies. He left them be.

He and Rose had agreed not to see each other until after the call with Tarn Susette, on the chance anyone was watching her or them both. Srodo, the midweek day, arrived with the need to ring Susette.

Yoan was already down the pub to open when Beo made his way to the communal telephone on the second floor of Yoan's building. The connection seemed to take forever, setting Beo's heart to a too-quick rhythm from anxiety; once, Irena had told Beo that there was almost no wait for telephone connections, but things were different now. He'd never stopped to think that perhaps the NPV had something to do with that.

"Overlook Galleria, how may I direct your call?" A young voice, probably a man, with a pleasant tone that erred just this side of outright boredom.

"Tarn Susette, please. This is Beo Mataya."

"One moment, please."

There was the sound of chimes on the line, followed by ringing.

"This is Tarn Susette."

"Mister Susette, this is Beo Mataya," said Beo. "You had asked me to ring you this week regarding space at the Galleria."

"Ah, yes. Thank you for your promptness. I would very much like to give you the northwest gallery space for an exhibition starting next week. We had an exhibitor pull out of the Galleria last minute. Can you deliver the prints this week?"

Beo's stomach did an unnerving flip-flop, leaping at the news that he would get the space he wanted—northern light, excellent foot traffic—and then sinking a moment later at the time frame. "I'm afraid I had a bit of a misfortune befall me this week, Mister Susette," Beo said carefully, considering. "My flat was broken into, and some of my equipment was destroyed. My negatives are elsewhere, but it will likely be next week before I can get you the prints. I kept inventory of the page numbers of my portfolio, so I can ensure the prints I choose are the ones you preferred."

He could almost hear Susette waving away his words. "That won't be necessary. You will have the space for between eight to fifteen prints, and I'll leave it to you to choose. I'm sorry to hear about your flat. If you are in need of space to develop, my colleague has an excellent darkroom and I am certain he would welcome you to prepare for the exhibition there. He is quite eager to meet you."

"That is too kind of you."

"Hardly a kindness. You do good work, and I have little interest in seeing your talent go unnoticed simply because some ruffian took liberties with your home."

There was a momentary silence. "Regardless, thank you."

Tarn Susette gave an address in the northern quarter of the city, and a name. Emon Sanhaya.

"Would it be possible to come on Popaxel to develop the prints?" Beo asked. "I'll need a day or two to travel."

"Your negatives are not in the city?"

"I'm afraid not." Beo thought of Irena, and how surprised she would be to see him.

"Very well. I'll tell Emon to expect you first thing Popaxel morning. He isn't one for early days, so first thing is likely tenth bell, mind."

"Please pass along my thanks to him," said Beo. "I'll be there."

"I look forward to seeing your work at the Overlook," Susette says. "It deserves a wider audience."

The line disconnected then, and Beo steadied himself next to the phone.

It wasn't until he replaced the receiver that he realised the only other person who could have seen his portfolio besides Rose and the pub patrons was Susette himself.

• • • • •

That afternoon, Beo met up with Rose in the city centre after finishing up a short shift at work. Her face looked troubled, but her eyes brightened when she caught sight of him.

Beo kissed both her cheeks, feeling her cold nose brush against his skin.

They took a turn around Plax Rynka, both keeping eyes out for NPV guards and speaking in low voices. He told her of his plan to travel to Viyarenyo that night. The final train would leave Sanmarian in two hours, and Rose insisted on helping him pass the time before he had to go.

"I haven't been back to the office yet," Rose confessed as they walked. "I passed by today, and it looked undisturbed, but I am afraid I'll go in and find the place torn apart like your flat was."

"You should go in," Beo said. "If you like, I'll take a later train and go with you tomorrow before I leave."

Rose shook her head. "I don't think that's wise." She looked wistful as she said it. "It's one thing to be seen strolling together, but if you were to go to the office, it could attract more notice for you. More risk. But thank you."

The lamps along the edges of the square flickered orange against the sunset stone and the sunset itself, and Market Tower rose high, casting a long shadow in the swiftly sinking light. The air looked warm in spite of the winter cold, and the sunset came earlier and earlier in these days before the longest night.

"How long will you be away?" Rose asked.

"Until Paxel," said Beo. "I'd like to have a full day with Irena if I'm going to make the journey."

Rose was quiet for a moment, adjusting her gloves to cover the gap between wrists and coat sleeves. "The gallery exhibition sounds like a wonderful thing for you."

They paused to let a cart worker go by, the wheels of the cart jangling against the cobblestones. Beyond where they stood, yet another shop had closed, the windows boarded up. Beo warred for a moment with himself about whether or not he ought to tell Rose what he had realised regarding Tarn Susette, then decided to do it.

He told her quickly, staring straight ahead and unconsciously tapping one finger on a button of his coat with a small *clickclickclick.*

The cart passed, and Rose started walking again. The crease between her eyebrows grew more pronounced. "You could be right," she said, a forcefulness in her voice he hadn't heard before. "How would you know whether to trust him or not? He marked down photographs, you said?"

"Yes."

"Do you remember which ones?"

Beo tried to think back, the awareness that he had moved from an unsuspicious life into a suspicious one saturating his thoughts. "Nothing of note," he said finally in answer. "He said my work deserved a wider audience."

Beo wouldn't have attributed the flattery to any kind of sinister intent before this week, but he couldn't help but wonder then.

"Be careful," Rose said, her words so soft the wind nearly stole them away.

They made a complete circuit of the square, pausing to watch workers set up for the midwinter market, where in a couple short weeks, merchants would open stalls and sell mulled wine and roasted meat and clamshells for shoppers. The market would be open until the running of the bulls for the longest night.

On sudden inspiration, Beo rummaged in his camera bag and pulled out a small notebook. He jotted down Irena's address, the home he had grown up in. "That is where I'm going. There are only one or two telephones in the village still, but the post moves quickly between Sanmarian and Viyarenyo. No more than a half a day—it runs at tenth bell in the morning and again around sixth in the evening."

"I've heard Viyarenyo is a nice village," said Rose, taking the paper between two long fingers and smoothing the crease before tucking it into a pocket on her satchel. She took Beo's pen and notebook and wrote her own address. "In case you don't remember."

It felt a bit silly to exchange addresses for so short a separation, but Beo couldn't help but notice the way Rose's hand lingered atop the pocket on her satchel where she had stashed the paper with Irena's address on it.

"What are your plans for the weekend?" Beo asked. It seemed so mundane a question that he felt silly even asking.

"I think I will do some office work," Rose said, looking around at the darkening square. She paused outside a bookshop with newly refreshed gold lettering on the plate glass windows. "Make copies and the like."

Beo didn't have to ask what copies she was going to make. The square seemed quieter than usual, the normal passers-by still moving with the direct swiftness and little conversation that had marked them since the protest. Or perhaps this had been the way of things for longer and Beo only noticed now. He wasn't certain.

"I may also call upon Amelie," said Rose, and her head turned in toward the southwest, where Beo thought her friend's home was. "I'm worried about her."

"If there is anything I can do, please tell me." Beo didn't have the faintest idea of what he might do to help in such a situation, but he couldn't help but imagine Rose's friend, trapped in a marriage that suffocated her with someone who caused her harm. He could too easily see himself in that same position, had things gone differently with Zara.

Rose looked at him gratefully. "Thank you."

"Will you go to—" Beo caught himself just before saying *the meeting* out loud.

Rose caught his meaning. "Yes," she said. "I need to understand more."

"I wish I could go with you." Beo knew she could go with Yoan in safety, but still he had hoped to go himself. He felt a surge of helplessness.

"I'm sure there will be other..." The market bells rang out five loud tolls, drowning out Rose's sentence ending.

His train left at sixth bell.

"I'll walk you to the station," Rose said.

Again as they walked, their shoulders touched.

• • • • •

The train ride to Viyarenyo was only three hours, but to Beo it seemed longer in winter as the early-setting sun made the landscape vanish into darkness, the train hurtling down the tracks without points of reference except the occasional platform.

Beo sat in his seat, an old woman snoring opposite him, and tried to calm himself. Speeding away from Sanmarian left him disquieted, as much as he wanted to be excited about his exhibition at the Overlook Galleria. His mind raced through possibilities that, a week ago, would have felt implausible. Tarn Susette as an NPV operative, the NPV clenching its fist around Kael as a whole. Was he being paranoid or simply realistic for the first time in his life?

It took the better part of two hours for him to pin down the source of what he was feeling, and when he did, it brought no comfort.

In his early days with Zara, there had been tiny moments where she would say something to him, perhaps not something outwardly cruel, but a tad disdainful, a bit hurtful. When he would ask her to repeat what she'd said, she would look at him blankly and say she hadn't said anything at all.

Later, much later, he let slip to Yoan what happened sometimes, and Yoan's shock rendered him speechless.

"You're not going mad, Beo," Yoan said to him with surprising ferocity. "That's not you. She wants you to not trust your own memory. My father used to do that to my mother and me."

At the time, it had felt almost more crazy to think of it that way, but Zara's behaviour hadn't gotten better. It had only worsened. It would pass for a while, and Zara would be the Zara he had fallen in love with for a time. She would be warm and funny, sweet and witty. And then some tiny perceived slight—asking how she was doing, maybe, or cooking the wrong fish for supper—would ignite her into an explosion of fury that sparked and fizzled for days afterward. If Beo expressed any emotion besides contrition (and in truth, even then), Zara would threaten to hurt herself, to cut herself, to kill herself.

Beo felt that same sense of helplessness and confusion now, though he did not share a bed with it this time.

The Sanmarian he knew, the Kael he knew—had it ever existed? Or had he simply brushed off its defects for so long that he'd missed the warnings all this time? Had Kael already tied its own noose, like Zara had?

Was it too late?

Beo stared out the window of the train into the darkness, unable to see anything but the memory of Zara's bloated, accusatory face, framed by rope and hanging from his ceiling.

• • • • •

Viyarenyo Station was barely more than a platform and a ticket kiosk, but the sight of it filled Beo with simultaneous nostalgia and displacement. Viyarenyo was where he had spent the first twenty years of his life; it was no longer home, though, and he didn't know if he even had one.

Getting off the train took longer than it should have, because the door to Beo's car stuck, and after ten minutes of the conductor attempting to open it, she finally gave up and funnelled the passengers through to the next car to exit.

The platform was cold and nearly empty, except of the few passengers waiting to board. Behind the kiosk, Beo could see the lit lamps of the village, sparse, but bright.

The ticket kiosk was still open for the train to return to Sanmarian after it went on past Viyarenyo to Sankael and returned in two hours, and Beo recognised the person inside. Lan Desette, an immigrant from Coret to the north who had brought her family to Viyarenyo when Beo was still in swaddling clothes. When Beo's mother had passed away, Lan had been the one to organise everything for the funeral ceremony. His father had been too distraught, staring into the distance for days on end, hardly rousing to care for Beo.

Lan looked up as Beo approached then, and he couldn't help but feel like a small child again. Her face broke into a welcome smile, and she rose from her seat inside the kiosk. Bundled in scarves to ward against the drafts in her tiny workplace, she energetically opened the door and tucked Beo into a tight hug.

"Beo Mataya, I thought I might be seeing you tonight."

"I beg your pardon?" Beo pulled back from the hug with a quick kiss on Lan's cold cheek.

Lan held up a hand and ducked her head inside the kiosk, propping the door open with her foot. "This came for you with the train. I reckoned if someone was bothering to post a letter to you here, you had either dared come to town without saying hello to me or I'd see you step on off it once they figured out how to open a door."

She looked as though she might spit in the direction of the train, but she didn't. Instead, she peered at the envelope.

The letter's direction was in Rose's hand, though it bore no sender name, and Beo took off his gloves before taking it, holding the envelope tight.

"Someone must miss you already," Lan said with a wink. "Way you're smiling, boy."

Beo hadn't realised he was. He tucked the envelope away in his camera bag. "Thank you, Lan."

"Fine, don't tell me about him." Lan stopped, then looked around. "I mean, her."

Beo felt something vile sprout in his gut. He thought of the manifest Rose had been given. As a boy in school in the village, Beo had dated both other boys and girls and those who considered themselves neither or both.

"Lan," Beo said, pitching his voice low, suddenly and painfully aware of the few travellers on the platform. "Has something happened?"

She gave him a tight smile. "Nothing I can tell you here. Ask your Aunt Irena, though, if you truly don't know."

"I think I might."

Lan looked at him closely, eyes brown against pink skin far paler than most Kaeli had. Her hair was Coretian blonde, a few shades darker than shadowed honey.

"I reckon you might, if you're back after all this time." Lan turned at the sound of footsteps, and her voice lifted into false cheer. "I've customers to tend to. Don't you dare leave this village without saying goodbye."

"I won't," Beo promised. Lan gave him a tight smile and ducked back into the kiosk, already greeting the customer.

Viyarenyo felt smaller.

Not just in the sense that it was objectively smaller—as Beo exited the tiny station and onto Rian Sanmarian, which was little more than a dual lane track for autocars passing through the village, Beo felt like the very buildings had shrunk. Viyarenyo had one main road, lined on either side by a general store that attached to the inn, a tavern on the other side of the store, and opposite that cluster of three, a bank, a barber, and the village school. The folk who ran the businesses lived above them, and while there were a few small groupings of houses that lay outside the city centre, most of Viyarenyo's population lived within pebble-tossing distance from those six main buildings.

Beo walked between them wondering whether the buildings had indeed shrunk or if he had grown larger or both.

His childhood home was one of the houses outside the central cluster, off a small side street and down a hill that iced over enough in winter that autocars couldn't pass that way.

A light glowed in the window. Beo hadn't expected Irena to have already gone to bed at just past ninth bell, but still, the sight of the lamp's light gave him a swirl of nervousness. It had been a long time since he and Irena had exchanged words that weren't written on paper.

He approached the door and knocked three times. A small window was set into the wood, and his knocking made the curtains quiver.

A moment later, the curtains drew back, and Irena's face appeared halfway from behind them. She dropped the fabric with a start, and the click of latches unlocking sounded from the other side of the door.

Beo didn't remember ever latching the door before.

It opened, and Irena stared at him, mouth agape. "Beo," she said. "What"

"I'll explain," he said quietly.

Irena moved to the side of the threshold to let him in, shock still angling her features. She latched the door again behind him and reached out to kiss his cheeks as if the only way she would believe he was truly there was to touch him.

He drew back, pulling his camera bag from his shoulder and setting it on the floor. The house had not changed since his last visit, a fact that Beo found more eerie than he would have had Irena remodelled the entirety of it.

She looked older. Her hair was now a mixture of silver and gold, and her left eye had a slight cloudiness to it. Alarmed, Beo motioned to it.

"Your eye," he said.

"Cataract," said Irena, waving her hand dismissively. "I'm a bit young for one, but the doctor says it's treatable."

"Irena," Beo began, but she cut him off with one sharp motion of her hand.

"You didn't come here to talk about how my left eye needed surgery. I'm quite all right. Sit. I'll make you some tea."

Beo obeyed, not knowing what else to do.

"I came to get a few negatives," he called over the sound of running water. "The Overlook Galleria is giving me exhibition space."

"The Overlook?" The soft poof of the gas burner followed a clank. For a moment Beo half-expected a warning from Irena, but she went on. "That's quite a to-do for you."

When she emerged from the kitchen, wiping her hands on a tea towel, Beo thought he saw a sheen to her eyes that had nothing to do with a cataract. She leaned against the arch that led to the kitchen.

"That's not all, is it?" The traces of pride vanished from her face as Irena looked closer at Beo.

He shook his head, then slowly related the events of the past week, from finding the pocket watch to losing it in the raid on his flat. But he didn't mention

Rose by name, only that a friend was helping him. Beo didn't know what he'd say. The smell of her hair—soft like chamomile—came to mind unbidden.

"You've changed," said Irena when he finished. She held a frown on her face, a frown that had appeared as he spoke, but not directed at Beo himself. It lurked in her expression like a rain-pregnant cloud rolling in from the sea. "You believe me now."

"I never doubted your warnings."

"But you never thought they would apply to you."

The teapot whistled, and Beo got up to beat Irena to finishing the cups. She turned round, leaning her other shoulder against the arch then.

Beo poured water over the tea balls. "Why did you leave Sanmarian?"

He'd asked the question before, and she had never answered.

She didn't change her pattern now. "It's not a story worth telling."

"If you know something that could help—"

"What help I can give you, I've already given." Irene's voice went flat like champagne left out overnight. "If I thought it would do any good, I would tell you to stay here and not go back."

Beo remembered Lan's self-correction on the train platform. "What's happened here?"

"The same thing that's happened everywhere else," Irena said simply. "The NPV has finally begun to show its true face."

"And what face is that?"

Irena looked at him as if he had overlooked a shark in the centre of the room. "They dislike women, and they would prefer if every couple were made only of a man and a woman. I am not certain if it has begun in the cities, but in the villages and smaller towns, certain officials and clerks have been replaced in the past two years. Those who fit party ideals have no trouble securing the necessary documentation for travel, marriage, employment, local political office."

"And those who do not?"

"They encounter unavoidable delays," Irena said, cocking her head to the side and affecting an expression of feigned sympathy. "Missing paperwork, lost documents, miscommunications. And it's not simply service workers. The teachers have all been replaced at the school."

Her eyes hardened, and her expression went flat.

"There's more," Beo said, his own voice sounding hollow.

"It hasn't happened here, and I can't be certain if the reports are substantiated," she said in preamble.

"What, Irena?"

"Harla Etiyen said her cousin is missing. He only favours the company of men. I cannot be sure, but Harla is not one for exaggeration or hysterics."

"Gods," Beo said. He thought for a moment of Rose's aunts. "Is it possible that he simply fled?"

"I suppose," said Irena, "but what reason would he have to flee Viyasurmar? In my experience, people seldom flee before it's far too late."

Irena seemed to realise that she had said something she didn't intend to. She sipped her tea in silence until it was gone, then rose and placed the empty mug in the sink.

"I'm quite tired," she said. "We can speak more in the morning, while you look for your negatives."

Beo nodded, then watched her departing back with a welter of emotions swirling in him.

When he heard the door close to her bedroom, Beo sat in his father's armchair near the banked fire on the hearth. He pulled Rose's letter from his camera bag.

The chair smelled of home, somehow still retaining what Beo remembered as his father's scent. Perhaps it was impossible. Perhaps all he smelled was old fabric and ash and stuccoed brick walls.

He slid his finger under the seal on the envelope and removed the letter.

Dear Beo,

You may think me strange for writing to you before you've even gone, but I asked the postmaster at the train station when the next post to Viyarenyo would be, and he told me it would be on your train. I thought it might be nice, in such a week as this, to arrive with something to greet you. Though you are going to your home village, so perhaps it is not needed.

We've only known each other a short time, and I think maybe it is easier to express oneself in writing sometimes than it is when there are eyes upon you. I wanted to say that I have appreciated your friendship. Not only have I had the chance to discuss my favourite stories with you, but you have proven yourself to be someone worth knowing for your own self. I am thankful that we met.

I hope your journey passed quickly and that you found a warm welcome. If by some chance neither of those things came to pass, then I hope this letter at least will show you that you are missed.

Warmly,
Rose

Beo read and reread her words, rocking in his father's chair as the embers in the hearth slowly died and the warmth in his heart slowly grew to flame.

CHAPTER FIFTEEN

Rose couldn't bring herself to start a fire in the office hearth. The chill in the air suited her mood, and she worked with dogged efficiency. The walls themselves seemed hollow, the room emptier than it should have been. Rose organised the existing orders, checked the post, laid out all the envelopes on her desk in order of postmark. There were regular orders to be filled, but the shop was closed and the aunts were long gone, and by now Rose was certain someone would know. Downstairs there was an old woodstove, and the flue stood open—though she had to tamp away some of the creosote that remained inside the stovepipe—so Rose built the fire there.

She opened the hidden closet where she had stored the business records. The crates were all just as she'd left them, neatly stacked and innocuous. Rose didn't bother to open any of the books. As the fire caught from her carefully constructed pyramid of kindling and scraps of packing paper, Rose put the first of the ledgers on to burn.

Strange, how simple it was.

Her whole life, Rosenni Abernethy had abided by the rules, the laws of Kael and Sanmarian. She sought out no opium, no drugs or medicines outside legal herbal tinctures or what her doctor prescribed for flu. When she drove her autocar, she kept it licensed and in working order. She paid her taxes ahead of their due dates.

And now, she sat and watched evidence turn to ash.

Evidence of what, she wasn't truly certain. Nothing Aleis sold was illegal. Most of the wares were only teas anyway. Some few medicinal herbs were meant to keep unwanted pregnancies from occurring; that was widespread and fully lawful. An even smaller amount were meant to end unwanted pregnancies or those sad and rare pregnancies that would harm or kill the bearer. Such things were rare, safe, accessible.

Maybe the NPV wanted to change that, but Rose could not fathom why.

Rose watched the ledgers burn, the pages licking up hot and bright against the black iron of the woodstove, and she felt something ignite within herself.

Anger.

It was not an emotion Rose had often given way to in the course of her life. There were times, of course, that as a child her frustration had become an awkward and immature tantrum. She had felt flashes of agitation and anger whilst driving her autocar when an inconsiderate driver failed to signal or cut off her route unexpectedly. But until now, Rose had never felt something she could rightly classify as fury.

It built within her, the heat of the fire drying and stretching the skin on her face taut and hot. She felt the wind of it, drawing the air from outside the stove much like Rose drew in fuel from Sanmarian to stoke her rage.

The National People's Voice. Again she wondered for whom they truly spoke, for it wasn't for her. It wasn't for Aleis or Helyne or Grenye. It wasn't for Beo or Yoan, or, she suspected, Taran Marpaxan. It wasn't for the Roa who had quietly left the city centre, or for her father, fifteen years dead.

For whom did they speak, if not these people? Were the people in Rose's life not Sanmarian citizens as well?

While the ledgers smoked and their pages and adhesives shrivelled and collapsed, Rose went upstairs and fetched an old typewriter from Grenye's desk. She placed it on a stack of crates in the cellar, pulling another crate to them to use as a chair. She sat the typewriter atop the crates, straightened the pile of blank paper she'd brought down, pulled out the NPV manifest from her satchel, and began to type.

It took five hours to burn thirty years of meticulously kept bookkeeping. During that time, Rose typed out five full copies of the NPV manifest.

So often did her eyes scan through the document that by the time she finished, her fingers cramping and her eyes burning from the heat and escaping wisps of smoke from the woodstove, she felt as if she had branded the poisonous words into her very soul.

Sociosexology. Gender purity. Reconditioning. Sexological stratagems. Reproductive integrity.

Her hands hurt, but she had five stacks of paper, copied truthfully from the original. As the embers died down with the last of the burnt ledgers, Rose looked over her work in the dimming light of the cellar. The lamp she had brought down was oil—there was no electric connection points in the cellar—and the oil was nearly gone, the flame guttering almost as if Rose's rage had consumed it.

Rose thought again of Beo's flat, the missing watch stolen away from his bedside table, cushions and mattress gutted and left with their cotton and feathered innards gaping open to the air.

This was not a world she wanted to be blind to.

Some small amount of her anger, Rose reserved for her aunts. Worried as she was for their safety, she resented the ignorance they had kept stuffed round her eyes and ears. They had clearly known for some time this was at least a possibility. Rose stacked the manifest copies with the original on top and placed them back into her satchel, hesitating before folding the leather flap over the opening. She took one copy out and held it in front of her.

The hidden closet was now full only of the empty crates the ledgers had occupied and the small pile of items that had inhabited it before Rose brought the books down. Taking the dying lamp in, she looked at the remaining contents of the closet. These were the things Aleis had deemed important enough to keep fully tucked away; perhaps they would hold something of interest or import.

Though they all seemed only to hold tchotchkes and heaps of warehouse smocks. Rose frowned. Perhaps Aleis had simply used the place for overflow storage. She set the copied manifest on the floor beside her to look more thoroughly.

The first crate was about twice the size of the crates she'd used to transport the ledgers, and it was full top to bottom with folded warehouse smocks of grey canvas. Rose rifled through the clothing, nonplussed. There was an entire credenza of such things upstairs, tucked in plain sight.

The second crate was much the same as the first, full of smocks and a few pairs of folded work trousers meant to fit most body sizes.

The third was full of books, and none that seemed to be of any interest. Surveys of Kael's flora, one herbal thesaurus that compared native plants from various regions of the continent for any similar usage—again, most of these titles also lived upstairs in plain sight.

Rose opened the top book and flipped through it. The pages smelled of dust and winter. They held only diagrams of herbs, pointing out which parts— root or leaf or flower or berry—could be used safely and to what end.

She picked up the one under it and opened it to a random page.

The book was hollow.

· · · · ·

The pages had not been glued together, only carefully excised of their meat. In the empty space they left behind, there was a small pouch that rattled when Rose took it out between two careful fingers.

Her breath stopped in her throat, and her fingers pried open the small drawstring.

She couldn't see well enough to tell what was in it. Rose brought it back out into the cellar where the fire burned low. The light glinted off something inside the pouch.

Rose upturned the small pouch on the makeshift desktop, and a small pattering of gemstones poured out.

Yellow rubies, from the look of it. Precious enough to fetch a good price and retain relatively stable value, but not so dear as to elicit notice if someone were to say, sell a small number of them for cash.

Rose looked from the small pile of stones to the hidden closet with new eyes.

Her hands shook as she folded a piece of paper to funnel the gemstones back into their tiny sack. She placed the sack in her satchel, in the zippered pocket at the back of the main pouch.

Going back into the closet, Rose bent to lift one of the crates of smocks. The large wooden crate bit into her fingers, and she heaved it up off the ground. She staggered under the unexpected weight of it and dropped it back to the floor with a poof of dust.

She hadn't noticed when she'd lifted the folded garments a few at a time to see what the crate contained. She looked now, eyes wide.

How much was in there? Rose had no doubt that the tiny sack of shining yellow rubies wasn't the only thing hidden in that space. To anyone looking in, they'd think it only extra storage. But now that she'd found something there, Rose knew she could not leave it.

Upstairs, the office was still cold and fireless. The sun had reached its zenith and begun its descent, and Rose was hungry. Her skin felt stretched and tight.

She made a snap decision. Hurrying downstairs, she pawed through the crate of books. She found five more that contained pouches and added them to the pile with the first hollow book, removing each small rattling sack to her own satchel. Rose piled the hollow books onto the woodstove's dying fire, watching it come back to life, hungrily licking the fluttering pages of the gutted books. A pang of regret touched her, discomfort at burning even already-destroyed books.

She thought of Veran's words in the library and decided these texts were shields against people meeting the same fate. Rose tucked one of the herb guides and a non-hollow thesaurus into her bag; it would be useful to have at home, and on the off chance someone stopped her, her bag would look simply full of boring horticultural texts.

Exiting the office and locking it securely—the old adage about poverty knowing security and wealth knowing fear suddenly made sense—Rose forced herself to walk home at a normal pace. She stopped at a food cart and bought a few clamshells stuffed with curried fish and one with lentils and cheese. She ate one, walking to her flat. Her shoulders ached from hunching over.

At home, one eye on the afternoon light that would quickly become twilight, Rose changed into more comfortable linen trousers and a long, flowing tunic she'd almost turned into washrags the previous year. Her clothes from the day smelled of smoke from the woodstove, and soon those she wore would follow suit, but if Rose were to carry out her plan, she wanted to be comfortable.

Her plan was simple: Rose wanted to transfer any items of worth from the office to her flat's cubby hole. Something told her that her aunt's offices wouldn't be allowed to stand empty and unsearched for long.

Rose placed the sacks of gems in the crate of *Red Sunrise* copies without opening any of the others to see what they contained, and then she hurried back to the office.

Rose refilled the lamp's oil when she returned and brought a second down to boot, latching the office's front door and shutting off all lights upstairs in case anyone ventured by and wondered who was in there so late. The chimney for the woodstove fed into the building ventilation system as a whole; in winter, a smoking chimney in the city centre would cause no notice.

She found no more hollow books, but when she examined the first of the smocks more closely, she discovered that the fabric was thicker than it ought to be. Rummaging about in the cellar—Grenye and Aleis always kept sewing kits about in case a button fell off or a shirt ripped—Rose found a seam ripper and a needle and thread, then sat back against the wall of the closet, unsure of what she could expect. She thought of Beo in the small village of Viyarenyo and wondered how he was doing. Whether he'd gotten her letter. What he had thought of it.

Rose then pushed all thoughts beyond the task at hand out of her mind and felt along the seam of a smock until she detected a slight change in thickness. It took two tries with the seam ripper to get the hang of it (sewing was never one of Rose's strong points), but the threads snapped and curled away like regrowing hairs, and Rose pried apart the fabric, not sure what she'd find.

Money.

Mostly hundred-notes, a few fifties and tens, folded into strips and tucked in seams and hems.

Rose ignored the value of what she was looking at and stacked the currency—all Kaeli marks—in neat piles according to denomination. Some of the minting dates were twenty years past, though the notes were still in circulation.

The project took her well into the night.

Rose reheated the clamshells she'd brought throughout the night as she worked, placing the paper-wrapped pastries on top of the stove to warm for a few minutes, then eating them quickly enough that she had to force herself to take smaller bites when she started to feel sick at her stomach.

Some of the smocks held Coretian crowns, which was not so inflated in value as Kaeli marks, all in high denomination bills. One hundred Coretian crowns was equal to between four hundred and six hundred Kaeli marks, depending on the markets on any given day. When Rose got through all the smocks and to the trousers, careful to tug out the torn threads and re-stitch the hems, she found something else, just as hidden but of nowhere near as clear a value.

Letters.

Some in her father's hand.

Tempted as she was to read them as she discovered them, Rose left them be, stacking them next to the money. She could not, however, keep them from her mind, and as she painstakingly re-stitched the hems on the garments she had searched through, her eyes sought them out, looking at the familiar curlicues of *l*'s and *y*'s, feeling as if she had stumbled upon something quite removed from time.

Finally, in the darkest hours of predawn night, Rose came to the end. She could not help but feel impressed—none of the garments had held items in the same place; In front of her on the floor sat thousands of Kaeli marks and Coretian crowns, enough to total at least two years' salary. She could not guess at the amount contained in the pouches of gems. Rose bundled the marks together, highest denominations, then smaller. She bound them and arranged them in the zippered pouch of her satchel. They didn't all fit. After a few moments of exhausted consternation, Rose took a now-lighter smock and folded the rest of the money and the letters up in the middle, arranging it neatly and placing it in her satchel's main pocket. She put another smock and a pair of drawstring trousers on top of it. Laundry, she could say, as long as no one tried to hold the satchel. Its weight had increased by a stone.

Never before had Rose considered someone stopping her to search her things.

Tired to the point of near-delirium, Rose made a small bed from smocks and trousers, curling up on her side with her head on a folded pile of fabric. Her fingers throbbed, and her joints felt like the creaking hinges of an old door. Her head upon the rough smocks spun with the dizzy heaviness of mental and physical exhaustion.

Try as she may, Rose could not sleep.

• • • • •

Rising at first light, Rose broke down the crates she had used for her desk and took the typewriter back upstairs. In the cellar, Rose considered leaving one copy of the NPV manifest between the wooden crates and the back wall. If she left it, she could see two possible outcomes, were it to be discovered. One, the NPV could think some party member long ago had used the hiding place and that Aleis and the other workers had never found it. Two, they could see it as a challenge, suspecting correctly that Aleis or Rose had placed it there as a way of saying, *I know who you are.* After a long hesitation, Rose opted not to leave it. She again closed the wall to the hidden closet and beat burlap dust over it to cover her presence, hoping that if and when the NPV discovered it, they would see only overflow storage and not look too closely at the hems. She had thrown all the spare threads in the fire.

It was Anpax, the last day of the work week, and outside the office, Rose could see Sanmarian stirring to face the day. Looking outside, the heavy weight of her satchel bearing down upon her aching shoulder, Rose took in the mundane bustle with bleary eyes.

The mail she had laid out on her desk sat there, bland and bureaucratic. Bills she could identify.

She no longer had a job.

She had enough money in her bag to last quite a long time, but Rose felt no connection to it. It wasn't hers, much as she knew her aunts would not begrudge her using it. There was no way they would flee Sanmarian without taking what they needed. Such caches of valuables used to be common, Rose knew. How many other citizens around Sanmarian had similar places?

Unable to process the past day on no sleep with a weary and pained body, Rose spent the morning putting the office into whatever order she could. She gathered some of her favourite teas into a canvas bag, wondering what would happen to the stores in the warehouse. On impulse, she found a large empty tin and filled it with medicinal herbs, then two more. The canvas bag, usually used for groceries, bulged with the tins.

Finally, just past midday, there was nothing left she could reasonably do. She locked the office, her fingers clumsy with tiredness, and made her way home. Once, an NPV guard rounded a corner just as Rose made to cross an alley, making her jump with too-real terror.

The guard, amused that he had startled her, simply gave her a smile. "Sorry, miss," he said, peering into her canvas bag at the tea tins. "Enjoy your weekend. Try not to have too much fun at your tea party."

Rose did her best to smile back at him, leaning on the sunset stone wall and watching a father wrangle three children toward the market square while her breath slowly returned to her lungs and her blood stopped racing. The canvas bag of tea tins swayed on her arm.

She made it the rest of the way home without incident, stopping only to open her flat's postbox.

There was a letter from Beo, a sight so welcome and at once unexpected that Rose almost sat down in the corridor to read it right there.

Instead, she forced herself to go to her flat, unlocking the door.

The very smell of home soothed her as she entered, a mixture of her own scent, herbs from work, and the wood of the floors and walls. Much as she wanted to, she didn't stop or sit. Rose latched the door behind her and went straight to her room, where she arranged the money in the cubby and placed the stack of letters she had found beside it.

Stripping naked and throwing her clothes in the woven hamper in the corner of her bedroom, Rose went to the washroom and turned on the bathwater, listening to the familiar clank of the pipes and smelling the familiar metallic scent of the pipes as the hot water splashed into the enamel tub. Usually, she tried not to overuse the hot water—she shared a boiler with the flat next-door—but today Rose indulged herself, filling the tub with it and filling the washroom with steam.

She sank into it, almost drifting off to sleep. Too soon, the water began to cool, and Rose made herself get out. She had done a lot over the weekend, but she had forgotten all about the Liberation Front meeting. Rose had no remaining energy to consider the implications of that. She bundled her sore body, prune-skinned and swaying on her feet, into pyjamas.

Beo's letter was addressed to her, stamped that morning. Rose pictured him taking the time to write back to her even after his train journey, getting the letter to the post early enough for it to be on the first train.

She was almost afraid to read it, but the long night and morning had left her starving for human connection and feeling adrift, lonely. She broke the seal on the envelope and pulled out the letter.

Dear Rose,

Thank you for your letter.

It's strange, coming home. It's at once home and not home, a place I used to understand and now wonder if I ever understood. My aunt tells me that many things have changed. The faces in the village shops, the teachers at the school, even the shape of the buildings feels different.

It's made me...melancholy is not the right word. Nor is nostalgic. Though this is just a short visit, it feels constraining already. Like I ought to be back in Sanmarian, with you.

I have appreciated your friendship as well, Rose. You have greeted me with openness and understanding; there aren't quite the right words to describe what that means to me either.

I'll be returning on the Paxel day train; it gets in at fourth bell. Would you perhaps like to meet me? If so, I'll see you there. If not, I'll call on you at home on Popaxel.

In friendship,
Beo

Rose meant to do more, to fully inventory what she'd found, anything, but the moment her head touched her own pillow in her own soft bed, she was asleep.

CHAPTER SIXTEEN

Beo woke earlier than he meant to, unused to the relative quiet of Viyarenyo after Sanmarian's background noise. Autocars, gulls, the occasional tram, even the faint but present sound of the waves of the sea. None of that existed in the village, only the winter wind in tree branches and the house settling.

Irena's door was still shut when Beo slipped down the hall. His negatives were still strewn about the dining area. Those he had set aside for the gallery show had been placed in a tidy stack on one end. He set the kettle on to boil and went about double-checking the negatives he wanted. One drew his eye on the table, and he held it up to the light. It was one from his portfolio, a photograph of Irena taken the last time he'd been back to Viyarenyo. Her eye wasn't yet clouded by the cataract; Beo had caught her gazing out the window, a rare look of softness about her face. She hadn't been thrilled with the photograph, but Beo kept it anyway.

After a moment of hesitation, he put it in the stack for the exhibition and placed the lot of the negatives in an envelope.

He tidied up the boxes as he waited for his water to boil. When he finished, he sliced onions and spinach to cook with some eggs. He seldom cooked at home for himself anymore. Beo wondered what it would be like to cook for Rose.

Irena had a small tray of flowers growing in the windowsill near the warmth of the fireplace. Beo trimmed a pair of them and put them in a bowl of water on the table, arranging the food on plates and making sure to finish the eggs with a bit of crumbly goat cheese, like she always enjoyed. Even in winter, a neighbour delivered the stuff.

When he finished, Beo padded down the hall to knock on her door. He knocked once, shoulder brushing against the doorjamb. "Irena, I made breakfast."

He expected to hear her moving around; she was usually an early riser, and she'd gone to bed before he had the night before. Instead, he heard nothing.

"Irena?" Beo knocked again.

No answer.

Beo went out to the salon. Irena's shoes were still by the door, her coat on the hook beside it.

Beginning to prickle with alarm, Beo trotted back down the hall and knocked harder.

"Irena, I'm coming in." Images of Zara hanging from the ceiling turned Beo's stomach as he twisted the doorknob and pushed, instinctively closing his eyes against a scene he couldn't bear to risk seeing.

"Irena," he said, eyes closed tight.

There was no answer.

Beo let out a breath, felt his lungs empty. He inhaled, expecting the odour of voided bowels and death.

Instead he got simply fabric, Irena's musky perfume, a hint of moth repellent from the chest at the foot of her bed.

He forced his eyes open.

Irena's bed was neatly made, everything in the room in perfect order.

Except her. She was nowhere to be seen. A piece of paper sat folded on her pillow, and even from the doorway, Beo could see his name scrawled upon it in her handwriting.

He didn't have to open it to know that she was gone.

Beo had not told Irena about Rose, so he had not told her about Rose's aunts disappearing. He felt a keen sense of dissonance when he opened the note.

There is something I should have done a very long time ago. You are a good man, Beo. You have all that remains of my love.

She was never one for verbosity.

Beo took the note with him back out to the kitchen, where he sat at the table and ate both plates of eggs.

He knew almost nothing about Irena's past. His mother had died when he was young, and from what his father had said, they were estranged and had been for ten years. His father's new husband had raised him, then passed away of cholera after eating some bad fish that had not been kept cold enough on a transport train from Sanmarian. Four other villagers in Viyarenyo had died, too. And then, a bare few years later, Beo's own father had fallen ill.

Irena had arrived around that time, when Beo was just barely into his adolescence, grown into his knees but possessing far more height than width. Beo hadn't even known he had an aunt before then, that he could remember. She had seldom spoken of her life—or at all—and Beo found that when she began to speak to him, it was only in the general warnings she gave.

Something she should have done a very long time ago.

Beo hadn't a clue where she could have gone, or what she planned to do.

He spent the next hour tidying up the house. He went outside and shut off the waterline so the pipes wouldn't freeze with the house unoccupied. He found an old carpet bag that he thought had been his stepfather's and filled it with clothing that miraculously still fit, though it smelled a bit of dust and moth repellent.

Allowing himself one tiny trespass, he went into Irena's room. Only then, when he opened her wardrobe, did he see that she had packed some things. It stood mostly empty, though organised by colour. He could see no other clue in her room that anything was amiss.

Beo shouldered his camera bag with negatives tucked into the front pocket, hefted the carpet bag of clothing, and, before he left, took the small tray of flowers from the windowsill.

He left it at Lan's home on his way out of town.

When she asked after Irena, he told her simply that she had business to attend to out of town.

Lan didn't look as if she believed him, but she helped him pass the time before his train, sensing he needed lighter conversation, until it was time for him to return to Sanmarian.

• • • • •

This time, it was light outside when Beo made the train journey. He had wanted to send Rose another letter, had hoped to find one in the postbox from her in Viyarenyo, but it had been empty. Would she be at the station to greet him?

The countryside of Kael flashed by the windows, revealed by the cloud-scudded daylight. Dormant olive groves, rolling hills that in summer would be the kind of verdant green one always had to relearn after winter's drab colours.

At Viyamar, a bare forty-five minutes from Sanmarian Central, the train held on the platform after boarding.

For the first few minutes, Beo thought nothing of it, drumming his fingers on the knee of his trousers and wishing he had a book. *Red Sunrise* was tucked into his camera bag, as always, but after what Veran had told them in the library, he wasn't certain reading it in public was a good idea anymore.

The sound of murmuring voices reached Beo's ears, and the man sitting opposite him stiffened. Beo met his eyes.

"What is it?" Beo asked, confused.

"The party has begun doing checks on train routes," the man said curtly.

It had been a year or more since Beo had taken a train out of Sanmarian, and he had heard nothing of such checks.

"Checking for what?" Beo looked over his shoulder in the direction of the murmurs. The door between the cars stood open, though a conductor stood in the opening, blocking Beo's view of anything but moving human shapes.

The man didn't answer. He was likely in his forties, hair grey at the temples and pulled into a low knot at the nape of his neck.

The murmurs behind Beo stopped, and a clipped voice sounded from the other car, words unintelligible.

Outside, the sun peeked through the clouds. Golden as it slipped toward the horizon, it glinted off a light dusting of rare snow on a bench back. Heavy footsteps on the metal floor of the car coupling thumped loudly. Beo's mind started to fret at the edges of his thoughts, worries swarming like ants on a discovered lump of bread. Would they search him? What were they looking for?

The car wasn't full, but wasn't particularly empty, either. One seat in two held a passenger, and now that the NPV guards were in his car, Beo could not stomach the thought of turning to look. He sat facing the front of the train, wishing his motion sickness did not dictate always facing forward in a moving vehicle. The presence of the NPV felt heavy and thick, like a dense white fog in the air that one could taste.

The murmured voices became understandable halfway through the car. Each time the same questions.

Where are you coming from? Identification papers, please. What is your business in Sanmarian? Where is your domicile? What is your profession?

Answers seemed to be recorded; Beo could not see, but he heard the scratching of a fountain pen, the occasional sound of breath drying wet inks, a rustle of blotting paper.

When the NPV guards reached the seat behind Beo, one stood directly next to his right elbow. Beo could feel the guard's warmth. Every fibre of wool in the guard's uniform stood out with crystalline clarity. Though they were spun of grey wool, small paler fibres showed in the weave. The guard's boot had a single white scuff on the otherwise pristine leather.

Beo tried to focus on those details, anything to calm the skipping beat of his heart.

"Good afternoon," the guard said then, stepping to the side to look down at Beo. His comrade moved beside him, watching, notepad in hand.

"Good afternoon," answered Beo automatically, his voice more self-assured than he had expected.

"Identification papers, please." The guard's politeness felt strange, foreign.

Beo opened his camera bag and unzipped the pouch on the flap where he kept his papers. He handed them to the guard without comment.

"A camera, eh?" The guard gave a sharp nod at Beo's bag. He had a clean-shaven face and hair in a club, his hat pulled down over his ears enough that the short bill at its front hooded his eyes.

"I'm a photographer," said Beo.

The second guard's pen scratched on the paper.

"Where are you coming from"—The guard paused to look at Beo's papers—"Mister Mataya?"

"Viyarenyo."

"What is your business in Sanmarian?"

"I live in Sanmarian."

"What was your business in Viyarenyo? It says here that is your place of birth?"

Lie. Beo felt the impulse like a lightning strike in his ribs, and before he could stop himself, the words cascaded from his mouth, smooth and fluid, water overrunning a bowl in a sink. "I was recently given exhibition status at the Overlook Galleria," Beo said, colouring the forthcoming falsehood with truth. "My parents are dead, but a few villagers in Viyarenyo helped raise me. I made a brief trip to share the news."

"Congratulations," the guard with the notepad said blandly.

"Thanks very much," said Beo.

"Photography is your primary occupation?" The first guard asked.

"I also work in a shop framing pictures."

"Very well," said the guard.

They moved on to the man opposite Beo with no other comment, and Beo sat back in his seat, trying to affect nonchalance. Fetching negatives would have been a reasonable mission by near any standard, but if he had admitted to doing so, it could have raised questions. More questions. Why would a Sanmarian photographer store photographic equipment in a tiny village three hours away? *Irena had impressed upon him that it was safer.* Why safer? What does a photographer in Sanmarian have to hide?

Beo tried to be a truthful person. In love, in life.

He could hear the scratch of the guard's pen recording the neighbouring passenger's answers. Those answers would end up in party hands, somewhere. If Irena had fled something so many years ago, something that had left her so certain of Sanmarian's teeth, if she had vanished to fulfil something left over a decade undone—Beo could not risk pointing the NPV at anything remotely connected to her in Viyarenyo.

He had never thought of it before, but her disappearance had told him one thing: Irena had spent the past years in Viyarenyo, a tiny village in the Kaeli countryside for a reason.

Beo was absolutely certain that she had gone there to hide.

He was starting to get an idea about from what.

The minutes ticked by, the guards moving out of Beo's car and into the next. The man across from Beo took out a newspaper and began reading, looking casual except for the still-stiff set of his shoulders.

On the platform outside the window, Beo saw six NPV guards gather near a lamppost. They had a man with them, one guard holding each of his elbows.

The train began to pull away, the whistle blowing brightly into the winter air.

Just before the platform winked out of sight, Beo saw the man in NPV custody double over, a fist in his stomach and a spray of vomit splashing onto the cobblestones of the platform.

• • • • •

Beo jerked in his seat, his skull hitting the headrest behind him. The man with the newspaper looked up, took one look at Beo's wild eyes, and looked back down at the paper.

He did not turn a page for the next fifteen minutes, his eyes glued on the print, but not moving.

Beo saw the man double over again and again. What had been his crime? He had been standing peaceably in custody, not resisting. The splash of vomit. The sharp movement of the man's body.

Never before had Beo seen the NPV guards turn violent.

Not only violent, but publicly violent. On a train platform. In front of the passengers on board, those waiting for their own trains.

Beo thought of the calculated, measured questions he had answered. The polite, "Good afternoon."

The remaining forty-five minute journey to Sanmarian seemed to take forty-five hours. When the edges of the city's outlying suburbs sprung up around the train tracks, Beo stood to get the carpet bag from where it rested on the rack above his head. He placed it on his lap, camera bag on top of it, and hugged it to his chest.

Would Rose be there when he arrived? He wondered if she had gotten his letter.

He felt like cobblestone mortar had turned to liquid beneath his feet, creating a sea of sinking stones upon which he tried to navigate his feet so he wouldn't disappear into the muck. It was a lack of control, Beo decided, the effects of seeing a system so fully outside his influence. Could he do anything in the face of what he was seeing?

Beo didn't know. All he knew was that he would breathe easier once he could be near Rose. She had come into his life so suddenly, but already Beo was not ready to see her leave it again. He could not shake the sense that she felt the same. The train had been twenty-three minutes delayed with the NPV questioning; would Rose be waiting if she'd come at all?

The train passed through the old city wall and into the Sanmarian city centre. Beo, near the exit of the car, almost didn't see the newspaper man fold his faux-reading and place it into his bag. When Beo saw the converging tracks leading into Sanmarian Central, he stood to take a place directly by the door. The train slowed, moving along the tracks under the wide glass dome that covered the boarding platforms like honeycomb.

When they pulled into Platform 3, the man beside Beo got to his feet. He looked once around the train car and the quiet urgency of passengers gathering their belongings.

"I don't know what you saw in Viyamar," the man said to Beo, so quietly it was almost a whisper. "But you are likely to see worse in the days to come."

"What?" Beo turned to him, steadying himself on the swaying train with a hand to the door's latch.

"You're too young to remember the worst of it. Remember this, if nothing else: it only seems to have gotten better."

"What do you mean?" Passengers were beginning to get up from their seats and queue to exit.

The man shook his head. "History repeats."

With that, the man again seemed to forget Beo's existence. An old woman with a cane stood behind Beo, and when he heard the doors open, he pulled the latch in front of him. He looked back once at the man before exiting the train, but the man wasn't looking at him, and the woman with the cane behind Beo needed help descending the steps onto the train platform.

Beo helped her down, nodded a *you're welcome* to her thanks, and looked around. There seemed to be more NPV guards about than usual, the sight of them causing almost visible apprehension in more than just Beo. An older couple, a man and a woman, stood near a news kiosk hand in hand, the man's eyes magnified by thick spectacles and darting back and forth from his partner to the guard ten feet away.

What history had the train passenger been speaking of repeating?

In spite of the clear glass above his head filtering in the final rays of afternoon sunlight, Beo felt as if the whole of Sanmarian weighed down upon him. He stood next to a twist-bread vendor, the scent of yeast warm in the cool air. Beo's heart sank as he looked around the station, toward the ticket counters and information boards. He could see no sign of Rose.

She must not have received the letter, he told himself.

Yoan would not be home; he worked weekend nights at the pub. Beo didn't like the idea of going back to Yoan's flat and sitting alone. The library was open. Beo had just decided to go there and read whatever recent histories he could find when something inexplicable made him turn. A feeling, a movement in the corner of his eye, a scent—he couldn't be sure. But when Beo turned his head, there was Rose, not ten feet away, just rounding a corner.

She smiled.

Somehow, in that moment, when Beo felt his own smile respond to hers, he felt like no matter what history was about to repeat in Sanmarian, they could face it together.

CHAPTER SEVENTEEN

"I did get your letter," Rose said. There was a quiet note in her voice that could almost be called shyness, but when she looked at Beo as he sat cross-legged on the floor of her bedroom, stacks of currency between them, she felt anything but shy.

"I reckoned you had, since you turned up at the station."

Rose took in his face, his angled jaw, the gold-brown of his eyes that was a near match for the tone of his skin, the curls that dropped down over his forehead.

He smiled at her again, and Rose couldn't help but wonder at it. She remembered the first time she approached him, her thought. That smile she saw now was meant for her, and she welcomed it into her sight and her memory.

Beo nodded down at the pile in front of him, and a scrap of paper where they'd tallied everything. "Totals."

He had shared with her in snippets the details of his trip. Irena's disappearance, the changes in Viyarenyo, the NPV guards assaulting a prisoner in full view of train travellers under the light of a winter sun.

She had in turn told him of what she had found, and now she showed him. Together they had counted and recounted the bills and gems from Aleis's cache. Except the letters. Those sat unopened in the cubby. Rose could not bring herself to read them. They were addressed to no one.

"Fifty-three thousand eight hundred twenty-seven Kaeli marks and another eleven thousand three hundred Coretian crowns," Beo said. "And these."

The gems they had laid out atop a white tea towel. Beyond the yellow rubies, there were sapphires, rare blood garnets the colour of a pinprick's first droplet, and moss emeralds that gleamed in the light with tiny cracks of iridescent fire.

Rose's first assessment of there being at least two years' salary in that cache had been correct. Neither of them could be certain of the exact value of the gemstones, but a single moss emerald in a gold setting often fetched upward of twenty thousand marks, the price of a gold band less than five thousand. Even a conservative guess would put the total at well over a hundred thousand marks.

"Kaeli money to live here," Rose said slowly. "Coret is our nearest neighbour and the only nation with which we share a land border."

Kael was a peninsula, surrounded on three sides by the Tarenr Sea. It was at least a week's passage by ship to any nation besides Coret.

"And gems could be traded anywhere. Their worth is stable, more stable than currency," Beo finished for Rose, plucking a single blood garnet from the tea towel and holding it up to the light.

"They must have prepared for a very long time," said Rose, thinking about her aunts. They lived simply in their flat above the tea shop. Helyne did her carpentry there; Grenye worked in the office and warehouse. They wore serviceable clothing, never opulent or ostentatious.

Rose thought of Aunt Aleis handing her a thousand-note to buy new shoes.

"They were prepared to flee the country completely," said Rose.

"They did flee," Beo reminded her. "Do you think they couldn't get back to the office to retrieve this?"

It didn't make sense. Rose had spoken to Helyne at their flat. They had a telephone in their home; Helyne had even said Aleis had planned to ring her from the office that very evening.

"Aleis and Grenye were going to the office that night," said Rose, her words coming out like chilled honey, ponderous and thick as she tried to process her thoughts. "Helyne said they were meant to ring her from there."

"Do you think they did?"

"They must have."

Beo got it as soon as Rose did. "They could have moved all this."

"And they didn't." Rose hesitated. "I told Helyne where I'd put the records. She knew I'd have to go back in there. She knew they'd already be gone by the time I did."

"Aleis wrote you a letter," Beo said gently. "She told you."

"She said I have everything I need." Rose stared at the piles in front of her, unable to make sense of it.

Beo was quiet, sitting in front of her. When Rose looked up, his expression was worried. "Rose?"

"They're not coming back," Rose said. "They're never coming back."

Everything spread upon the floor suddenly looked like nothing more than a goodbye.

• • • • •

Rose splashed her face with water in the washroom, trying to regain some sense of calm. In the space of a week, her life had cracked in half. No job, no family. Her flat was paid for, and her aunts had left her quite enough money to pay for essentials, but as the ice-cold water dripped from her lashes and chin into the basin, Rose would have handed it back, down to the last centime, just to have Aleis and her partners here to tell her what she was supposed to do.

One tiny letter from Aleis was meant to show her everything she needed? She didn't need money; she needed the people she loved.

Think, Rose.

An NPV manifest that implied her life, her family, and her contributions were no longer valued in her own country.

A stack of money, able to be used in Sanmarian or anywhere, if she were careful.

A stack of letters, from her father to no one, which Rose couldn't even force herself to read.

A letter for her, left sitting on top of a crate of books.

Rose's hands fell from the sides of her face and clasped the edges of the sink.

The water ran into the ceramic basin, swirling clockwise down the drain.

She didn't bother to wipe her face with a towel. Beo was perched on the side of her bed, thumbing through one of the books Veran had entrusted them with at the library.

"She could have left that note anywhere in my flat," Rose said. "She knew I open that cubby every so often. She showed it to me once before. If she went missing, if I'd noticed she was gone before I found that note, I would have looked in there. She knew I'd find it in there sooner or later. She put it exactly there for a reason."

"In a secret cubby?"

"In the place I keep those books."

Something dawned on Beo's face. His sleeves were rolled up, and from where she stood in the threshold of the washroom, she could see his tattoo, bold and dark upon his skin.

"The NPV keeps an eye out for *Red Sunrise*," Beo said.

"There's something in there they don't like." Rose wiped her still-wet face with her hand, mind whirling. "They took the pocket watch, Beo. The only thing they took from your flat, aside from your general peace of mind."

"It wasn't the only thing of value in my flat." Beo stood, stepping over the money on the floor to close the distance between them. "They left my darkroom equipment."

"Did any of the photographs in your portfolio have anything to do with the book?"

Beo shook his head, looking bewildered. "Nothing. There aren't any self-portraits in it, and even if there were, my tattoo is almost always covered. I'm not even sure I have any self-portraits where it shows. It's personal."

Rose looked at him, her gaze falling involuntarily to the tattoo on his arm. She understood how it would be personal.

The curtains were drawn in her bedroom, though they'd turned on the floor lamp near the bed.

"It's past eighth bell," Rose said. "Marpaxan said we ought not be out after dark."

"Too late now," Beo said, his smile going crooked and wry.

"Would—" Rose cleared her throat and looked Beo directly in the eye. "Would you like to stay?"

Beo's lips parted ever so slightly, and Rose saw his chest expand with a quick breath. She swallowed.

"I would," he said. "But Yoan is expecting me, and I think I ought to be there when he gets home."

Rose nodded, though for a moment she wondered where the air in the room had gone. "I understand."

"I have to develop the prints for my exhibition tomorrow morning. It will likely take most of the day, but if you'd like to meet me at fourth bell, we can get supper together. If you'd like."

"I would," said Rose. "Very much."

She saw Beo to the door. "I'll reread the book," she said as he shrugged himself into his coat. "I want to see if there's something there. Or perhaps to know if we're just entirely mad and paranoid."

Beo glanced over Rose's shoulder in the direction of her bedroom where several years' worth of money lay spread out over her floor. "The NPV may not be about to start killing civilians, but you've evidence enough that you're not mad. As have I."

Abashed, Rose pressed her lips together. "You're right. I'm sorry."

"You don't have to apologise to me, Rose. Not to me." Beo buttoned his coat, then reached out and cupped Rose's cheeks in his hands. His skin was warm upon her skin, so warm she thought she could stay there and fall safely and comfortably to sleep if need be. That is, until his lips touched her cheek, and suddenly the warmth was heat and she was very, very awake.

Beo kissed her right cheek, then the left, and then pulled back. His eyes met hers, and Rose found she couldn't speak.

"Stay safe," said Beo. "I'll see you tomorrow—at the library?"

Rose nodded. "You stay safe as well," she said.

When the door closed behind him, Rose latched it with a shuddering breath. She could not pull apart the threads of emotion woven through her, for they were a tapestry of every colour and texture. Yellow fear and blue peace, purple anger and grey like Papa's jumper that was comfort and warmth and love. Something beneath it all, a red-orange like sunsets that burned hot through it all, and Rose could not tell where one ended and another began.

She thought she heard his footsteps hesitate outside her door, but the sound returned a moment later and vanished down the corridor.

Rose packed away the gemstones and money back in the cubby, then went into the salon. She turned on the radio, listening to it crackle. The sound drove her mad, but she wanted to hear if there was a broadcast. Paxel was not a normal day for any party addresses, but many things had changed in the past week.

She opened *Red Sunrise* again, listening to a staccato dance number on the radio that felt incongruous with the book. She felt like she was hunting ghosts. Maybe she was.

The book had been Papa's before she claimed it as her own. How could it possibly hold answers when it was fiction written fifteen years past?

Rose read late into the night, a notebook by her side, jotting down anything of interest that she could find.

"You cannot truly mean it when you say it will not affect you!"

"How can you know what I mean?"

"You help them in every word," Remir Roxa's voice carried the weight of censure. *"They have come for me, and you did nothing. You said nothing. Do you truly believe that they will not one day come for you?"*

"They will not. I can protect you."

"Can you protect Yosif?" Remir pulled her sleeve to the elbow, revealing the black lines on her scarred skin, the tattoo that had once meant hope, love, a future. A new day.

She looked into the face of her lover and felt fear.

Regret and rage lit the edges of her words. "Yosif is dead. Would you have me follow him for the sake of your pride? You loved him too. We three were love, together. But your fear, Vitar, your fear is poison. It will taint every time you try to love, just as it brought death to ours."

"That was not love." Vitar spit the words back at her. He touched his shirt over his heart, then over Remir's. "This was love. This is love. You will not meet the end he did, I swear it."

Remir pulled away, pulled her sleeve back down to the wrist, buttoned it over the fluttering pulse that beat frantically under the thin skin. She could not let Vitar see what she felt. Not the terror that had sunk its talons into the beating muscle of her heart, and not the grief that sought to rend her in twain where she stood. She looked at Vitar and at once saw what they were, what they had been. Soft kisses and wonder. His face near Yosif's, eyes shining love.

And now, those eyes that shone only with anger and denial, two things borne on the fleeting feet of fear.

Remir spoke sadly, her body heavy and tired. "There are many ways to die, Vitar."

The meaning there was clear enough to Rose. No one is safe.

The thought chilled her. Her flat was warmed by the heating system, yet she felt cold. If Aleis and the others had fled, should she? Could she?

Rose thought of Amelie, shackled to Tomas, stripped of the business she had built and her every stake in it taken from her. How Rose wished she could pull Amelie to her then, in the tinted light of her flat, the radio crackling in the background.

As children, they had slept over together, huddled under the blankets and giggled, told scary stories. Now they were part of a story, one that indeed scared Rose, and she had no idea what part in it she was to play.

Aleis had said Rose had a choice.

Rose sat with one hand holding the pages of the book open on her lap, staring past the bookshelves and into her kitchen.

What choice would she make?

She wished she knew, but more than that, she wished she could be certain it would be the right one.

• • • • •

Sleep evaded Rose until late into the night, late enough that morning came calling. As many times as Rose had read and reread *Red Sunrise*, she had never looked at it as anything more than fiction. Powerful fiction. Fiction she felt was made for her as if the writer—about whom no one had ever seemed to know— had seen the whole of her life and soul and every figment of her mind and tailored the book to her exact measurements. But now, reading it once more, Rose couldn't shake the feeling that there was something true lurking in the fictional lines.

Try as she may, though, she could not pinpoint it.

Exhaustion muddied her thoughts as she lay in bed, *Red Sunrise* propped on her chest. Her nose was cold in the morning air, the flat's heating gone quiet for the time being.

Papa, Rose thought, *what would you do if you were here?*

What had her father done? Picturing Aunt Aleis's note in her mind—Rose had not burned it yet, could not bring herself to do so—she saw again Aleis's words. *Your parents stood against them once.*

Somehow, in the heavy silence of predawn winter, something became clear.

Beo would be working for most of the day. Rose climbed from her bed and tugged the blankets up to her pillows, smoothing the edge of the quilt.

It took very little for her to decide what to do then. Rose again pulled the hanging clothes from the wardrobe, pulling out a pair of trousers the colour of wet ash, a long white tunic, and a short-tailed waistcoat that looked like the clear Tarenr Sea after the summer storms. The waistcoat was far too fine for the average Popaxel stroll, but it had one thing to recommend its use that day: a series of pockets meant to hold what money or small items the wearer needed.

In those pockets, Rose carefully placed the pouches of gems, spreading them out within their tiny sacks so they wouldn't bulge the fabric overmuch. Pulling her hair back from her face, she secured it with a comb without looking in a mirror, instead watching the way the light glinted off the small sample of stones she had removed from their pouches. Those she placed in a small bone box that sat on her bedside and put the box into her satchel.

Rose wasn't certain. She could not with any true security of heart be sure that what she planned to do was the right choice. What she did know, down to the bedrock of her self, was that she would not do as Vitar had done in *Red Sunrise*. She would not betray those she loved by standing silently by while they vanished or died.

A chill seeped through her, wondering how much of that book was based on the real Sanmarian, and not, as she had always thought, a Sanmarian apart, a more dangerous Sanmarian. A deadly Sanmarian. A Sanmarian that devoured.

For a moment, Rose swayed on her feet, exhaustion warring with fear in her gut like a ponderous lead weight.

The bell rang out eight. The sun would be up soon, and the shops would be opening.

Rose bundled her coat and scarves about her and set off into the cold.

The first stop she made was the jeweller. Farras was his name, and Rose knew Aleis had done business with him before. She reached the shop as he drew up the heavy iron gate from in front of the door, meeting her with a sleepy look that didn't quite turn to recognition. He motioned her into the shop, which was already toasty warm for the day, the lights a soft glow that accentuated the sheen of gold and the glitter of inset gems.

"What can I do for you, friend?" Farras raised a wood plank and ducked under it, dropping it back into place as a countertop at the edge of the displays.

"I would like to see if you could appraise a few stones I have. I inherited this box from my mother," Rose lied. "It was at the bottom of a steamer trunk and under a few decades of scientific magazines."

"The box is nice bone work," Farras said, taking it between two stubby fingers. He peered at the maker's mark etched into its bottom. "Ah. Yuli's work."

Rose started, surprised.

Farras opened the box, aiming the light of an adjustable lamp toward a bleached leather mat. He upturned the box on the mat, where the colours of the gems stood out brightly against the leather.

"Your mother, was she one to secret away valuables?" Farras turned and pulled a pair of spectacles from a cashmere sleeve and nudged them up onto the bridge of his nose. "These are good quality."

"She was one for secrets in general. I used to think no one in the world knew her." That was true enough; Rose herself knew very little of Miko Abernethy, who had run off when Rose was a toddler. She had given Rose and Andreas her surname, given Rose birth, and that was all.

Farras drew out a sheet of paper from a drawer, fumbling behind him for a fountain pen. He scratched a few figures on the paper, then picked it up by the edge and shook it to dry the inks. "This was a nice little find for you," he said. "I'd personally buy them from you for the price listed here."

Rose looked at the numbers Farras had written on the paper. As she had expected, the moss emeralds would fetch the highest price at over six thousand marks for the one she had brought—which was one of the smaller stones. The total he had listed for five stones was over twenty thousand marks.

"Thank you, Mister Farras," Rose said. "I'll need to think about it. I may like to do something else with the stones."

"Of course. That offer stands for a month complete."

Of all the people Rose had encountered in the past week, Farras was the first who appeared totally unperturbed by the current goings-on in the city. She left the shop with the stones newly tucked in their own pouch provided by Farras, feeling disconcerted, though her resolve remained.

Rose planned to pass the morning at the library, hoping to see Veran and ask her more about the books. But when she entered the library antechamber, only one of the older women remained at the circulation desk. The papers that had been strewn about before had long since been gathered and binned, and the library was free of rubbish. Even from where she stood, Rose could see the large gaps in the shelves, glaring and obvious.

"Pardon me," she said to the librarian at the desk. "Is Veran working today?"

The woman's grey hair was pulled back in a severe bun, tight enough that it tugged at the edges of her face. "Veran no longer works here."

Rose tried for nonchalance, but her voice wobbled when she asked, "Did she find a new job somewhere else?"

The librarian shrugged, but the casual air of the gesture shattered on the sharp edges of the woman's unrelenting stare into Rose's face.

"Can you direct me to the local history books then?" Rose asked, steadying her voice and pretending not to notice the librarian's hostility. Distrust for Rose? Attempting to protect Veran? Or was that disgust in her demeanour aimed at Veran herself? Rose could not be sure.

"Second floor, turn right from the stairs. First two shelves on the right." Her lips showed white round the edges for a moment, and she turned back to the catalog in front of her. Ceramic dinnerware.

Rose thanked her and went up the stairs, following her directions.

The first thing she noticed was that the local history shelves had no gaps.

The second was that every single book on them bore a familiar stamp. Three stylised silhouettes of human busts with black lines leading from their heads to form an arrow pointing upward. Voices joined together to one goal. The National People's Voice symbol.

Rose made herself read until noon.

When she finally left the library, having checked out three archival manuscripts of newspapers from fifteen years ago, the librarian's hard edges seemed to have smoothed somewhat, but Rose felt dirty. Having read the NPV manifest, she could almost taste the flavour of their ideals in the party-sanctioned history texts. Rose remembered Tiraya, Rinan, Hersectus—all well-known and respected historians from Kael and beyond—and not a single one of their names had been listed on the book bindings at the library.

The Lionfish Pub had been open only for a few minutes when Rose stepped through the door. Yoan's back faced the bar, counting liquor bottles. He called a friendly, "Good day!"

Rose sat near him. She was the only person in the pub so far. "Hello, Yoan."

He turned, the expression on his face slipping from *greet customer* to surprise. "Rose. What brings you here?"

"Can I speak freely here?" Rose asked quietly.

"We're the only ones in the building."

Rose let out a breath and darted a glance at the door. "I need to speak to Marpaxan."

Yoan's expression turned wary. "Why?"

His shift in mood confirmed something Rose suspected. "She is near the top of it, isn't she?" Rose meant Liberation Front, and she knew Yoan knew it.

He looked back at her but said nothing.

"You're in this deeper than you've let on to Beo."

Yoan hesitated, tucking a free strand of hair behind his ear. "Beo trusts you. I barely know you."

Rose's breath shuddered as she breathed in to speak. She reached into her satchel and pulled out the bone box of stones. Yoan watched it as Rose slid it across the bar, curious but not intrigued enough to ask.

"My aunts are gone. My parents are long gone. I have no job, and the NPV came to my flat not long ago. They signed away my best friend's business to her abusive husband. My aunt said my father used to fight against the NPV. I don't know how I can help, but I want to. And there is one way I know I can." Rose opened the bone box, feeling as if she were walking the length of Sanmarian's sea-facing wall, two hundred metres above the rocks and waves with no parapet between her and the fall. She closed her eyes for a double beat of her heart and could almost hear the surf.

When she opened her eyes, Yoan was peering into the box.

Rose handed him the paper Farras had scratched on. "This is their approximate worth," said Rose. "I've helped my aunt run her business since I left school. If there's anything I can guess, it's that someone running against the party current will need funds. I don't know what my aunts intended me to use these for. To flee Kael, probably. But this is my home. Sanmarian is my city. It may be rotting from the inside out, but if I can help stop that, I will."

Yoan's expression had gone blank at the figures on the paper. "This would help. This would help tremendously."

He took a pen from behind the bar, turned over the paper from the jeweller. He wrote a column of numbers down the side. "That is the house number," he said, pointing to the number third from the top, his voice sticking in his throat as if he were as afraid as Rose was. "I won't write the street names. You'll have to remember them."

Rose nodded.

"Moraya, near the corner of Progress Way."

"That's right by the fortress." Rose couldn't help but gape. "I don't know whether to be impressed by your gumption or terrified that I'm about to walk into a trap."

"It's not a trap," Yoan said. "Beo would murder me if it was. And you won't find Marpaxan there. Tell them the locksmith sent you with an invoice. They'll take you to her."

Rose nodded and put the box of stones away. The other sacks were heavy in her waistcoat pockets, out of sight, present.

"Rose," Yoan said as she turned to walk to the door.

She stopped and looked over her shoulder.

"Be careful."

· · · · ·

It didn't take long.

Rose did as she was told, knocking on the door with the practice of someone who spent two years just out of school delivering invoices for tea orders. When a woman with her hair bound in a red scarf atop her head answered the door, Rose affected an air of boredom as best she could.

"The locksmith sent me with an invoice," she said.

The woman looked her over. "Do come in." She motioned through the door. "No need for you to wait for payment out there."

The house was much like any Rose had ever been in. Nothing suggested it was a hinge point for an underground opposition party. There was an NPV newspaper on the table by the door.

Rose waited for fifteen minutes before a man emerged from the rear of the house, his face bearing some small remnants of Roa look—his eyes were hooded, his nose shorter and straight, his hair more blue-black than brown-black. His clothing was Kaeli, though, and when he spoke, it was clear he had been born and raised in Sanmarian.

"Yoan sent you," he said bluntly. "I'll take you from here."

It was a strange thing to say, but Rose nodded, again feeling that wave of vertigo that came with the implicit trusting of an unknown human being with her life.

The man didn't introduce himself, only walked with Rose outside and kept a brisk pace across half of Sanmarian until they reached the very sea wall Rose had imagined walking upon. The sunset stone shaded them from the weak sunlight, and the man led Rose to a row of houses that backed up against the wall itself.

She had watched him as they walked, observed his wariness, his crisp but casual gait, the way he'd scan the street for guards whilst pretending to look both ways for autocars as they crossed the streets. Now, he bent to tie his shoe. When he stood, he gave Rose a warm, friendly smile and, to her surprise, kissed both her cheeks.

"There is a guard house across the street," he said in a low tone, beaming at her. He looked at his watch. "They change in one minute. Count to sixty, then knock at the door. Don't turn around. Count."

Rose began counting in her head, her heart beating twice for every number she reached.

He touched her cheek like a lover and smiled again. "I've known Yoan for most of my life. If he trusts you, I am willing to give you a chance. This is no game we play."

"I know," said Rose. *Twenty-seven. Twenty-eight.*

The man's face still shone with seemingly genuine affection. "The NPV killed my brother two months ago. They keep the killings quiet as they can. They silence those who speak against them. No one is safe."

Forty. Forty-one.

"My aunts are missing," murmured Rose, giving him a crooked smile in response. *Forty-nine.*

"You don't know yet. But you will." With that, his fingers left Rose's cheek, and he walked away, looking back once over his shoulder, looking for all the world like a wistful lover leaving a promising date.

Sixty.

Rose walked straight up the stairs of the house, knocked, and was ushered in at once.

Marpaxan was waiting for her in the house's kitchen, long legs propped up on the table itself.

"I have brought you something that may help," said Rose.

"We shall see," said Marpaxan.

CHAPTER EIGHTEEN

He couldn't be certain, but Beo felt as if Emon Sanhaya had been watching him since he came into the workspace.

Emon had greeted Beo with plenty of friendliness—he had an infectious smile and sparkling brown eyes so dark the light reflecting off his irises looked like starlight—but he had not said much, and he showed Beo his darkroom and left him to do his work.

Beo worked through the morning and into the early afternoon, finally finishing up the developing so the prints could dry on their line. He emerged from the darkroom with a strange sense of warring familiarity and oddity. The smells were the same, but the equipment set up just slightly different. The distance from one item to another, from the rinse basin to the chemicals, the tables to the drying line. Beo didn't miss his flat. Not really. But he did miss his darkroom.

Emon Sanhaya's workspace was an artist's dream. His flat had been remodelled to remove almost every wall; only the washroom and the darkroom had escaped. It gave Beo a tickle of precarious intimacy, to move about someone's private space. Sanhaya's bed was unmade, and as Beo ducked under the heavy curtain at the darkroom door, Emon was pouring soup into a bowl. A second bowl, Beo noticed.

"I'm very sorry," said Beo. "I didn't realise you were expecting company. I'm finished, but I'll need to come back later and fetch the prints once they're dry."

"Please, sit." Emon set the second bowl down on the table next to the first. His hair was straight and fell to his collarbone, all one even length like a cascade of black water. "That's for you. I could hear you finishing up and thought you might be hungry."

"That's very kind of you." Beo had been about to shoulder his camera bag to leave, but now he stood with it in one hand, shifting the weight of it somewhat awkwardly. He hung it over the back of a chair and sat opposite Emon at the table.

"I must confess, I'm very happy to have gotten the chance to meet you," said Emon.

"I beg your pardon?" The soup in front of Beo smelled hearty and spicy, like chile sausage and smoked peppers. He took a bite.

"I've seen your work before. When Tarn told me you were getting the open space at the Galleria, I was overjoyed to hear it."

Beo shifted in his seat. "Thank you. I've only ever done smaller exhibitions before."

"I know. I've been to a few of your shows around the city."

A pepper caught in Beo's tonsil. He coughed, then cleared his throat. "You seem to have me at a bit of a disadvantage."

"Hardly, though I can try if you'd like."

A jolt went through Beo, and this time when he swallowed, it had nothing to do with stray peppers. "Erm."

"I'm sorry. That was a bit forward of me." Emon gave Beo that same infectious smile, and Beo couldn't help but smile back.

"No need to apologise. I'm flattered; I simply don't know anything at all about you other than that you keep your darkroom in enviable order."

"Unlike the rest of my flat," Emon agreed.

"How long have you known Tarn?"

"Years. I apprenticed to his lover about ten years ago, but his lover passed away, and Tarn took me on at the Galleria. I've been there about seven years now."

"Do you like it there?"

"It doesn't give me as much time to paint or work on my own projects as I would like, but I do enjoy some of the perks." Emon winked at Beo.

Beo asked questions about the Galleria and about Emon's art and about Susette until he finished his soup, all of which Emon Sanhaya answered readily and with aplomb. When he asked after the time and Emon told him it was a quarter after third bell, Beo started, almost sad to leave.

"Thank you very much for the use of your space. And for the meal and conversation," Beo said, meaning it. Emon's eyes glowed, and Beo felt a heady dizziness.

"I trust I will see you again at the Overlook Galleria." Emon pushed back his chair and took Beo's bowl to place in the sink, the moment diffused. "If by some chance we don't meet there, however, I would welcome you here any time. To work or to talk."

"I'd like that." Beo was somewhat surprised at himself to discover that he meant that too. He warred for a moment with himself, then decided that if Emon could be forthright, so could he. "I should let you know that there is someone in my life. Newly, but she is...important to me."

Emon Sanhaya gave Beo a long look, a smile playing about his face. "That is quite fair enough for me. If she is agreeable to the idea and you decide you are interested, then I am, certainly. The photographs caught my eye, but you caught my fancy."

Beo couldn't think of anything to say to that. He bid Emon farewell, feeling somewhat shyer than he had in his recent memory.

The walk to the library to meet Rose seemed to take no time at all, and when he saw her standing outside the main door of Market Tower, her troubled face chased away the lighthearted banter with Emon Sanhaya.

Beo's heart gave a now-familiar turn at the sight of her when she looked up and saw him coming, her handsome face and the pensive draw of her lips. He kissed her cheeks, and the touch of her skin felt like home.

"I did something," she said without preamble. "Something big. But this isn't the place to talk about it."

"We can speak of it later," he said. "I've got something to tell you as well."

Beo's mind spun through possibilities. He didn't hear the footsteps until they were right beside him.

"Beomir Mataya," said a voice.

Beo and Rose both turned quickly. An NPV guard had spoken.

"And Rosenni Abernethy. Please come with us."

· · · · ·

Us, as it turned out, was a small contingent of four guards. Without a word, Beo nodded, his stomach turning on the soup he had eaten at Emon Sanhaya's. Rose looked straight ahead, her face resolute as if she were steeling herself.

She had done something big? Big enough to warrant arrest?

"Excuse me," Beo said to one of the guards. "Have we done something wrong? Are we under arrest?"

"You are wanted for questioning," the guard said, and would say nothing else.

Beo could not help but admire Rose, who glanced at Beo once with grey eyes that showed no fear. His own body felt full of it, roiling, churning, toiling in his gut. His mouth tasted of metal, and his fingers felt numb even through his gloves as the guards marched them down Alcazar Avenue.

They were being taken to the fortress.

Beo's throat tightened with each step, feeling the weight of eyes upon him as he walked, flanked by the NPV guards.

Rose seemed to have steel in her spine as she walked. She did not look embarrassed or cowed, and Beo envied her that. The wind blew bitter cold up the street from the sea wall, and the fortress loomed to their right, a giant, domed edifice of towers and sunset stone that looked like dusted rose gold in the winter light.

The guards at the gate nodded sharply as they passed through into the fortress courtyard. Beo could see the map of Sanmarian inside his mind, the circular city wall, the lines of the five main streets that led to the market at its centre, the towers at each spoke's end. And here, the fortress, circular wall inside circular wall, towers within like the gears of a clock grinding inexorably onward.

Where would this lead?

The guards escorting them stopped at the entrance to the main fortress, a heavy mahogany door that took two guards on each side to open. But they did not open it. Instead, three of the guards stood at attention while the fourth disappeared around a corner. Beo allowed himself to look at Rose. She looked back, her eyes unreadable. It was only then he saw a small crack in her façade, a longing look that vanished in an instant. She wrapped her arms around her chest, and Beo thought he saw a moment of relief, also gone forthwith.

The fourth guard returned a few minutes later with a curt nod, leading them around the corner where he had gone to a smaller door at the south side of the fortress. It stood open, another guard holding it.

Beo had never been inside the fortress walls. He had had no idea what to expect.

The corridors were warm and lit with electric lights in false sconces. The floors were the same dark mahogany as the main door, polished to gleam on either side of the gold runner rug that stretched down the entirety of the corridor's length. Each step on that carpet felt ominous. Questioning, the guard had said. What did that mean to the NPV?

Just before the end of the corridor, the guards stopped at a door and opened it. "Go in."

Once Rose and Beo were through, the guards shut the door behind them, leaving them alone.

"Are you all right?" Rose asked softly.

"I don't know. You?"

"I don't know either." Her face was blank again. What was it she had done?

The room they had been brought to contained a gleaming table, a pair of chairs, and a sofa. Beo suddenly felt tired, but there was no way he would sit when an NPV guard could return at any moment.

"Did you get your work done?" Rose asked.

It was a safe enough subject, Beo thought. "I did," he said, wanting to tell her about Emon, but deciding that was not a safe subject for the present. "I'll have to go back to get the prints once they're dry."

It remained unspoken that doing so was conditional upon them ever leaving the fortress.

The minutes turned into an hour as they stood in the empty room. Once, Beo considered trying the door, but decided against it.

Just after the bell at Fortress Tower chimed half past fifth, the door opened.

The man who came through was of medium height. His hair was salt and pepper all through, so evenly it looked intentional. His eyes were hazel with hints of green at the edges, and his left cheek bore an old scar, long since healed into a pale line that only showed when he turned toward the nearest light.

Beo recognised him.

He was Rico Samson.

Rose recognised the man as well; Beo could see it in her face and the way she took half a step back.

"It appears you both know me," said Rico Samson. He wore the same uniform as any NPV guard. Nothing to mark him as what he was, at least not on the surface. It showed instead in every move of his body. At average height, shorter than Beo and eye level with Rose, he was not a physically imposing man.

And yet when he moved into the room, he commanded it. His presence filled it, from the way he surveyed the space to see if anything was out of place to the unblinking look he affixed on Rose's face. His voice when he spoke held the absolute certainty of conviction. He did not speak loudly or forcefully, not now. His command of space came from his command of self. To this man, to the leader of the National People's Voice, command of self and command of space were one and the same.

"You are a photographer," Rico Samson said to Beo.

Beo nodded.

"Tell me, how do you find your subjects?"

The question was a simple one, yet it sent a chill through Beo's body. He thought of Emon Sanhaya's jovial smile and animated curiosity. Rico Samson's query held none of that, only the bedrock knowledge that the question would be answered to his satisfaction.

"It depends," Beo said slowly. "Some volunteer for sittings, but I prefer candid portraiture. Those I find throughout the city. Sometimes I speak to them, other times I do not."

"So you do not personally know your subjects."

"Not all of them, no."

Samson knocked once on the door, and it opened a crack, wide enough for him to take a proffered folder through the gap before it closed once more. He strode to the table and set the folder upon it, opening it to display photographic paper, face down.

Upon it was a small numeral one in a tidy circle. Beo's finger twitched at the sight of it, because he had drawn it. It was one of his photographs.

Samson turned the photograph over to display a close portrait of a woman. Her hair was dark gold, her expression distant, pensive. Only a billowing curtain showed behind her, and a windowsill with an empty planter.

"How did you come to take a photograph of this woman?"

Beo's mind spun, and he couldn't keep the bewilderment from showing on his face even as he carefully wove words together into a sentence. "I don't fully remember," he said. He remembered every second. "It was some time ago, when I was touring the countryside to broaden my subject base. I think she was in one of the villages near the Coretian border."

Rico Samson displayed no discernible emotion. "You do not recall which one?"

"I traveled the length of it," said Beo, this time in full truth. "I shot nearly one thousand portraits in two months."

"You do not know who she is."

It was not a question, but Beo felt that he needed to answer. "I'm afraid not."

Samson knocked once again on the door. This time it opened the entire way. "Search them," he said.

The same four guards entered the room, and Beo drew a sharp breath as one held his arms out to the side. Another did the same to Rose.

Their hands patted the entirety of his body, from his neck where the guard unwound his scarf and placed it on the table to Beo's boots. The same guard opened the camera bag, then, the first still holding Beo's arms outstretched as if a reminder not to interfere. Beo's bag held only his camera. He had left his books at Yoan's flat, and the relief that filled him almost made him sigh. Beo could not see the guard rifling through Rose's satchel, but he hoped, hoped, hoped that she had done the same. What would happen if one of the guards found a copy of *Red Sunrise*? Beo did not want to find out.

Rico Samson observed the search with flat eyes.

"Abernethy," Samson said. "That is an uncommon surname."

Beo's blood seemed to stop in his veins.

"Quite, your honour," Rose said, affording him a formal address Beo had not thought to use.

"What are your parents' names?"

"My parents are dead," said Rose. "At least I think my mother must be. She left when I was a child."

"I did not ask whether or not they lived," said Samson, and this time Beo saw the fear on Rose's face. "I asked their names."

"Miko and Andreas Abernethy," Rose said softly. Her voice cracked on her father's name.

"There is nothing here," one of the guards said.

Samson took a step toward Rose. "I can see him in your face. It appears his spirit was directed elsewhere, however. Andreas Abernethy was never so easily frightened."

Rose's mouth parted, and even from where he stood with his arms still spread wide, Beo could hear the small intake of breath.

"My father died in a car crash when I was fifteen," said Rose after regaining a bit of face. "I never knew how easily he frightened or not."

"Indeed," said Samson. His eyes glowed in the electric lights, and he looked back and forth between Rose and Beo. "How did the two of you come to know one another?"

"Beo took my picture," said Rose. "I was a bit out of sorts that day. I had gotten injured after stumbling into a protest. I was hurt and late for work and my autocar had broken down."

What was she doing? Beo watched Samson, the knot of terror in his chest growing as the party leader's eyes stayed trained on Rose.

"That sounds like a rather difficult day, indeed," Samson's voice held a note of pity, but Beo could not help but think it was not sympathy, but disdain, having decided Rose was pitiful. "It shall come perhaps as some reassurance that those who organised the protest have been brought to justice."

"Yes, your honour," said Rose. "Thank you."

There was a long silence, and for a moment Beo thought Samson would turn to him to corroborate the story. Instead, he motioned to the guards.

"See them out."

They gathered their things, and Beo stopped to rewrap his scarf around his neck. Rose's shoulder brushed his as they collected their bags, but neither said a word.

When Beo turned back to the door, Samson was already gone. The guards looked bored, waving a hand to indicate Beo and Rose ought to follow.

Silence reigned between Rose and Beo as they walked, without needing to confer, to Rose's flat. It followed past the click of the latches on Rose's door, to the centre of her salon. She double-checked the curtains at the windows and flicked on the radio. It filled the room with crackling music, and she turned up the volume.

"I need to tell you what I did," she said. "I was afraid they knew, when they took us. But they didn't."

Her face shone with something fierce and triumphant.

"The gemstones," she said. "I gave them to Taran Marpaxan. She's the leader of Liberation Front. I gave them all but a few, which she insisted I keep."

She opened her satchel and pulled out a bone box, opening it to show him that it was empty. Rose pawed around at the bottom until Beo could see what she was pointing to. At the very bottom of her satchel, where the lining was bunched and seamed, was a tiny hole. Rose ran one thumbnail along the hem, and out came five moss emeralds.

"I thought they had followed me," said Rose. "I thought that was why they wanted to question us."

"Turns out it was my fault," Beo said. He smiled, but he could feel the smile was lopsided. He would tell Rose about Emon, would absolutely, but this was far bigger, far more important. "The woman in that photograph is my Aunt Irena."

CHAPTER NINETEEN

"Your aunt," said Rose. She had said it three times already, but it still felt unbelievable. The radio played an orchestral waltz, crackling on each downbeat as if the static were part of the music. "Why is Rico Samson interested in your aunt?"

"I don't know," Beo said. "But after the way she left Viyarenyo, I couldn't let him know I knew her. What I said about taking portraits along the Coretian border was true, except I did it five years ago, and that photograph is from year before last."

"He knew my father," Rose said faintly. "It seems everyone knew my father. Except me."

They were silent again for a moment.

Rose walked to the sofa and sat on the edge of the cushions, her eyes prickling with unwelcome tears.

"One somewhat amusing thing happened," said Beo. "The man who lent me his space fancies me."

Rose blinked away her surprise, then looked at Beo. He still stood, looking at her with some anxiety pervading the small smile on his face.

"Do you fancy him too?"

"He's interesting. Joyful," said Beo. "That is a trait I don't often share."

"Oh," said Rose. She couldn't quite know her own feelings, so swirled together were they. The lip of the sofa beneath the cushion dug into her upper thighs, and she pressed her knees together.

"I told him there was someone in my life," Beo said. "You."

Rose's heart stopped for a silent second, and for that brief space of time, Rose felt as if the crackling waltz of the radio kept her blood flowing. "Me?"

After a brief pause, Beo came to sit beside her, close enough that his shoulder touched hers. Rose leaned into the warmth, her movement almost imperceptible even to herself.

Part of her wanted to ask what this meant. The rest did not care to put words out onto the air.

She thought of Aleis and Helyne and Grenye, all so happily in love for decades. Their family was not abnormal in Sanmarian, though in Rose's life, her relationships hadn't taken that course. Rose felt as if she were standing in a room she thought she knew only to have a hidden door opened, a door that led somewhere she herself had yet to explore.

Rose turned her head to meet Beo's eyes. His face was so close she could feel the whispers of his breath upon the soft tiny hairs on her cheek. Was that fear in his eyes?

Was there fear in her own?

Of all the things she had to fear, Rose suddenly felt certain that this was not one of them. She knew what she felt, what seemed to exist between herself and Beo Mataya. She thought she could trust it. Trust was a choice.

She made the choice. "You told him about me," she said.

"I couldn't not," Beo said. "It's likely a terrible time to even be thinking about romance at all. I only just met him."

"You really only just met me," said Rose.

"That doesn't feel true. Even if it is." Beo looked away but did not move his shoulder from where it sat against Rose's.

"I know what you mean." Gazing down at his knee, Rose gently took his hand. Something inside her felt full to bursting, something that became somehow complete with the touch of her skin on his. "Does it matter, truly? The timing?"

Beo shook his head, his thumb tracing a vein on the back of Rose's hand. "There is only the time we have, whatever that may be."

He didn't have to say that neither of them could be sure how much time they had.

When she had stood waiting outside the library for Beo, after leaving Marpaxan and dropping off the history books at her flat on the way, she had felt as if there were too many words to say. What she did with the money her aunts had left was, of course, her own business. But there was one important bit she had not yet shared.

"I told Marpaxan that the gift was from the both of us," Rose said. "I thought...you would like to be a part of it."

Beo's head turned quickly back to face her, his thumb squeezing her hand. "You didn't need to do that."

"I ought to have asked you first," said Rose.

"You did the right thing," he said. "So we are in this."

Beo swallowed, the sound audible over the crackling radio, which now played a bright reel.

"We are in this."

"Thank you."

The music from the broken radio was an incongruous counterpoint, about as romantic as a herd of children playing stickball in the city centre, yet when Rose met Beo's eyes again, her lips were on his with a shock of sweetness that turned the incessant crackling of the radio to velvet silence. Their mouths met with heat and hunger, suffusing Rose with a sort of warmth she had only read about, never thought truly possible.

Beo's hands found her cheeks, his fingers twining with her curls as he turned the caress to run them through her hair. Rose mirrored him, her own hands seeking out his curls, the softness she had wished to touch for what felt like eons instead of days. Her fingers traced the skin of his neck, discovered how his pulse fluttered against them, and it wasn't enough. Rose turned on the sofa, pivoted on one knee, the other sliding down on the other side of Beo with her atop his lap.

His kisses tasted of fire and hope, and Rose struggled to breathe. She pulled free with a sharp gasp, rained kisses down the length of his jaw, followed the trail her fingers had trod over his neck, laid her lips against that fluttering heartbeat.

She felt him beneath her as he leaned back, pulling her with him against the back of the sofa. His hands still tangled with her hair, he took them back, placed them over her waistcoat where her ribs met, his thumbs finding the precise spot over the fabric where they split, and Rose could not help but wonder what it would feel like if there were not layers of clothing between them.

A cannon shot rang out through the city, and Rose jumped. Beo's hands tightened on her waist, but this time not from passion.

A moment later, it sounded again, the boom loud enough that the window rattled. Rose looked at Beo, the moment shattered between them like glass. She climbed off his lap, feeling unsteady on her feet, and went to the window. Her flat overlooked Palm Street, which curved to the southwest, toward the harbour.

"That did not sound like it came from the fortress cannon this time," said Beo.

Rose shook her head. "It didn't."

Through the window, in the darkened sky, Rose could see an orange glow against the deep blue of night. It was not the yellow-orange of the streetlights, and it was far too big to be caused by a lantern.

"Fire," she said. "Toward the harbour."

"You're certain?"

Rose pointed. "Look. Smoke."

Sure enough, the smoke rose to the southwest.

"Why would cannons fire on the harbour?" Beo shut his mouth as if he felt stupid for asking. "Could it be a ship firing on the city?"

"I don't think so," said Rose. "Too far inland."

They stared out the window, desire dissipated into anxiety and nerves, and this time when Beo took Rose's hand, they squeezed one another's fingers for comfort.

• • • • •

Niepax dawned with Rose's head popping off her pillow, a panic about her chest and the too-familiar sense of oversleeping sending her heart into her throat. Except she no longer had a job, so after a moment of terror, she lay back against the pillow and shut her eyes. New work week. No work. Her bed, which had always felt like it was the right size, now felt too empty. She knew it was because she wished Beo were in it with her.

He had left at eighth bell to retrieve his prints from Tarn Susette's associate, which left Rose with an unfamiliar sense of exposure. That someone else was interested in Beo was far from surprising. Rose appreciated that Beo had told her. In spite of everything going on in Sanmarian, Rose could not begrudge anyone in some small quest for happiness. Jealousy was something Rose hadn't often experienced, and she wasn't sure if she experienced it now.

Pushing all thoughts of love out of her mind, Rose got out of bed, showered, and made her way to the city centre. She picked up a newspaper on the way. It said nothing about the cannon fire from the night before, nothing about the fires. The smoke had died down in the night, and Rose felt certain that it had taken Sanmarian lives with it. The newspaper in her hand, devoid of mention of those events, felt like a betrayal in paper. Rose remembered the archival composites she'd brought home the night before. She would have to go through them, but later. She was nearly certain they would be as useless as the one she held in her hand, but perhaps there would be something.

That day, she wanted to find a small gift for Beo to celebrate the exhibition, which would begin with a launch party that evening. It seemed so very fast, but Beo had said someone had pulled out of the exhibition space, leaving it open for him.

Rose also wanted to pay Amelie a visit. After a moment's reflection, she decided to do that first. Amelie's and Tomas's shop was on Carino Avenue, outside the city walls. Rose walked by briefly, peering in the window long enough to establish that Tomas was there—Niepax was the only day of the week that he usually spent in the shop instead of the home office—and Rose's decision was made. The streets were busy for the time of day, though still the tense silence crowded through the passers-by.

She knocked on the door at Amelie's house. Could she tell Amelie everything that had happened? For most of her life, she had told Amelie everything in general. Rose heard a shuffle of footsteps, the clink of the peep cover being pushed aside, and then the clank of the latch.

Amelie's face was puffy and red. She had a small cut on her right cheekbone.

Rose forgot about the NPV and everything outside of her friend's home.

She didn't ask, only stepped through the door and locked it behind her.

• • • • •

I don't know what to do.

They were Amelie's words, not Rose's, but Rose felt them too. She felt them crawling around in her stomach as she tried to keep the quaver out of her voice and the tears out of her eyes. She had to be strong for Amelie.

"The bank accounts are in his name now. All of the money we saved together from our business."

From your business, Rose wanted to say. It was Amelie's ideas, Amelie's work that had made their living. Beneath the gaping chasm of sorrow and disbelief was a white-hot kernel of rage. Rose tamped it down like she tamped down the tears.

"You can come live with me. You can."

Amelie looked up, her eyes full of something that wanted to be hope, but couldn't.

"I should never have told you. There's nothing that can be done."

Rose wanted to scream. "There's always something that can be done, love. You didn't do anything wrong."

The clock on their mantelpiece chimed the quarter hour. "You need to go, Rose. He'll be back soon."

"I'm not allowed to visit you?"

Amelie recoiled, her chest rising and falling with a slight wheeze Rose didn't remember ever hearing before.

After a long pause, Amelie shook her head. "Not when Tomas isn't here."

"When did this happen? When did this change?"

Eyes distant, Amelie looked away. "A while ago. After he first hit me. He told me he didn't want to burden you with our troubles, at first. Then he said you wouldn't understand, that he was trying. He said he needed time to fix things and told me that if a visitor came when he wasn't home, I should pretend not to be here."

The kernel of rage sprouted into a spiky vine in Rose's core. "Amelie, that is twisted. That is not how you treat someone you love."

"Sometimes it's normal," Amelie said, still not meeting Rose's eyes. "Sometimes he's the Tomas you know, and things are good for a while."

For a while.

Rose sat silent, listening to the tick of the clock. "Do you ever feel safe?"

Amelie's shoulders jerked, and then she froze.

That was all the answer Rose needed.

"I'll go," said Rose, her voice low and urgent. "Because I don't want him to come back and see me here if it would put you in danger. I'm going to help you. I promise, Amelie. I'll come back soon, and I'll help you."

Amelie looked as though she were agreeing out of politeness instead of any real belief.

When Rose left the house, she heard Amelie's footsteps retreat from behind the door, and she couldn't help but feel like her friend was getting farther and farther away with every step and every breath.

A plan took shape in her mind.

• • • • •

Rose marvelled at the difference a few days could make. As she walked along Carino Avenue, more than a few shops were closed. Café Maya had been boarded up, a potter's shop had a CLOSED sign on the window, and at least three others Rose saw in the space of a few streets had the same. How, she wondered, did the people remain silent?

A buzz pervaded the air as she walked, the day warmer than usual for winter. Soon it would be the longest night, only three days away. How many people would be running with the bulls this year, hoping to gain Larsi's favour and turn their luck?

Rose watched the passers-by as they went about their business, their eyes downcast and their steps hurried. Had the citizens of Sanmarian always walked with such purpose? Had Rose simply never noticed? No. This was new.

When she set foot onto the city's market square, she saw why.

A massive NPV banner had been displayed on the side of Market Tower, the party symbol as high as three people together. But that was not what stopped Rose Abernethy in her tracks.

Someone, somehow, had splashed red paint over the lines meant to symbolise the voices of the three silhouettes on the banner. The red had blocked them out, shocking and bright, running in rivulets down the white background until it trickled onto the silhouettes' heads. A massive red explosion with trails of blood downward. Was it red paint? Rose swayed on her feet as she stared, unsure if it were paint or truly blood.

The breeze changed direction, and the scent of chemicals reached her nose, answering the question without removing her anxiety.

No one moved on the market square. The tower tolled out tenth bell, the sound ricocheting off the buildings and closed shops. An older couple stood near Rose, their eyes glued to the tower's macabre clash of party and rebellion, the black and red and white stark against the soft colours of the sunset stone around them. Rose wanted to ask them about the past, ask them how Sanmarian had gotten here, to this.

To Rose, it seemed to have happened as quickly as a splash of red paint, but when she saw the familiarity and fear in the eyes of the couple near her, both men clutching hands as if doing so would wake them from some terrible dream, Rose could feel that it was not sudden, it was not quick. It had been happening for some time, and in their eyes was not one ounce of surprise.

Across the square, the sound of movement reached Rose's ears, of heavy footsteps marching in time. NPV guards, it had to be. As the first guard moved around the edge of Market Tower and into view, out of the corner of her eye, Rose saw the old couple drop each other's hands like a choreographed dance as they flowed apart, the barest few inches, from intimates to acquaintances.

When Rose met one of the men's gazes, she saw in his eyes only pleading. He looked to the guards, then back at Rose, and that pleading stare remained. Rose didn't know what to do. She looked back at the man, her heart brittle and breaking, and she placed one hand softly to her chest where she could reassure herself that her heart still beat.

The man relaxed, if only by a hairsbreadth, and he and his love turned away from the square and walked away, their movement slow and calculated, their shoulders bearing witness to the tension within.

The NPV guards, ten of them at least, stopped beneath the banner. One looked up, where high above on the tower's mostly unused lookout, a pair of guards saluted with a clenched fist, elbows bent at a ninety-degree angle to their bodies. The guards cut the lines holding the banner, sending the top of it rippling forward, exposing the white expanse of the banner's back.

Rose could not stand to watch any longer. She would have to think of another way to celebrate Beo's exhibition. As she turned away, taking care to copy the old men's calculated gait, Rose stifled a panicked laugh from burbling out of her. How was anyone to simply go about their lives as the city began to boil?

• • • • •

Somehow, the day did go on. Rose went home and tried to quiet her mind by tidying her flat, though it did little to help.

She discovered the cakes Helyne had given her the night the aunts fled Sanmarian, stale and sticky in the icebox. Rose had left them there, unable to throw them away. Helyne's carving was with them, and Rose, feeling silly, had removed it from the icebox and held it until the intricate wooden piece warmed to her hands. She placed it on her bedside table where the small fish appeared to be leaping out of the wood grain of the table itself.

At seventh bell in the evening, Rose arrived at the Overlook Galleria. Beo would already be there, and Rose had little to give him but a small bundle of teas she had picked out herself.

How the galleria manager had gotten a launch party ready over a single weekend was a mystery to Rose. The galleries were, if not full, well-trafficked. Rose peeked into a few of the other exhibitions before making her way up the stairs to the northwest gallery where Beo's work had been displayed.

She would have spotted his photographs even if she hadn't known which gallery they were in. The first she saw was a young child in a sling on their father's back, expression oblivious while the father laughed sheepishly and wiped away a pigeon splat from his own cheek with a lace handkerchief. It brought a smile to Rose's lips, the baby's preoccupation with something far in the distance and the father's ability to laugh at a bird shitting on his face both. Rose didn't remember seeing such a photograph in Beo's portfolio.

The next was one she recognised, and the photograph made her ache for some reason she could not quite reach. Perhaps it was the man's smile, which looked as though it had conquered a thousand tears. Or the summer Sanmarian sun that shone so bright and golden even though the photograph had no colour. Perhaps it was the contrast so unlike the wan light of winter. Rose did not know. A few other people milled about in the gallery, their soft conversations a quiet buzz in the background.

"Heartbreaking, isn't it?"

The voice that cut into Rose's observation was deep and mellifluous. Rose turned. The man who had spoken was of a height with her, with hair tied back from his face.

"Heartbreaking," Rose said. "I didn't have the word for it. I think you're right."

The man came to stand beside her, not so close as to be overly familiar, but close enough that Rose could feel his presence.

"It's the Sanmarian I want to believe is possible," he said quietly.

If Rose felt surprised to hear such a vulnerable statement from a stranger, she could not bring herself to fault him for it. He seemed to be in earnest.

"I'm not sure it has ever existed." Rose was wary of saying too much, so she left it at that, and they stood side by side for a time, both looking over the lines of the photograph.

The man pointed to another at the far end of the gallery, this one blown up to the size of the door to Rose's flat.

"This one I love as well," he said.

Rose followed him toward the photograph. In that one, the sky dipped low with heavy clouds, weighed down with rain. A summer storm, a familiar storm, the kind Rose had seen hundreds of times growing up. The clouds, deep grey in the photograph, would be near purple as they cracked down the centre with lightning. Beo had captured that lightning, those clouds, framed by a pair of arms. There were no faces in the photograph, only the arms, joined together by clasped hands. To get such a shot, Beo would have had to have his stomach flat to the cobblestones of the market. Rose had no doubt that he had done exactly that.

"It looks like love," Rose murmured.

"It does, precisely." The man turned to her, put out his hand. "Emon Sanhaya."

"Rose Abernethy."

"It is a pleasure."

"Likewise," said Rose. "Are you from Sanmarian, then?"

"From birth till now," said Emon.

A loud crash sounded from below.

Every occupant of the gallery turned to the door, and all conversation ceased. Beside her, Emon Sanhaya's face drained of colour.

A chime rang out through every room, and confused chatter bubbled from the people.

"Guests," said Emon loudly, turning back toward the visitors, "do not be alarmed. It seems there may be a fire somewhere on the premises. Please move to the exits in an orderly fashion. Likely one of the cleaners was smoking inside again and set off the warning system."

A chuckle rippled through the gaggle of people in the room, but they had all been facing the opposite direction when the chimes were heard. Rose had seen Emon's face.

As the people filed past him, Rose grabbed his arm. "What do they really mean?"

"What? Rose, I must ask you to follow the rest of the visitors outside, even if it's likely just a precaution."

"You work here. This is my friend's work in this room. Please, is Beo in danger?"

Emon's face lit with shock once more, though he recovered quickly. "My boss will make sure of his safety. If you are who I think you are, I must make sure of yours. Come with me."

CHAPTER TWENTY

The first thing Beo thought when the chimes went off through the whole of the Overlook Galleria was *Rose.*

She had to be upstairs already, while he was here in Susette's office sorting out payment. And, naturally, waiting for Susette to accompany him upstairs and introduce him, which was the bit of the evening Beo looked forward to the least—until the crashing sound of the galleria's front door shattering.

Tarn Susette shook the glass shards from his gloved hand, the hand he had used to smash the cover on the alarm system. Beo would never forget the calm that slid across Susette's face like a fog across the Tarenr Sea.

"I'm very sorry, Beo," Susette said, pulling off one glove, then the other. "Had I known this was coming so soon, I would never have invited you to show your work."

"Mister Susette," Beo said.

"There's no time, lad." Tarn Susette handed Beo an envelope. "It's cash. I do not expect any of my promissory notes to be taken by banks after tonight."

"I don't understand what's happening."

"In less than a minute, NPV guards are going to come through that door." He pointed. "Go out the side door, through Emon's office. On the third floor behind Nisat's largest painting, there is a passageway that leads out of the galleria and onto the street. Emon should be already there."

"My friend should be upstairs," Beo said as Susette pushed him toward the door.

"If Emon was upstairs, he would have told everyone it was the fire alarm. Go. You don't want them to see you with me."

"But why? You could come with me!" As far as Beo knew, Tarn Susette was a respected member of Sanmarian's artistic elites, an artist himself in his younger years, though he had moved into buying.

"Get out!" The older man barked it at him, fury and desperation flashing in his eyes.

Beo obeyed, slipping out the door as he was told, trying to keep the sound of his feet quiet on the stone floors of the galleria. Behind him, he heard the heavy tread of guards' boots. When he found the stairs, he ran, ignoring the people who streamed down the stairs. One of them called after him, "Fire alarm! Turn round!"

He ignored that too.

There was more than one stairwell, but this was the closest to the gallery where his work was displayed. Rose's face was not among those he passed.

The gallery with his work was empty, free of any signs of people, silent except for the soft hum of the electric lights.

Beo's throat was devoid of moisture, his tongue sticky with fear.

Beo's photographs were on the third floor. In the southeast gallery was Nisat's oil paintings, most of which were larger than a person standing upright. The largest of these took up half a wall, ceiling to floor.

The frame was well-made but looked like an ordinary frame. Beo tugged at one side of it, but it did not budge. He could not see how it was mounted to the wall. When he tugged at the opposite side, the painting swung outward. Behind the canvas was a handle, and nothing else but darkness.

Beo went through and pulled it shut behind him, wondering to what fate he had abandoned Tarn Susette.

• • • • •

The darkness was complete and palpable.

Beo made his feet move forward, feeling himself certainly between the walls of the gallery, wondering how he would descend to street level without plunging downward to break his bones.

He had no torch, no lighter, nothing that could illuminate his path. His spine crawled as he wondered what might be around him in the dark, and though Beo stretched out one hand to guide his steps against the sandstone wall, he flinched from the dust and cobwebs his fingers encountered. He walked for some time before realising that the wall curved to his right, and the floor beneath him sloped. Once, something skittered by his foot, close enough to bump him. A rat.

The Overlook Galleria was a circular building, made of sunset stone like the rest of Sanmarian's city centre. Never before had Beo considered that those thick stone walls could be hollow. Sanmarian was a breathing, living city, and secrets were its blood.

Beo's steps grew faster as he descended through the passage, the floor he walked upon even enough that he did not trip, though twice he scraped his knuckles against the wall. Had Rose left the gallery with the visitors to the exhibition? He thought of the NPV discovering her there and the thought twisted his stomach to knots.

Tarn Susette had said that the passage led to the street, but where? Beo lost all sense of place, kept only the movement of his feet and the feel of stone beneath his fingertips. If there were a hell, some place of torment, Beo could imagine it being like that passage. Always moving, unable to see or hear, fearing for the lives of those one loved.

The comparison nearly stopped Beo where he was. *Do I love Rose?*

She had said herself that they had only just met, and too she had said herself that it did not seem true.

How much time love needed to grow, Beo did not know.

His throat tightened again, dried by fear and mouldering dust.

Love before Rose had felt like this tunnel, stumbling through the darkness with feet leading him through he knew not what. It had felt like fingers grasping in the night, unsure whether they would encounter a soft kiss or a spider's bite. Love had been pain, had been fear, had been blame, shame, and guilt.

A voice whispered through Beo's mind, soft like the cobwebs that brushed his fingers, that such things were not what love was made of.

He stumbled on, ever forward, uncertain and unsure, but somehow his feet found their way.

• • • • •

When Beo came to the end of the passage, he kicked it with his foot by accident. His fingers, sanded by the wall and swollen, found a door in front of him. Beo fumbled for a knob, a latch, anything. He found a lever and pushed it. It did not move. He pulled upward instead, and a rusty creak answered his labour, the clank of metal greeting his ears along with a breeze of outside night air that leaped through the crack into the tunnel itself.

At first, Beo thought he could have cried tears of joy to have that scent meet him. He drew a deep breath, and his nose caught something beyond sea salt and winter.

Smoke.

Beo pulled open the door, scooting backward to give it space, then wedged himself through it. It slammed shut the moment he let go of it, and there was no handle on the outside for him to return.

Tarn Susette had said the tunnel gave way onto a street, but in truth it was more of a tight, crooked close. There was bare enough room for two average-sized people to stand shoulder to shoulder, and something skittered off to Beo's left. Another rat, most likely.

Beo blinked, his eyes adjusting to light again. From where he stood, he could see no streetlamps, only the twists of the close. He didn't know which way to go.

He looked up, feeling lost. The wall rose high above his head, but it did not look like the Overlook Galleria. Beo decided to turn left, stepping over a dislodged cobblestone the size of his head. It had rained or snowed, and the stones smelled damp.

The choice to turn left was the correct one, spilling Beo out onto Palaxo Circle, which ran along the circumference of the fortress itself. Beo had been right again—the wall out of which he had emerged was far to the north from the Overlook itself. The passage must have led through several adjoined buildings in order to deposit him where it did.

He needed to find Rose.

He had no idea where to look.

When Beo reached Alcazar Avenue, he heard the first screams.

Smoke rose from buildings all over the city. Alcazar rose toward the fortress, which sat on a hill, and as Beo walked southward toward where his flat had been on Altas Street, he could see plumes of smoke white against the night's clouds. He had no bag with him for once, and his fingers itched to photograph the city. Beo was afraid he wouldn't believe his own memory if he did not capture it on film.

There were some few people on the streets, rushing to their destinations without looking back.

He could go to Yoan's, where his things were, where Yoan might have some answers, but Beo had taken no more than a few steps with that in mind when he turned down a side street to cut due south, skirting the market square and aiming at Marian Road, which became Carino Avenue. Beo's nose twitched each time the wind blew smoke his way, and his ears prickled each time he heard someone yell. Three or four times, he saw a scuffle down the street and changed his path, heart thumping.

The only thing he knew was that he needed to get to Rose. If she had gotten out of the Galleria, she would likely go home. He would wait there if she wasn't there already.

Around him, Sanmarian burned.

• • • • •

Beo reached Rose's flat as eleventh bell tolled through the city, taking the stairs two at a time to get to her floor. His scraped knuckles stung from sweat, and his legs ached with each step upward, but he ignored the pain.

He knocked on her door with his uninjured left hand, the sensation a strange one. When only silence answered him, Beo turned and slumped against the wall beside the door.

The door opened.

"Beo?" Rose's voice, dreamlike after the surreal path the evening had taken, seemed to float through the air.

He forgot the pain in his legs and hand and leaped to his feet. His lips found hers, and she kissed him back, her hands at his face as if trying to reassure herself that he truly stood in front of her. Pulling away from the kiss reluctantly, Beo cupped her cheek in his hand, ready to ask what had happened. But behind her, Beo caught sight of movement.

"Emon," he said, surprise erasing any other words from his vocabulary.

"Come in," Rose said. "He helped me escape the gallery."

Beo obeyed, latching the door behind himself.

Two mugs of tea sat on the coffee table, and the radio was on again, scratchy static overlaying the boom of a man's voice instead of music this time.

"The NPV has been playing Samson's address from last week, beginning to end, over and over," said Rose. "I've kept the radio on in case something changes. Every channel has been over-broadcast."

"You helped Rose get out," said Beo. He walked to Emon and embraced him, smelling the same scent of smoke on the man's hair as he had smelled on Rose's. "Then you know about Susette."

Emon's shoulders slumped against Beo's embrace, and he pulled away. "He told me such a thing would likely happen. He didn't know it would be tonight."

"He said as much to me. What did they want with him?"

Emon gave Beo a disbelieving look. "Do you truly not know?"

Beo looked back and forth between Rose and Emon. Rose's curls were dampened—from the rain Beo had missed inside the tunnel?—and Emon's straight hair was still pulled back from his face, though the joyful exuberance Beo had seen in him over the weekend was gone, lost into quiet contemplation that seemed to be directed at Beo's face.

"Please," said Beo. "Tell us."

"When was the last time you had a relationship with a man?" Emon asked.

Beo started at the question, but after reading the NPV manifest Rose's aunts had left for her, he could not wonder at the reason for it. "Not since my school days, not seriously, anyway."

Emon's eyes showed a glimmer of surprise, quickly suppressed. "The NPV knows that art, literature, music—all are things that contain the soul of a people. Of all of a people. They have been collecting books from the Market Tower library for over two years now. The books vanish, and they aren't replaced."

"I know. I've seen."

"The books they have been taking contain what the NPV sees as objectionable content." Emon's mouth quirked. "They think if they can erase the kinds of love, the kinds of families they despise, they will be able to erase us from existing. Create what they want to be normal."

"The history section at the library is full only of NPV-approved texts," said Rose. "Like these I borrowed."

She gestured to the table in front of the sofa, where a stack of three books sat.

"I'd hoped to learn something, but I don't know if they will be of any use."

Emon went on. "Those of us who have been involved more seriously in relationships with people who share our gender—and those of us who have moved to another gender or both or neither—have known for some time that the NPV does not want us in their society. Susette's lover died five years ago after visiting an NPV-chosen doctor. He had influenza. Susette believed the doctor treated him with the concentrated extract of apricot kernels instead of the medicinal mould tincture."

Beo stared at Emon. "You cannot be in earnest. A doctor?"

"Willa was my tutor and my friend," Emon said. "He did not die of influenza by itself. His symptoms changed and showed evidence of cyanide poisoning."

"Five years ago," said Rose. "You believe this has been happening for five years?"

"Longer than that. Over the past fifteen years, ever since the NPV seized power, they have quietly disposed of anyone who disagreed with them. Some they got rid of through bureaucratic means—"

Rose jumped at that, and Beo knew she was thinking of her friend Amelie and the way the NPV had taken her business out from under her with no care for lawful ownership.

"—and others have vanished or died of disease that should have been curable." Emon made the pronouncement blandly, but Beo saw the pain in his eyes.

"Why do the people not fight back?" Rose squeezed Beo's hand, leaning her shoulder into his. The touch was slight. The comfort it brought Beo was not.

"People don't notice what doesn't affect them," said Emon. If seeing Rose and Beo's closeness bothered him, he did not show it. "Liberation Front tries, but they are disorganised and lack knowledge and the infrastructure they need. No one really knows what the NPV is aiming for, other than the sweeping social changes. If that is all they want, however, I'll eat your radio to get that blasted crackling to stop."

Rose cracked a grim smile. "It's been like that forever. I ought to get a new one. My aunt tried to fix it, but she said it wasn't fixable."

Beo looked at Rose. "Mikael Iris saw this coming," he said. "The entire book is about this."

At Emon's confused look, Rose ventured an explanation. "It's a novel. A tragedy, about people in love torn apart by fear. It takes place in Sanmarian, with a fascist party in power."

"I should very much like to read such a book," said Emon. "Especially since right now it doesn't quite seem safe to leave this flat."

Rose was quiet for a moment, and Beo could feel his heart scudding in his chest, wondering if she would share a book—that book, her book, that apparently infamous book—with a near stranger to her.

"I'll go get it," she said, voice quiet and almost shy. Rose pulled her hand from Beo's and gave him a small smile, then turned toward her bedroom.

"Thank you," said Beo when she had gone. He could hear her opening the wardrobe even through the closed door. "For making sure she got out. We were questioned by the NPV not two days ago, and they let us go after only searching us. They wanted to know about a subject in one of my photographs. I don't want to think about what might have happened if they had found her there tonight and knew she had already been brought in once."

Emon's eyes widened as Beo spoke, and he went to sit on the sofa, scratching at the linen of his trousers with a fingernail. "I didn't know who she was at first. She and I were speaking about your photographs; I was merely excited to see someone who seemed as taken with them as I am. And," he said almost ruefully, "I thought she was...magnetic. It wasn't until the alarm sounded that she mentioned you, and I knew she must be the person you had spoken of. You are beautiful together, you know. It cheers me to see it. She is a remarkable person."

"She is," said Beo softly. "I told her about you."

"Is that so?" Some of Emon's spark returned, and he gave Beo an assessing look. He smiled then. "I may have gotten her out of the gallery, but she knows this city like she sculpted it from clay herself. She helped us avoid whatever is happening in the city centre."

"I'll have to thank her for that as well, then." Beo returned Emon's smile, feeling as if a tightrope were stretched beneath his feet. He didn't know if he would fall to either side if he kept on, and if he did, how far down he would have to go.

"Willa used to say that nothing we do controls anything in this world," said Emon. "And because of that, all we can control is what we do."

Rose's soft footsteps returned, and she held out what Beo knew to be her own current copy of *Red Sunrise*. "It can't leave this flat," she said. "The NPV doesn't like it."

"In that case, I love it already," said Emon. He met Beo's eyes as he took the book from Rose's hand.

Emon's words rang in Beo's head.

CHAPTER TWENTY-ONE

Rose had considered what it might be like to first share her bed with Beo, but her considerations had not included what it might be like to do so on a night they were forced to flee a public gallery, with a man who fancied him reading on the sofa in the salon.

Even so, when Rose closed the door to her bedroom with Beo in it, a thrill went through her in spite of the fear and exhaustion that had plagued their night.

"How are you?" she asked Beo, as much to say something at all as to find out. Beo looked haggard, dark circles under his eyes and his hair in disarray, dust muting the dark curls in the light of Rose's lamp.

"I don't know where to start," he said. "Yoan will be worried that I don't come home, if he's even all right himself. I don't know where Irena went or what she meant to do. I'm not certain I even understand what's happening tonight. Worse, I don't know if it can be stopped, or what happens to us if it can't."

"I know," said Rose. Her trousers were dusty from brushing against the walls in the passage Emon had led her out of, and her feet ached from all the walking. She swallowed, thinking of Amelie. "I don't know how we will make it through this, if the NPV is taking people openly."

"Nor do I." Beo raised his hand as if he wanted to rub his eyes, then thought better of it. "May I use your washroom?"

"Of course," Rose said. She wanted to do the same.

Her trek out of the galleria with Emon had been harried and strange, the fear of being alone in the dark with a stranger almost outweighing the fear of encountering NPV guards. Rose did not think they would be so accommodating were they to question her a second time.

Once she had found out who Emon was, Rose had felt an almost indescribable relief. Even from the little Beo had told her of him, she was disposed to like him, but spending three hours navigating Sanmarian at his side had made her not just thankful, but something else. She could tell he cared for Beo, and not only in the way one admires an artist one likes. His own home was too far away, so she had invited him to her flat, knowing it likely that Beo would make his way there if—when—he got away from the Overlook.

Perhaps Emon Sanhaya had helped her only to increase Beo's opinion of him, but Rose didn't think so. Regardless, she was grateful.

She listened to the sound of water running in the washroom, gathering clean pyjamas to change into. She was several inches shorter than Beo, but she thought he might fit in a longer pair of pyjama bottoms. When Beo emerged several minutes later, drying his hair with a towel and with a second towel wrapped round his waist, Rose caught her breath at the sight of him. He smiled at her, a real smile, that smile that lit something deep inside her. Rose returned it, motioning to the pyjamas on the bed.

"Those are for you, if you'd like," she said. "I didn't think you'd want to put your other clothes back on straightaway."

"Thank you."

Rose left it unspoken that he was welcome to share the bed and slipped into the washroom. There was still hot water, and Rose used it liberally, washing her hair quickly and scrubbing the dust and cobwebs from her skin. The water running into the drain turned grey. She hadn't realised she was so dirty.

Her pyjamas felt like comfort and safety against her skin, and she joined Beo back in her room feeling as if the water had washed away more than just surface grime. He was sitting on her bed and had been gazing at the floor until she came back. The pyjama bottoms cleared his ankles, and he wore no shirt. His chest was slim, not overtly muscular. A line of hair ran from his navel to the waistband of the pyjamas.

"I know you asked me to stay the other night as well," he said. "I want you to know that I don't take anything for granted, between you and me. I care about you. The situation has become...a little unique."

For some reason, Rose was sure he didn't mean Emon in the salon at all.

"I understand," Rose said. "And likewise."

She hesitated for a moment, then went to sit beside him. "Tonight, I think, it would be too much to do more than sleep," she said, and she saw relief in his face, which caused her to mirror it, her body relaxing and releasing tension she hadn't realised she was holding knotted in her muscles. Rose didn't think she had to explain that another night, a less complicated night, there was nothing she would want more than him.

Beo looked at Rose, and she looked back, could not look away.

"I feel foolish for having not seen what was happening," he said after a beat. "Even though Irena warned me about this city."

"I have lived here my whole life." Rose traced the line of stitches on her quilt, her finger following a whorl of blue and green. She thought of Amelie. "It's easy, I think, not to see things when they don't happen in front of you."

"I want to do something."

"I do too."

They sat quietly, the mattress creaking slightly whenever their weight shifted.

Rose got up and walked to her side of the bed, fingers quivering as she pulled back the blankets and sheets. The linens were cool against her skin, and her cheeks felt warm from the bath and nerves. It had been some time since she shared her bed with anyone. She seldom wanted to.

Beo hesitated before climbing in. Rose felt his warmth immediately, reaching for the pull-cord of the lamp on her bedside table. The jingle of the metal cord plunged the room into darkness.

"How are you?" Beo asked. Rose felt him next to her, could almost sense his bare shoulder even though she could not see it.

"Lost," said Rose. "I feel as though I'm attempting to cross the sea in storm season on a pair of floating wooden shoes. Taran Marpaxan could take the gems I gave her and run away to Coret with them, or cross the Tarenr Sea and join the Risati Empire and I will have taken that risk for naught. I don't know how we got here."

"Neither do I." There was a pause, then Beo went on. "If I have to be here, Rose, I am thankful you're here beside me."

Rose reached out her hand and touched his arm, hesitant, hungry for the warmth and comfort of his skin. "May I—" She didn't quite know what she was asking.

The bed creaked, and Beo's arm lifted, making a space for her.

Rose found the crook of his arm, and Beo moved his shoulders until their arms encircled one another and somehow neither held more or less than the other. She could feel him breathe, the movement of air against her still-damp hair, the rise and fall of his torso, the life-beat of his heart.

In that moment, some might have said that the world outside ceased to be—the NPV, the broken glass that littered the floor of Tarn Susette's office, aunts missing, businesses lost, people taken—but in the circle of Rose and Beo's arms, the world dwelt large and full. Sanmarian's rounded buildings and jagged teeth and blood-secrets lived in that circle, surrounded that circle, became that circle. The world existed in that circle. But in that place, so crowded with fear and concern and helplessness, Rose held tight to the fierce fire of gratitude, to live in such a world and still find something warm. Something peaceful. Something true.

· · · · ·

Rose found Emon on the sofa, *Red Sunrise* clutched to his chest with both arms. She stopped in the open door to her bedroom, Beo behind her, and something in her heart melted at the sight.

"I don't want to wake him," Rose murmured to Beo. Beo's lips touched Rose's shoulder, and he slipped by her to the kitchen.

"I'll make tea."

"I'm already awake," said Emon, stirring. "But thanks for the thought."

He sat up, eyes puffy as if he had wept and failed to sleep. Judging by the state in which Rose had found him, she guessed that was precisely what had happened.

Emon told them that the radio had gone over to staticky silence at third bell in the morning. "It finished a cycle of Samson's address," he said. "It was deliberately cut off."

Rose looked out the window, her mug of tea in her hands, the curtains drawn back for once. "It looks quiet out there."

It wasn't, but they would soon find that out for themselves.

In the stillness of Rose's flat, Emon stretched, finally setting *Red Sunrise* on the table in front of the sofa.

"Thank you for this," he said, touching it with two long fingers. "I couldn't sleep until I'd read the whole thing."

Rose and Beo exchanged a glance, and Rose went to sit beside Emon on the sofa.

"You liked it?" she asked.

"I don't know if that's the right way to put it." Emon rubbed one hand over the stubble growing on his chin, pushing his now-loose hair back from his face. "It felt real."

"I know what you mean," Beo said, leaning against the doorframe that led to the kitchen. "It always feels real."

Rose reached over and turned the radio back on. Static crackled through the salon for a moment before she turned it back off.

"Did you try the other channels?" Rose turned to Emon, who shook his head.

Flicking the radio back on, Rose turned the dial through the channels, trying to find any frequency that was broadcasting.

"I've never heard of this happening," she murmured. "Except—"

"Except in the book." Emon leaned back against the sofa, and Rose could hear his breathing, quick and almost ragged in the way of people who haven't slept.

"I need to check on Yoan," said Beo. He took a sip of his steaming tea and winced.

"I'm not sure you ought to go alone." Outside, the sky was overcast with low hanging clouds that formed a grey ceiling, a swirling ceiling that Rose could see moving, changing. "I'm not sure anyone ought to be alone right now."

Was Amelie okay? Rose knew what she wanted to do, but she didn't know how to start. She needed to see Amelie without Tomas present. And Beo was right—they needed to check on Yoan. Beyond that, Rose knew she needed to find Liberation Front and see what she could do to help.

"We'll all go," said Emon, looking at Beo with more reserve than Rose had seen in him. "If that's all right, that is."

"Of course," said Beo, his own face just as reserved.

They left Rose's flat shortly after, and the streets felt hollow like a cave, every step seeming to echo. There was no dull roar of autocar traffic, no exhaust pumping into the air, only the rain-dampened cobbles and the swiftly moving cloud cover above and gusts of wind that brought both the scent of the sea and the dusty smell of oncoming snow.

On Carino Avenue, the silence evaporated.

It began with what sounded simply like voices in the distance, but as Rose, Beo, and Emon stepped through the city gate past the walls of sunset stone, the voices became yells.

"Café Maya," Rose said with a gasp she could not help. She froze on the footpath, her hand seeking Beo's but accidentally finding Emon's. It was smoother than Beo's, and Emon gripped her hand tight. Rose reached for Beo with her other free hand, but even holding both she felt she might fall.

Café Maya's boarded up windows had been set aflame and scorched, the hasty coverings torn away. Broken glass haunted the cobbles in front of the café, dull in the grey morning. The dining room tables lay in charred heaps on the floor, ash dusting through the hollowed-out space with the breeze.

At the sound of voices approaching, Rose dropped the men's hands, swallowing the bile that rose in her throat.

"Maybe we should go around the market," said Beo.

"My son!" A man's voice cut through the air, and a figure appeared at the corner of the market, fifty yards away. "Where's my son?"

A pair of NPV guards appeared from the opposite direction, faces grim and the brims of their hats pulled down low.

"Where's my son?" The man cried out, running toward them. "You took my son!"

Rose stood stock-still, watching the man cross Carino Avenue toward the two waiting NPV guards as if time had slowed. She saw the man's hysterical panic, the jerky motion of his grief-stricken body. She saw the guard on the left pull a baton from his belt. She saw the moment they collided, the guards clearly prepared. The guard on the right caught the man's arm and spun him, and the left guard's baton fell once, hard, onto the man's head.

The man slumped onto the cobblestones.

The guard slid his baton back into its holder on his belt, looking up to see Rose and the others, still frozen on the footpath. "Go home," he said. "Leader Samson will address the city at noon bells."

More of desperation than any feeling of emboldenment, Rose called out, "Home is north of here. We got stuck last night. Can we get through?"

Beside her, Rose heard Beo's sharp intake of breath.

After a moment of hesitation or assessment, the guard gave a curt nod. "Walk straight through the square," he said, then nodded at his fellow guard, who stooped with him to grab the fallen man by his arms.

"Go," whispered Emon, and Rose heard the sickness in his voice even though she could not see his face.

Somehow at the front of their small group, Rose looked straight ahead, her legs unsteady as much as she tried to keep them moving. Out of the corner of her eye, a flash of blood on the cobblestones stood out against the grey.

They made a sharp right at the edge of the market square. The giant banner, yesterday stained red over the symbol of the National People's Voice on the side of Market Tower, had been replaced. It seemed somehow larger, ephemeral in the morning light, slow-evaporating mist curling around the edges of the tower like Sanmarian's breath in the winter air.

• • • • •

Walking across the square, Rose's body felt as if it were the inner workings of a machine. Her legs moved, her lungs drew breath, her heart beat, but she kept her face as blank as she could, trying not to react to what she saw.

Burned storefronts, broken glass—paper and debris scattered across the stones. The only pristine sight was the NPV banner, stark white and black against the pink-orange of the tower itself.

More splashes of red stood out against the cobblestones, and this time as Rose walked apace with Beo, Emon half a step behind, no reassuring chemical paint smell reached her nose.

The occasional cry rang out, loud and sharp, and as much as Rose tried, each made her jump. She flinched away from the guards, keeping her head down and her expression neutral, futile as her efforts were. Rose couldn't help but quicken her pace. Yoan's flat was off Sankael, and the path to it would take them past a familiar place.

Her stomach sank with every step as they approached Sankael Road, and though Beo didn't reach out then to take her hand again, he moved closer, the heat of his body a warmth that sought to reassure her.

Aunt Aleis's tearoom had been smashed in.

Rose saw it before they reached it, the glass blackened with soot on the ground beneath the window frame.

"Keep walking," Beo said, his voice gentle. "Don't stop."

"My gods." Emon's own words reached Rose's ears, but they sounded far away, farther than the short distance between them as they walked.

Rose swallowed, then swallowed again. Her throat was sticky and dry. The cold seeped into her nose, the wind finding gaps in her scarf to bite at her neck. The walk to Yoan's seemed to take an age.

The smaller square where Yoan's flat was housed—Plax Kael—was deserted. No laundry hung on lines stretched between buildings, no people peeked out of their homes.

"I have a key," Beo said, pushing open the door to the building. He said nothing of Yoan, but Rose knew his thoughts were exactly where her own were: whether or not they would even find his friend at home.

Somewhere in the city, a clock tolled out eleventh bell. One hour until Rico Samson planned to address the city. What could he possibly say?

At Yoan's door, Beo paused, moving ahead of Rose. He dug in his pockets for the key, and Rose couldn't help but think his figure looked unfinished without his camera bag slung over his shoulder. Visions of Beo's smashed flat flashed unbidden to mind as the key clicked in the door.

Yoan was on the other side, a heavy club in one hand and a wary expression on his face. "Beo," he said. He dropped the club on the sofa and ushered them inside.

Emon earned a quizzical look, but Yoan didn't wait for any introductions. "I heard about Tarn Susette," Yoan said. "He was a friend of Mar—"

He didn't finish the name.

"I know Taran Marpaxan," Emon said quietly. "I haven't been active in Liberation Front due to my work at the gallery, but I know her."

"Emon has worked with Susette for more than half a decade," Beo said, and Yoan's shoulders slumped.

"I'm very sorry," Yoan said.

"Was," said Rose. "You said was a friend of Marpaxan, or you started to."

Emon went very still.

"You haven't heard." Yoan's quiet declaration sounded sick.

"I know Susette was taken last night. He helped me escape the Overlook Galleria. Emon himself helped Rose get out. The rest of the patrons seem to have believed there was simply a fire alarm." Beo latched the door with a harsh-sounding click, looking to Emon Sanhaya with the kind of preemptive pity that occurs when someone knows bad news is coming.

"Susette and five others were executed last night. Publicly." Yoan sat on the arm of the sofa, looking as though he wished he could sink into it and not come out. "They charged them with sedition, named off connection with a few others as 'proof' and shot them in the head."

"Oh, gods." Rose took a step backward and ran into Beo. "Emon."

Emon's face lost its colour. "Nikan Alerpax," he said. He turned to look at Beo, ashen. "His exhibition was pulled last week; that's why you got the space. Susette saw his work had taken an...unpleasant turn. Last minute he changed out what he had planned to show at the galleria, and Tarn said he could not in good conscience display Alerpax's work."

"Who is Nikan Alerpax?" Yoan asked.

"He's a painter, and a good one, but his work has recently been commissioned by the NPV." Emon ran his fingers through his hair once, then again, violently the second time, as if the strands falling in his face could be enough to shatter his remaining calm. "He did the most recent round of propaganda posters. Tarn stayed out of the NPV target zone for years by making sure he invited party-sympathetic artists to exhibit. I didn't see Alerpax's newest work, but if it was enough to make Tarn—if it was enough—"

Emon's voice caught, and his throat seemed to close like a fist around his next breath. His shoulders convulsed, and Beo darted around Rose, catching Emon just as his knees buckled and he sobbed. They sank to the floor, Emon's hands grasping tight at Beo's coat, hard enough that his fingernails bent back.

Rose looked at Yoan, whose eyes were on Beo and Emon. For a long moment, Rose was unable to speak. Finally, she found words.

"Someone burned my aunts' tearoom. And Café Maya. Was it the NPV?"

Yoan's head turned slowly to face her, and then he nodded. "Directly or indirectly, yes. The NPV itself or their supporters. They chased everyone out of the square last night after the executions. No one else could have gotten through their perimeter."

Rose stood in silence, listening to the quiet gasps of Emon's sobs and trying to find purchase on a new view of a world where, in the city where she had been born, she could see a grieving man clubbed by guards and know that in the night, citizens had died without trial, slain by means of public execution.

CHAPTER TWENTY-TWO

It was strange to miss the static crackling of Rose's radio when Yoan turned on his own, which stood in the corner opposite the front door of his flat and gave forth only a hushed whisper. It was Torek, one of the days of the week Beo usually went to work framing pictures, but that day he did not think he would be missed. Emon sat in a chair in the corner, face puffy but empty now. He met Beo's eyes.

Rose stood beside the radio, her coat unbuttoned, absently fiddling with a fraying buttonhole. "Noon bell, the guard said."

"It's noon bell just now," Yoan said just as the clock tolled out the time. No sooner had the twelfth bell sounded then the radio chimed to life with a descending triplet of notes.

Beo had never really noticed before that those notes played before NPV addresses; he so seldom had listened to the radio at all. He didn't own one.

"Attention," the radio said. "This broadcast is mandatory for all citizens of Sanmarian and surrounding villages. This message will repeat."

"Here it goes," Beo muttered.

"Sanmarian is my home," said a deep voice Beo didn't recognise. "It is the duty of all citizens to protect their home."

"We deserve a safer Sanmarian," said another, a soft alto. "Safer for our children to grow up in."

"We must protect our children from deviants," a new voice boomed. "We must protect the natural families."

"They keep using that word," Rose said over the voice's continued sentence. "Protect. They believe these things are threatened? Truly?"

Beo himself had stuck on the word *deviants*.

There was a pause in the broadcast, differentiated from the cutoff silence by a swelling of three notes in harmony in a minor key.

The next voice that spoke, Beo knew. He had been face-to-face with the man not two days before. Rico Samson.

"Too long," said Samson through the radio. "Too long has this land suffered. Our families toil but are unable to feed their children. There is no one at home to care for the children, no one to tend them when they finish their school days."

"That's not even *true*—" Yoan spat, but Beo raised a hand to quiet him.

"There is an ill-kept secret in our city, in our country, my friends. There is not enough work for all." Samson delivered his line in a conspiratorial tone, as if he were confirming something everyone suspected, but no one knew. "There is a solution, and your government is working toward it. We are your voice, the National People's Voice. We see your fear, and we see your anger. You do not need to doubt that we work tirelessly to ensure your safety."

The sick feeling in Beo's stomach grew stronger. He thought of Irena and wondered where she was. Could she have known this was coming?

"Our silence this past day must have come as a shock. For those of you who did not yet hear, we are proud to announce that today, with only two days before our midwinter celebrations, we have finally conducted a successful raid and brought several known seditionists to justice." Samson's voice swelled, grew more resonant. "Together we will build a stronger Sanmarian. Together, we will ensure the safety of our city and citizens from those who seek to unbalance the stability we have cultivated these past fifteen years. The National People's Voice has been your advocate, your protector. We have worked long to bring a brighter future to you, and we will not tire or slake in our desire to see those who would threaten that stability to meet your judgment."

"What does he mean?" Emon, still sitting in the chair, had both hands splayed on his knees. He looked as though he might vomit. His fingertips showed white against the dark grey of his trousers.

"This Ctoro, two days hence, we shall celebrate the longest night in true Kaeli fashion, with the running of the bulls. This year, however, entrance shall not be open. Only those selected by the party shall be allowed to compete. But fear not!" Samson's voice now held a deep timbre and a hint of a laugh. "Larsi's luck shall favour our city."

Music swelled again behind Samson's voice, this time a major key in thirds and fifths, a swelling of sound that took a moment for Beo to register as a chorus of voices.

"We will fight for you, Sanmarian. Stay vigilant. Raise your voice with ours."

The first three notes replayed, descending, and the broadcast began again.

Rose's hand flicked out and spun the dial to turn it off so quickly, her hand seemed to blur.

Beo couldn't blame her. For all the reassuring words, for all the talk of care and safety, the Sanmarian of the day was full of danger. More than Beo had ever thought possible.

"Do the NPV have any reason to connect you with Tarn Susette?" Yoan asked Emon carefully. "Any reason to believe you would be his supporter?"

"Of course they do," said Emon. "I was apprenticed to his lover, who we both suspected they had a hand in killing. I expect that if I had not been helping Rose out of the passage from the galleria, had I been instead with Tarn in his office, I would also have had my brains shot out last night."

He said it so calmly that it took Beo a moment to process his words.

"Bloody hell," Beo said, his voice hoarse.

Yoan's face shifted a fraction of an expression. He turned his right ear toward the front door. "Quiet," he said.

Beo shut his mouth, held his breath. He couldn't hear anything but three people's ragged breathing.

Yoan took three steps toward the kitchen table, where Beo's camera bag sat. He snatched it up and handed it to Beo in one smooth motion.

"You three. Out the window."

"What?" Rose asked, head swivelling toward the door. "I don't hear anything."

Just then, Beo did. Footsteps. Heavy ones. Boots.

Beo slung the bag over his shoulder, his heart taking up a new residence in his throat. "Rose," he whispered. "Do it."

"What are you doing?" Rose buttoned her coat as she walked to the door, Emon rising from his chair, his face sick with grief and fright.

Beo went to the corner where his belongings were still bundled in the bedsheets he had carried them in from his flat. The footsteps in the corridor grew louder, and he heard the window open behind him.

"Get out," he heard Yoan say. "They can't find you here."

Somewhere outside, a chorus of shouts rose up. Beo rummaged through his clothes, frantically throwing them to the side.

"Beo," hissed Yoan. "Beo!"

They have to be here. Beo pawed at the garments, small clothes, waistcoats, shirts. His hand struck something hard. He grabbed it, both books bundled, still wrapped in a clean pair of drawers.

"Beo!" The footsteps stopped outside the door, and Beo bolted to his feet.

"If they found you with this book, they would kill you," Beo said, looking his friend in the eyes and knowing his words to be absolute truth.

Yoan looked back, his face unreadable. He clasped Beo's hand just as a loud knock sounded at the door. Yoan's grip was firm and strong, his muscles defined under his shirt. Yoan's beard was neatly trimmed, his hair in its usual knot, just as if he might be heading to the pub to serve beer and soup and sourbread to customers for the day.

Outside the window, Beo could see Rose's and Emon's faces.

He squeezed Yoan's hand once more, afraid to speak, willing the *come with us* to show on his face.

Yoan gave Beo a small smile, then gestured sharply at the window.

"Coming!" Yoan called brightly in the direction of the door.

Beo crawled over the windowsill, feet landing in mulch just shy of a small leafless hedge. Rose's hand found his shoulder.

Yoan had paused at the door, waiting for Beo to get out. *Run*, he mouthed.

Emon and Rose pulled at Beo's hands, their feet churning upon the courtyard.

Gods help him, but Beo ran.

· · · · ·

Beo lost sight of where they were going. He didn't think Emon or Rose knew either. They only managed to escape Plax Kael before the shouting caught up with them.

They had slowed to a walk, not wanting to be conspicuous, and Beo's mind reeled. He wanted to stop. He wanted to sit. He wanted the chance to try and make sense out of some of this, any of it.

At first all Beo saw was a throng of people moving toward him down Sankael Road. The sides by the footpaths were lined with autocars, but no one was driving today. The throng filled the street from side to side.

They were moving fast, a brisk walk bordering on a trot, a crowd of Sanmarian citizens. Beo couldn't help but think of the Liberation Front protest that had caught him up, only a week past, his only-just-healed bruise and his meeting with Tarn Susette.

Tarn Susette was dead.

"What do we do?" Emon asked. "What can we do?"

"Who are they?" Rose looked ahead at the crowd, eyes searching out any signs, squinting up the road.

Some of the flats that lined Sankael Road showed thin slivers of light in the windows. When Beo looked up, he saw a face, made eye contact with whoever it was for the barest instant, and then the person bolted from the window, leaving only swishing curtains.

"I can't tell," Emon said to Rose. "They could be Lib Front. They could be NPV supporters."

"They've certainly seen us," Beo said. "If we turn and run the other way..."

"Whoever it is might decide to chase us."

Fifty metres.

"Keep walking toward them, slowly," Beo said. "Stay together."

"NPV," Rose said. "They're NPV."

At first Beo couldn't tell how she had come to that conclusion, but then he saw it, a white armband with three silhouettes, three lines joining in an upward-pointing arrow. As they drew closer, more armbands appeared.

"What do we do?" Emon asked again.

They were in the centre of the footpath, equidistant between the nearest cross streets.

Rose thought the quickest as the crowd reached them. She balled her hand into a fist, raised her elbow to shoulder level, and she saluted the crowd.

A cheer went up, and the crowd of people marching began to chant. "NPV speaks for me! NPV speaks for me!"

Beo wanted to vomit. He mirrored Rose's movement, every inch of his fist's path to his heart a betrayal. Emon, beside him, stood stock-still. Too long.

"Emon," Beo said, doing his best not to move his lips.

Ashen, Emon raised his fist in salute.

"Fall in!" Someone called to them, gesturing emphatically.

Ten metres.

"First chance we get, split off," Rose said, mimicking Beo's soft speech without moving her lips.

Emon gave a terse nod, and the NPV march swept them up.

At first, Beo couldn't relax. His heart beat so heavy and so high in his chest that he thought any moment he'd taste blood on his tongue. The crowd pulsed with energy, their steps unmetered but steady, the pace quick and exacting. They would reach the market shortly, where the open spaces would make it difficult to leave unseen, if anyone was watching.

He assumed someone in a crowd like this would be watching.

Stay vigilant, Rico Samson had said.

The heat from the crowd's bodies and breath sent tendrils of silver steam into the winter day. The clouds had lowered yet more toward the city, and the air grew brittle, promising snow not far behind. The NPV supporters marched close to one another. More than once, someone trod on Beo's foot, and more than once, he trod on a heel in front of him. No one turned to say anything about it, only kept on marching toward the market.

Halfway there, Beo felt secure enough to look round at the people walking around him. They looked like average Kaeli citizens, though judging on where they were walking from, they lived outside the city centre. Many were in mended coats and clothing, a few men in shirtsleeves rolled up to the elbows, braces holding up trousers that hung only just noticeably loose on their hips. There were women among them, wearing trousers of slate grey wool and long tunics with layers of overshirts or long jackets. Beo thought of the NPV manifest he had read and suppressed a shudder. Did the women here know? Did they understand that to the NPV they were to be subservient? Would they exchange liberty for a promise of security that was as likely to be realised as the direct hand of the gods?

But more than anything, surrounded by the NPV supporters, Beo noticed—and could not help but notice—how like himself they were. There was nothing that would set them apart on the streets of his home village or in the Lionfish with Yoan behind the bar.

Then Beo thought of Yoan, and his heart hardened. He still felt the strong grip of Yoan's hand, the certainty in his friend's face as he had all but shoved Beo and Rose and Emon toward the windows.

Rose reached forward and leaned close to Beo's ear. "Next street," she murmured.

Beo nodded, looking over at Emon, who still looked on the verge of sicking up, his hair hanging lank and flat over his right eye as if he had given up on pushing it away or wanted to hide behind it out of shame.

Up ahead, Beo could see the street Rose meant. Temple Street, which cut south parallel to the market and held Sanmarian's city temple. Even now, Beo could see the glass dome and spires rising over the lower buildings that surrounded it.

He started to edge his way to the right side of the crowd, hoping for a gap to squeeze out of the throng and into Temple Street, but the marchers surged forward. The market came into view ahead, and the NPV supporters reacted with callbacks and chants, their speed increasing with renewed vigour. Someone pushed between Beo and Rose, and Beo tripped and was pushed sideways, the crowd pressing in on every side of him. Beo's head ducked when he tripped, and someone clipped his shoulder and spun him. Hands reached out and spun him back around, supporting him and keeping him from being trampled, but moving him unstoppably, inexorably to the left.

"Rose!" Beo called out her name and felt the word sucked into the din of hundreds of other voices.

He was tall enough to see over most heads, but he could not see her or Emon. Not her black mass of curls, not Emon's straight, collar-length bob. Temple Street appeared on his right, and Beo watched it pass, helpless, lost in a sea of people he couldn't be certain would not do him harm.

· · · · ·

Sankael Road spit the marchers out onto the market square, and only then could Beo breathe again, gulping cold air and feeling the prickle of new-falling snowflakes lighting upon his stress-heated cheeks. It would be his luck, he thought, to be swept up in two different mobs in a week, to be in precisely the wrong place at the wrong time how many times now?

When he caught his bearings, however, Beo saw that the crowd marching down Sankael for the city centre was not the only one. Groups of NPV-armbanded citizens converged on the market from Alcazar Avenue, from Marixo Road, from Carino Avenue, wherever the width of the street would bear them passage.

The shock of his situation met him like a cresting wave, and Beo walked silently to the edge of the market, to a closed café he had sometimes visited. Its windows were neither smashed nor boarded up. From behind the plated glass, its owner watched the people on the square with wide eyes that met Beo's, held them. For a few seconds, Beo felt more kinship with a stranger on the other side of a pane of glass than with those that had surrounded him with their body heat minutes before.

The owner turned away and drew the shutters, breaking whatever ties had bound them.

Rose and Emon were gone. They must have managed to escape the crowd and move off into Temple Street, and they had no plan in place, nothing to tell them what to do in case of separation.

Beo was alone.

He had some money and he had his camera bag, but he could not go back to Yoan's, he had no key to Rose's flat, and he had no idea where to start searching for Liberation Front, if they would even help him.

If nothing else, he thought he could offer them information about Yoan. What had Emon said? That Liberation Front was poorly organised.

Snowflakes began to fall in greater numbers, tiny and cold enough that when they struck the panes of the café's window behind Beo, he heard their minuscule pitters upon the glass even over the crowd.

At a loss of anything to do, Beo opened his camera bag and assembled his camera. He had a single length of film with perhaps twenty exposures remaining. Raising the camera and twisting the lens to focus, he began to shoot.

He caught the NPV banner against Market Tower and wondered if Veran was safe. Rose had told him that she no longer worked at the library.

He caught the crowd, gathering in a swirling maelstrom of people at the base of the tower itself and wondered where they had come from. Sanmarian and wider Kael were not like Coret to the north, where their leaders were elected by ballot. Kael's rulers had emerged out of a series of city-states—only in the past hundred years had Kael formed together as one nation. Beo had wrongly assumed that the population remained apathetic.

Or perhaps his quiet, background distaste for the NPV was something he had only hoped he shared with the people of his city and his country.

A shout rose up from Market Tower, and the crowd parted to reveal a phalanx of NPV guards and a pile of something Beo could not quite recognise. He looked through the lens of his camera, zoomed in on the dark-coloured heap beside the guards.

When he realised what it was, he froze.

The pile on the ground, which reached waist height on the guards around it, was a pile of books.

Beo closed his eyes, lowering his camera. Emon had said something else, the previous night.

If Beo's actions controlled nothing, all that lay in his control was what he did.

Beo stopped, camera in both hands at a level with his chest. What he could control in that moment, that was simple enough. The NPV may have been tightening their fist around the throat of Sanmarian. They may have left Sanmarian's library toothless and painted over history to suit their own ideals. But Beo had one power he could muster, alone and separated from the people he knew and trusted.

He had his camera.

He raised it once more, focused the lens just as a citizen in an NPV armband stepped forward with a tin of kerosene.

The pile of books went up like a bonfire with an audible *whoosh*.

The shutter of Beo's camera clicked and clicked and clicked.

CHAPTER TWENTY-THREE

Rose couldn't quite catch her breath.

Snowflakes swirled in the wind around her, dotting Emon's black hair with white.

The march had made it to the market square—that much Rose could see, and smoke rose in a thin column over the top of Sanmarian Temple, thicker than the chimney smoke from homes and the few businesses and banks that were open. Snow rarely fell in Sanmarian. It seemed to portend sorrow. Standing in the temple's shelter, Rose couldn't help but remember a parable about snow, how the gods once covered Kael in snow to mute the voices of their subjects.

"We ought to have had a plan," Rose said. "Something in case we got separated."

"He will likely go to your flat," Emon told her. "I don't reckon there's anywhere else he would go."

A group of NPV supporters passed, eyes falling curiously upon Emon and Rose where they stood in an alcove beside the wide staircase that led to the temple's entrance, but they did not speak or otherwise indicate any suspicion.

"What about you?" Rose's question left her mouth and seemed at once to vanish and hover in the air like a ghost. "Do you have anyone else in the city?"

"A few friends," Emon said. "No one I would want to endanger with my presence."

"You can't go home." Rose swallowed. "If you are so certain you are in danger from them—" she avoided saying *NPV*, "—that would be the first place they would look for you."

"If they find me with you, you will be in danger." Emon's face bore no hints of humour, only a weariness Rose could too-well understand.

"I am already in danger," said Rose. "With or without you."

Emon looked at her, long enough that Rose had to break eye contact and glance away for a moment. When she met his eyes again, he nodded. "What do you want to do?"

Rose's mind raced. She needed to get to Taran Marpaxan and wasn't certain how—she would bet her left foot that Marpaxan would be moving around and not found easily where Rose had last seen her. She had never seen NPV rallies happen in the city before, and Rose felt as if the world around her had spread out so far that she could not touch anything. *Beo.*

There was no way to communicate with him, but Emon was right. Likely he would go to Rose's flat, and they could meet there together. Finding Taran Marpaxan would have to wait until the city calmed down, though a voice in Rose's mind whispered that Sanmarian's calm days had passed. She thought again of Samson's address and shuddered.

Perhaps there was one thing she could do.

"I have another friend who is in danger," Rose said after wrestling with herself for a moment. "A different sort of danger. Her husband hurts her and just helped the NPV take her name off their business ownership papers. I need to get a message to her, but he'll certainly be home on a day like today. Would you help me?"

Amelie's home was on the way back to Rose's flat. Rose's mind turned quickly, checking her plan. The scent of smoke reached her, unlike the chimney smoke that formed the usual winter backdrop. This smelled of trouble and rage.

Rose could do nothing about that smoke, but perhaps she could do one small thing for good.

Something lit in Emon's face. A spark. His eyes grew more focused, and his lips curled into a mischievous slant that could almost be called a smile if it weren't for the heat of cynicism powering it. "I think I can manage to distract him."

Rose had been about to say that she could go alone if Emon wasn't comfortable, but his answer made her bite her tongue on the statement. Instead, she nodded.

"What message are you planning to give her?" Emon stepped out of the alcove, waiting for Rose to follow.

Beo and Rose hadn't told him about the money, and Rose felt strange saying that she had a cubby full of wealth in her flat, especially for what she intended to do with it.

"I'm going to give her a way out of this place," Rose said simply, looking up over the glass dome of Sanmarian Temple at the column of thick grey smoke rising into the air.

· · · · ·

Navigating Sanmarian proved easier than Rose had expected. The oddity of seeing no autocars on the streets proved a constant reminder of the troubles, but so many citizens remained inside that there was no one to impede them as Rose and Emon made their way to Amelie and Tomas's home. Behind them, the smoke still rose from the market square, and Rose could not keep Beo from her mind.

"Maybe we ought to have gone to search for him," she said once to Emon as they walked.

"I doubt we would have been able to find him in that crowd," he replied, but he slowed his steps and looked toward the smoke. "But it would make me feel better to know where he was, just the same."

"You like him." It wasn't a question, and Rose knew that Emon also caught the dual meaning of the word *like*.

Emon paused. They were about two streets from Amelie's, and Rose felt like a burr in her own sock for bringing the subject up then.

"I do," said Emon. "But I respect what you share with him, and I have no wish to come between you."

A small amount of pressure Rose hadn't recognised as dwelling in her chest eased with his words. "I'm not familiar with wading through these waters," she said. "But I think Beo has had enough pain in his life."

At that, Emon's expression grew guarded, and Rose hurriedly went on.

"I only mean that if we can bring him happiness, it is worth it to me. I wish that for him." Rose swallowed against a growing lump in her throat. "It seems absurd to say such a thing when we are at such a moment in this city. You must think me very foolish."

To Rose's surprise, Emon closed the distance between them and reached out a hand to touch her face. His fingers were ice cold, but gentle. He wiped away a tear that clung to her lashes with the pad of his thumb.

"Only fools let fear destroy love," he said. "Fears grow when they are kept hidden. Sometimes sharing them can shrink them."

Rose covered Emon's hand with her own, a surprising ripple of gratitude and warmth suffusing her at the touch in spite of the chill in the air and in their flesh.

"That's a very wise thing to say," she said.

Emon gave her a sad smile and let his hand drop. "Tarn used to say that."

Rose had nothing to say to that, only brought her hand to Emon's shoulder and squeezed.

"Besides," Emon said, his pitch rising to some semblance of attempted cheer. "The gods give us one life. Who are we to waste our desires for joy simply because others choose to fill the world with woe?"

There could be no disagreement with that; Rose had thought something similar herself, lying in Beo's arms. She had a new sense of wanting, of wondering, of wishing Emon could be there to share in a future moment.

She realised that he would be welcome.

The sight of Amelie's and Tomas's door looming closer chased all comfort from her skin, and the wind took that moment to pick up and cut right through her.

"That's their house," Rose said. Her stomach felt queasy—when had she last eaten?

She closed her eyes without knowing what she did. Rose did not know how to reconcile Tomas Prysbos, the gangly, short child who couldn't play stickball but could outrun anyone to tease him for it, with someone who had turned her vivacious and playful friend into someone so afraid.

Someone who Rose had not noticed coming into being. Rose felt guilt, sickly and swirling, while she stood in self-made darkness with snowflakes touching her cheeks like a legion of infinitesimal fingers belonging to winter itself. She could not tell if those touches were a caress or a warning.

"Rose?" Emon's voice made her open her eyes.

"I'm sorry," Rose said. "I'm a bit nervous."

Emon looked at her but didn't speak.

"He was my friend," said Rose, and her voice hitched on the past tense.

"Loving someone doesn't always stop them from hurting us."

Emon's words found a way into Rose's heart and stayed there, repeating quietly. He was right. *Only fools let fear destroy love.*

Rose was going to fight for what love she had. She walked past Emon and up the stairs to the door. She made herself knock.

And knocked again, this time louder and with urgency.

Thinking she should have asked Emon for his ideas on how to distract Tomas, she knocked a third time.

As it turned out, she had no reason to fret.

Tomas himself flung open the door, irritation turning to alarm when he saw Rose.

She pushed through the door, past him into the foyer. Amelie stood in the corridor leading to the kitchen, anxiety written large across her face.

"I'm sorry to disturb you," Rose said, "but—"

"I'm hurt," said Emon. He gasped the words so convincingly that Rose turned quickly to make sure he was actually okay—and saw his left arm hanging limp by his side. "My shoulder. It's dislocated."

"How did this happen?" Tomas asked, looking back and forth between them.

"There are NPV demonstrators in the city centre. We were afraid to try and get all the way to my flat." Rose said in a clipped tone. "Can you help him?"

"I can try," Tomas said, and gestured toward the salon.

"Thank you." Emon's voice came through gritted teeth.

"I'll fetch some water and a hot compress," said Rose. "Amelie, will you help me?"

"Of course." With Tomas's back already turned, Amelie's eyes held nothing but confusion and questioning.

Rose went down the corridor, feeling as though it was tilting beneath her feet. She turned on the faucet in the kitchen and started running water into the tea kettle. "I'll be quick," she said, careful not to speak too loudly. "My aunts knew the city was on the verge of something catastrophic. They left money enough to get to Coret and live there for some time. It's yours."

"Rose, I can't—what's going on with you? Who is that man?"

"He's a friend," Rose said, certain of that if nothing else. "The money is yours, and I need you to take it. It's cash. It will get you out of Sanmarian safely, until all this subsides. If it comes to it, and Kael truly falls to this new version of the NPV, I hope to join you one day."

"You could join me now," said Amelie. Her face held something wild and waking, like bright eyes blinking away sleep.

"I can't." Rose left the water on, putting the kettle on the stove with a clank. Her body felt light and tingly. Her mind felt as clear as the glass dome on Sanmarian Temple. "I don't know why I have to stay, but I do."

A cry of pain came from the salon, and Amelie flinched. "Your friend—"

"Emon is fine." Rose hoped that was true.

"Do you have it here?" Amelie whispered.

Rose didn't have to ask what she meant. "It's at my flat. But you don't have to go there. Tell me a day, and I will bring it to you, and you can leave straightaway."

"Rose, I can't."

"You can, Amelie." Rose felt time slipping into the drain with the flowing water.

Amelie looked down the hall, toward the salon. Rose imagined that her friend could see through the walls themselves. She imagined that Amelie's entire body was attuned to Tomas's presence and whereabouts. She imagined it and knew it to be true.

"I'll be okay," Amelie said. She gave Rose what seemed to be a reassuring smile.

But Rose had seen the wild hope in her. "The offer stands," Rose said. What determination she had felt slipped into a hollow echo. Her own words sounded far away.

"Amelie?" Tomas's voice called from the salon. Amelie flinched, but tried to hide it. "Can you bring the compress?"

"The water is heating!" Rose called back, then turned to Amelie. "Please. I am afraid for you."

"I'm okay," said Amelie.

Rose wanted to hold her, to coax her to cross the gap between them, to convince her it was safe to trust this one unknown, but there was nothing she could say.

Then, after a pause, Amelie's quiet voice came. "I've never been alone."

"Alone you are stronger sometimes," said Rose. "The right partner makes you stronger."

She couldn't bring herself to say to Amelie what she knew they both knew: Amelie was more alone now than she would be by herself in Coret.

Numb, Rose poured hot water over a towel as soon as the water boiled, holding it by a single corner until it cooled enough to wring out. Amelie watched her from across the kitchen, silent.

In the salon, Emon's shirt was off, and a sheen of sweat covered his face, but he flexed his left arm and shifted his shoulder.

"Thank you," he said, grimacing.

"You should be more careful," Tomas said to him as Rose handed Emon the compress.

"I imagine I should," Emon agreed. "Or perhaps people ought to consider not being an angry mob."

Tomas laughed, and Rose jumped. They made small talk while the compress slowly cooled, and Rose felt time slip by like water. Beo could be waiting for them.

Forever I will find you.

"We ought to get home," said Rose. "The streets aren't safe just now."

"You could stay—" Tomas began, but Rose shook her head, thinking of Beo.

"We'll be all right." Rose looked to Emon, who nodded gamely.

When Amelie hugged Rose goodbye, Rose thought her friend's grip might dislocate her own shoulder.

· · · · ·

"It happened when I was a lad," Emon said as they entered Rose's building an hour later. "I was playing in the square with a bunch of other children and I felt it pop out. I've been able to dislocate it on command ever since."

"Useful, but painful," said Rose. "Thank you. I should have asked what you planned to do."

"It worked out. Did you talk to her?"

The corridor to the stairwell rang with their words, hollow and echoing. Rose nodded, hurrying up the stairs. Her heart expanded with every step, imagining Beo leaning against the doorjamb, imagining his face flushed with gratitude to see them, imagining him, his presence, his warmth.

But even as Emon and Rose left the stairwell, the hallway stood empty.

Each step toward Rose's door, her feet felt heavier. Neither she nor Emon voiced the fear Rose knew they both felt.

Rose unlocked the door, and Emon followed her inside, latching the door himself once he was in.

It felt strange to be there, wondering where Beo was. If he was safe.

The atmosphere in her flat felt foreign. Rose suddenly burned in her outerwear, too hot, the scarf against her neck moistening with perspiration. She shrugged her satchel off her shoulder and unbuttoned her coat. Rose's fingers untwined the length of fabric at her throat, first slowly and then with burgeoning desperation. Her breath came faster.

"Easy," Emon said. He was somehow at her side, his hands stilling hers, finding the end of the scarf and unwinding it from her throat where it had been tied.

The air against her skin was a cooling touch, and Rose felt Emon's breath besides. She swallowed and took a deep breath. Emon helped her out of her coat and hung it on the coat rack, draping the scarf over it before seeing to his own.

Dizziness swayed through Rose's head, and she couldn't seem to draw breath.

She knew this feeling; it had happened many times after Papa died. The rising tide of panic, the heartbeat she couldn't catch up to, the sense that the very air ran away from her lungs as they gave chase.

Rose closed her eyes and crossed her arms over her chest, palms to her shoulders. She counted to three as she breathed in, then to four as she breathed out. She counted five with her inhale, six with her exhale. Breathe in, seven. Breathe out, eight. In. Nine. Out. Ten.

When Rose opened her eyes again, Emon was watching her.

"I'm okay," said Rose.

"I see that," said Emon. "What would you like to do now?"

What Rose wanted to do was fall asleep, but as tired as her body felt, she didn't expect her mind to quiet enough to allow such a thing. "I suppose we wait. See if Beo finds us here."

She didn't like the if, and she didn't think Emon did either.

Her brain's fog clearing, Rose looked around the flat. Something still didn't feel quite right, the same way Rose had felt when she looked at the bookcase the NPV guards had rifled through and left the spines askew. Unable to stomach sitting, Rose went to the radio and clicked the dial on.

"*Today we celebrate the beginning of a new day...*" a voice came from it, stark and powerful and...clear.

Emon didn't seem to notice, but Rose immediately turned the radio off, then back on.

"*...It is with great pride that the National People's Voice reaffirms the will of Kael's people, for a safer Sanmarian and a safer Kael.*"

No static.

"Emon," said Rose. She moved the radio out from the wall, peered behind it. Nothing seemed amiss. "There's no static."

He came to stand by her side and squinted at the radio. "Could it have just been some kind of interference?"

"It's always sounded that way, for as long as I can remember. It was Papa's radio."

Turning to look at Emon, Rose saw the coffee table over his shoulder clearly for the first time.

"Someone's been here," she said.

"How can you be sure?"

She pointed at the empty table. "The book. It's gone."

CHAPTER TWENTY-FOUR

The camera weighed heavily at Beo's side. Around him, whispers of silver breath tufted through the frigid air, bright in contrast to the clouds of ghost grey smoke that rose from the pile of still-smouldering books. The people had gone from boiling to an excited simmer, and the air crackled with the energy of a lightning storm, while the flakes of snow dusted gently down, oblivious.

Out of film, Beo's fingers still itched to shoot. He wanted to capture this moment, more than he already had.

He needed to find Rose and Emon.

The obvious place was Rose's flat, and Beo felt certain that was where they would have gone. Without the distraction of the burning books or the anger of the crowd, the apprehension and anxiety returned to flood him. He tasted ash on the air.

A haze of smoke lay low over the market square, hemmed in by the heavy cover of clouds. Beo moved toward Carino Avenue. If he hurried, he could get to Rose's in a quarter of an hour.

But as he passed through the sunset stone gate leading out of the city centre through Xaran Tower, Beo turned his head and caught a glimpse of grey wool, quickly out of sight around a corner.

It's nothing, he told himself. There were hundreds—maybe over a thousand—people on the market square. If Beo did not have an NPV armband over his jacket sleeve, so too others lacked. He kept his pace as measured as he could manage, unsure how he could be so sure that the flash of grey wool had anything to do with him.

The crowd lessened as Beo increased his distance from the city centre. Minutes passed, punctuated by only the sound of his shoes on the paving stones of the footpath. As he crossed Harbour Road, he heard a sound he hadn't heard yet that day: the engine of an autocar.

His ears registered the noise just as he saw the three NPV guards moving toward him on the footpath from the left. They did not wear dutiful expressions of patrolling Sanmarian's streets.

Every one of them had his eyes trained on Beo.

Beo turned to the right, deciding whether to run. But the street was straight, and there was nowhere he could hide.

Three more guards approached from the right.

Beo stopped, thinking of Yoan, thinking of Irena and Emon. *Rose.*

A strange stillness overtook him as Beo watched the guards approach, as if this was the reality he had known faced him and the glimmers with Rose had been only illusion.

Happiness had always been an illusion. Beo closed his eyes and saw Zara's dead face.

He felt an impossible smile and tried to keep it from curling over his lips.

He expected the guards to say something, to identify him somehow, to tell him what they planned.

Beo didn't see the black sack until it scratched roughly over his face. His body jerked, the feeling of hands all over his arms and torso, holding him still as dark fabric blocked out the light. He gasped a breath, breathed in fibres of dyed burlap. He said nothing.

The autocar engine drew closer, coming to rest close by in a thrumming roar. Beo choked, tongue pressing against the top of his mouth as the guards turned him the opposite direction and shoved him forward. He heard the latch of the autocar door, smelled a blast of dusty heated air and leather.

A guard pushed him into the autocar, and a gust of cold air accompanied the sound of the opposite door opening. The seat under Beo gave way as a guard slid in on either side of him.

It had to be the pictures he had taken; someone had been watching. Beo thought he should have felt stupid for doing such a thing, but what he felt instead was pride. The NPV could destroy his camera and his work, but at least he had done something.

He had seen what they did to the books in the square, had seen the fire Beo believed Veran had been right about, the fire intended in the end for people.

Rose.

Beo felt the doors of the autocar close as much as he heard them, the sound sealing him between the guards that flanked him. The purr of the engine grew louder, and the autocar began to move. The wheels dipped between the cobbles on the road.

"Are you not going to ask where we are taking you?" The guard to Beo's right asked the question warily, as if disconcerted by Beo's complete lack of resistance.

"Would it matter if I did?" The black burlap over Beo's head rubbed roughly against his lips when he spoke. The steam of his breath gathered on the fibres.

"I suppose not."

"Is this sack on my head necessary?"

"We were told that the faces of prisoners should not be visible to passers-by."

As far as explanations went, Beo supposed it would do. He nodded, if not in assent, but resignation. The sack smelled sharply of dye, and a headache began to prickle at his sinuses.

It occurred to Beo that he had accepted the oncoming eyes of death.

Had it been the moment he was separated from Emon and Rose, or had it been sooner? He couldn't tell and didn't care to try. In some ways, Beo thought he had accepted it the moment he saw Zara's body hanging from his ceiling. That what she had done was nothing but forewarn him. Something in him had died in that moment, and wherever Beo had gone, he had carried that death with him. It only made sense, sitting between the two NPV guards, Beo could feel that unfurling seed of death grow within him.

He wanted to ask the guards how things had gotten to this point in Sanmarian, but he could not drum up enough disbelief to pose the question. People saw what they wanted to see until the world around them caused them direct inconvenience. Beo was no different than any other citizen in Sanmarian or Kael at large; he had given little thought to the NPV. They had been Kael's only party for fifteen years, and they had utilised their power even before that.

More than his own inability to see, though, Beo knew he simply hadn't wanted to see. He kept to himself, ignored the whispers and outright outbursts from Yoan.

So he sat, in the NPV car with a black-dyed burlap sack over his head and the acrid scent burning in his nostrils, and Beo Mataya waited to see what would become of his life.

• • • • •

They took him to the same room he had been to with Rose. Again the guards left him with his camera bag unsearched, and again they left him to sit by himself.

Once inside the fortress walls, the guard to Beo's right had removed the sack from his head, though Beo could still feel the prickles of the burlap fibres, and his throat itched with irritation from breathing fibres and fumes alike.

He waited.

He could never later be sure how much time passed in that room. It at once felt solid and fluid, like something built minute by minute to unnerve him and yet something that slipped by before he could touch it. With it came a certainty that bordered on relief.

What could be more exquisite a torture than to find something so potentially glorious only to have it taken swiftly away?

Rose was not an it. Rose was a person, and whatever they felt for one another had only just begun to form. In spite of the short time they had known each other, though, they had experienced more side by side than he had with nearly anyone else he had known.

And now he'd never get to find out what could have been.

Beo memorised the texture of the walls, the tiny imperfections in the room's deep red-brown table. He had naught else to do but wait.

When the latch at the door finally clanked, Beo expected guards to come through it.

Instead, it was again Rico Samson.

Beo stood, his knees creaking from the amount of time he had spent in the chair. Twice now he had been face-to-face with the leader of the NPV himself. He felt certain it had to do with Irena, with the words she had left behind when she vanished from Beo's childhood home not days before. Had she been Samson's enemy? He knew her; that much was clear.

"I had hoped not to see your face again under such circumstances," Rico Samson said, closing the door behind him. He wore tight grey gloves a shade lighter than the darker grey of his woolen uniform. In person, his voice sounded little as it did on the radio. More weary, though just as calculated. Quieter. Samson had no need to convince or reassure anyone here.

Beo wasn't sure what gave him the nerve to be cheeky. "Under what circumstances would those be? If you'd hoped it to be different, you might have sent an invitation rather than thugs to put a sack over my head and drag me in."

"They hardly dragged you. I was told you cooperated very nicely." Samson's tone ran with the undercurrent of *stupid boy*.

Beo began to understand something of Tarn Susette's wave of calm, which had struck him as disingenuous at the time. But now—whatever would happen, would happen.

"I did not care to become a smear on the cobblestones," Beo said finally, anticipating Samson's next words before the man could say them.

That still may be.

Except Samson did not say them. Instead, he walked to Beo's camera bag, and Beo felt the first spike of true fear cut through his calm.

Samson pulled open the brass buckles that held the bag shut and flipped back the cover. Instead of pulling out the camera, Samson pulled out Beo's love-worn copy of *Red Sunrise*.

Rico Samson's fingers actually quivered for the slightest of moments as he held the book at chest level, eyes on the new copy from Rose beneath it.

"What a strange man you are, Beomir Mataya."

"I beg your pardon?"

"Where did you get this?"

"It was a gift, a long time ago."

"From whom?"

"My father's sister."

"Whose name is?"

"Roban Mataya." Beo pulled the name of Rose's aunts' assistant out of his memory.

"You lie like you were born to it." Rico Samson's fingers tightened on the book, ran the length of the pages and the tattered cover, the thong of leather that kept it together. "This book has been much read."

"It is one of the few family mementos I have," said Beo, feeling as if his feet skated on ice that could break at any moment, that he could slide into something yet more dangerous.

"That is not a lie." Samson placed the book on the table and turned to face Beo again, but he did not stray out of arm's reach of the book.

"No, it is not." The walls of the room entombed him. Beo wondered if he would ever see the outside again. If not, perhaps Rico Samson would speak his mind. "You killed Tarn Susette."

"I personally killed no one."

The qualifier stuck in Beo's ears, both because it was unnecessary and because Samson had felt the need to use it anyway.

"On the radio you said you executed insurgents. How was a simple gallery owner an enemy of the NPV?"

"You are either incredibly naïve or incredibly bold. Or both." Samson tilted his head to the side and met Beo's eyes.

"What was Susette's crime?"

"I never said he committed one." Rico Samson placed three fingertips on the varnished tabletop. His nails were impeccably trimmed, his fingers straight and long except the shortest, which had a bulbous joint as if it had long ago been badly broken and set worse. "What makes you think he's dead?"

"You haven't yet plucked out all the eyes in Sanmarian."

"None of them, in fact. Would you like if I started with yours?" Samson slid his fingers over the wood grains of the table. "I tire of this conversation. Who gave you the book?"

"I told you." Beo's skin prickled from fingernails to hairline at the idea of Samson plucking out his eyes.

"You lied."

"What reason would I have to tell you the truth when you've just had several people murdered?"

"There is a difference between execution and murder, Beomir."

"Not to the one it happens to."

Beo's stiff knees wanted to wobble, but he tried to keep any sign of uncertainty out of his body. Naïve or bold—perhaps it was indeed both. If Beo's life bought Irena's, or Rose's, or Emon's, he would gladly give it.

If he expected Rico Samson to be impressed by his wit, though, Beo was quickly disabused of that notion. Samson did not visibly react to Beo's philosophical lumping together of human-caused death. Instead, he picked up *Red Sunrise* once more.

"The last time I saw this book," he said, "it had fallen down between the mattress and the headboard of my bed, which in itself is unremarkable."

Beo froze, caught off guard.

"The remarkable thing is that the bed was new, and the book was most decidedly not mine."

"Perhaps it was a gift from your furniture builder."

"That woman in your photograph," Samson began. "You know her. She gave you this book."

"I told you I do not know the woman, and the book was a gift from my Aunt Roban, may the gods carry her to peace."

"The gods carry no one to peace."

"I thought the NPV a pious party."

"Piety is not my concern."

Beo saw then something in Rico Samson that he could not place. "What is your concern?"

Rico Samson dropped the book onto the table as if it had somehow affronted him, or—Beo couldn't help but think—as if Samson were stalling to find words that eluded him.

Beo didn't get a chance to find out which. An NPV guard burst into the room, making Beo jump and Samson merely look over with an expression devoid of emotion.

"Sir," the guard said, "you asked to be informed if the freq—"

"Indeed." Samson cut the guard off. "See this man downstairs."

• • • • •

Downstairs was a dungeon.

Beo had known the fortress was exactly that—a fortress—but he had thought that all criminals in Sanmarian went to the gaol outside the city walls, on a promontory that overlooked the sea. Some few minor infractions resulted in a night at the city guard station, but Beo had not realised the fortress still housed an actual dungeon.

He had to think through that series of thoughts. The odour of moulding straw and human waste quickly filled his nostrils as the guard led him down the stone stairs, another guard following to make sure he remained cooperative. His bag they had kept.

Each step downward felt like it confirmed every ill thought Beo had ever had about what he deserved from this life.

Rose and Emon felt like the fantasy. This was the reality.

It was almost a comfort.

He wished he could have spoken to Irena, found out what it was she had meant to do. He hoped she managed it, whatever it was. Irena meant to fight. Fight what, Beo didn't know. Her own demons, maybe.

In that moment, Beo hated himself, hated whatever poison he had taken into his heart to make him such a coward. The guards opened a metal door and kicked Beo through it, slamming the door behind him. Beo tripped on the uneven floor but narrowly avoided landing face-first in a pile of straw that smelled of piss and rot.

There was movement in the dungeon. Rats probably accounted for the smaller rustling, but it was certain that Beo wasn't alone.

I could have loved you, he thought. He wasn't sure who he meant he could have loved.

He could have been braver. It wasn't until that moment, locked into a dungeon under the NPV fortress, that Beo could see the cracked shell of the life he hadn't managed to live. Zara's suicide had hollowed him out—left him jagged at the edges and empty in the middle—where his heart had been. What was there now? Anything?

He could have run when the NPV guards came toward him. He hadn't.

It was perhaps too late to ask himself why.

Through the metal door, eyes glinted in the dim light.

"What'd you do to get this honour?" A scratchy voice came through the darkness, a woman with what sounded like a severe case of laryngitis.

"Lied to Rico Samson. You?"

Her voice became a harsh laugh. "I don't even know, son," she said. "Sometimes I think my only real crime was living at all."

Beo wished he didn't know what she meant. More bodies moved in the distance, down the corridor. One voice yelled for quiet and was given a series of curses in return from the surrounding cells.

"What happens next?" His voice came out so softly that he wasn't sure if she had heard him or not.

"Wish I could tell you."

"What do the NPV want?"

The woman snorted. "They're zealots," she said. "Zealots want power."

Something about that didn't sound quite right, but, Beo supposed, he wasn't going to find any real answers in a dungeon.

CHAPTER TWENTY-FIVE

High dark came and passed, and Rose could not sleep. Emon drowsed on the sofa. Rose sat with eyes trained on the door, knowing with each passing hour that Beo would not be knocking upon it.

In *Red Sunrise*, Remir and Yosif had known what they were about. They had known the threats they faced and stood close enough to feel the breath of their enemies upon their skin. Even when their lover Vitar betrayed them, they had known what it was they were meant to do. It had cost Yosif his life, but Remir had gone on and saved Sanmarian.

Rose was none of those people.

She did not know who had taken the book from the table, nor why her radio no longer crackled with static.

She sat on the floor of her flat and closed her eyes. Her head felt heavy and full of thoughts that warred with one another. When she thought of Beo, too quickly the image of his lifeless face on the cobbles of the market square invaded her thoughts. She still fancied she felt that cord between them. Rose raised her arm where she sat and held it out, pointing to the north. Emon stirred on the sofa, and Rose dropped her hand to her lap, her cheeks heating with embarrassment. It was a foolish thing, a child's wish, to think that just because she cared for someone she could close her eyes and point to them.

The hours passed, and Rose opened her eyes when it was still dark to find that she had fallen asleep on the rug. Emon sat awake, staring at the curtained window.

"I didn't want to wake you," said Emon when he saw Rose stretch. "Not that you looked comfortable."

"We should have gone back to look for him." Rose didn't know what else to say.

"I know."

"We don't have any way to get a message to him." Rose swallowed, again feeling the panic rising. "Even if he comes here, if we're gone, he won't be able to get in."

"Rose," Emon began, but she cut him off.

"How did it come to this? Two weeks ago, my biggest worry was whether the shipment would be on time and intact at the office and if they'd send the right amount of star mint this time." Rose scrambled to her feet. It was just past fifth bell, and the morning sun was still a long way off. The longest night would be the next one. What was usually a celebration of the passing of the winter dark, the running of the bulls for Larsi's luck and holiday markets throughout the city—Rose could not imagine joy or luck this year. "I have to do something."

"Do what?"

"I need to find Taran Marpaxan again."

"Liberation Front? They haven't managed anything useful in fifteen years, Rose."

"We don't know that. They organised that protest."

"The protest did nothing but get people killed."

"Was Tarn at the protest?" Rose already knew the answer, and Emon's lips flattened.

He shook his head.

"My family is gone," said Rose. "Beo's aunt vanished as well. We don't know where Beo is. My best childhood friend can't escape my other best childhood friend. I've no job, and the NPV has begun executing people in the city centre. As I see it, I have two choices. I can take the money my aunts left me and flee the country. I could take you and Amelie and go. We could leave Sanmarian, leave Beo, and leave Kael itself behind and never look back. I could go alone and leave everyone I've ever known."

Emon looked at her, waiting.

"Or I could do something. I don't know if Liberation Front is worth anything, Emon. I don't. I gave them a heap of money this week, and for all I know Taran Marpaxan herself buggered off to Coret with it. But if she didn't, if she's still here trying to keep our city a safe place for everyone in it, I want to help." Exhausted dizziness made Rose's head swim, but she swallowed the gummy flavour in her mouth. "I think it is what my Papa would do."

Rose couldn't really be sure. She had only known Andreas Abernethy as a loving father, a quiet man, a sometimes very sad man, but if there was anything she knew about her father's character, it was that he put those he loved first. He'd given up his surname in favour of a woman who left him to parent a young baby within a year or so of her birth. It was a lesson Rose intended to put into practice.

Emon drew a breath, and even from where she sat across the room, Rose heard it quaver. "So," he said. "Where do we find Liberation Front?"

• • • • •

Sanmarian's streets were devoid of autocar traffic and pedestrians alike, but to Rose it seemed as though she could feel the city itself breathe in the cold winter air. The sun had not yet risen. Twenty-six years Rose had lived in these streets, had felt the sandy texture of the sunset stone surround her. This was her home, just as it had been her father's. It was Emon's home, Amelie's, Aleis's and Helyne's and Grenye's. And Beo's.

Rose tried to push thoughts of Beo from her mind, avoiding the image of his face as if by doing so she could remain convinced that he was still alive.

Rose and Emon reached the house where Yoan had first sent her just before fifth bell. The sky above was a blue-black bowl dotted with stars, the snow clouds from the night before long gone, leaving only the sliver of a waning crescent moon and a vast sprinkling of tiny lights that shimmered in the haze of the city's chimney smoke.

The house's curtains covered the windows; there was no telling if any lights lit the interior. Rose raised her hand to the door and knocked hard. Counting to ten, she knocked again.

The door cracked open.

Rose hadn't heard anyone approach, and she nearly jumped back from the door.

It was the man who had taken her to Taran Marpaxan the last time, the man whose brother had been killed by the NPV two months before. He looked at her, then looked at Emon.

For a moment, Rose thought he was going to slam the door shut in her face. Instead though, he opened it and beckoned them through.

The house was much as Rose remembered it, if muted with morning darkness. There was still an NPV newspaper on the table by the door, and still an air of being staged about it.

"If you are here about Yoan, we can only say we know about his arrest." The man said the words quietly. "My name is Maro. Who is your friend?"

"My name is Emon Sanhaya," said Emon. "My mentor and friend was executed this week. Tarn Susette."

Maro's face showed a brief flash of grief, quickly erased. He clasped Emon's hand. "Tarn was not much involved with our work, but he helped fund us for several years."

"I need to see Taran Marpaxan," said Rose.

"Your gift was very generous, but I'm afraid we cannot simply allow access to her."

"Our friend is missing," Rose said. "Yesterday when Yoan was arrested, we were at his flat. He told us to climb out the window. We got caught up with an NPV march toward the city centre, and Beo got separated from us. We waited for him all night at my flat before coming here, but he didn't turn up."

"Beo. Beomir Mataya?"

"Yes," Emon said, jumping in. "You know of him?"

"Of course he knows of him," Rose said. "The donation I gave to Marpaxan was in both our names."

Maro shook his head. "Yes, but that is not why I asked."

"What?" Rose stood still on the runner rug inside the door, dread filling her from her feet up, weighing her in place.

"He was on last night's arrest list."

"Arrest list."

"We have someone at the fortress who reports to us about who the NPV has taken. Beo Mataya was on the list." Maro folded his hands in front of him as if unsure how Rose and Emon would react.

Rose couldn't quite catch her breath. "Arrested?"

"Did your contact say why?" Emon's voice came out hoarse.

Maro shook his head.

"It has to be the photograph of his aunt," Rose said. "That was why we were brought in the first time. Samson must not have believed that Beo didn't know her."

"Why would Rico Samson be interested in Beo's aunt?" Maro asked.

"I don't know."

Emon touched Rose's shoulder urgently. "If he's been arrested, they got him with his camera bag."

Rose didn't have to wonder what that meant. "They'll have found the book."

"What book?" Maro asked.

"*Red Sunrise*, by Mikael Iris," said Rose.

Maro's blank look was almost reassuring, but a moment later he unfolded his hands and beckoned to them both to sit in the salon. "Wait there. I think I will have to give you what you came for after all."

Rose felt no triumph, only fear.

Emon took her hand as they sat on a small sofa with its back to the curtained window, and Rose took a tiny amount of comfort in the warm grip.

• • • • •

Maro did not lead them back outside, as he had done with Rose before. Instead, he took Rose and Emon through a door in the centre of the house that led to the cellar. The small hairs on Rose's back prickled with apprehension as they descended the stairs, the scent of musty damp pervading her nose. The cellar was lit by candles instead of electric lamps, and it smelled of soot and wax alongside the damp winter stone.

In the farthest corner of the cellar, behind a brass boiler and a loud furnace, was a door. Just inside it was a wooden crate with several oil lanterns.

"Those who built this city had many secrets," Maro said, picking up one of the lanterns with a clank and lighting it. "Now the city herself hides many of them. We utilise the ones we find as best we can."

Rose glanced at Emon and knew he was thinking of the passage out of the Overlook Galleria.

In *Red Sunrise*, the resistance made use of such passageways, but Rose had always thought them to be a simple convenient fantasy. Now, walking in line with Emon and Maro in a passage cramped enough that she felt the ceiling brush against her hair, Rose considered the possibility that Mikael Iris, the author of *Red Sunrise*, had known more of Sanmarian's secrets than she herself ever would.

She wondered what other truths lay woven in amongst the fiction and wished she had had the time to read the history books she had taken from the library.

As they walked, Maro told them about the book burning at the market square the day before.

"The smoke we saw," Emon said.

"A few days ago, there were fires toward Southharbour," Rose said. "I saw the smoke from my flat. Do you know what happened?"

"The NPV raided a Roa enclave," Maro said immediately. "There were about eight families living in a tenement, which is the way of things in Southharbour, except that two adolescents joined the Lib Front protest last week and were marked by the NPV guards."

"Did they—" Emon sounded as if he didn't want to ask.

"They pretended to be running cannon drills with dummy balls. They aimed a cannon with exploding shot at the tenement."

Rose remembered hearing the cannon fire that night, and she shuddered. The flickering lantern light on the pink-orange walls cast shadows like fingers that reached back from Maro to where Rose and Emon walked behind him. Maro didn't turn back to look at them, only kept walking straight ahead.

"It was late evening, just around supper time," Maro said. "Everyone was home."

Rose couldn't bring herself to ask if anyone had escaped.

In front of her, she could see the tightness in Emon's shoulders. After a pause, he burst out.

"Are you so foolish that you would hold a protest that endangered the people in it?"

Maro didn't stop. "The protest was not arranged by Liberation Front," he said. "Those who marched that day know little about what it is we actually do. We have operated in silence for two decades, but there is no way to keep things fully quiet. Words and stories have a way of growing, mutating into myth and legend."

"The protest was real enough," Rose said, thinking of that day and how far away it seemed now. "I still have the remnants of a bruise to prove it."

"People know our name. Sometimes they start their own groups, and those groups take on new life."

Rose was very quiet, listening to the sounds of their footsteps.

"If that many people want to help, why stay so secret?" Emon asked.

"Because the other groups are perfect decoys," Rose said softly, and this time Maro did look over his shoulder. His expression was one of pain, not pride. "You said it yourself, Emon. Everyone thinks Liberation Front are directionless fools. The NPV takes heads when it feels threatened even by young people who don't know any better. This way they never come close to the real Liberation Front."

Emon stopped walking in front of her. "You're saying that Tarn Susette died as some kind of decoy?"

"Everyone who has died at the hands of the NPV is dead no matter how they were caught," Maro said sharply. "We save who we can."

"You know Yoan," Rose said.

"Yes."

"Beo thought Yoan didn't know the real Liberation Front."

"He didn't, not at first. He was new to the real centre of it."

"Because of you." Rose pushed past Emon to look Maro in the eye. "Because two months ago, the NPV killed your brother, but they didn't kill you."

"Obviously."

"Liberation Front found you after it happened, didn't they? They recruited you."

"It didn't take much. My brother was killed because he shouted at an NPV guard when they came to take our mother's business away. I already had reason to want to fight them." Maro's dark eyes flickered in the lantern's light. "As does anyone in this city, were they to know what the NPV has truly done."

"How do you ever expect to truly fight them if you hide in underground tunnels like rats?" Far from the joyful man Beo had described to Rose, Emon's voice was ragged and raw like a sheet of steel torn down the middle.

Rose knew the answer to that, too. "Because as soon as the real Liberation Front does show their face, all those decoy groups will flock to them." She thought of *Red Sunrise*, of the book's aching ending, of blood running across the market square in rivers of red between the cobbles, of Remir Roxa's grief, Vitar's betrayal, Yosif's death. "Because myths and legends have power."

Maro did not answer, only met Rose's eyes. She knew she was right.

The Roa man turned and kept walking up the tunnel. After a moment, Emon and Rose followed.

• • • • •

Rose could not be certain if the house Maro led them to was the same she had met Taran Marpaxan in before. They came up through the cellar, as expected, and somehow Taran Marpaxan was already waiting for them in the salon. Though they had seen no others in the house they had left, Rose felt disconcerted knowing someone must have rung a private telephone to inform Marpaxan they were coming.

"I was sorry to hear of the Mataya boy," Marpaxan said in greeting.

"You say that as though you know he's dead." Rose hated those words that fell from her mouth, wished she could burn them before they met the air.

"He's still alive. For now."

"And for all that you have someone in the fortress, you have no way to rescue him?" Rose asked. "You're going to leave him there?"

"He is in the dungeon beneath the fortress itself. The fortress houses not only Rico Samson's personal guard of two hundred NPV guardsmen. The dungeon has only three entrances, all of which are from the main floor in the centre of the guard quarters. There is no way for anyone to get any prisoner out unseen, and if being unseen were not a requirement, no way for anyone to get any prisoner out alive. Each of those two hundred NPV guardsmen carries a revolver, two daggers, and often a poniard. Beomir Mataya is alive, for now." Taran Marpaxan gestured to a pair of chairs in the salon. "Sit, if you please."

Rose sat, the weariness she felt sapping any remaining strength from her. Emon hesitated a moment before sitting.

"I need you to tell me whatever you know about Beo Mataya's aunt," Marpaxan said with no further preamble.

Rose blinked. "Why?"

"If Samson sought him out personally, as I believe you and I both know he did, it was for a reason. If she is that reason, we need to know about it. Samson has almost never set a toe out of his usual mode of operation. He has no family, no personal life. He keeps no lover—male or female, certainly not male—and has no children. He is dangerous because he holds interest in nothing but the party. A man like that who appears to want nothing but power has nothing to stop him from seizing it."

"And he showed interest in her."

"Precisely."

"You think she is an enemy of his?" Emon spoke quietly, his tone hollow. Somewhere in the house, a clock chimed sixth bell.

"She must hold some threat to him, or he would not seek her," said Taran Marpaxan.

Rose remembered what Beo had told her, that Irena had left Viyarenyo to do something she had meant to do long ago. Could it truly have been about Rico Samson? Who was this woman, who could live for over a decade in a tiny Kaeli village and yet inspire so much fear in someone as powerful as Rico Samson?

"How do I know I can trust you if I tell you what I know?" Rose asked. She thought of Beo in the fortress dungeon, how frightened he must be, knowing that at any time he could die. "Will you swear to me that you will do everything in your power to help Beo?"

"I can and will do no such thing," Marpaxan said. "I have worked too long to save this city from the National People's Voice. I will not jeopardise that to keep one single heart beating."

Something twisted in Rose's chest, a sickening wringing of bone and blood and muscle that nearly made her cry out. "What good is anything you do, if not to keep one single heart beating?"

For a moment, Marpaxan's face softened. "I have no other choice. You may tell me what information you have, or you may keep it to yourself. This city is my home, and I have made it my life's work to redeem it and prove I deserve my place in it as well as others like me."

"Prove you deserve your place?" Rose caught those words and repeated them. "Why?"

Taran Marpaxan gave Rose a wry smile. "I am *deviant*," she said.

Rose looked at Emon reflexively, thinking of her three aunts and whatever may have been beginning to form between herself and the two men who had so suddenly become part of her life. "That does not set you apart from us as much as you think."

"It does, I think. You may have more than one lover, but my very body is an affront to the NPV."

And then Rose understood. She thought of Grenye's words to her so long ago. All three of her aunts, as business owners who were women and had no children of their own, would be considered in violation of the NPV's considerations of their *sociosexological roles*, but Grenye, to them, lacked gender purity. To the NPV, Grenye would never be a woman. Nor, it seemed, would Taran Marpaxan.

Rose was not quite sure what to say.

"You understand," Taran Marpaxan said. "If I am to live, I need to fight them."

"If I tell you what I know, will you at least swear that I myself may try to rescue Beo if I get the opportunity to do so? That you will not stop me?"

Marpaxan gave Rose a long, hard look. "You ask permission to do the impossible."

"I ask permission to do nothing but try."

"Rose," Emon began.

Rose looked at him, and she reached out and took his hand. "I can't just leave him there," she said.

"I'm not asking you to. If you go, I'll go with you."

Nodding, Rose looked back to Marpaxan. "Do you agree?"

Taran Marpaxan looked like she wanted to do nothing of the sort, but she stood and extended her hand to Rose. Rose shook it.

"I don't know much," Rose said as soon as Marpaxan was seated again. "I think Rico Samson targeted Beo because of a single picture of her. Beo and I were at the Lionfish, and someone stole his portfolio. Less than twenty minutes later, Beo's flat had been ransacked. They destroyed his photography equipment and slashed every cushion. The photograph of Irena was in the portfolio. I wouldn't think it was connected if we hadn't been taken in and questioned about the photograph."

Marpaxan shifted in her seat, crossing her left leg over her right. She leaned back, crossing her arms as well. She said nothing.

"I don't know anything about Irena herself, except that she lived in Viyarenyo for the past ten years or so." Rose scratched at a hangnail on her thumb. "I'm not even certain how much Beo knows of her. I know she arrived in his village not long before his father died."

"That is all you know?" Marpaxan asked.

"I told you it wasn't much."

"Maro," Marpaxan said, turning her head.

Rose started. She hadn't realised Maro was still nearby. He entered the salon, nodding at Taran Marpaxan.

"Take them upstairs and see that they get some rest."

"We can go back to my flat—" Rose began, but Marpaxan shook her head sharply.

"You must understand. If the NPV are looking for you, I cannot have you lead them to me. You will stay here until we are able to ensure whether they are looking for you. It is likely they are looking for Emon."

Emon nodded, his chest deflating as if he had been expecting this.

"There's only one room," Marpaxan said. "I apologise."

Maro led them upstairs, and when the door shut behind them, leaving Emon and Rose in a small room taken up mostly by a comfortable-looking but unfamiliar bed, Rose couldn't help but feel as if they were prisoners.

She thought of Beo, beneath the NPV fortress.

I will find you.

CHAPTER TWENTY-SIX

B eo didn't know when he had ever been so cold.

The cold seemed to grow inside him the way frost patterns grew on a window in winter. As a child he had watched them, seen the way the misted moisture of his family's breath gathered on the glass. Beo had always marvelled at the way the cold from outside reached through the windows and touched the condensation, splaying tiny beads into paisley patterns that wound their way up from the windowsill.

He felt like that now, except instead of gentle whorls of frost, it felt like he had jagged pieces of ice filling his hollow body with sharp points of pain. He could no longer tell the difference between pain and cold.

Beo had found a somewhat clean corner of his cell to sit, but the wind whipped down the corridor in the dungeon from he knew not where, and there was nothing to shelter him. They had not stripped him of his coat, but the fabric was not made to withstand a winter night without respite.

The only reason Beo knew that morning had come was that someone yelled it from the other end of the dungeon. Someone who, as it seemed, had a crack in their wall or window enough for light to get through. Perhaps that was also the source of the wind.

Not long after, the door to upstairs banged open, and two guards came up to the metal bars of Beo's cell.

"No trouble," one of the guards said.

"Do I look like I could cause any?" Beo's voice scratched his throat. He couldn't remember the last time he had had anything to drink or eat.

"No trouble," the guard repeated, jerking his hand at Beo.

Beo rose to his feet, moving slowly to avoid overstretching his cramped back.

The guard opened the door to Beo's cell and motioned him out. The woman in the cell opposite Beo's watched, her eyes unreadable in the dimness.

Beo tried not to look back. He followed the guards up the stairs, and his knees hurt with each step upward. His tailbone ached from sitting on hard stone all night, and the farther away from the cell, the more he could smell himself. His trousers reeked of mould and urine. Though there was a wooden bucket on the side of the cell, he wasn't sure the cell's previous occupant had used it.

The guards took him down a fortress hallway—it might have been the same one he'd come down before or it might not have. Beo couldn't tell the difference.

To his surprise, they led him to a room with a large table laid out with food. Plates of clamshell pastries, their dough buttery and flaky. Smoked fish in rows on pristine platters. Summer fruits from the hot house, kumquats and slices of melon and bright red strawberries. Roasted tomatoes, sausages, decanters of juice, steaming teapots, a hand-thrown carafe of coffee. Beo's eyes swam with the sight of it, and his stomach gave an audible gurgle.

"Sit," the guard said. "Touch nothing."

Those final two words withered Beo's tongue in his mouth.

He did as he was told, sitting at a chair on the far side of the table. He had meant to choose one as far away from food as he could, but there was no seat that was not in arm's reach of the beautiful array.

The guards left, and again Beo waited.

His mouth watered, which did nothing to wash away the foul taste from the night. He considered ignoring the guards—if they meant to kill him, surely taking a smoked fish and a clamshell wouldn't make that sentence any more final.

Yet he was still uncertain. Something about Rico Samson had told Beo that the man still wanted something from him. Probably that something was that Beo still breathed.

Warmth slowly returned to Beo's body, and with it, a dizzying hunger. He kept his hands in his lap, held them as still as he could. It took every grain of self-control Beo possessed not to fall on the food face-first in spite of his hands being clenched together.

He was not surprised when the door opened several minutes later to admit Rico Samson himself. The NPV leader wore immaculate brushed wool in the same pale grey his gloves had been the previous day. The man sat at the opposite end of the table from Beo and immediately filled a plate with food.

There was no other plate.

"Tell me about the woman," Rico Samson said conversationally, just before placing a meticulous bite of clamshell pastry in his mouth.

"I have nothing to say that you haven't already heard."

Samson chewed, wiped his mouth with a pressed square of linen, and swallowed. "I am not certain that you fully understand your situation, Beomir. You are not my guest."

"If I were, it would reflect quite poorly on your hospitality."

"Are you familiar with Larsi's Luck Run?"

"Everyone is."

"Then you know that on the longest night—tonight, in fact—those hoping to gain favour with the luck god will race the bulls through the city in hopes that she will grace them with good fortune."

Beo watched Samson over a decanter of cranberry juice. "I said I was familiar with it."

"Did you perhaps hear my radio address this week?"

"Yes."

Rico Samson raised one eyebrow at Beo, then continued eating for several minutes.

Beo was not certain what the man meant about the bulls. The only thing that struck Beo with any kind of certainty was that Samson wanted information from him, about his aunt. Absurdly, Beo knew almost as little about Irena as anyone. She was neither forthcoming nor one to share her feelings.

"You seem awfully afraid of this woman," Beo said, not caring for the rashness of his words. "I hope that whoever she is, she brings you precisely what you deserve."

Nothing seemed to get a rise out of the party leader. He again wiped his mouth, swallowed politely before talking, and then took a sip of his coffee. Beo's stomach cramped with the torturous smells of the roast tomatoes Samson reached out for. Beo imagined biting into one of them, feeling the hot seeds spill on his tongue and a hint of coarse sea salt against the roof of his mouth. When Samson bit into a tomato, Beo could almost taste it before the stale taste of his own tongue wiped the fantasy away.

"If you live long enough," Samson said, "you will come to find that certain choices will come back to you like spirits. There are few enough times that a man is given the chance to settle those old choices. And your time, Beomir, is looking as though it will not be long enough to settle the choices you are making now."

"If you were looking for someone concerned with lengthening their time, perhaps you have chosen the wrong person to break your fast in front of," said Beo. "Whatever fate I deserve, it was decided long before you knew my name."

"That is the second time you have used that word." Samson leaned back in his chair, for the first time smoothing the right angles of his body into something softer.

"What word is that?"

"Deserve."

Beo felt an uncomfortable tingle spread down his arms. "What of it?"

"You do not think you deserve to live."

"You have already decided that I don't."

"I think you decided it first."

Beo did not know how to respond to that. "What is it to you?"

"I am curious."

A laugh threatened to leave Beo's throat, but he swallowed it back, wishing he could freshen his mouth with anything on the table. If he could not confess himself to a man about to kill him, who could he ever tell?

"I killed the woman I loved," he said, and to Beo's surprise, the words did not lodge in his throat. They bubbled out over his lips like the way the egg tart halfway down the table had overrun its crust.

Rico Samson showed no surprise, only waited for Beo to go on and asked, "What was her name?"

"Zara. She told me she would kill herself if I left her. I left her. I came home and found her hanging in the kitchen of my flat. I may not have put the noose about her neck, but I killed her." Beo had never said those words out loud to any other soul. The absurdity of it struck him, and he had to swallow a laugh again. He feared that laugh, feared the way he felt it in his voice box like a whirling ball of knives, ready to leap out and cut him to shreds.

Beo couldn't tell if Samson was even listening. His gaze had moved to the edge of his plate, where he plucked a strawberry off it with his fork and moved it to his mouth. When was the last time Beo had seen a strawberry at all, let alone one as sumptuous as this? For a moment he thought he might tell Samson everything he knew about Irena, just for the chance to taste a strawberry one last time. The strawberry vanished into Rico Samson's mouth, and Beo's neck flushed with shame. His stomach turned.

"It doesn't matter if you kill me," Beo said, anger taking hold in the void the confession had left behind. "There's nothing to kill."

But Samson looked up, not the tiniest dribble of strawberry juice escaping his precise mouth. In his face, Beo saw not the leader of his city's oppressing party but Rose reflected in his eyes, Emon beside her.

There was yet something in Beo that could die.

And Rico Samson saw it.

CHAPTER TWENTY-SEVEN

Rose had thought there was no way she could sleep, but sleep she did, Emon next to her, their bodies close enough to touch without touching. She felt his warmth, and Rose could not help but remember the feel of her head on Beo's chest and the sound of his heartbeat beneath her ear. Would she ever hear that again? Did his heart even still beat?

When they woke again, Rose and Emon both lay in silence, eyes locked in a helpless staring contest.

"What do we do now?" Emon asked after a long while.

"I don't know," said Rose.

She did not think that Taran Marpaxan would let her leave the house. Rose thought of Amelie. What would happen if her friend worked up the courage to go to Rose's flat to get the money, only to find that Rose wasn't there?

Downstairs, a torrent of hurried footsteps began. Rose sat up straight, throwing her legs over the edge of the bed.

Emon followed her lead, but neither of them moved toward the door.

"Do you think the guards are here?" He nearly whispered the question, and Rose shook her head.

"It's coming from inside the house."

Rose didn't care if they weren't supposed to intrude. She pulled open the door to the bedroom and strode down the stairs, smoothing her sleep-wrinkled clothes on the way.

Maro and Marpaxan stood in the salon around a radio with several other people. One looked up when they entered but said nothing.

"You're certain that was the frequency," Marpaxan was saying to an older woman who had to be nearly Aunt Aleis's age.

"I couldn't forget that if I tried. It's been nothing but interference for fifteen years. Weak, but present. The interference is gone now. Nothing's been broadcast on that frequency since. It's the same tune. I'd know it anywhere."

"Who could have done this?" Maro pointed at the radio. "The NPV controls all the major channels. If this was the opposition channel back then, why is it showing up now?"

"It's a trap," one of the others said, his voice dry. "They know we're getting close."

"You think the NPV has controlled it all this time?" Maro laughed. "That's giving them more credit than they deserve."

"Take a look outside and tell me they're not capable of planning their moves in advance."

Maro's laugh stopped, though he didn't look wholly convinced.

Marpaxan saw Emon and Rose and pursed her lips. The expression was so like Aunt Aleis's that Rose had to blink away a sudden prick of tears.

At first, Rose thought Marpaxan was about to order them back upstairs. Marpaxan murmured something quietly to the others at the radio. She beckoned to Rose and Emon.

"It seems you've gotten the honour of being present for one of our more exciting moments," Marpaxan said. "That particular frequency has been dead since the NPV seized control of the city. By all our experience since, it ought not be broadcasting anything."

"What is it broadcasting?" The volume was turned low enough that Rose couldn't hear it.

"A dulcimer waltz in a minor key, on repeat. It's very faint, as if the signal isn't particularly strong, but it's there."

Rose, who had read the book several times a year for almost twenty years, felt something go through her at Marpaxan's words. Beside her, she sensed more than saw Emon's own reaction. He had only just read *Red Sunrise* for the first time, but it would have been fresh in his memory.

No one else in the room seemed to understand. Rose could see the scene in her mind's eye, see Remir Roxa and Yosif Milabr in the dim cellar beneath the city. Surrounded by candlelight out of necessity instead of romance. Rose had first read those pages with quivering fingers, felt the longing between the two of them like the electricity powering the radio. The radio in that fictional cellar broadcast a dulcimer waltz, the notes mournful and haunting. The waltz was a tribute to their fallen comrades, and in that cellar, it became the song that sweetened love between two heavy hearts.

In that storybook cellar, the radio faded away and left behind a resonant stage, a series of dulcimers played by masters with felted mallets in their hands. In that cellar, there was only a pair of lovers finding a moment of joy in dusty tunnels of sorrow. There was nothing to fear. There was only love.

"I don't think it's the NPV," Rose murmured. It could be a trap, if the NPV truly did know the book. But somehow, Rose didn't think so.

Taran Marpaxan frowned.

"Guard change in five," one of the others said.

Marpaxan frowned more deeply, then looked at Rose and Emon. "If you would like to leave, you may do so when the guard changes across the street. Go left and walk until you meet the wall, then turn right and go into the city. Stay away from the market, and if you see guards, get away."

"How can we reach you again if we need to?" Emon asked. "Or is it for good if we leave?"

"There is no point of contact. But if you truly wish to be of service to us, be at the fourth turn of the bull route tonight at the exact moment the bulls are released. Eighth bell. Maro will be there, and he will tell you what to do." Taran Marpaxan looked to Maro, who hesitated before nodding.

Rose nodded. They could go to her flat, find some food, see if somehow, some way, Liberation Front were wrong and Beo had gone there to wait. Perhaps Rose could get a message to Amelie.

Maybe. Maybe. Maybe.

• • • • •

The city was quiet.

In all the years before, Rose never remembered the longest night being a quiet day. Before, Sanmarian had bustled with movement. Rows of candles lined the main streets, set out by those who lived in flats or owned shops along the thoroughfares. They would fill the city with light along with the streetlamps, a sight Rose had always felt was magical.

Until now. Now she saw it for what it was, something created by human hands. When those hands instead stayed at the hem of curtains or window shutters, the owners obscured except for an occasional peeking eye, those lights did not appear.

Emon and Rose made it to Rose's building without encountering a single passer-by or guard, and the streets lacked candles.

At the door, they stopped. Neither of them voiced it, but Rose knew Emon was wondering the same thing. If they could still leave the city. Were trains even running? If there were a chance to rescue Beo, how would they do it? What would happen if they met Maro for Larsi's Run?

They should have asked. Rose unlocked her door. She felt as though she had come upon something too late to affect it herself, and she paused with the key in the keyhole. Perhaps she and Emon should take the money, get Amelie, and flee the city. Rose's hand shook on the key. Could she live with that? Leaving a man she had, in truth, known only for a pair of weeks?

"Rose," Emon said softly. "Are you all right?"

She shook her head. "For a moment I thought we could do it."

"Do what?"

"Leave. Take the money I have and go build a new life in Coret."

Emon was quiet. "We could. It's not a question of whether or not we could do that. You could even leave me here and go yourself, with your friend."

He said it so simply. Was this what trust was, to know full well that your life was in someone else's hand and that they could clench their fist and crush you or upturn it and drop you at any moment? Rose thought of Beo. She had no knowledge of the dungeon under Sanmarian's fortress, but she could not imagine it was a pleasant place. It was strange now, knowing precisely where he was and yet having no way to get to him.

When Rose had closed her eyes and pointed to the north whilst sitting on her floor the night before, she had indeed drawn a straight line between herself and Beomir Mataya.

"It's not a question of can," Rose agreed. She thought of her words to Taran Marpaxan. What was the point, if not to save a single beating heart? "I won't leave him. Or you."

"No one would blame you," Emon said.

"I would."

Rose turned the knob on the door and stepped through it.

Emon locked the door behind them.

A floorboard creaked in the kitchen.

"Emon," Rose whispered. "There's someone here."

Rose stepped forward into the salon, where the radio played the same dulcimer waltz. No static, just soft tones of haunting melody that grew louder with each footstep.

Perhaps it was that she felt helpless in the face of her city crumbling around her. Perhaps it was being unable to rescue a man she could feel, even now, even from across Sanmarian. Perhaps it was sheer foolhardiness.

Rose opened the broom cupboard in the foyer and took out a broom, clutching the handle in both hands. "Who's there?"

Her heart jumped, unsure if an NPV guard or Aunt Aleis or Beo were about to greet her.

It was not an NPV guard, or Aunt Aleis. It was not Beo.

It was his Aunt Irena.

With a revolver pointed directly at Rose.

• • • • •

"Wait," Rose said.

She had never stared down the barrel of a gun before. She saw it more clearly than she had seen anything in her life, the dark steel, the sights at the tip, dented from wear. Irena's finger was on the trigger, not near the trigger. On it, her index finger already strained against the small tab of metal that could end a life.

"I'm sorry," Irena said.

"Irena, wait!" Rose knew she should dive to the side, but she couldn't move.

A loud bang went off, and something hot flashed through Rose's arm.

"Rose!" Emon was at her side, and dimly Rose heard the click of the revolver cocking again.

"I know Beo," Rose said, pain and heat and a tickling sensation spreading through her upper arm.

She couldn't seem to focus. Her field of vision was taken up by a thin woman's torso and knees, well-dressed in green woolen trousers and a grey wool jumper that fit her form to her neck and bore black buttons diagonally from shoulder to ribcage.

"What did you just say?" Rose heard Irena's voice.

"You shot her," Emon said.

A loud thunk made Rose jump. She was on her knees, Emon's arm around her shoulders. The revolver now sat on the floor, the source of the noise.

"Your name is Rose," Irena said. "You said you know Beo."

"I live here," Rose said. Her words didn't seem to fit what Irena had said.

"Get a towel!" Emon barked. He unwound Rose's scarf and began to unbutton her coat.

Irena vanished into the kitchen and reappeared a moment later with a towel.

Rose couldn't move the fingers on her left hand. The towel pressed against her arm, and she cried out.

"I think the bullet is still in there," Emon said. "It shouldn't be, from this range. It's a damn good thing you missed."

"I didn't miss." Irena knelt and moved to Rose's side, her fingers prodding behind the towel. "I moved the gun because she knew my name, and I wanted to find out how."

"My gods," said Emon.

"The bullet went through," Irena said. "There is an exit wound."

She pointed to the wall behind Rose, but Rose couldn't turn to see. Her brain wouldn't seem to clear.

"I know Beo," Rose said again. Her arm felt as if it had been set on fire.

"The bullet didn't hit the bone." Irena prodded Rose's arm again, and Rose almost didn't recognise the high-pitched keen that came from her own throat.

"Be gentle with her!"

"I need to make sure that the bullet did not hit her artery," Irena said. She moved the towel, and Rose felt a trickle down her arm. "I don't think it did. You. Keep pressure on the wound."

Emon scrambled around to Rose's left side and took the towel from Irena's hand.

"You took the book," Rose said. Her thoughts flitted from corner to corner of the past few days. "You were here before."

Emon looked up, still pressing the towel against Rose's arm. "Is that true?"

Rose managed to focus enough to turn toward Irena, who knelt on the carpet by the coffee table and watched Rose bleed, an unreadable expression on her face.

"How did you get in?" Rose asked the question feebly, then drew a breath, trying to ignore the pain in her arm.

"I have a key."

"Rose, maybe you should lie down," Emon said, but Irena shook her head.

"She should sit up until the bleeding stops. If she lies down, it will get worse."

"You shot me and came into my home. I want to know why. Did you follow Beo here?" For the first time, Rose's voice sounded somewhat steady.

"You know who I am." The statement almost rang like a question.

"You're Beo's aunt. That's all I know."

"Where is he?"

Rose swallowed. Her mouth tasted of metal. "He was arrested by the NPV. I don't know why. We were with him yesterday and got separated."

Irena went very still. "How do you know he was arrested?"

"First tell me why you are in my home." From Irena's surprise, Rose realised the older woman had no idea that Rose and Beo were connected.

"What is your surname?" Irena asked.

"Abernethy."

"My gods." There was wind in those words, like Rose's name had pulled them from Irena's lungs. They whispered through the salon, at once soft like a breeze and as loud as a hurricane.

To Rose's utter shock, Irena covered her face with both of her hands and began to laugh.

• • • • •

"Is something funny?" Emon's grip tightened on Rose's upper arm.

"Your name is Rose Abernethy, and you know my nephew."

Rose wasn't certain if her fuzzy head was from exhaustion, blood loss, pain, or shock at finding an intruder in her home. "Yes. I only just met Beo recently, not long before he went to see you in Viyarenyo."

Irena's quiet laugh was like petals falling on ashes. "He did not mention you." Then her face turned thoughtful. "Or perhaps he did."

"You left rather suddenly." Rose winced. Meeting Emon's eyes, she placed her right hand over his on the towel and nodded at him to remove his. "I can hold this."

"Was your father called Andreas?"

The sound of her father's name went through Rose like a flash of fire in a pan. "Yes. He died, fifteen years ago in an autocar crash."

This time Irena's breath was a sharp intake.

"Did you know him?" Rose could feel her pulse heavy against the towel in her hand. Her arm throbbed in time with it, louder than she was used to feeling her own blood.

Irena's expression seemed to shift like grains of sand, her eyes full of helpless sadness and her mouth opening and closing. She straightened from her kneeling position and crept closer to Rose, coming to sit in front of her on the carpet.

Rose felt Emon tense with alarm beside her, but she herself felt no threat. The revolver still sat on the floor, out of arm's reach.

"You said you live here. This is not Aleis's home?"

Rose felt a shock again. The towel drooped, and she hurriedly pressed it back against a new surge of blood. "I have lived here since I finished school. We bought it with the money from Papa's house—"

Irena gave a sharp shake of her head. "Aleis lived here, long ago."

Rose sat, feeling the warmth of blood seeping through the towel against her fingers. The money she had found, the money intended for her by her aunts. She had a vague memory of how much Papa's house had sold for. With the total amount of the gemstones, it would be that, near enough. This flat had been Aunt Aleis's. And something else, far deeper than the money, far beyond anything Rose could comprehend. The room receded around her, blurred at the edges.

All Rose could see was Irena's face.

"My name is Rosenni Irena Abernethy," she said. "Who are you?"

A thousand thousand possibilities went through Rose's head.

"Your father was my lover, a very long time ago."

Emon looked back and forth between Rose and Irena, his expression bordering on horrified. "Is Rose your—"

"No," said Irena, and some bit of relief found Rose's heart. "Rose's mother's name was Miko, and she left when Rose was barely out of swaddling clothes."

"My father was your lover." Rose repeated the words in a daze. "For how long?"

Irena gave Rose a soft smile, softer than anything Rose had yet seen from her. "Seventeen years." She paused as if knowing full well the weight of the revelation. "I'll tell you as much as I can, but there's not much time before I have to go. There is something I must do that cannot wait, and if I am successful I can save Beo as well."

"You think you can rescue him?" Rose asked, a wild hope taking root in her centre. "Then go now and tell me later. Please help him."

"It has to be tonight, when the city gathers to run the bulls. There is no one who could reach him now."

The hope shrivelled as quickly as it had begun, and Rose blinked back the sting in her eyes. Next to her, she saw Emon do the same.

"Then please," said Rose. "Tell me what you can. My aunts...they never told me."

Irena nodded, moving to sit cross-legged on the floor. For the first time Rose noticed the slight glaze to her eye, the cataract forming on its surface.

"I met your father two years before you were born. I was married at the time, and both my husband and I fell in love with Andreas from the moment we saw him. Such things usually don't work out so neatly, and for three years, we lived in near-perfect bliss. We all should have known it would never be so simple. You were born, and Miko left—I never knew why she left, if she couldn't bear Andreas's relationship with us or if there was something else—and right around then was when the National People's Voice began to take hold in Sanmarian. They started here, you know."

Rose knew.

"My husband joined the party. He was always proud of Kael. He joined before you were born, but it wasn't until he began to rise through the ranks that it caused problems. None of us knew, back then, what the NPV's true goals were." Irena peered at Rose. "If this is too much for you right now, please say so."

She didn't apologise for shooting Rose, which Rose found to be a strange comfort. Rose had a feeling that Irena knew precisely what she meant to do. *I didn't miss. I moved.* She reminded Rose of Taran Marpaxan in that way.

"I'm all right," Rose said. "Go on."

"When your mother left, my husband was initiated into the NPV's inner circle. At that point, they were growing and gaining the trust of their followers. You must understand that they are master manipulators. They promise their adherents power, yes, but more than that, they promise them a place. A role. Something to be part of that is bigger than themselves. They admitted my husband even knowing that he loved a man and a woman both, and slowly they began to twist his feelings for us. For Andreas, and for me." Irena spoke with conviction and no small bit of cynicism. There was poison in her words, a kind of poison that had been there long enough to turn to dust on her tongue. She swallowed as though it still tasted bitter. "They told him that true love was only for one person. They taught him of gender purity and confessed these things as if they were great scientific secrets they were granting. They spoke of the corrupt leaders of Sanmarian at the time and how their invitations to the Roa were seditious. Everything they said was meant to fix their people with one truth, their truth. They used that word a lot, truth. The problem with truth is that if only one small group can find it, it has dual power. It makes people hunger for it, for truth is a worthy thing to seek. And it discredits anyone who gainsays them, once the small group has enough power and followers, regardless of whether they are right or wrong."

"My father," said Rose.

"My husband broke off his relationship with Andreas. I won't tell you more, except that it happened. I was there, and it devastated me. I was young, and I was stupid. I was weak. It wasn't long after that my husband demanded I end my relationship with Andreas as well." Irena's eyes grew distant. "Times were uncertain then. Violence in the streets was more common. I was poor and dependent upon Rico for my home, as party members' wives were discouraged from working—"

"Rico," said Rose at the same time as Emon said, "Your husband is Rico Samson?"

Irena blinked as if she had lost track of what she was saying.

"That's why he took Beo," Rose breathed. "He saw Beo's photograph of you."

Samson's words rang in Rose's memory, something about her father not being so easily frightened.

Irena collected herself, visibly steadying her breathing. "The man I married was called Rico Vitar. Samson was his father's name, the name he took when he joined the NPV."

"Vitar," Rose said, feeling faint. "My gods. You're Remir Roxa."

The book. *Red Sunrise*. Rose didn't need to know more of Irena's story. She already knew it. She had read it a hundred times. She looked to the radio behind Irena, where the dulcimer waltz still played softly in the background.

Suddenly the faces of Yosif Milabr and Remir Roxa were not the faces she had always imagined as she read.

One was slender and strong, with eyes like warm peat and hair the colour of honey in shadow. The other had an oval face, squarish on the jaw, with eyes that saw right through you and wavy dark hair pulled back from his face.

"I am not Remir Roxa," Irena said, her words breaking Rose from her reeling thoughts. "Remir Roxa was who your father always hoped I would be. Someone strong enough to fight. Someone brave enough to leave Rico when I ought to, instead of staying ten more years while Sanmarian slowly rotted."

There was no sound in the salon but for the dulcimer's haunting chords.

"When I saw the book here that first night, I thought Aleis must have still read it. It had been a long time since I opened it. I didn't think any other copies existed."

"I have a whole crate," Rose said. "Papa made sure I had them. I read it so much I went through six."

Irena leaned back in surprise. "He had them printed?" Then she closed her eyes as if something hit her, raising one hand to her mouth. "Ah."

"What is it?" Desperation boiled up in her, and Rose shifted until she was on her knees, still pressing the towel against her arm as tightly as she could.

"You said your father died in an autocar crash," Irena said. "It was not an autocar crash. Rico found the book in our home; I thought I'd kept it hidden enough. I hadn't. We got a new bed, and I hid it there in haste. He spilled something and went to remove the sheets and found the book. He knew immediately what it was, but he read it anyway."

"What was it?" Emon asked.

"A love letter to me. Andreas wrote it for me. And for Rico, I think, as a warning, though he never expected Rico to read it at all."

Rose closed her eyes. She remembered Papa's face the moment she had asked him if it could be possible for a book to be written just for one person, remembered the sadness that crossed his face. *I think this one is for me.*

Then it is.

"How did Papa die?" In that moment, Rose was nine years old again, sitting in the plush red chair, her back cramped from a full night of reading, eyes puffy from crying over the story in those pages, watching the prism rainbows dance across the room. *Papa's own story.*

Irena reached out and touched Rose's cheek. "It was Rico's fault. He found the book and went berserk. He broke nearly everything in our flat, and I fled into the city. Rico was incoherent in his rage—he had believed my relationship with Andreas over for more than ten years. He spit out his anger at another party member, who took Andreas's name. That was the Burning Night, fifteen years ago. The party decided to move on Andreas, who was one of the leaders of the opposition. They spared you and Aleis out of pragmatism, not compassion, because they knew the city was not yet ready for what they planned. They burned a publisher, several opposition strongholds, and they killed Andreas and set him in an autocar to burn too."

"And you?" Emon asked.

Rose could not speak. Tears ran hot down her cheeks like steady streams, the kind of weeping that floods one's soul. The NPV had spared her, and Aunt Aleis. Aleis knew, had to have known. Rose could still remember her great aunt's face when she told Rose of Andreas's death.

"The city was alight with fire that night," Irena said, and in her eyes Rose could almost see sparks against the midnight dark. "Many people died. I simply...pretended to be one of them. I made certain that NPV guards saw me in the city centre, pretended I was fleeing in terror. They never thought to question, and I went to Viyarenyo."

"Mikael Iris," Emon said. "Why did Andreas write under that name?"

"He loved this country," Irena said. "Mikael, my Kael. And the *iris* is the promise of the gods not to forsake their people."

Rose remembered the prisms in Papa's study that cast rainbows on every wall when the sun shone through them. Back when people left their curtains open in Sanmarian. Before people hid behind them.

"What did you come back to Sanmarian to do?" Rose asked. "You couldn't have known Beo would be arrested."

"Rico has thought me dead for fifteen years," said Irena. She stood and walked to the radio. "This waltz was Andreas's and my song. Andreas was an engineer. He and his fellows recorded it on a transmitter that would block the opposition's frequency whenever we used it. This was your father's radio. I was amazed the transmitter was still in place."

"The static," Rose said. "The transmitter would cause interference. You moved it."

Irena nodded. "I brought it back here, though, to transmit the signal. I want Rico to hear it. I thought you were intruders here," she said.

Rose wanted to laugh at that but couldn't. "So you shot me."

Irena's face softened. "I wouldn't have, had I known."

Rose figured that was as close to an apology as she would get. "What brought you back here?"

"I'm going to do something I should have done long ago." Irena's hand caressed the arched wood of the radio. "Rico has gone too far now, caused too much death."

"Irena," Rose said.

"I'm going to kill him."

CHAPTER TWENTY-EIGHT

I remember when time was not a river, but a pool.

I remember dwelling there with you in the endless heal of dark, where there was naught but souls. There time was around us, and there we floated. Now, time is up, down, left, right, and forward.

I remember dwelling there with you. Where we had no breath and yet could breathe, and where around us was the possibility of infinity.

I remember dwelling there with you, and then the gods broke the dam and time spilled forth, and we split at our unseen seams and time washed us forward.

I remember dwelling there with you, forever before the gods tore us in two or three or four or more.

Forever I will find you. Forward took us, but I remember.

Beo had read those lines over and over as he grew into an adult, but never had they seemed more real than they did as he huddled in the dungeon cell under Sanmarian's fortress. When he closed his eyes, it was as if he could remember that pool of time, where there was no forward or back, only floating.

Except no one was going to find him.

When the guard had deposited him back into the cell, the woman across had startled in her own. She had come to the bars of her cell once the guards were gone, looked enquiringly at Beo, but Beo had not wanted to answer any questions.

He hadn't betrayed Irena, and Beo wouldn't. His stomach had gone from gurgling to cramping after an hour of sitting at the table full of food, and even though Beo knew that going a day or so without food was not nearly tortuous in truth, being taunted with food was painful.

Hours passed in his cell, the cold settling back into Beo's bones.

When he looked up, the woman across the stone was still looking at him.

"What do you want?" Beo asked.

"I want to know who you are. Most, they just throw in here and leave to rot. If they take someone out, they don't come back. But you they took out and brought back."

"I'm no one."

"You have something they want."

"They're not going to get anything from me."

"Son, have they really tried?"

Though the woman's face was dirty, her eyes were alert, and her hair had been plaited back from her face. Beo couldn't have guessed at her age—in the dim unlight of the dungeon she could have been twenty-five or sixty—but she did not seem overly distressed by her situation. She was right, as well. They had not resorted to any more effective means of obtaining information from Beo.

Beo looked at her and shook his head.

"What is your name, son?"

"Beo Mataya."

From the end of the corridor, Beo heard a rustle of straw and the clank of metal.

"Beo?" A voice came from a distant cell. "Beo?"

"Yoan!" Beo scrambled to his feet and grabbed at the bars for an instant before pulling his hands back from the freezing metal and shrugging them into the sleeves of his coat. "Is that you?"

"Gods, Beo, why are you here?"

"Same reason you are, I reckon."

The other prisoners moved closer to their doors to peer out, and Beo couldn't blame them. Probably two of their prison-mates knowing each other was more entertainment than any of them got in a week.

"I told you to run," Yoan said. His voice sounded weak, and he coughed.

"We did," Beo told him. Yoan seemed to be on the same side of the prison as Beo was, and all Beo could see was one strong hand dangling out between the bars of Yoan's cell. "I got separated from the others, and the guards took me just outside the city centre."

"Why?"

Beo didn't want to answer in the dungeon, uncertain of the other pairs of ears that occupied the same space. He changed the subject. "What are they keeping us here for? They executed people not two days ago. Surely they would have done the same to us already if they meant to kill us."

"I imagine they have a reason for waiting," Yoan said. He coughed again, longer this time. His cough sounded tight and dry to Beo's ears, and after a moment he remembered that Yoan had asthma.

"Are you okay, my friend?" Beo asked, alarmed. "Your asthma."

"It's made worse by the cold," Yoan said. "If it kills me, it saves the NPV a bullet."

The woman across from Beo barked a laugh. "Have you any kind of scarf or fabric you can put over your face?"

Beo looked at her from where he stood. She angled her body toward Yoan, peeking out of her own cell.

"Yes, that should do," she said, nodding approvingly.

"You can see him?" Beo asked. It gave him an odd relief, to know someone could see his friend's face.

"Yes," she said. "Yoan, is that your name? Put it to your face and keep it there. It ought to help you breathe more easily. The moisture from your breath will help, and it should trap some warmth."

"Thank you." Yoan's voice came a bit more muffled, and he cleared his throat. "That feels better."

"Why are you in here?" Beo asked the woman.

She raised one shoulder in a partial shrug. "I am a physician and was attempting to ally myself with Liberation Front," she said frankly. "I helped women with contraceptives and also those the NPV deems of impure gender. I am many things the NPV does not like."

"You do not seem bothered by the notion that we are all about to die," said Beo.

"I have done as much good as I can. If I live through this, I will try to do more. I am proud of the life I have lived, and if it ends, I will leave this world knowing that I did what I could."

"I envy you that," Beo said before he could stop himself. "I have done nothing of worth."

The woman looked at him with a piercing gaze. "You have said you will not give the NPV what they want from you," she said and waited for Beo to nod his assent. "If that is true, you have done something of worth."

One of the other prisoners snorted, but the woman turned to him. "And you? You are here simply because the NPV disapproved of your choice of executive in your business. Don't pretend you've done anything particularly noble."

"None of us deserve to die," the man said.

There was that word again.

"Yoan," Beo began, but just then the door clanked open again, and two guards entered. They moved right to Beo's cell again, and again one of them looked at Beo.

"No trouble," he said.

"No trouble," Beo said, wondering if the guard knew any other words.

His cell door unlocked, Beo followed them, aware of the many sets of eyes upon his retreating back.

$$\bullet \bullet \bullet \bullet \bullet$$

Again, the guards led Beo to the same room, the same table covered in food. Again, they told him to touch nothing.

Beo sat, his heart thudding hollow thump after hollow thump in his chest. A sense of foolishness washed over him for his previous hopeless oblivion. It wasn't that he had found hope of any kind—he was quite certain his remaining lifetime scrawled itself out in hours instead of days or weeks or years—but seeing a glimpse of Yoan, hearing even a few of the charges laid against the dungeon's inhabitants had given Beo some part of himself back.

As he waited for Rico Samson's inevitable appearance, Beo pondered what it could be. It took some time, and his mind flitted between thoughts of his dwindling future and the sumptuous foods he could not touch, inventorying the new spread of food in front of him. A bowl of deep red cherries was the closest, stems deep green and fresh. Beo still could not get to Rose or Emon, a thought that made his heart ache so much his vision swam. A basket of sourbread covered in linens sat next to the cherries, one spongy fold peeking out from under the fabric. Beo had little power to do anything, however much he resisted Samson's questions. Would Samson resort to other means? There were more fish—this time curried and roasted as well as smoked—and halved oysters topped with capers and olive relish. Would Samson torture him? A salad of fresh greens. Was this itself torture? Ceramic pots of stewed spinach and lentils and white beans with saffron.

The food meant nothing, and Beo could not concentrate.

He wanted to scream, to smash every dish on the table and eat none of it. He wanted to photograph it and call the print *Hunger*. He wanted to eat all of it. His stomach burned with bile, and his still-stuffy mouth tasted of phlegm and the odours of the dungeon.

This anger differed from despair, and it took Beo too long to see why.

People.

When he had sat at this table for Rico Samson's breakfast, he had felt as though he were totally alone. Samson had thrown him in a dungeon, but there were others in that dungeon.

It had been Yoan's voice calling out Beo's name that reminded him. He may never see Irena or Rose or Emon again, but he was not alone, not yet.

Rico Samson opened the door to the room, still in his immaculate suit of brushed grey wool, still perfectly composed as he had ever been.

Beo was not alone, but looking at the leader of the NPV as he strode into the room and pulled out a chair opposite Beo, he was certain Rico Samson was.

Rico Samson was alone, totally and completely.

For the first time, Beo watched him and tried to actually see him. Not as a party leader or as someone who had been pushing Sanmarian with propaganda and populist fear, but as a person.

He was neither tall, nor was he short. His hair was cropped close and neat, nearly shaved at his neck and combed straight back from his forehead. His hairline showed no signs of retreating, in spite of him easily being in his fifties. Beo wished he had his camera. He wanted to look through the lens at this man, see who he was and what he wanted. Samson's eyes were clear and focused, and Beo could see them on film. In that unassuming, neat body, Rico Samson had the charisma to capture the emotions and trust of much of the city, to get them to turn against their neighbours and family members. How many other couples like Rose's friends had the city seen? How many wives or partners cut out of their livelihoods? And somewhere in Rico Samson was a pit of sadism, to lay out so much food in front of a prisoner who could eat none of it. What calculations had gone into Samson assessing whether leaving Beo alone here would make him try to sneak bites—and whether Beo would trust that the food was not poisoned?

"It is rude to stare," Samson said.

"It is rude to set a hungry man in front of a table of food and tell him he is to eat none of it." Beo leaned back in his chair, one hand on each knee, displaying far more bravado than he felt. "Of the two transgressions, yours is worse."

"Only if you are an innocent man, and we both know that is not true."

Beo fought to keep his face blank. "Who decides who is innocent?"

Samson pulled off a chunk of sourbread and with it, scooped up some stewed spinach. He smiled. "I do."

"Do you think yourself a god then, to decide the fates of mortals?"

Samson smiled again, wider, as if Beo had unwittingly made a joke. "Hardly. You hyperbolise."

"I'm not the one who sets a table with enough food for ten just to serve myself."

"Tell me about your friend."

"Which one? I may not have many, but I do have more than one."

"The woman with you the first time I brought you here." Samson ignored Beo's cheek, which made Beo wonder how far he could push the NPV leader.

Not enough to try. "What exactly are you asking?"

"You seemed close. You behaved protective of one another, which belies that you trust each other. Trust is not something that comes easily, so I assume you have reason to trust her, and she you. I would like to know about her."

"Trust can be a function of proximity," Beo said. "She was with me the day you raided my flat."

It was a guess, but from Rico Samson's lack of surprise, Beo was right.

He steeled himself and went farther. "It was her watch you stole. It was one of the only mementos she had of her father, who died fifteen years ago."

Something passed across Samson's face, gone so fast Beo almost missed it. "I stole nothing," he said calmly. "And if your flat was indeed raided, it was likely the work of common thieves. Deviants, perhaps, or Roa."

Beo thought the leader of a political party ought to at least sound like he believed what he was saying, but Beo got the sudden and strong impression that Samson was only saying what was expected of him.

"Tell me about Rose Abernethy." Samson said then. "Or I will have my guards go fetch her, and she can join you downstairs."

Beo had to respect the way Samson continued with the euphemism of *downstairs*. He thought for a moment. "When you met her, you insinuated that she was a coward. She is not. When she has the chance to help others, she takes it. I took a photograph of her the day she lost that watch, when she was weeping. She had every right to be affronted at that, but instead she sought me out and befriended me. Your party's desire to condemn women to the singular role of houseworker has condemned Rose's best friend to an abusive home, and Rose has done what she can to try and help her friend escape, even though thanks to you, this friend has no money in her own name, and the business she has built has been snatched out of her hands and put in the control of her abuser.

"Rose is kind. She is strong and intelligent. She has had opportunity and means to leave this place behind, to escape the NPV and its poisonous, exclusionary ideals. And yet she stays and tries to make some good happen for those she knows and loves." Beo swallowed, hating the taste in his mouth and the lump in his throat at once. His words felt like fire, and he wished they would burn away the stale coating of his tongue. "She is the exact type of person you are responsible for harming. More than me, more than anyone down in that dungeon."

Beo thought of Emon, of Tarn Susette and Susette's lover, whose death both Susette and Emon had lain at the NPV's feet.

"And you don't care, do you?" Beo asked. "You don't care who you hurt or what burns while you sit here in your fortress. Nothing threatens you; you kill anyone who so much as disagrees. Those executions this week, they were nothing new. They were only visible, available for others to see for the first time because you believe you have grown strong enough that no one will risk standing up to you."

Rico Samson did not respond, only listened with his head tilted to the side, a slight angle of someone who could very well be memorising every word they were hearing.

"Someone will," Beo said. "Whether you think so or not, someone will stand up to you eventually. You cannot strip rights from your populace with impunity. You can kill me and everyone else *downstairs* and that will not change that you are alone. At least I will be missed when I am gone."

"You keep assuming I mean to kill you."

That stopped Beo's next words in his throat. "Don't you?"

"You may very well live through the night, though perhaps a little worse for wear."

Dread took hold like the cold of the dungeon's stone floor.

"What is it you plan to do to me?" Beo made himself ask the question, certain he did not want to hear the answer. He could not have said then whether it was better to know or be left in ignorance.

"I personally plan to do nothing to you whatsoever." As if on cue, the guards returned then, opening the door with decorum, as if they were interrupting Samson and the city magistrate or someone else of such importance. "But as you were so eager to point out this morning, it will make little difference to you either way."

Samson nodded at the guards, and the dread swirled through Beo like muck from the bottom of a pond. Each guard grasped one of Beo's arms.

"No trouble," Beo said. "I'll walk."

Samson gave a sharp gesture with his left hand, and the guards' grip on Beo's upper arms did not lessen. A third guard appeared through the threshold of the door, a man with a slight figure and quick, almost jerky movements.

The third guard pulled out his revolver, and Beo froze, his body going rigid.

Out of the corner of his eye, he saw Rico Samson nod.

The guard brought down the butt of the revolver on Beo's head.

CHAPTER TWENTY-NINE

Never in Rose's life had she ever thought she would hear someone say they intended to kill a person and mean it. As she showered for what felt like the first time in weeks, careful of the bandage Emon and Irena had wound about her wounded arm, Rose couldn't decide if she could stomach Rico Samson's murder or not.

Emon and Rose could turn Irena in to the NPV. They could try and barter her life for Beo's. It was a thought others would have, so Rose made herself have it, if only to know that she had thought through every possibility. She thought of Tarn Susette, and she thought of the others executed in the market square of Sanmarian, under the shadow of the library's gutted tower, and Rose decided that she could stomach Rico Samson's murder more than she could cope with the idea of likely causing Irena's.

She would never forgive herself if she made that choice, and if he survived, neither would Beo.

She wondered what her father would do.

Rose dressed herself in comfortable clothing, unwittingly choosing wool trousers almost the same shade of green Irena wore. She paired the trousers with a loose black shirt that wouldn't show blood.

Emon and Irena were still out in the salon, and Emon had showered before Rose, leaving her some space.

She looked around her bedroom with new eyes.

Aleis's flat, Irena had said. Her aunt had a key, and Rose had never really wondered at why. She didn't mind, and Aleis was never the sort to invade Rose's privacy. And Irena had a key. How long had she had it? Had Andreas and Irena used this flat to meet without Rico knowing?

It was a strange feeling, disconcerting and not entirely welcome, to think of her father and his lover stealing moments in the same bedroom where Rose had slept for eight years. Were her father still alive, Rose could imagine joking with him about it, jabbing at him and pretending disgust where she felt none.

But Andreas was dead, and even if it had not been Rico Samson—Rico Vitar, gods have mercy—who killed him, it was, as Irena had said, Rico's fault.

Fault.

Such a strange word. Again, Rose reeled with the knowledge that *Red Sunrise* was true, down to Yosif Milabr's death. Andreas had not died by public execution as Yosif had, but Rose's body chilled at her father's prescience. Had Papa somehow known? After a decade of secretly loving Rico's wife after their triad had been poisoned and broken apart by fear and control and the NPV's promises of power and purity, had Papa seen his own death as somehow inevitable?

Was that the reason for the crate of books left behind? Had he wanted to somehow ensure his own story was told?

Rose did not know and could not say.

What would Papa do now?

Rose could not imagine her Papa, her gentle Papa with his warm hands and smelling of wool and pipe tobacco, grim-faced and planning a murder.

Yet Beo was in the hands of the NPV, and a twisting vine in Rose's very centre whispered that for someone he loved, for those dearest and closest to his soul, Papa would have turned Sanmarian's sunset stone walls to sand and scattered them in the Tarenr Sea.

Rose's arm hurt, and she wanted to do nothing but sleep. She needed food, and she needed rest. Food she could obtain. Rest would have to wait.

A quiet peace came over her. She could not fully feel the fingers in her left hand, but Irena said the feeling should return.

Someone knocked at her bedroom door. "Come in," said Rose.

Emon pushed the door open. "I think you need to see this," he said, his voice cloaked with sadness.

Rose stood, her body screaming for the comfort of bed. She ignored it and followed Emon into the salon, where Irena had drawn back the curtains.

"The mastery of the NPV," Irena muttered, pointing down to street level. "They have spent fifteen years to come to this point."

Moving close enough to Irena that Rose could feel the older woman's warmth, she looked out where Irena indicated.

Red paint splashed a shop window. A specialty shoe shop, one that made work boots for the dockworkers and always smelled of leather when she walked by. The red paint spelled out PERVERT.

"The NPV have always been smart," said Irena, still staring out the window. "In their internal correspondence, they use pseudoscience and flowery language, like sociosexology and gender purity and patriotic geneticism. What they whisper to their public supporters, those folks who feel disenfranchised and unappreciated and trapped in poverty, is this. Pervert, deviant, invader. Succinct, divisive. When there are groups within groups who are visible, they are easily scapegoated."

"The Roa," Rose said, and Emon tensed.

"And families made of combinations of adults outside the NPV's patriotic genetic ideal." Irena's eyes grew distant. "Their tactics run deeper than that, as well. The propaganda I'm certain you've seen. They have also quietly changed teachers, expelling some in favour of those who share the NPV's values. Those teachers deemed far enough outside those values vanished. The NPV did the same in public offices, magistrates and justice officials, physicians and herbalists."

Herbalists. Physicians. Rose remembered Doctor Carixo's warning and how frightened he had seemed. "A chirurgeon came to warn Aleis and her partners," Rose said slowly. "Why physicians and medical professionals?"

"The National People's Voice seeks to create a society where every pregnancy results in a 'genetically pure' Kaeli child," Irena said. "They wish to stop anyone from ending their pregnancies."

"But what if anti-conceptions fail?" Rose asked, aghast. "What if someone's partner is violent? What if it would risk the life of the person carrying the child?"

Emon looked at Rose, but Rose could only see him out of the corner of her eye. She tried to imagine a Sanmarian where Amelie would be forced to give her violent husband a baby. Or just as terrifying, be forced to remain pregnant with a spouse who beat her, to know each time that he could end the pregnancy with his blows. That such a thing could mean the trauma turned septic and no chirurgeon would help save her life. Rose didn't know Doctor Carixo well, but she did know he helped people who miscarried or whose infants died in the womb and needed to be removed before sepsis set in.

Horrified, Rose blinked back sudden understanding. "That's why Aunt Aleis fled. They sell a tincture of pennyroyal."

"Likely that was not the only reason Aleis left Sanmarian." Irena turned away from the window and drew the curtains again, cutting off Rose's view of the paint-splashed storefront. She looked around the salon, her fingertips ghosting over the polished wood of the radio that still softly played the dulcimer waltz. "Rico never found this place. I thought for a long time after I left the city that he would go after Aleis. Or after you, Rose. It seems he put all of us out of his head."

"You still love him." Emon's voice, absent for what felt like most of the past day, seemed to float in the morning air.

"I'm not sure that is a true statement," Irena said. "I never stopped loving Rico, even when Andreas and I deceived him. He was a hungry man, desperate to prove himself and be found worthy, but without the discernment to know whose approval was worth seeking. He was a gentle lover, a hopeful lover, always eager to please at the expense of himself. He believed my love and approval were worth having, for a long time. Until he didn't, and the NPV gave him a concrete path to their approval that included hurting those he loved. Fifteen years is a long time to think a loved one is dead."

"You think he never stopped loving you," Emon said.

"I know less than nothing of what's in Rico's mind. From his actions I can only assume he left love behind long ago."

"I won't help you kill him," Rose said. "I can't do that. But I want to help you save Beo."

Emon nodded his head vigorously. "If there is anyone worth saving in this city, it's him. What can we do?"

• • • • •

Rose did not recognise the Sanmarian outside.

Smoke rose in plumes at intervals throughout the city, some grey or white and some ink-black and oily. Just before they reached the city centre, Rose saw why. The gunshot wound in her arm felt hot and full of fire, and the city she saw bore its own wounds. She wore her old winter coat, a heavy burnt orange woolen number that had once been Amelie's and was always a bit too large. For the extra space, Rose was grateful. For what lay outside her clothing, Rose felt nothing but anger and fear.

Café Maya had been petrol bombed again, the formerly immaculate plate glass shattered into thousands of shards on the cobblestone footpath and what remained of the varnished wood of the frame blackened with soot. The fire had been put out, but the air stank of wet ash.

The sun had yet to melt over the horizon, though the sky lightened above with a few scattered clouds, enough to see the welts and bruises from the night before. Rose felt the ripples of repetition, like the time an earthquake had shaken Sanmarian and brought shivers of earth in its wake for days after. Except this time, Rose did not think the real earthquake had yet come.

"How did we not hear any of this happen?" Emon murmured. He kept close to Rose, and the warmth of his shoulder was a comfort.

Rose walked with Emon on her right to avoid bumping her shoulder, and Irena walked ahead of them both, trying to keep pace with them but occasionally dipping forward as if her feet sought to set their own hurried rhythm.

"We were beneath the city," Rose said. "Too deep to feel these blows."

"It's likely worse outside the walls," said Irena. "Hurry."

Irena had asked Rose what felt like a hundred questions. Having learned that Aleis, Helyne, and Grenye lived near the square, Irena wanted to go to Aleis's flat, because it was closer to the city centre. Rose had a key to the tea shop and not to the flat, but Irena waved off the concern.

"Is it wise to go straight through the market square?" Emon asked. "Yesterday it was full of NPV crowds and guards."

"The guards will be preparing for the Longest Night and Larsi's Luck Run," Irena said. "It is early. They will be sparse enough in the square. They will know that most people will be indoors, waiting for the celebrations or simply hiding."

A set of massive speakers had been erected on a large dais in front of Market Tower, where the NPV's banner still hung, this time unsullied by paint. When was the last time Rose had walked Sanmarian's streets without smelling fire on the wind?

Already Rose could see where the streets were cordoned off for the bulls. Each year they began at Marixo Road from the south and ran through side streets to loop around the market square like a luck spiral. The path deposited them on the northeastern corner of the market, where Alcazar met the promenade. There, a wide corral was already in place. The dais faced that way, where anyone important enough to be granted a seat would see the fortunate—or the very stupid, as Aleis would say—who had managed to stay afoot throughout the entirety of the run. It was said Larsi granted ten years of luck to whoever reached the end of the run. Rose was not certain any of the gods were so beneficent, and making someone risk death for the possibility of unguaranteed good fortune smacked of caprice, if not outright sadism.

This year, Rose felt as if luck had naught to do with any of it. What should have been a day of celebration had become a day of ruin.

She thought of Maya's café, and the stab of pain she felt was not for the bullet wound. Maya's café was far from the only business near Plax Rynka that had been burned. Glass littered the cobbles, reflecting the city like windows into a broken world.

All thoughts left her head as they rounded the tower. There was a rack with a series of spikes, and upon each was a human head.

One was Doctor Carixo, the chirurgeon who had told Rose to warn her aunts. A seagull sat perched atop it, pecking at what remained of the doctor's eye sockets.

Rose could not look away.

She heard Emon gasp, his eyes wide enough to show white all around his brown irises. He was looking past Carixo at another spike.

"Emon," Rose said, forcing herself to turn her back to the obscene display. "Emon, look away."

"That's Tarn," he choked. "That's Tarn Susette."

Rose's left arm was nearly useless, but she threw her right one around Emon's shoulders. "I'm sorry," she said, repeating it, meaning it, knowing it meant nothing.

The speakers above the dais crackled into life. Emon froze in Rose's embrace, and she felt him breathe in, but he did not breathe out.

"*Attention citizens of Sanmarian,*" came a pleasant-sounding voice. "*Let it be known that all citizens are required to attend Larsi's Luck Run this evening, to join in the celebrations of a new Sanmarian and a stronger Kael. The bulls will be loosed at eighth bell.*"

"Can they do that?" Rose said. "All of Sanmarian will not fit on the market square."

"That isn't the point," Irena said.

Rose looked around the market over Emon's shoulder, taking in the corral for the soon-to-be lathered bulls, the dais, the space that would hold several thousand, but far from the total population of the city. "They want the people panicked and afraid of them," she said. "And unable to move quickly through the city. Which means..."

"Whatever anyone else plans"—Emon did not have to specify Taran Marpaxan, and his voice cracked on his words—"they'll hardly be able to move to do it."

Rose did not want to let go of Emon, but she knew they could not linger.

"Hurry," said Irena.

They quickened their pace over the cobblestones of the market square. Rose began to wish she had drunk some of Aunt Aleis's valerian tea before leaving the house, something to dull the pain in the absence of modern medicinal options. Valerian made her tired, and Rose hoped she would find aspirin of some sort at her great aunt's flat.

She should have been prepared for the sight that greeted them on Sankael Road, but Rose had not stopped to consider. Aunt Aleis and Helyne and Grenye were beloved in Sanmarian.

Or Rose had thought so.

The front window of the tea shop was smashed, and Rose had seen that before, had expected the sight again. The door—the hand-carved door that bore Helyne's careful touch in every curve of wood—now said DEVIANTS in white paint.

Rose reached for the door, and it nearly fell off, hanging by one hinge as if someone had looted and then made a bizarre attempt to close the door behind themselves. The weight of the door threw Rose off balance, and she cried out from the pain of the quick movement. Emon grabbed the door and steadied it, waiting while Rose ducked out from under it. Her eyes stung. The door had hit her right shoulder and not the left, but every muscle tensed in anticipation of more pain. Her right sleeve bore a new swath of white. The paint was still tacky.

She led the way into the dining room of the tea shop, forcing herself ahead of Emon and Irena. She had to see first. The pastry cases, always so meticulously wiped free of fingerprints, were pounded into glass shards and torn backing fabric.

The tables had been overturned or smashed outright. There would have been little to steal; perhaps whoever had come in was even more angered by the lack of theft-worthy items and settled for destruction.

"Rose," Irena said, glancing behind them. "You can grieve later. We ought to get upstairs, see if there is anyone in your aunts' flat."

"For the sake of the gods, give her a moment," Emon said. He came around Rose's side to stand in front of her, taking her face in his hands. "This place is not your aunts. Remember that they escaped before this happened. They were not home. Wherever they are, they are safer than we are."

Rose could not nod, but she met Emon's eyes and felt something like gratitude wash through the shock and pain of everything else.

In her periphery, Rose saw Irena remove the revolver from her pocket and check the chambers. There was a clink as she replaced the bullet that had gone through Rose's arm.

The sight and sound brought Rose back to the present.

"Let's go," she said.

CHAPTER THIRTY

At first, Beo could not be certain that he truly awoke. His eyes felt as though they were open, but no light shone in. For a moment, he hung suspended in darkness, unsure if he was alive or dead.

"Beo." Yoan's voice brought him back to life.

Life was moving around him and dark and smelled of acrid body sweat and waste.

"Yoan?" His own voice sounded bulbous and wrong, and his head lolled against something hard.

"He's awake." Beo recognised the voice as coming from the woman in the cell across from him.

Something sharp and hot rose in Beo's throat, and his stomach heaved.

"Turn him on his side!"

Beo couldn't tell who said it. He felt hands on his shoulders pushing him at the same time the sick came up, spilling out of his mouth and down onto the floor. Down was a direction; gravity still existed here. He coughed, spitting and choking. He had had no food in two days. All that came out was bile. His throat felt raw. Tears dripped from Beo's eyes, stinging along with the welt he could now feel on his head. The world swayed, jostling him enough that Beo almost fell face forward into his own sick.

"Easy," Yoan breathed, and Beo felt his friend beside him, pulling him away from the vomit as far as he could.

It wasn't far. Wherever they were was cramped and small and moving about. Emon's arms steadied him. Beo's mind didn't seem to want to work right. Not Emon. Yoan.

"Rose," Beo said.

"Shh," said Yoan. "Is he going to be all right?"

"He has a concussion," the physician said. "And they may have given him laudanum as well, as they did with us. Together that would addle him more than a simple blow to the head."

There were more bodies, more people. Beo could not tell if they were conscious or not. Or dead.

Rose wasn't there. Beo remembered the dungeon, the surreal spreads of food with Rico Samson. Did that happen, or had he only imagined it? It seemed like something he would dream. He felt at his face, where the wetness of bile smeared on his cheek. He wiped it away. The lump on his head was real enough, as was the solidity of Yoan's grip holding him upright.

"Where are they taking us?" Beo was trapped in the swelling of his own head, trapped with the sense that any moment, he would heave his entire stomach onto the floor, trapped in this box. Panic rose, heady and hot, and it sounded like a drumbeat rising to frenzied tempo. It could have been his heart.

"We don't know," said the physician.

Beo swallowed the again-growing lump in his throat. "Rico Samson made me watch him eat."

Yoan's fingers grew tighter on Beo's shoulders. "You saw Rico Samson?"

"He wants my aunt," Beo said before he could stop himself. "Damn."

"Your aunt?" The physician asked. "Who is your aunt?"

"No one," said Beo. His jaw worked as he struggled not to throw up again. "She's no one."

"Beo." Yoan moved so Beo could lean against him.

"That's why they broke into my flat," said Beo. "They saw my portfolio and stole it."

"Gods."

Sound began to return to Beo, seeping into the traveling crate from the outside world. The rumble of tyres on cobblestones. The growl of an engine.

"How long have we been driving?" Beo asked.

"We don't know." The physician's voice moved closer, her movements uncertain with the rolling gait of the lorry.

"Could be half an hour, could be a day," Yoan said. "Ani woke up first."

"The benefit of having taken laudanum daily for chronic pain," she said cheerfully. "I have a high tolerance."

"Ani," Beo said. "I wish we were meeting under better circumstances."

"As do I, Beo. We're not dead yet."

No light came through the box that held them. "How many of us are there?"

Slowly, Beo's head cleared, though he felt still that at any moment he might pass out or vomit.

"Twelve," said Ani. "Only one other has woken up, and he went straight back to sleep."

"But you two are awake."

"High tolerance for laudanum," Ani repeated.

"I was worried for you," said Yoan. "Though I feel as though I could sleep a week and not wake rested."

"We are in a lorry, and not a train. They gave us nothing for use as a toilet. We cannot see, but this place is not airtight or we would suffocate. They either mean this to be a short trip or..." Beo struggled to hold his own weight up, pulling away from Yoan to sit upright. He regretted it instantly when the lorry dipped into a groove of cobblestones and Beo had to throw his hand down into his puddle to stay sitting. He wiped his hand on his trousers.

"We are in the city centre," said Yoan. "Cobblestones."

"Then we cannot have been driving long." As if Ani's words had made it happen, the lorry slowed, crawling forward, then stopped. Outside, someone shouted an order that Beo couldn't quite hear. The vehicle moved forward again.

A moment later, the lorry halted.

More voices sounded outside. Beo could not look at Yoan, for there was no light, only the warmth of his friend's body beside him.

"If this is the end of our time together," Yoan said, "know that dying by your side is an honour, my friend. I would rather we live to be cantankerous old farts, but if that is not to be the way of things, I'll meet my death proud to have known you."

"We're none of us dead yet," Ani barked. "Look your deaths in the eye with flowery speeches if you must, but until the moment it takes you, be ready to spit in its face."

Beo's lips stretched with a smile.

• • • • •

It was not death whose face greeted them when someone opened the cargo hold, but a phalanx of NPV guards.

A gust of crisp winter air flooded the hold, washing away the stink for the barest of moments. Beo blinked into the sudden brightness and resisted the urge to spit in the guards' faces nonetheless.

"Some are awake," one of the guards said. "We don't want no trouble from you."

"No trouble," Beo said, tasting irony right alongside the bile that still haunted his tongue.

The splash of vomit glinted in the sunlight. Near midday, it must have been. Beo could not be sure. He'd heard no clocks chiming the bells.

The guards began pulling the still-unconscious prisoners from the hold, grasping them by the wrists and yanking them out. Ani and Yoan stayed back with Beo. The prisoners' bodies seemed to be liquid. Their shoulders reached the edge of the lorry bed and they rippled out, flopping as if they had lost their bones instead of their consciousness. Beo shuddered.

When the last of the unconscious prisoners was out—some had begun to groan as guards hauled them out of sight of the vehicle—two of the guards beckoned to Beo and the others.

Standing took help. Yoan pulled Beo to his feet and steadied him to help him navigate his way out. Ani moved faster, though Beo could see a stiffness in her movements he wasn't sure was just from the laudanum.

One guard grabbed Beo's arm hard.

"Have a care!" Yoan said. "You'll bruise his brain more than you already have."

The guard sneered, but he helped Beo more gently after a muttered command from the other guard. Beo clambered out of the lorry, trying to get his bearings through the nausea that swirled within and around him. He couldn't see where they were. The city walls were right in front of him, huge and pink-or-ange and sparkling demurely in the sun. They must have been just inside the walls, but Beo had no idea of where.

He didn't have much time to try and find out. Ahead, NPV guards in their grey wool uniforms already pushed Ani forward, and Beo was next. He heard Yoan's wheezing behind him and tried to keep his bearings with the effort of walking.

The guards brought them through the side door of a house and down a staircase into a cellar. There the unconscious prisoners were already present, a pair of them sitting up. No one seemed to be bound or shackled. In the far corner was a toilet—a proper toilet with its tank nearly too tall for the cellar's ceiling and the pull-flusher intact. It stood out in odd contrast to the rest of the cellar. There was nothing to give its user privacy. Only a few feet from the toilet was a table covered in bread and cheese and pitchers of water, guarded by a pair of men with revolvers drawn.

They weren't alone, either. NPV guards with revolvers studded the cellar, which spread out before Beo. Prisoners of all ages and genders were already present, some eyeing the new arrivals, others eyeing the food. Most were gaunt. All were frightened. Beo felt their fear like his own, the uncertainty of walking along a precipice with death and wondering when it would simply shoulder you off the edge.

"No trouble," one of the guards said loudly. "Form a queue if you want to eat."

One of the half-awake prisoners from Beo's transport snorted, wiping drool from his face. "Last time one of you fed me, you drugged me and I woke up here."

The guard nearest him kicked him in the face. It was the same guard who minutes before had made his fellow treat Beo more kindly. Blood sprayed from his nose, spattering the still-sleeping prisoner next to him. "Eat or don't, but if I were you, I'd want something in my belly before tonight."

"So we can void full bowels when you shoot us in the back of the head?" One of the others asked, her voice cynical and unafraid.

She was standing, and thus not easily accessible to the guard's boot. When he stepped over to stand in front of her, Beo flinched, expecting him to hit her.

He didn't, only smiled. "I'd eat if I were you." The guard was taller than Beo, making him taller than average. He motioned to the other guards. "The door will be barred behind us. We will come back to get you at fifth bell. We will shoot anyone who gives us trouble. Come quietly, and you live."

No one in the cellar dared ask how long.

Beo stepped aside to let the guards reach the stairs, his heart throbbing and his head pounding—or perhaps the other way round.

The head guard—for he had to be in charge—stopped in front of Beo. "The Leader told me to ask you again. Who is she? Tell me and I will let one of these people go free."

Beo bit off his answer before it could escape his mouth. One slight shake of Ani's head, and Beo met the guard's eyes. "I told him. I don't know."

The guard shrugged. "See you in four hours."

They stomped up the stairs in their heavy boots, each footfall bringing a new wave of pain and nausea to Beo's head. He blinked, still feeling the tightness on his forehead where the skin stretched above the lump.

The door slammed shut, and almost immediately the prisoners began to buzz.

"You have information they want," the woman who had spoken out about the food wove through the prisoners to get to Beo. No one yet moved toward the table. "And you haven't given it to them? I don't know why I'm still alive, but that explains why you are."

She was around Beo's age, his height—taller than Rose—and long-haired with a flat nose and small eyes. She looked nothing like Zara, but something about her reminded Beo of her. He took an unconscious step backward.

"I'm not going to hurt you," she said. She glanced at the others and raised a stick-thin wrist to her face, wiping away a stray hair. "Whatever they want, don't give it to them."

"They said they'd let someone go." Another one of the prisoners from Beo's transport was waking up, groggy and bleary-eyed. "One of us could go free."

"They say a lot of things," said the woman.

Ani nodded, then went directly to the table of food.

"It's probably poisoned," someone said.

"I don't think so," said Ani. She picked up a loaf of bread and sniffed it, peered at the water, dropped a taste onto her tongue from the tip of her finger. The cheese she also examined. "I can think of two reasons why they would feed us. One, it is a final mercy before we die. Two, they want to return some small bit of our strength before making an example of us."

"I think I know which one to put my money on," muttered Yoan, looping an arm around Beo's waist to help him to the table. "But I'll take it either way."

Beo's stomach still roiled like the Tarenr Sea in early spring, but at Ani's insistence, he choked down a slice of bread and a square of cheese. There were three pitchers of water, which was hardly enough for everyone to have their fill, but Ani solved that problem by climbing on top of the toilet seat to remove the lid on the fill tank. She peered into the ceramic tank.

"Nothing growing in here, and it's flushed enough that it's probably as fresh as any of the city's water. Everyone should drink some."

Everyone did.

Slowly the unconscious prisoners awoke, and to Beo's surprise, those who had been there longer—some said they had been in the fortress dungeon for a month or more, fed three times a week and watered only once a day, which Beo hadn't experienced—made certain the newer prisoners got something to eat. Kindness was not something Beo had expected.

Ani seemed to see him watching. "There are always choices," she said softly. He didn't need to ask what she meant.

No one knew what the guards had in store for them. The hours passed, with prisoners swapping stories about who they were and how they were taken. Some were Roa from Southharbour just outside the city, folk who had dared stand up to the NPV. Beo had not heard how the NPV had restricted Roa employment in the city, nor had he heard the extent of NPV influence outside Sanmarian's centre. He thought again of the marchers who had caused him to be separated from Rose and Emon, dockworkers and labourers, almost all from the working classes of the city, evidence of toil in their bodies and attire.

Some of the prisoners were like Yoan and Beo, Liberation Front sympathisers caught in the past week. Most were academics, physicians, creatives. Many were working-class themselves. One confessed that she and her wife had arrived to their small shop in Southharbour to find that the NPV had signed the deed over to one of their male workers in the night. When they went to report it to the magistrate—she laughed bitterly at her own naïveté for that choice—the magistrate had them wait in an anteroom, and guards had come to arrest them. She hadn't seen her wife since. One of them started at Beo's name, then shyly admitted to liking his photographs.

Not everyone was friendly. A few people only grudgingly shared a name, and several of the prisoners who had arrived with Beo and Yoan and Ani looked as if they were ready to storm up the stairs and try and push through the heavy door themselves. Beo wasn't certain what stopped them, but he was thankful no one resorted to violence.

The afternoon passed that way, in a somewhat wary surreality, until the door banged open again, and the head guard put his head through.

"Mataya," he said. "One last chance. Who's the woman?"

"I said I don't know. Tell Samson to get his ears checked."

The guard actually laughed, a laugh so resonant and pleasant that under other circumstances, Beo would have felt the urge to join in.

"Very well, but this is your chance to let one of these other poor fools go live their life in peace." The light came from behind the guard, framing his silhouette and obscuring the angles of his features. Beo could not see his expression.

Beo looked up at him and shook his head.

"It's his aunt!"

Beo turned so quickly that his head spun, and he nearly threw up the bread and cheese he had painstakingly fed himself. The man who had spoken was from his transport. Beo had thought him unconscious when they arrived, but the man's eyes darted back and forth, and he scrambled to his feet to stare up the stairs at the guard.

"It's his aunt! I heard him say Samson was looking for his aunt! He didn't mean to say it, but I heard him. I heard him!" The man scuttled up the stairs until his face was at knee level with the head guard.

There was no air in the room. Beo tried to draw breath and failed.

The head guard laughed again and beckoned to the prisoner, who eagerly tripped over the stairs and caught himself on the thin railing. The guard helped him up and over the threshold.

Beo did not think he was the only prisoner holding his breath.

He heard a sharp slap, like someone clapping someone else on the back.

"He's going to get to go home," someone whispered.

A shot rang out. Then a thud.

Not a single sound left a prisoner in the cellar.

No one moved.

A moment later, the head guard appeared, wiping the barrel of his revolver with a silk handkerchief.

Beo no longer had any inclination to laugh with the man.

"I offered Mister Mataya that honour. The prisoner took away young Beo's chance. One of you could have gone free. Pity." The guard still loomed in the threshold, backlit by the rapidly dimming afternoon light. "There are rules. Remember that. With Larsi's luck, some of you may live to follow them. I will return shortly, after this mess has been cleaned."

The door slammed again, and Beo was not the only one who jumped.

"I know what they plan for us," Yoan said. He swallowed, looking as though he wanted to sick up as much as Beo had and more. "Do you remember what Samson said on the radio, about the Luck Run?"

Beo looked past Ani and the other prisoners to meet Yoan's gaze. "He said it was not open to all this year."

Yoan nodded, and Beo understood.

Rico Samson would force the prisoners to race the bulls for the chance to live.

CHAPTER THIRTY-ONE

Aunt Aleis's flat had been opened, but there was little taken or broken that Rose could see. The blown glass bowls Rose had often admired—those were worth half a year's salary and were long gone, but it wasn't like the shop downstairs where people had destroyed without purpose.

They found food still in the pantry and Rose found aspirin in the washroom. She swallowed three with a glass of icy water and stripped off her coat to check her bandages.

Irena found a small radio in a wardrobe that had not been stolen and plugged it in above the kitchen worktop. Emon stood in the spacious salon, looking as if he felt tremendously out of place.

"This feels wrong," he said.

"Everything about this is wrong," said Rose. Her wound seemed to have clotted, but the flesh around the entry hole was red and swollen, and a few black pocks stood out in her flesh. She would wear those beneath her skin for the rest of her life. Just then, she thought they looked somewhat like the stars in the sky.

Irena came over to examine the gunshot. "I'll look for some clean fabric to redress it," she said, and vanished into one of the bedrooms.

"Emon," Rose said, listening to her retreating footsteps. "Do you think Beo's alive?"

Emon looked at her. Behind him, there was a large painting of marsh lilies blooming in purple and blue. It was worth more than the bowls, and Rose allowed herself to be surprised that it was still there. She wondered what Helyne would say.

"What do you think?" He asked the question with eyes like comets.

"That's not an answer," she said. "He's alive."

Emon nodded and closed the distance between them. "Trust what you feel."

"I might be wrong."

"You might, but do you really think you are?"

Rose held a cold compress to her arm.

"Let me," said Emon. He took it from her hand, and Rose let her arm drop, leaning against the solid wood table in the dining area. The table didn't budge. Helyne knew how to build something sturdy, though Rose didn't wonder that no one had stolen the table. It would take several strong folk just to get it out the door.

Emon dabbed at the wound with the compress, peering at it. The tips of his fingers danced over the black spots in her skin. He traced them in a sketch of a design. "It's like the Sleeping Tiger," he said.

Rose tried to see, if they really formed the pattern of the constellation, but moving her arm hurt too much. "I'll take you at your word." She paused for a moment, then said, "I think they look like stars too."

For several minutes they sat in silence. Irena returned with strips of ivory muslin, far more than Rose needed.

"Keep them with you, just in case you need to change your dressing again." Irena bundled most of the strips up with the aspirin and tucked them into Rose's satchel, which Emon had been carrying. She retreated from the kitchen again.

Rose remembered what Beo had said about Irena, that she kept to herself and volunteered little. How lonely had this woman been for the past decade and a half?

Looking up at Emon as he began to wind the muslin around her arm, Rose raised her uninjured hand to touch the side of his neck. "Thank you," she said.

"For what?"

"Everything."

"I'm not certain I deserve thanks," said Emon. "Were I not with you, I'd likely be in that dungeon."

"At least you'd be with Beo," Rose said, cracking a smile.

"One day I hope to see you smile in earnest," he said.

Rose felt the expression fade, and she watched as Emon's own face took on a ruddy flush. "When I first met Beo, I thought the same thing about him. None of us have had much cause to smile lately."

"I hope that will change," said Emon.

"As do I." A strange feeling came over her, and Rose could not decide if it were hope or longing. For what, she was not certain. She could not know what would become of her and Beo, whether Beo would survive whatever was about to descend upon Sanmarian. And she could not know what would become of her and Emon, or of Emon and Beo, or of the three of them together. But as she and Emon looked at one another, Rose was certain that thoughts of Beo hung clear and present for them both, and she decided that the longing she felt was simply to find out. For a future in which they could, if nothing else, see if they could make one another smile.

Irena returned and flipped on the radio.

"What now?" Rose asked. The moment between her and Emon still swayed in the air like kelp in the sea's waves.

"Rest," said Irena. She fiddled with the frequency on the radio until the dulcimer waltz poured through the speakers, then nodded her approval that the transmitter she had left at Rose's flat had not yet been discovered. "At fifth bell, we will move closer to the fortress. For now, we ought to be able to keep an eye on the square. You can see it from Aleis's bedroom."

Rose and Emon moved into Aleis's room, the large bed still made as if Rose's three aunts were simply out for a walk and might return to it after Larsi's Luck Run, full of ale and spiced rum as they often were on the longest night. The curtains were drawn, but Rose pulled one end back to reveal the market square. She could see one edge of the corral, and the angle allowed a view of where Alcazar Avenue spilled onto the square.

More than that, though, it afforded her a view of the throngs of people moving along the streets. Some wore NPV armbands; most did not. Every person Rose could see moved with uncertain wariness. From the kitchen, the radio crackled as Irena changed the stations and found an NPV channel where an announcer regaled the airwaves with the story of the fortune god Larsi and her fabled run against the bulls to prove her canniness to the gods she had angered. The announcer's voice was jubilant, celebratory, like any other year.

But this was not every other year.

Below, on Sankael Road, Rose could see the suspicion like the silk threads of a spider's web, zinging with tension between those who walked there. She took Emon's hand and hoped it was not too late to save Sanmarian.

• • • • •

Irena had said they would leave at fifth bell, but as Market Tower tolled out half past three, Rose called to her.

"The square is teeming with people," Rose said. "If you hope to be any-where near the fortress for the run, we ought to leave now or we won't get to the end of this street."

Irena looked out over the square, then at Rose. "Are you certain you are up to this? You can stay here and rest. No one would blame you for doing so."

"I would blame myself," said Rose, though the knowledge that she would have to navigate the steadily increasing crowds below where people were certain to jostle her left shoulder filled her with trepidation.

"Very well." Irena beckoned to Emon. "Help me pack up the supplies we need."

Rose let herself lie back on Aunt Aleis's bed, staring up at the ceiling. She had lain there when she visited and overate. She had once spent a week in her aunts' flat when they still had their old white cat and went to Coret for a holiday. The bed smelled of herbs and sawdust, of Aleis and Grenye and Helyne. Rose turned her head and plucked a dark hair from the pillow nearest her. It lay next to a flax-en one, and she hunted for a moment until she found a grey that she decided to believe was Grenye's. It was a stupid fancy, but Rose held them above her face and plaited the three strands together, feeling foolish all the while.

She missed her aunts. She missed Aleis's bustling purpose and Helyne's strong grip and soft hugs. She missed Grenye's birdlike movements and the way she showed her love through doing small things for those she cared for. Rose wiped away tears from her eyes and sat up.

If Irena was right, if tonight would truly change Sanmarian, perhaps the sun would return tomorrow with a safer city for Rose's aunts to come home to.

She stood, looking one last time out the window at the burgeoning crowd thronging down Sankael Road. Then she drew the curtain and turned to follow Irena to whatever the future might hold.

• • • • •

At Irena's orders, Emon and Rose stayed behind her, following the gold-en cap of her hair through the crowd. She had wound a scarf around the low-er half of her face, ostensibly to help keep warm in the frigid air, but mostly to eliminate the chance of someone recognising her. Irena thought—and Rose and Emon agreed—that if a single off-duty NPV guard had recognised her portrait after fifteen years, the risk was too much to take. It wasn't before dawn now, and the streets were far from deserted. The noise from the crowd had already reached a roar like the waves against the cliffs at high tide.

"They loose the bulls at eighth bell, correct?" Emon asked.

Irena nodded, pushing past people.

In spite of the massive crowd and the air of anxiety that thrummed through it, there were vendors selling clamshells and bottles of carbonated juice. Some peddled hot tea with berry liquor. Rose wasn't hungry at all, but she watched the vendors shout about their wares with a mix of fascination and horror. This single consistent detail with the many, many other Luck Runs Rose had seen in her quarter century struck her as at once a comfort and an obscenity. She could not reconcile the conflict inside her.

Rose could not say how Irena managed to find the holes and flows of the crowd, but she led them with surprising speed across the market. It wasn't until they skirted the corral that Rose's ears picked up something that made her stop short in the centre of it.

"They closed the run to the public. Samson's pitting his political prisoners against the bulls."

Rose's ears rang like they had when Irena shot her. Her eardrums popped, and she froze. Dimly, she was aware that Irena and Emon had not seen her stop, and she opened her mouth to call out to them, but no sound came out.

Whoever had spoken wasn't far away and wasn't speaking loudly, but Rose heard them as they went on.

"He's going to turn the bulls loose on them," the voice said.

Rose could not move.

"Emon," she managed to get out. And he was there, miraculously, at her side. "Beo's not at the fortress."

"What?"

Irena pushed back through the crowd. "Why did you stop? Is it your arm?"

Rose shook her head, speaking low, aware of the hundreds of people who surrounded them. "Beo isn't at the fortress," she said. "Someone just said—I heard someone say—the prisoners are the ones doing the Luck Run."

"Who did you hear?" Irena looked around sharply.

"I don't know," said Rose. "I couldn't tell who was speaking. If it's true, and I think it must be, they will have already moved the prisoners to the starting point on Marixo Road. They bring the bulls in from the west, outside the city, and they start them on the ring-road where Marixo hits the city walls. There are usually at least a hundred runners. Moving that many prisoners through the city when Samson has ordered every Sanmarian citizen be present—"

"You don't have to go on," Irena said. Her voice had taken on a heavy darkness. She stood on her toes and looked over the crowd as best she could. Rose could almost see the older woman reformulating her plans. Irena moved close to Rose and whispered in her ear. "You said Marpaxan planned something tonight. Do you think they have any chance of success?"

"I don't know," said Rose, speaking softly in return. "I believe them to be far more organised than they have let anyone think up till now, but that could mean many things. We were told to meet at the fourth turn of the run."

Rose closed her eyes, trying to shut out the crowd and visualise the route the Luck Run would take. She opened her eyes again. "It would be where the run meets Alcazar, halfway up the avenue between the fortress and the square, right as the bulls are released."

"What do you want to do?" Emon asked Irena. "We've five hours yet."

Rose didn't have to ask. "Do you think the prisoners are being held on Marixo?"

"It would be a small window, if there's one at all. Samson will parade through the city along the Luck Run route with his entourage. If it's anything like the other years—"

"They'll bring the prisoners here first, so the crowd can see them."

Rose tried to imagine the usual Luck Run with prisoners instead. The runners on a normal year trained for it. It wasn't a hugely long route, but the bulls could run as fast as an average autocar drove in the city centre on the cobblestones. Those who reached the end of the run ahead of at least one bull or young steer were fêted for the remainder of the day, said to have Larsi's own luck. To think of prisoners who could already be injured or starving attempting the run...

Irena pulled back from their small knot. She and Rose exchanged a long look. "We can't be sure they won't just keep the prisoners near the start. Moving them here and back seems to be an unnecessary risk."

"Then we ought to go. We have to try—"

"Rose!"

Rose turned too quickly, spinning to see who had called her name. Over the heads in the crowd, she saw dark curls. Amelie.

An errant thought took over. Rose looked to Irena, waving at Amelie and Tomas above the crowd.

"Rose, what are you doing?" Irena asked. "We haven't time for a chat."

"Make sure you're ready to move as fast as we can," said Rose. "I need to do something that is probably foolish."

Her fingertips tingled as Tomas's face came into view.

Irena touched the small of Rose's back. "What are you doing?"

"You stayed with Vitar for ten years," Rose said, using Samson's former name. "Amelie shouldn't have to reach a decade with Tomas."

She fumbled in her pocket until she found what she was searching for.

Tomas and Amelie pushed through the crowd, with Tomas brightly calling, "Lady with a baby! Lady with a baby!"

Emon's face flickered like lightning deep in a thunderhead, and then the expression vanished and he beamed at Tomas.

Rose greeted Tomas first, kissing each of his cheeks. "Good afternoon," she said.

"My friend!" Tomas went to Emon next, but Rose noticed how his gaze lit first on Amelie with a sharpness that made Rose's stomach turn.

Rose went to Amelie and embraced her. "My shoulder is injured. Amelie, this may be your only chance. Listen to me closely." Rose pressed her flat's key into Amelie's hand. "At eighth bell, the NPV will run the bulls behind their political prisoners. I've a friend among them. We are going to try and save him, but there is risk to all of us. You deserve a chance at something better, and I'm going to give that to you. Go to my flat. In the wardrobe you'll find everything you need to start a new life in Coret."

"Rose—" Amelie's voice cracked with shock, her eyes on the old coat that had once been hers, and her hand closing tight around Rose's key. Rose saw the way she looked around, the way she took in the crowds, Tomas talking jovially to Emon, Irena scanning the crowd.

Believe, Rose thought, willing her friend to see that a day like this where the city was washed in clamour and confusion was a day a lone person could slip away.

"Get out of the city. Your home is not safe, and neither is Sanmarian." *Or anywhere in Kael, most like.* "Write to me when you arrive in Coret. If I am still able, we will join you after we do what we must."

Amelie leaned forward and kissed Rose's cheek. The moment seemed to float in time.

And then Rose's closest friend turned with an old glint in her eye and pushed through the crowd toward the south, toward Carino Avenue, toward Rose's money and toward freedom. She vanished almost immediately.

Rose had to believe she would make it.

Tomas noticed her absence a bare moment later. "Amelie?" His eyes settled on Rose, and his body tensed. "What have you done?"

"Friends don't hit friends," Rose said, and she punched him as hard as she could in the jaw. Papa had taught her to throw a punch. Rose put the total of her strength behind it. Tomas went down cold.

A murmur began in the crowd.

"This man beats his wife," Rose said loudly, and the murmur turned angry. People had heard Tomas as he approached. From someone, she heard a shocked *his pregnant wife.*

Irena had hung back, pretending not to be part of their group, but she met Roses's eyes with a meld of exasperation and respect.

"Move," she said.

This time Rose followed, hoping Amelie would truly go. Rose looked back once, but she caught no sight of Amelie's curls.

CHAPTER THIRTY-TWO

One of the other prisoners vomited in the toilet before the head guard returned, lurching toward it with his hand over his mouth. Beo couldn't blame him. In all their minds until now there had been some illusion that Sanmarian was ruled by law, if not justice of a sort. The fifth bell had tolled out moments before, and around him Beo felt a surge of energy, of the prisoners trying to find hope that they could live through this run.

It wasn't every year that someone died, but those who ran in usual years trained for it. Beo could hear Yoan's wheeze next to him and see other prisoners for whom outrunning a small herd of cattle would not come easily or naturally. And of course, himself. His head still felt heavy and thick, and there was nothing for it but to try in spite of it.

Those who ran in previous years also knew that they would live if they ran. Beo could not count that a certainty. To fail in a normal year meant that a runner reached the square after all the bulls had entered the corral. To fail this year—Beo knew it meant death.

He dreaded the door of the cellar reopening, but in all too short a time, it did.

The head guard no longer laughed or smiled, only looked down from a darkening doorway. "Queue up," he said. "Leave an arm's length of space between each of you. No trouble."

No trouble.

Beo wondered how it was that they could say that and it would be so. He wondered what Rose was doing, and Emon. And Irena. Had Irena come to Sanmarian at all?

A chill went through him as he positioned himself behind Ani and ahead of Yoan to climb the stairs, halfway back in the queue of prisoners. The NPV knew who she was now. It was only a matter of time before that information was transmitted to Rico Samson. What would Samson do? What did Irena plan?

The first of the prisoners reached the top of the stairs and vanished, taken in hand by a pair of guards. Yoan placed a hand on Beo's shoulder.

"Are you all right?" He asked.

Beo wanted to laugh. "Far cry from last year."

"That it is, my friend."

Then Yoan said something that made Beo's urge for laughter turn the other way round altogether. "It's not your fault."

It was the same thing he said after Zara died by suicide. Immediately Beo was there again, on his knees in the Lionfish on the hard wood floor, patrons staring and conversations silenced. He looked over his shoulder at the man who had been his closest friend in the years he'd spent in Sanmarian.

"Of course it was my fault," Beo said. "Had I not left her—"

"It would have happened anyway. Or she would have killed you." Yoan nodded at Beo to look ahead, and Beo obeyed. "I know something of this. There is nothing you could have done that would have saved her. You are fortunate that you did not fully lose yourself."

Beo could not agree with that. He cracked a smile. "Fortunate?"

"Poor choice of word," Yoan said, a touch of his old humour in his tone.

They reached the bottom of the stairs, a few folks ahead of Ani. She turned to look Beo in the eyes.

"I don't know you well," she said bluntly, "but if what I'm hearing is correct, allow me to place my vote with Yoan. You loved someone who hurt you, did you not?"

Beo hesitated, then nodded.

"Many of us have done the same, whether it was a parent or a lover or yet someone else. You are not responsible for what she did. Did she tell you she would kill herself if you left her?"

"Yes."

Ani shook her head, one eye on the prisoner who moved up the stairs. She was next. "Take some peace, Beo Mataya," Ani said. "Someone who says that to you, that is not love. That is abuse."

The physician straightened her shoulders, and Beo could see the pain in her movements. Could this woman survive a run with bulls?

Clammy perspiration formed on Beo's back as Ani mounted the stairs. He waited until she was halfway up, then began to climb.

• • • • •

Outside, the air tasted of ash.

Beo still could see no street signs, though the lamps were lit like tiny golden suns in the swiftly falling dark.

The wooden rails, he saw. Sometime since the prisoners had been brought, the fences for the run had been erected. The prisoners all stood on the street with their hands on their head. A guard snapped an order, and Beo followed Ani, his palms flat against the back of his skull.

Three hours still stood between the prisoners and the bulls' release. What was it the NPV planned for them?

Beo waited in a queue of prisoners, standing in silence. Ani did not turn to look at him, though Beo could feel Yoan's presence behind him. Rose was somewhere in this city, perhaps still with Emon.

Forever I will find you.

Beo closed his eyes and wished it to be true. Somewhere in Sanmarian, there was a woman and a man Beo thought he could possibly love. People who understood him in a way he thought no one could. A breeze blew round the sunset stone of the city wall, brushing Beo's lips with cold air, and as that breeze touched him, he fancied he could feel them, out there. Searching for him.

When he opened his eyes, no one was there.

No one was coming. He was on his own.

A large lorry waited on the street, this time not a closed hold but an open freighter that had a cage built round the flat bed. The guards ordered the first of the prisoners to climb up onto the bed.

Two guards flanked the lorry with revolvers drawn. Even though they could not fire quickly enough to shoot every prisoner, there were two more guards clinging to the metal frame of the cage from the outside and another dozen pairs at intervals along the wooden fence that would keep the bulls from goring on-lookers. There were no crowds yet, though Beo could see windows that must have belonged to citizens overlooking the street where they were gathered. He did not wonder that no one was brave enough to peek out.

The prisoners filed onto the bed of the lorry, climbing up one after another until they were all present, and the pair of guards clinging to the outside of the metal cage jumped down to shut the rear door. The head guard stepped back a few metres to survey the lorry.

"I mentioned there were rules. Here are your rules," he said. He had donned a hat, and the brim obscured his eyes where Beo peered out at him between the bars of the lorry's cage. "When we reach the ceremony, you will not speak, you will not shout, and you will do nothing other than stand and hear your charges. You will be silent. If you are not silent, you will be shot."

He did smile again then, and the smile chilled Beo more than the wind.

"Simple enough," said the guard. He nodded to the reflection of the driver in the side mirror, and the engine of the lorry turned over and roared to life.

Beo clutched the metal of the cage to hold himself upright as the lorry began to move. He hadn't noticed the gate until they pulled forward. The guards who were left behind scrambled to move the weighted wooden fence into place to block the driveway, and then the lorry turned to pass through the city wall, and they were moving.

"They mean to parade us in front of the city," one of the prisoners said. "Like—"

"Like criminals?" Yoan craned his neck to look at the man. "To them, we are."

• • • • •

The lorry wound through the run route. Not far into the journey, Beo caught sight of a flurry of movement ahead. NPV guards moved fencing aside, and a second lorry pulled onto the route behind them, its caged bed full of prisoners who peeked out between the bars at Beo's group.

"How many of us are there?" The tall woman who had reminded Beo of Zara asked the question in a murmur, clearly not expecting an answer.

As the lorries made their way to the city centre, seven more joined that Beo could see. Each time they passed a cross street, more and more onlookers could be seen off to the sides of the route. They all stood silent, watching the parade of prisoners toward the square.

After the first few lorries, Beo was not certain if there were more or not. The route turned, cutting off his view of the end of the caravan. When they turned on Alcazar, Beo caught a glimpse of the fortress to the northeast, high on its hill with every window lit with candles. It sparkled in the twilit dark like a shining beacon.

"Nine lorries," someone said as they approached the market square. Beo turned and counted himself as theirs clattered over the cobblestones of Alcazar Avenue, now able to see the entirety of the caravan stretching out behind them.

"What did we do to deserve this place of honour?" Yoan asked sarcastically. Drums pounded in the distance, toward the market.

"Nine lorries, with a score of prisoners in each," said Ani. "That's near two hundred prisoners. If the bulls don't trample us, we may well trample each other."

What sort of cruel game was it, to force human beings to compete in desperation for a chance at life? *There are rules.*

Being in the first position of the caravan, Beo saw when they advanced upon the market square. From Alcazar Avenue to Market Tower on the far diagonal end, the square was a seething mass of people. Lanterns topped each of the fence posts in the corral, and it was there the lorry driver took them, turning right as they hit the square to skirt the edge of the corral. Their lorry stopped at the head of the corral, and Beo could see the others behind them alternating right and left when they turned in. Not far from the corral, a dais sat, a band at one end and a phalanx of NPV officials and their wives at the other. In the centre was a black podium with a white circle on its front with the NPV logo stark and clear.

Drums and dulcimers played, the heavy beat of bass a tonal heartbeat in the flickering lamplight. An old Kaeli bow-harp sat on the far end, its musician guiding the soft bow across strings nearly as tall as Beo himself. He could scarce see beyond the dais except for the glimmer of light reflecting from the eyes of citizens. As the final lorry pulled into place, the crowd began to roar, and Rico Samson mounted the dais, striding toward the podium.

He wore pure white wool with gold buttons down the front. He wore a banded collar that did not overlap and exposed the hollow of his throat. A smart black cap with a short brim, similar to the guard cap but finer, sat atop Samson's head. His gloves were as pristine as the rest of him, his black boots shined to such a state that Beo could see the dancing reflections of gas lamp flames in the patent leather.

The band quieted, and Samson stepped up to a silver microphone.

He raised his arms and smiled beatifically at the citizens on the square. Beo marvelled at the difference in the man's composure. Every NPV guard in Beo's sight immediately made a fist and saluted to their heart. Samson did not return the salute, but he acknowledged it, beaming out at the gathered citizens of Sanmarian. In private, he was soft-spoken and deliberate, his expressions stoic and his tone even. On the dais, looking out to survey the crowd that had gathered around him, Rico Samson drew every eye to him.

Beo could hear the breaths of a thousand people draw in when Samson raised one hand and adjusted his glove. The clock in Market Tower boomed out sixth bell. There was no crackle of feedback in the microphone, only a sharp beginning as Samson began to speak, his word booming out of the square's speakers on a slight delay.

"Citizens of Sanmarian," Samson said. "My beloved Kaeli people. Tonight, you must be uncertain. But I urge you, fear not, my friends."

The crowd shifted like ocean currents, almost zigzagging with movement. No one called out, and Beo could see why. Even if there were dissenters present—and there must have been—NPV guards surrounded the square, posted at every street corner and on small raised platforms across the cobblestones. Each had revolvers at their hips. And there—at the top of Market Tower, more guards atop the library, the silhouettes of rifles visible against the deepening blue of the sky.

"Tonight, the National People's Voice will show you that we are the party of justice, the party of order. Before you, you see prisoners. These seditionists have been arrested over the past month, in the widest and most successful attack on insurrectionists that this city has ever seen. Nearly two hundred traitors, deviants, and perverts have been found in your city, and your NPV has brought them to you for public trial."

A hum began in the crowd, and among the prisoners who surrounded him. Beo could see people wearing NPV armbands, but hundreds did not. The crowd rippled with tension, apprehension, fear. And eagerness. Beo saw the shifting bodies of the NPV supporters, some wiggling up on their toes to try and look over the heads of the others in the crowd to catch sight of these prisoners. In the cage with him, the prisoners—whose stories Beo now knew, in whole or in part—clearly remembered the guard's warning, and they said nothing, though Beo saw throats pulse as they swallowed and saw veins moving in foreheads, saw the uneasy stance of the prisoners' feet. Though the lorry had stopped moving, no one had their balance now.

"This night has ever been a night for those who sought fortune, a night to prove one's worth to the gods themselves. Tonight, your NPV is here to show you that we are not without mercy. Even these seditionists and traitors may be redeemed by Larsi's luck." The crowd's voices began to pick up, and Samson raised his hands, placing his palms downward to quiet them. "Those who are successful will be granted amnesty. They will be given the chance for rehabilitation and welcome back into our community, if the gods favour them."

Rehabilitation. *Reconditioning*. Beo remembered the NPV manifest.

They say many things, Ani had said.

Beo saw what little hope the prisoners had flicker and die like a guttering flame.

He could not find his tongue, though he wanted to speak. He wanted to shout. He wanted to scream defiance at this man in his snow-white suit. Beo listened as Samson went on, his voice rising and falling in cadence like waves. Beo could not have measured the emotions of the crowd. Beyond the wooden fence of the corral, there were thousands of Sanmarian citizens, and Beo could not know how many hearts soared at Samson's words—or how many soured and turned brittle with terror.

Minutes passed, and the hum of voices in the square became a background roar, Samson's words somehow still audible above them.

"Bid farewell to these prisoners. When you next see them, they will be redeemed, or they will be reclaimed for our justice. Tonight is the longest night, my friends," Samson said. "Tomorrow we greet the returning sun with a new Sanmarian, a stronger Sanmarian. Your NPV will speak for you, and for all of Kael."

It did not matter then if any of the prisoners opened their mouths, for a great clamour of voices arose on the square, and Beo could not sort out any dissent from affirmation. The lorries started their engines once more. It took a long time for the noise of the crowd to fade from Beo's ears.

The journey to the beginning of the route seemed to take longer than had the journey to the market square. Beo and Yoan clung to the rungs of the cage with near-frozen fingers.

"Move around," Ani instructed everyone. "Warm up your limbs. You will need blood flowing if you hope to have any chance of survival."

"What does it matter?" Someone spat out of the cage, nearly falling over when the lorry hit a bump.

"It may not," Ani said, her voice grim. "But at least you will have tried."

Beo could not be certain that was a comfort.

They did not return to where they had come from, not exactly. Beo was not sure if they passed the house where they had spent the day, and he supposed it did not matter. Strange details stood out at him as the prisoners were herded into a paddock together by the score. The guard stationed at the forefront of the paddock, picking his nose with his thumb. A sign on a nearby building that advertised an industrial cleaner. A heart dug into the sunset stone, its edges deep enough that it had not been eroded, the initials at its centre long since scratched away.

"Stay close to me," Beo said to Ani and Yoan. "Stay close."

His head ached from the noise and the jostling movement. Someone bumped him even then, and Beo caught himself on Yoan's shoulder. Yoan moved on his toes—he kept himself well and was far from out of shape—but Beo could hear the tight whistle of his friend's breath.

Around them, people as old as seventy and as young as puberty formed a thronging mass, crowded into the small area by the guards. Beo's breath came faster, and he tried to warm himself. Sweat that was not from heat beaded on his brow.

"We can do this," Yoan said. "We can do this."

Beo had lost sight of any familiar prisoners beyond Ani and Yoan. Ani had a sad look on her face. She opened her mouth as if to speak, and a horn blasted through the air.

"That's it," a guard bellowed. "Prisoners ready yourselves! Reach the square ahead of the bulls, and you live. Arrive behind their tails, and you die."

"Mind the horns," another guard laughed.

At the front of the paddock, six guards hefted the wooden fence sections on each side of the opening. One guard counted, and they all heaved, moving in time, opening a passage.

But not all the way. They stopped after creating a funnel wide enough for perhaps four prisoners across. Beo's heart skipped, and Yoan sucked in a breath.

"The front," Ani said, grabbing both Beo and Yoan by the hands and pushing forward. "Get to the front, or we will not be through when the bulls arrive, and they will gore us to get past the fence."

A few of the guards were laughing, pointing at the panicked prisoners. Beo couldn't help but notice that others were not.

Ani was not the only one with the idea to push ahead. Someone shoved Beo from behind, and he pitched forward, Ani's hand the only thing that kept him upright. She may have been small, but Ani was strong. She yanked Beo and Yoan toward her, and they squirmed against the people in front of them.

Never in his life had Beo felt more like an animal. He could not breathe. His head swam.

"In," Ani said, opening her mouth and drawing a breath, eyes on the guards to await the second horn that would allow the prisoners to begin running. "Out."

Beo breathed with her. He wasn't the only one. Another woman and a man on either side of their trio did the same, eyes frantic.

The horn sounded.

• • • • •

The prisoners surged forward toward the small opening in the fence, and Beo immediately tripped over someone's heel.

He felt the pulse of bodies surround him, and Beo focused everything in his body on simply staying upright. Ani's hand in his was tight like a wire. He tried to remember to breathe.

"Gods," someone said, pushing forward. Someone caught an elbow on the wooden fence ahead and cried out as the press of prisoners behind them pushed them.

Beo saw a flash of blood. Ani edged them to the right, centring them in front of the path out, and suddenly the force of bodies pressing upon Beo's back seemed to double.

He did not have to ask what that meant. The frantic shouts behind him did enough.

The pressure built around him, people everywhere, at his shoulders, at his back, in front. The crowd carried Beo forward until suddenly the taut stretch of bodies gave way, and they spilled out onto Marixo Road, air enveloping them.

Still somehow grasping Ani's hand, Beo chanced a single look back just as someone screamed.

He met Yoan's terrified eyes over Ani's head. "Run."

The cobblestones were not made for sprinting, and with each step Beo feared he would lose his footing and send his ankle twisting to the side into a dip of stone.

"Go!" A voice yelled out behind them, and they ran.

More screams erupted from the paddock as Beo ran. He knew he should try to pace himself, but he also knew bulls were fast, and they had nearly two miles throughout the city to cover.

Beo was not a runner. He was a photographer, and most of his exercise came from walking the city at an ambling pace. His body rang with the metallic feel of adrenaline, and his lungs heaved with air that burned.

They ran, feet pounding the cobblestones. Each street they passed was filled with onlookers who watched with wide eyes. None cheered the way they would on a normal year. Beo locked eyes with a child sat atop their father's shoulders, bundled for the cold, and then they slipped past him, and the child was gone from view.

Ani dropped his hand. "The bulls are coming," she said between breaths. "Don't get in their way, and don't touch them if you can avoid it."

Beo wanted to know how she knew what to do, but he just nodded. Yoan panted beside them.

"Speed up," Ani said. Her face shone with perspiration already, and she suppressed a grimace of pain. "We'll want to be past the first turn when they catch us up."

Beo tried to increase his speed. His legs burned, and ahead, he could see the market square crowded with people. They were not yet even a quarter of the way to the end.

Someone hit Beo from the side, and Beo connected with the ground, sprawling.

"Beo!" Yoan half-yelled, half-growled his name.

Beo rolled, clambering to his feet and stumbling ahead, his feet churning at the stones and his head feeling as though his brain were made of rubber.

Hoofbeats.

Beo shook himself and lurched forward, chasing after Yoan and Ani.

They made the first turn. Market Tower appeared to their left as they hit the square, and the sound of thousands of voices spilled through the night air. Beo did not recognise this Sanmarian.

He could not tell if they cheered because he had gotten up, or if they cheered for the prisoners' blood.

CHAPTER THIRTY-THREE

Rose could hear a distant cheer spread over the market even from where she stood, in a spectator position at the corner of Alcazar. The fortress loomed to the northeast, bright with candles and looking far more welcoming than it ought to.

No sign of Maro yet, and the bulls had been released.

They had not been able to find Beo, not a sign of any of the prisoners until they saw the lorries parade up Alcazar for the square. Irena and Emon and Rose had all searched the metal cages for any sight of Beo, but they caught none.

"He has to be there," Emon had said, and Rose felt in her gut that it was true, but none of them saw a familiar face at all.

At eighth bell, they had been at the fourth turn of the run, and through the crowds, Rose still searched for Maro's face, unsure if they were already too late.

"You're certain this is where they said to be," Irena said. She still wore her scarf over the bottom half of her face, but her eyes were brown and bright in the lamplight.

Rose nodded. The crowd around them felt like a harp string about to snap. The air seemed to vibrate, and Rose could not have said where it would break when it did.

"There!" Emon pointed, calling out urgently.

Rose spotted Maro, nearing the edge of the fence at the run. He wore all black with a scarlet scarf at his neck.

He wasn't alone. Suddenly, Rose looked about and saw others filtering through the crowd. There were people with NPV armbands, yes, but for every one of those she saw, Rose marked a figure in all black. They were not uniforms; those wearing black were clothed in average wools and linens, no two alike, but for the look in their eyes. Purpose.

"Liberation Front," Irena muttered.

Maro looked up and spotted Rose, giving her a grim nod and beckoning her with a sharp gesture. Rose pushed at a shoulder in front of her with her good hand, ignoring the disgruntled exclamation she got in response.

"You came," Maro said as she reached him. He looked over her shoulder at Emon and Irena, then back at Rose. He frowned. "You're hurt."

"Is it that obvious?"

"You're favouring your right arm more than usual."

"I'm fine. Tell me what to do."

Maro glanced around, but there were enough people and enough noise that his words did not pass farther than their small circle. "You don't need to do anything. We are going to attempt to rescue prisoners as they run by. There are some of our people there."

"This is your plan?" Irena asked, scorn in her voice. "What then, turn the bulls on the guards?"

Maro looked at her. "Who is this?"

"Beo's aunt," Rose said, knowing Maro would understand her.

"You're—" Maro breathed. "You're Irena Vitar."

Irena nodded tersely. "I would have thought in fifteen years, you lot would have formulated an actual strategy."

"We have." Maro stood on his toes and looked around as if searching for someone in particular. "I have to get you to Taran."

"No one is getting anywhere," said Emon. "They're coming."

Rose tried to see over the crowd. She knew it was foolish, but she needed to get closer. She ignored the constant throb in her shoulder and nudged past Maro and the other onlookers, some Liberation Front and some not, until she reached the fence just beyond.

"Rose," Emon said. "If you see him, you'll not be able to help him in that state."

"Someone will," Maro said. "What state?"

"I shot her," said Irena. "I didn't know who she was at first."

There was no time for Maro or anyone to respond to that, because the first of the bulls appeared, a pair of energetic young specimens, nostrils flaring and brass septum rings glinting in the lamplight. She could smell them, the scent of fur and skin and manure and hay, and they came pounding over the cobblestones. Behind them ran struggling prisoners, their faces masks of terror. Rose heard the sound of hoofbeats and feet. Her eyes darted over the people approaching, but she could recognise no one. Her heart beat faster, desperate, seeking out one face.

A scream cut through the air, long and drawn out and curdling.

The crowd grew hushed.

"That's the signal," Maro said. "They're moving."

Rose didn't have time to ask who. "Beo!" His name tore from her throat with a force she hadn't known she contained.

There he was, running, half-limping, his face a measure of horror and exhaustion. Blood ran down his forehead and dripped off his nose. Beside him was Yoan. Rose felt a surge of gratitude and fear at once.

"Get his attention," Maro said. Across Alcazar, two Liberation Front members pulled a woman over the rail and out of the path of a bull.

"Beo!" Rose didn't care if any NPV supporters heard her. On the square, the clock chimed the half hour. "Beo!"

He looked up.

Rose saw his eyes like amber fire. She felt Emon beside her, pushing through the crowd with Irena.

Forever will I find you.

The words from *Red Sunrise* burst through her mind, and Rose put out her hand over the rail.

A Liberation Front member grabbed Yoan's hand and yanked him to the fence. Someone began to shout in alarm.

"Here, Beo!" Emon bellowed the words, and Beo turned their way, his face frantic.

A woman ran beside him, her face contorted in pain, snot running from her nose. In her fifties or sixties at least, her body moved like Rose felt, and not just the movement of her shoulder like Rose's gunshot had caused. Beo and the woman veered toward the fence, his eyes darting away toward the woman and then back to Rose as if the mere sight of her healed him.

Time froze with the sound of hoofbeats and drumbeats from the market square melding into one pounding rhythm.

Beo looked up at Rose and Emon across from five metres away, four, three. He smiled, a smile so sweet Rose thought she could taste it, his eyes shining with unshed tears and sweat gleaming on his brown skin.

He shoved the woman into the fence, and Rose caught her arm. Emon caught her other arm and Rose yelled in pain as they hauled her over the rail.

"Get her help!" Maro yelled it at someone, but Rose could not see who he was talking to.

The woman they had pulled over the fence wept in shock. "He shouldn't have saved me," she said over and over. "He shouldn't have saved me."

When she looked up, Beo was out of reach.

He did not look back. Rose saw his back vanish behind the glistening pelt of a running bull, and he was gone.

The last of the bulls passed, and prisoners still sprinted to catch up. Liberation Front grabbed who they could coax to the fence, called out to people they knew and those they didn't alike. The sound of an engine came on the heels of the prisoners, and the first shot rang out.

The crowd began to scream, jerking away from the gunfire.

Maro's face went grim. Two Liberation Front members appeared, and one scooped up the woman they had pulled to safety.

"Your name," Rose said to her, unable to form any other thought. "What is your name?"

Her eyes were glazed, and her body seemed to spasm with agony. "Ani," she said. "My name is Ani."

The Liberation Front members, two women, gave Rose a look of thanks and melted into the crowd.

"Where are they taking her?" Emon asked.

"Somewhere safe," said Maro. "If you want to try and save your friend, you better hurry. It's about to start."

"What's about to start?"

"The revolution."

$$\bullet\ \bullet\ \bullet\ \bullet\ \bullet$$

There were too many bodies.

Rose could not understand how the members of Liberation Front had parted the crowd like waves. She fought up the fringes of Alcazar, shoving past anyone in her path. Emon and Irena followed, Maro close behind. Throughout the crowd, Rose could see people in black. Were they truly all Liberation Front members? How had they possibly grown so large without attracting more notice? Rose remembered what Taran Marpaxan had said, that those who had gathered round the legend of their existence had served as decoys for the real resistance, but until now Rose hadn't believed it.

For weeks, Sanmarian had felt like a city with bubbles gathering at the bottom of it, ready to launch into a boil. As Rose desperately pushed south toward the market square, she could not help but feel the heat and steam of a thousand bubbles reaching the surface. White NPV armbands showed support for Samson and his party, but those in black moved with direction and purpose, while the former simply drifted, awash on the surface of Sanmarian's humanity.

It was like the city was full of oil and water both, writhing against each other over the heat of conflict that could send anyone spilling out into the fire.

The first of the bulls had reached the square. A cheer went up, and Rose could not tell the reason behind it. Toward the fortress, the sound of a lorry engine still rumbled in the bull run, and people screamed as more shots fired.

Rose's arm panged with each gunshot, and she couldn't help but flinch. She pressed on, wondering when her body would stop listening to her commands to keep moving.

"What are your people doing?" Emon asked Maro.

Each step brought them closer to the market and an uncertain future.

"Even as we speak, some are taking the fortress. All that was left to hold it was an honour guard of older men. Our sources said tonight was the best moment to strike." Maro kept his voice low, and Rose strained to hear him over the din. "Outside the fortress, others are taking guard stations."

"When you say taking—" Irena said.

"They are capturing, not killing." Maro sounded as though he did not truly believe that was the best course of action. "At least to the best of their abilities. The Roa in Southharbour have already taken the NPV artillery; that was the first stage, completed as Samson gave his first speech at sixth bell."

Rose glanced once behind her at Irena, whose half-covered face still managed to bely her surprise.

"I'm impressed," Irena said, not sounding at all grudging.

"Southharbour," Rose cut in, her thoughts turning to Amelie, for any fighting to the southeast of the city could jeopardise her friend's escape.

The crush of people continued to jostle around them, some citizens slipping northward and climbing over the fences to cross the street, but most didn't dare, fearing the NPV lorry not far behind.

"Low guard numbers," Maro said. "There was little conflict. Unlike we are likely to face here."

"Do you have so many people that you can face the brunt of the NPV guards here?" Emon asked.

"We have some advantages," Maro said, glancing at Irena. "Numbers, by a hair. The second is that the NPV are so against anyone who isn't a 'genetically pure' male taking up service duties that they have forgotten anyone else is capable of fighting. The third is that they will not expect us to move tonight."

Irena nodded, then pointed up the street. "Guards ahead, Maro."

Emon squinted. "How can you tell?"

"I lived among the NPV for fourteen years," Irena said softly. "I know their training, how they carry themselves. In or out of uniform, I could mark one from across the square."

Rose could see them. These were in uniform, but with their backs to Alcazar. "What are they doing?"

"The prisoners must have all reached the square," said Maro. "Marpaxan will move soon, after Samson makes his speech. Hurry."

Irena slipped through the crowd, leaving a path for the rest of them to follow. Rose wished then to see inside the other woman's mind, to know what it must be like to be seeking the life of one's nephew with one hand and the death of one's husband with the other.

CHAPTER THIRTY-FOUR

A ni had made it to safety; that much, Beo knew. He thought Yoan had as well. The cobblestones were cold against his cheeks. Around him, the bulls snorted and pawed the ground, but they did not charge. Beo imagined they were nearly as tired as he was.

He didn't know how many prisoners had been gored or shot. He heard the shots ring out behind him as the first few stragglers fell too far back to catch up with the running cattle. The sound—gods help him—had given him new strength. Now, though, the world tilted under his aching head.

He had seen her. She had found him.

Against all odds, Beo had seen Rose and Emon's faces once more.

Beo was under no false hope that the NPV would keep their promises; there was too much that had gone against their rules. Prisoners escaping, yes, but as he ran, Beo had seen citizens brawling in the streets, and he could not have guessed which might be on his side.

Other prisoners had made it too. The tall woman who looked nothing like Zara and yet had caused such a visceral reaction in Beo, she was here. Like Beo, she lay sprawled on the damp stones, one hand bloody where a bull's horn had caught it, but alive. Larsi's luck.

Beo remembered what Ani had said about death. *Be ready to spit in its face.*

He couldn't do that if his own face was on the ground.

Beo put his palms to the cobblestones. Every muscle in his body ached. He had long since stopped smelling the stink of his own body. To him, the lathered heat of the bulls smelled nice. Like the ranchland outside Viyarenyo, where his parents used to take him for picnics as a child. A soft swell of lush grasses with cattle grazing beyond in the sunlight.

It had been a very long time since Beo had thought of his mother. Irena's sister, so long dead. They had been estranged—or must have been—for Beo had not even known his mother had a sister until she arrived fifteen years before at their door.

He pushed, his knees wobbling on the cobbles. He almost gave up, then, wanting to fall back on his face on the square. Beo struggled, his arms shaking with the exhaustion of his muscles. Adrenaline had left him as unsteady as a newborn calf.

Some other of the prisoners also stood, holding themselves up on the wooden fence. The bulls' muscles twitched, steaming in the winter air.

A path had been cleared from the corral to the dais, and a shiny black autocar waited at the head of the corral. Rico Samson stood behind it at his podium. The podium was no longer on the larger dais, but instead on a small platform, where he stood flanked by six NPV guards on each side. Their revolvers were not drawn, but each had his hand upon the butt of the gun in his holster.

Rico Samson needed no gun.

Beo saw the man's face change, an unplaceable emotion crossing over it before disappearing as if it had never come. Beo met Samson's eyes from where he stood.

The ground slanted beneath Beo's feet, so sharply that Beo gasped and caught himself on a bull's shoulder without thinking.

The animal snorted and hit his hoof upon the square, but it did not startle enough to charge.

Beo's hand was grateful for the touch of warm flesh. Something alive. He gave the bull a pat and stepped forward to lean against the fence. Rico Samson began speaking into the microphone, but Beo could not listen. He heard vague praise of the runners' bravery before Samson's words devolved into a mere background hum.

In the distance, there was a stirring of motion, somewhere toward Market Tower. Beo could not see what it was, and at the moment, he did not care.

Samson's tone became reassuring, warm, welcoming. When he stopped speaking, there was applause, but not the kind one would have expected for a beloved leader. The crowd thrummed with apprehension. People glanced over their shoulders, at the guards, at the guns.

Samson nodded to the guards around him, and they gestured to others just out of Beo's sight. The crowd parted to reveal the head guard from Beo's group, the man who had laughed at the death of the prisoner.

He bowed to Samson, then saluted, fist to chest. He had no microphone, but said something to Samson, and Beo did not have to be in earshot to know what it was. Rico Samson spun on his heel and looked straight at Beo, his face ashen. A moment later, Samson snapped his fingers, and the guards sprang into action.

Beo could not have run if he tried.

Two guards shouldered the fence apart just wide enough to grab Beo through. Another opened the door of the shiny black autocar. A third jumped in the driver's seat. Beo dimly felt the rough grip of the guards who had taken him, but his concussed head had given into the ebbing wave of adrenaline that had carried him through the day. Head lolling on his shoulders, he smelled leather as the guards shoved him into the autocar.

He supposed someone got the bulls out of the way. The autocar's engine revved. On another day, Beo might have appreciated the luxury of a vehicle that moved so smoothly on cobblestone streets, but instead his head swivelled against the leather headrest behind him. Rico Samson was with him, murmuring directions to the driver. Outside the windows, Beo heard shouting. Rose was out there somewhere, as were Emon and Irena.

The car gained speed as it headed northeast on Alcazar, down the pathway that had been cleared for the bulls. Some few citizens sprang out of the way, clinging to the wooden fences. The lorry that had followed the prisoners swerved to the side, narrowly missing a head-on collision with Samson's vehicle.

Later, Beo would realise that he could have opened the door on his side and fallen straight out of the autocar onto the cobblestones. Later, he would find out that behind the autocar, the market square of Sanmarian erupted into chaos. Later, Beo would learn that the sharp *rat-tat-tat* of semiautomatic rifle fire that burst through the air was not the NPV's doing, but Liberation Front firing on the guards who raised their revolvers to shoot the surviving prisoners.

At that moment, however, Beomir Mataya did not escape, nor did he have any awareness of what lay outside the car aside from the sounds of shouting and gunfire.

For the second time that day, Beo lost consciousness.

• • • • •

Beo had only been knocked unconscious once in his life before that day, after falling out of a tree.

When he opened his eyes, startled by the sound of a clock gently chiming the hour—though he could not count the bells—he wondered in a flash of dreamlike incoherence if he were in the grass of Viyarenyo and the intervening twenty years had not happened at all.

Instead, Beo found himself on a plush bed atop the coverlets. He had been bathed and clothed in garments he did not recognise, grey trousers and a soft, band-collared white shirt that fit him as if it had been made for him. His entire body ached.

"Forgive the trespass of unclothing you," said Rico Samson, his lips an ironic slash that was almost a half-smile. "My servants are quite discreet, I assure you, and the physician needed to see to your wounds."

"What is the hour?" Beo asked.

"Just after tenth bell."

"Why did you bring me here?" Beo hadn't the faintest idea where *here* was, though the room seemed vaguely familiar. Someone must have cleaned his mouth, for his tongue tasted of fresh water and herbs, if a bit stale.

"I wanted to talk with you. Why did you not tell me that Irena Vitar was your aunt?" Rico Samson's voice held genuine curiosity and no small amount of bafflement.

Vitar. Beo closed his eyes and bit the inside of his cheek. He was not awake, could not be. That name did not belong to his aunt.

"My aunt's surname is Viatr," Beo said, and then a beat later, "Oh."

"You thought her surname was Viatr. Tempest. Curious of her. She always did surprise me."

Beo struggled to sit up, but Samson raised his hand.

"Where is this place?" Beo asked.

The bedroom in which they sat was larger than Beo's entire flat, with gleaming ironwood bookshelves better stocked than Sanmarian's city library at present. Rico Samson sat in a blue wingback chair next to a round table that matched the wood of the shelves. A tumbler of amber liquid rested on a Risati soapstone coaster beside him, half drunk.

"My villa. We are just north of the city walls, on the cliffs above Conch Shell Cove." The readiness and ease with which Samson answered the question made Beo wonder again if he was dreaming.

Beo's bruised brain struggled to keep up. Vitar was the name of the lover in *Red Sunrise* who betrayed Remir and Yosif to the fascist party. *Vitar* meant life source, or something similar. He had always thought the name to be a simple irony on the part of Mikael Iris, who had written the novel. Why would Aunt Irena share that name?

"Why did you tell me your aunt was a simple Coretian woman when I asked?"

Beo wanted to laugh. "You are the leader of a fascist party and a tyrant. You have had people like me killed. Do you truly think I would betray my own aunt into your hands?"

Confusion lit Rico Samson's features, and for once, he made no effort to alter or hide the expression on his face. He studied Beo for a long moment, so intently that Beo could almost see clocklike gears clicking through the NPV leader's mind.

"Ah," said Samson. "She never told you."

"Told me what?"

"Who she was. Is, legally." Samson opened the small drawer on the table beside him and pulled out Beo's copy of *Red Sunrise*. "And yet, you have this."

"I haven't the faintest idea what you're on about." Exhaustion and pain made Beo blunt. He was tired—so tired he thought he could simply decide to end the conversation by falling asleep, even if the house burned down around him.

"You truly don't." Rico Samson breathed in, then let the air out in a long sigh. "I understand your behaviour now."

Beo didn't answer that.

"Were I in your position—well, perhaps I would not have made the same decision. I am a different person, clearly. But I do understand why you withheld that information from me. What reason would you have to trust me?"

"None," agreed Beo. He remembered as a child how one of his drawings had been pinned on a sunward wall for several years. When one day he went to take it down and replace it with one of his photographs from his very first camera, the paper had crumbled, brittle from the sun. Beo felt like that paper.

"Would it help you if I mentioned that my surname was not always Samson? I changed it to honour my father, a party tradition."

Beo thought he was supposed to ask what name it had been previously, but he found he didn't have the will.

"Previously, it was Vitar."

Beo suddenly felt very stupid, and he wasn't certain he could blame the concussion.

"Irena is your sister?"

Samson started, then laughed. "No. She is my wife."

• • • • •

She is my wife.

Beo could not quite process the words Samson had said. Rico Samson was his uncle by marriage.

And something else.

Remir Roxa was the wife of Vitar Roxa in *Red Sunrise*. Vitar was responsible for their other lover's death.

"Who is Yosif Milabr?" Beo asked, near-terrified of the answer.

Samson blinked again, still holding the book. When he spoke, his brows knit together, but his tone was gentle. "I assume you mean in life, and not this... fictionalisation."

"Who is he?"

Rico Samson looked for a moment as though the entire world had been crafted as a singular cosmic joke, with him as the butt of it. "A man called Andreas Abernethy. I believe you know his daughter."

The room was silent but for the quiet ticking of the clock on one of the bookshelves.

"The watch," said Beo.

Samson lifted his hip to reach in his pocket, pulling the watch out. "Ah. I'm afraid I did lie to you, too. I gave this to Andreas long ago as a token. I was unaware he had kept it."

"You killed him."

Samson looked up at Beo's quiet accusation.

"Not directly, though I realise you may not believe me." He paused, thoughtfully opening and closing the watch. Beo saw the starlike glint of the watch's hands from where he lay. "Though it was my fault he died."

Beo could not speak.

Tapping the cover of *Red Sunrise*, he said, "I believe you have read the story. Enough of it is true that I ought not have to explain further."

"And Irena?" Where was she? What was it she meant to do?

"I have thought her dead for fifteen years. This," Samson said, indicating the book again, "obviously has some holes. Andreas was eerily prescient about his own death, though I believe he meant to live. He didn't quite get it right in the book, and I'll never be certain if it was my interference that caused his death or if his own activities with the opposition would have led him down that road without me. Irena did not follow the path of Remir Roxa. She must have found some way to make the guards think they saw her die. She vanished, and there were so many fires in Sanmarian that night that she could have burnt to ash in any of them.

"She has haunted me these past weeks. When one of my guards saw her portrait in your portfolio—I have it here, by the way, it's not been destroyed—he recognised her. He was one of the party's first guards. He knew me when I was Rico Vitar, and he is one of the few people in this city who would have known her face. He and Aleis Nicaro, likely Aleis's wives as well." Samson finished so casually that Beo had to stop for a moment.

"Rose's aunts. You have not—"

"They are safe, or as safe as one can be in this world." Samson's face became anguished. "I have caused Rosenni Abernethy quite enough harm for one lifetime."

A helpless laugh escaped Beo's throat. Aleis must have known. Beo could not have believed someone so quick to desert their family in such a time had they not at least suspected outside help.

"Irena and Andreas had a song," Samson said. "A dulcimer waltz. Andreas was an engineer, and he created a transmitter that would play it on the radio. It was a game to them, when the three of us were in love. And later, it became a tool of the opposition when my party forced them underground. It was a popular waltz by a Roa musician; Andreas could play it for Irena from across the city and no one would bat an eye. But she knew. I think I did too. Since yesterday, that song has been broadcast across the city on a frequency that has been jammed since Andreas died. She's in the city, is she not? She found his transmitter?"

"I don't know." This time, Beo was only telling the truth. "Truly, I do not know."

Samson frowned. "I cannot be sure if you are lying to me or not."

"Believe me or not, I don't care." Beo swallowed. *Rose.* "If it's true that you care for Rose, help me find her and make certain she is safe."

Samson gave a small smile, a wistful smile, turning his head as if he heard something Beo could not. "I'm afraid I'm in no position to do such a thing at present. Though I hope that you will believe me, nephew, when I say that I wish I were."

Nephew.

Beo opened his mouth, but whatever he had been about to say vanished into the sound of pounding footsteps and the crash of the bedroom door splintering off its hinges.

A tall woman Beo had seen before strode into the room, clothed in all black and flanked by a dozen others with semiautomatic rifles. Taran Marpaxan, the leader of Liberation Front.

"Rico Samson," said the woman. "You are to be executed for crimes against the citizens of Kael."

She looked over at Beo, eyes lighting for a moment with surprise, then, deciding he was no threat, turned back to Samson.

"Taran," Rico said, the wistful smile still ghosting about his lips. "Hello."

CHAPTER THIRTY-FIVE

"He was in that autocar, I saw him!" Rose shouted. "With Samson!"

"Rose, calm down." A few others in the room looked up. Maro held up a hand as if he were about to place it on Rose's injured left shoulder, and she slapped it away with her left hand.

She instantly regretted the action for the pain that shot up to her shoulder, but there was little an angry person resented more than being told to calm down.

"I believe you," said Emon. "Whatever you need to do, I'll be with you."

Rose nodded to Emon gratefully, but it wasn't Emon she needed to convince. Irena was across the room speaking to another Liberation Front member.

"You are wasting time," Rose said, taking care to modulate her volume.

"We can't stop in the middle of a revolution to save one person. I'm sorry." Maro put his hands up. "You don't even know where Samson took him, if Beo was in that autocar at all."

"I know what I saw."

"The street was chaotic, and you're injured."

"Gods damn it, Maro, I'm right."

Irena glanced over her shoulder and turned toward Rose. Her scarf no longer covered her face, and everyone in the small room seemed somewhat in awe of her. She strode to them, her left hand clenching and releasing at her side. She was a walking storm.

"They will not help me," she said. "Follow if you wish."

Rose cast one anguished look back at Maro, who gave her a helpless shrug. Rose and Emon followed Irena out of the small room into a smaller corridor, where it was quieter.

"You are certain you saw Beo in that autocar." Irena looked at Rose with the intensity of the sun.

"I have never been so certain of anything." *Except that we need to get Beo back.* "He was with Samson. By now they could be anywhere."

"I think not," said Irena. She beckoned to Rose and Emon to follow her.

Outside, the air stunk of gunpowder and death. Rose tried not to look at the pair of legs she saw sticking out behind a rubbish bin.

A Liberation Front autocar sat on the kerb.

"Tell me right now if you want to stay here," Irena said, looking back and forth. The people had scattered from the city centre. For all the thousands who had obeyed Samson's order, the streets of central Sanmarian were deserted except for the fighting and the dead.

"I want to save Beo," said Rose at the same time Emon said, "I'll go wherever you go."

Irena jerked her chin at the autocar. "Get in."

Rose didn't think, only obeyed, sliding into the front seat with Emon beside her.

Irena reached under the steering wheel. The ignition buttons sat to the right, but Irena did not punch in the sequence to start the autocar. Instead, she felt around beneath the metal until her fingers found what she was searching for. She yanked, and a handful of wires came out. Four were attached to the ignition buttons.

"Irena," said Emon, alarmed. "Do you know how to do that?"

"My papa was a mechanic," Irena said. She pulled a pocket knife from her coat pocket and stripped the coating at the base where the four wires connected. Within seconds, the engine hummed to life.

There was a muffled shout from the building they had just left, but Irena ignored it. She put the autocar in gear and pulled away from the kerb, pulling on the acceleration lever hard enough that the vehicle jumped forward.

"Let's hope they don't decide we're better off dead," Emon said, but his tone was almost joyful. Rose smiled at him through gritted teeth as the autocar hit a bump.

"Where are we going?" Rose asked.

"I know exactly where Rico would go."

• • • • •

The streets were near empty, but Irena immediately pulled the autocar off the main thoroughfares and instead chose back streets. Somewhere in the city, a clock announced tenth bell.

"Rico and I lived in a villa just north of the city," Irena said. "His family was very wealthy; mine was very poor. His parents both died of consumption just after we were married, and his father hadn't had the time to disinherit him. We lived in their house until he began to rise in party ranks, and he took a set of apartments in the fortress. I often stayed at the villa."

"How do you know he would go there tonight?" Rose asked.

"How are you so certain Beo was in Rico's autocar?"

"That's different," said Rose.

"You believe because you saw him. I believe because I knew Rico for twenty years. We both have our evidence."

"You still mean to kill him." Emon shifted his weight on the bench seat, taking Rose's right hand almost absently.

Irena didn't answer that.

She drove through the streets as if the map of Sanmarian were the same as the map of her veins. Rose squeezed Emon's hand.

"We'll find him," she said.

"I know."

Sanmarian was built on the edge of a cliff that stretched north and south both until the sea swept around the peninsula. There wasn't a beach for an hour's drive in any direction, but wealthy landowners had built villas along the mournful cliffs for centuries.

Ocantilaxo Road ran the length of the cliff for a score of kilometres, studded by privacy trees to the northeast and olive groves to the southwest of the road. A pair of enormous ironwoods guarded a turnoff, and it was there Irena steered the autocar to the right, through the gateway of those trees and toward the bluff to the north.

There were no lamps to light the way, only the headlamps of the autocar.

"Is it strange?" Rose asked softly. "Coming back here, I mean."

"Yes," Irena said.

That was all she said.

After several minutes, they came to an enormous fountain with a cobbled driveway circling it. The sound of splashing water joined with the sound of the autocar's engine. Beyond the fountain was one of the largest villas Rose had ever seen. The shiny black autocar sat between the fountain and the house.

"You were right," Emon said, and Rose wasn't sure if he was talking to Irena or to her.

Rose peered into the darkness outside the autocar as Irena pulled up behind the fountain.

"Irena," Rose said. "We're not the only ones who were right."

· · · · ·

Beside the villa was an NPV lorry, the exact type that had paraded the prisoners through the streets of Sanmarian.

"I don't suppose Samson would store those here, would he?" Emon asked.

Irena pulled her revolver out. "We'll move in slowly and quietly. If there are guards, and they see us, they will likely take us directly to Samson anyway."

That did not sound like the best plan to Rose, but she could not think of a better one.

The front door of the villa was locked. Irena nodded to the side of the house where the lorry was parked. "There is another door."

"You have a key to my flat, but not to your own home?"

"I never intended to come back here," she said.

The implication was that she had intended to return to Rose's—Aleis's—flat. Rose wondered why.

The garden door on the side of the house had a slate path leading away from it. It was strange to Rose to see a home made of something other than sunset stone; the villa was made of ivory stucco and red clay roofing tiles that formed rounded gables. Ivy climbed the side of the house, leafless for winter.

Rose could hear no noise from the inside of the house. The aspirin she had taken had long since worn off, and her shoulder felt hot and swollen, pressing against the sleeve of her shirt. The shirt fit her loosely. She tried not to think of how much her arm must have grown in size for the sleeve to be uncomfortably tight.

Irena depressed the latch on the side door, and it moved easily under her thumb. The door swung open silently on well-oiled hinges.

"Where would he be?" Rose asked.

"Beo is injured," said Emon. "Unless he has already killed him, Beo would need somewhere to lie down. Or Samson could have put him in a dungeon again."

"Rico has no dungeon," Irena murmured. "I hear footsteps above us, in Rico's bedroom."

Irena led the way to the servants' staircase. Rose had never seen so fine a house; the servant passageway had more ornate detail on its frescoed walls than one of the luxury wardrobes Helyne sometimes crafted for the wealthy. The climb to the first floor was skirted by a pastoral scene of the cliffs outside, an olive grove with the Tarenr Sea beyond.

"I hear voices," Emon whispered. "Up ahead."

"They are in Rico's bedroom." Irena stopped in the corridor, eyes closed to listen. "I can't tell how many there are."

"Those lorries held at least twenty prisoners," said Rose softly. "Your revolver does not hold anywhere close to twenty bullets, and I see no other guns."

She didn't mention that she had no practice with shooting anyway; Rose thought she would be more effective with her bruised fist, which had turned purple since using it to knock Tomas unconscious.

The voices in the room grew louder, and Rose started forward, her heart leaping.

"Rose, wait!" Emon caught her right arm.

"I know that voice," she said. "It's Taran Marpaxan."

• • • • •

Emon dropped her sleeve, and Rose had to convince herself not to run down the corridor toward Beo. An image of him dead on Samson's bed intruded into her mind. She tried to snuff it out. No. He was alive.

He had to be alive.

Forever I will find you.

Rose did the only thing in her power with a gunshot wound and a bruised fist. She raised her voice.

"Taran Marpaxan! It's Rose Abernethy. We're coming into the room. Please"—her voice caught on the word, almost gasping with a sudden shock of terror—"please don't shoot us."

Someone gave a sharp order, but Rose couldn't hear it.

Heavy footsteps approached, and a moment later, Marpaxan came into the corridor, a rifle in her hand.

Rose thought she could go the rest of her life without looking down the barrel of another gun. She could not have told anyone what she felt in that moment, but she could only imagine how pleading and desperate she must look.

Taran Marpaxan lowered the gun.

"We won't shoot," she said, "but you better have an excellent explanation of how you found out we were here."

"We didn't," said Rose. "We came to rescue Beo from his uncle."

Marpaxan assessed her, then nodded. "These people are under my protection unless they do something stupid."

She did not seem surprised that Beo was Rico Samson's nephew, nor did she seem perturbed by the fact. She looked over Rose's shoulder and made eye contact with Irena.

Rose happened to turn at that exact moment, saw the disbelief on Irena's face just before it faded into recognition and understanding. Marpaxan gave her a wry look, then beckoned them into the room.

Granted leave to not get shot again, Rose dashed into the bedroom with Emon close behind.

There.

On the bed.

His forehead was bruised and bandaged, and his lower lip swelled on one side. But he was alive, and he was Beo.

No one had to ask. Emon climbed onto the opposite side of the bed, and Rose the closest.

They were alive. They were together. It didn't matter where they were. Rose was home.

· · · · ·

Rose couldn't speak. She pressed her lips against Beo's temple. His skin was hot and feverish.

His eyes found hers, and Rose wept. "We found you," she said.

Beo's right hand sought out Emon's, his fingers interlacing with the other man's. Rose met Emon's gaze and smiled through her tears. He leaned over and kissed her gently on the cheek.

A dozen pairs of eyes were on them. Had anyone said anything in that moment, Rose thought she would have damned her already-bruised knuckles and punched them too. No one did.

Perhaps, she realised a moment later, there was a reason why.

Beo's eyes had gone to the doorway, and Irena stepped through.

The Liberation Front guards—or soldiers, Rose could not tell the difference on a day like this one—were mostly large people, men and women who had trained their muscles to fight. Compared to them, Irena was almost waifish.

And yet, when she entered Rico Samson's bedroom under the gaze of fifteen people and two warring party leaders, she held every ounce of power there.

Rose had not looked at him yet, had not been sure she could bring herself to do so. She looked then, tearing her eyes away from Irena to seek out the man Irena had fled so many years before.

Rico Samson closed his eyes, something like relief on his face.

"It does me good to see you alive, Irena," he said.

"It's not for you that I am." Her quiet voice invaded every corner of the room.

"I know."

His acceptance of her statement seemed to take Taran Marpaxan aback. She leaned on a bookshelf, seemingly content to watch whatever would happen play out.

"I'm sorry," Rico said.

"It's too late for that." Irena crossed the room and stood two metres from him.

"I know."

Irena's gaze turned to Beo, and she did not smile, but Rose saw the relief writ in her face. Rose lay another kiss on Beo's forehead and felt him lean into her.

"What have you done, Rico?" Irena asked him sadly. "I never thought you would grow to believe the poison of this party. What have you done?"

Rico chuckled, a bitter sound. He looked past his wife to Taran Marpaxan, who raised a cynical eyebrow as if waiting to see what yarn he would spin from the past fifteen years of thread.

"I don't believe it," he said finally. "I did, for a time. Andreas's death cured me of that."

Rose started, and she felt Emon's arm reach around Beo's shoulders to touch her right arm. Beo squeezed Rose's hand a little tighter.

Beo looked up at her as if to ask, *do you know?*

Rose could do nothing but nod.

"Bullshit," Marpaxan said. "You believed it then, and you believe it now."

But Irena shook her head, her gaze clear even if one iris was clouded. "Fifteen years, Rico."

"I don't believe it. How could I? It destroyed my life."

"How many lives have you destroyed?" The ache in Irena's voice was beyond anything Rose's swelling shoulder could fathom. "How many families? How many loves? For fifteen years you have worked for the aims of the NPV, led them for ten. It does not matter whether you believe the poison you have injected into this city and this country, Rico. Their lies and pseudoscience may be false, but the harm you have done is not. That is your legacy."

Where before, Samson had responded with his quiet admission of guilt, this time Irena's words seemed to flail him like a cat-o'-nine-tails. He flinched under the barrage of her declarations.

"Today alone," Irena said. She looked at Beo. "My nephew could have died because of you."

"I didn't know he was your nephew."

"Each person who died today was someone's nephew! Or their son or daughter or parent. But their worth was not in who they were to others, Rico Vitar, their worth was in who they *were*. They were each of them people. What you have done to this city is tell them that some lives are worthier of living than others. You have enabled the worst kind of fury, the kind of fury based solely in fear of those who are different, and you have aimed it at some of the most vulnerable among us. The Roa, who came here after being exterminated in their homeland. People like Taran, who you call *impure*. People like Beo and Emon who you call deviant. People like me, Rico! People like you!" Irena's anger was far more than fifteen years in the making, and it poured out of her like cleansing fire. "You—and the NPV—were so blind with your hatred that you did not stop to consider that you could be hating people you loved."

Rico Samson sat silent under the barrage of her words, his throat convulsing and wetness forming at the corners of his eyes even though no tears yet spilled over his cheeks.

"Andreas loved you," Irena went on, relentless. "He kept that watch you gave him until he died. He wrote it into that blasted book. I don't know how Aleis got it—"

"She was with him," Rico said dully. "Aleis was with Andreas when he—when the guards killed him. He must have told her to give Rosenni the watch."

Rose didn't know why, but for some reason when Rico said those words, he looked at Beo before looking at Rose. It took a moment for Rico's words to sink in.

The night came flooding back to her. Aleis's hollow words, the way she pressed the watch into Rose's fingers. It had smelled of rubbing alcohol, and Rose had never understood why. The sudden image of her great aunt painstakingly cleaning Papa's watch of blood was almost too much for Rose to bear.

How she must have known as she worked just how close she had been to death herself. Rose remembered the way Grenye held her tight that night, one of the only hugs the woman had ever given her.

"You loved my Papa," Rose blurted out. In that moment, she was fifteen years old again, the impression of the rising sun on the pocket watch embedded into the palm of her hand.

"I was wrong," Rico said, and at first Rose thought he meant for loving Andreas, and she almost flew at him. But he went on. "You are so like your father, child. You are as brave as he ever was, and far, far braver than I. I cannot make it right. I don't even deserve the chance to try."

"Stop it," Irena said. "You are not a martyr, Rico. You have made yourself the villain of this city."

"Which brings us to why we are here in the first place," Marpaxan said, straightening.

"Do what you must," Rico said.

"Wait," said Rose.

Every pair of eyes in the room turned to look at her.

She kissed Beo once more and slid off the side of the bed. Her arm felt like a hot water bottle inside her coat, and she had not noticed till then that she had begun to perspire.

"You plan to execute him," Rose said. "Here?"

Marpaxan was silent for a moment. "Not here, no."

"You have just taken over the city, am I correct?"

"Yes."

"How do you plan to be any different from the NPV if you begin the same way they ended?"

Rose's words hung in the air, heavy and ponderous, and the Liberation Front soldiers in the room shifted under the weight of them.

"He deserves to die," said Marpaxan finally.

"He deserves the consequences of his actions," said Beo from the bed. "There is a difference, and no one in this room is the correct person to decide what those are."

Emon, thus far silently watching with tears in his eyes, nodded.

"Do you want justice, Taran Marpaxan?" Rose asked. "Or do you want vengeance?"

Marpaxan, oddly, looked at Irena. She appeared to think for a long moment, and something passed between the two women that Rose could not guess at.

Marpaxan motioned to her people. "Take him to the gaol at the fortress. Not," she looked at Beo, "to the dungeon. He will await trial for his crimes."

Her face said that it would likely be some time before anything was in place to try him. Rico stood and held himself upright.

Before they led him away, he looked at Rose, his eyes asking a question of Irena and the Liberation Front soldiers. They released his arms for a moment.

Rico pulled the watch from his front pocket, his left pocket. The same pocket Rose had ever kept it in. He reached out to her with a tentative hand until Rose, her heart beating as fast as a caged bird's wings against bars, could muster the strength to take it from him.

"I am sorry," Rico said. And then to Beo, "These things are my fault. What you told me, however, is not yours, nephew. The past is not the future. That is a lesson I ought to have learned long before now."

Rose could not answer, feeling Andreas Abernethy's watch—Rico Samson's watch—warming to the skin of her palm. When she looked at Beo, he could find no words either.

CHAPTER THIRTY-SIX

The longest night, it was called. And it was, in truth, from sundown to sun-up, but to Beomir Mataya it felt as if it took the entirety of a year.

Taran Marpaxan had her guards transport Rico Samson to the gaol, as she had said, and next she had insisted upon bringing Rose and Beo to the infirmary at the fortress, which Liberation Front had taken over hours before.

In spite of being unconscious twice in one day, Beo's injuries were not severe. Rose, on the other hand, had to be sedated for the physician to clean the bullet wound in her arm, which had already become infected.

"Bacteria from clothing sometimes gets in with the bullet," the physician said. "She'll keep the arm, though she'll have the injury long as she lives."

Rose woke from her half-drowse sometime early in the dark of morning, her eyes puffy and frantic until she looked over to see Beo in his bed, awake and smiling at her, and Emon asleep in the chair between them.

Two beds over from his own and Rose's was a familiar face. Ani had awoken when they were brought in, and though she did not speak so as not to disturb the other patients, her face when she met Beo's eyes said she was grateful for the very stupid thing he had done.

Beo found he could not sleep.

He slid from his bed and shuffled out the door, Rose drowsing beside him and Emon sleeping in silence as well.

Irena was in the corridor. Someone had dragged in a very opulent chair that looked out of place on the sterile infirmary hardwood, and Irena was quite small enough to curl up in it. She opened her eyes as soon as she heard the door swing.

"You should be sleeping," she said.

"What are you doing up?"

"I was catching up with Taran Marpaxan."

Beo started. "You know her?"

"I did, long ago. She was once an NPV guard."

"But she is a woman. They don't let women in as guards."

"Ah, yes. Well. I think she had not quite admitted that to herself at that time." Irena paused, her face holding the kind of amusement that accompanied one surprise too many. "The NPV would not have welcomed such self-knowledge. I am glad she found her way."

Beo was silent for a time, and then he asked what he needed to ask, his voice melding to the predawn quiet. "Why did you never tell me?"

Irena pressed her lips together, as if she knew the question had been long overdue but had hoped it might hold off a bit longer.

"Shame," she said. "I lost my entire family to marry Rico. Your mother hated him for his wealth, said he would never understand our lives. But he was kind, and he always tried. When I came back and she had passed, I thought I was being punished."

"It's a family trait, I think," said Beo. He thought of Samson's words to him. "But you don't get to be the martyr any more than your husband does, Irena. You should have told me."

"Would you have listened?"

Beo coughed a laugh that hurt his head. "You saw the book and how many times I read it. You told me in that way. Had you told me that story was true?"

"It's not true, Beo."

"Perhaps not factually, in whole, but it is true. It is one of the truest things I've ever read or seen."

"Why do you say that?"

"Something Rico said before they took him to gaol—the past is not the future."

Irena smiled then. "Andreas used to say that. He was an engineer with a penchant for physics—did Rose ever tell you that?"

"Not yet," said Beo. "What else did Andreas say?"

"His actual thoughts on time were much longer than a pithy statement," Irena said. "But because it's almost morning, I'll try to sum up. He said that there was harm in fearing the future when we felt the present resembled the past. He would say that every variable is different now, and there is statistically no way to repeat the exact circumstances that caused us pain in the past. We have to trust whatever lessons we learn from it and try to build a better future."

Beo liked that.

The door swung open, and Rose's mussed curls appeared through it. "Beo?"

"I'm right here."

She slipped out of the door, Emon behind her mid-yawn. Rose's left arm was bound in a sling to her torso, and she winced.

"If the three of you are serious about not resting, there's a place I'd like to show you. You can greet the dawn, if you like."

"That's the most romantic thing I've ever heard you say," said Beo.

"I won't let it happen again."

Irena led them through the hallways of the fortress, out of the infirmary and into the living quarters, past familiar-looking doors and through an open courtyard to a glass atrium that reminded Beo of the dome atop Sanmarian's temple.

It was warm in the atrium, warmer at least than outside by a fair bit. But Irena didn't stop there. At the far side of the atrium, there was a spiral staircase leading up.

"Go to the top," she said. "Don't tell the physicians I told you to climb stairs."

"Your secret's safe," said Emon.

Irena looked at the three of them with something like reserved hope, if there was such a thing.

Up they climbed, no one speaking, whether out of suppressed pain or sheer exhaustion.

At the top was a glass dome, misted over from the sea's spray and facing east, where the sky had begun to lighten to grey.

They stood there for a long while in silence, watching the slow return of light to the winter world.

"You beat the bulls," Emon said finally. "Does that mean you will have ten years of luck?"

"It better," Beo said. "I'll share if I get it."

Rose smiled, leaning against the rail by a door that opened onto a balcony. She leaned on her right side, and Beo noticed her grimace when she moved.

"You didn't tell me how that happened," Beo said. Going to her side, he gently ran his fingers along her collarbone, trailing off before he reached her injured shoulder.

Rose gave him a bewildered, startled look, then put her face in her good hand. Emon shifted his weight as if to say, *You tell him.*

"Irena shot me," she said.

"What?"

"Irena shot me," Rose repeated. "Papa and Irena used to meet secretly at my flat, which was Aunt Aleis's then. She still had a key and thought Aleis lived there. Emon and I came in, she didn't know who we were, and she shot me."

"I thought she was a better shot. Maybe you have Larsi's luck." Irena used to hunt hares around Viyarenyo, not as much since Beo was in school, but she had always had a good mark.

"I recognised her," said Rose. "From the photograph. I called her by name, and she...adjusted her aim."

"She shot you on purpose."

"I don't really blame her."

Rose had stopped Rico Samson's execution with her words alone, and Beo caught himself before voicing what he thought. He had been about to say that he didn't deserve her, or Emon, who had stayed by Rose's side since the galleria. Beo promised himself right there that he would strike the word *deserve* from his vocabulary.

Instead, he changed the subject. "Irena was telling me about your Papa," he said. "About what he said about time." Beo repeated it as best as he could remember, and Rose shook her head.

"Papa was a scientist and an artist both." She paused, and all three of them knew she was thinking of *Red Sunrise*. "He used to say that people think of time as a line, like a river or a road, but that it's wrong. We think of it as just forward, but it's really more than that. We exist in our pasts, because we were there. We still feel the time that is no longer. We exist there. We exist in the swiftly passing present. And we exist in all the shining possibilities of our futures. Time is more than a line, and we experience far more than time alone. A line is only one dimension, and we exist in four."

Beo considered the book that Andreas Abernethy had written—his own past, present, and future—and he thought Andreas would be proud, to see what they had wrought of it.

"What will happen to Rico?" Emon asked. "Perhaps I oughtn't pity him, but I do. How he must have hated himself for so long, to do what he has done. What was he talking about when he left, Beo?"

Beo knew he could brush it off, shut those conversations with Rico Samson into a corner of himself and never open them again.

"A few years ago, I loved a woman called Zara. She abused me, and when I said I wanted to end our relationship, she threatened to kill herself. I stayed for a time, until I couldn't any longer. The day after I broke off our relationship, I found her hanging from my kitchen ceiling." Beo got those words out, but for some reason the rest felt stubbornly lodged somewhere deep in his chest, under his ribs where his heart lived. "When the NPV took me, I knew I was going to die. I thought I deserved to. Rico asked me why, and I told him I killed Zara."

"But you—" Emon started, but he stopped himself before he went any further.

"What Rico said when he left, that it wasn't my fault, that's what he meant."

Rose's face held no pity, and for that Beo was thankful. Instead, her features were lit with concern. "Do you believe him?"

"I don't know," Beo said honestly.

"I do," Rose said, and Emon nodded.

Emon put his arm about Beo's shoulders, and Beo took Rose in his arms. Together they stood that way, watching the sun paint the sky.

CHAPTER THIRTY-SEVEN

For all the silence, Rose's mind was loud.

There was no certainty in the coming dawn, and nothing she knew would be the same after the night.

Aunt Aleis, Helyne, and Grenye could come back from wherever they had gone—Taran Marpaxan had promised to find out, if she could, when questioning Rico—but Rose wouldn't blame them if they wanted to stay away for a time, or forever. The same went for Amelie, who Rose hoped had escaped the city. Marpaxan said that Liberation Front had conducted similar operations in other Kaeli cities, where the NPV was in control but not yet as extreme. Rose trusted that her friend was smart enough to take precautions. She wouldn't know for some time what had happened, and she would have to check to find out what had befallen Tomas. Rose knew he would not be happy that she had punched him.

She thought of her father's letters, hidden away in her wardrobe cubby. Rose would make sure they reached Irena's hands. Rico had given Rose the watch once more, Rico's watch that Papa had carried with him until death.

Perhaps the letters were not only for Irena.

As she thought it, she flexed her hand and cringed.

Beo tightened his hold on her waist, careful not to jostle her bound left arm.

Rose turned her head to look at both of them.

"What is it?" Emon asked.

"I'm thinking about uncertainty," said Rose. "And the three of us."

"The past is not the future," Beo said.

Rose frowned. "What do you mean?"

"Rico poisoned everything he loved because he hated himself," said Beo. "I could see myself in him, and it terrified me."

"You're not Rico Samson," Rose murmured.

"I know." Beo appeared to be struggling with something. "After Zara, I felt like I had been hollowed out inside. I wasn't sure I was capable of loving anyone again. No. That's not it."

"Loving is easy," Emon said. "It's accepting that someone else can love you sometimes that feels impossible."

Beo let out a breath, and Rose felt the movement of his chest against her back. Her wounded arm gave her a pang. She ignored it.

"If you'd been anyone but who you are, this love wouldn't have lasted beyond first sight, Beo," Rose said softly. Her eyes met Emon's, and he smiled.

"It's okay," he said. "Wherever we go, we go."

"I know." Rose smiled back at him. She couldn't predict what would happen, but with them, she felt like she had found her home. "What I mean is that none of what we feel—between any of us—it's not any less real for how quickly it began. Unless it is to you. It's not to me."

"It's real," Beo said, and Emon nodded.

"I couldn't have gotten through the past few days without either of you," Rose said. "I don't know if I'm the author of this story or if I'm just a character, and I don't know if we're the heroes or just secondaries passing through each other's lives. I don't know how it ends, just that I don't want it to end yet. I know I want you in every chapter. I want you on every page. In every word and between the ink's lines. As long as we all want that, I do."

Beo looked out through the window, and Rose could feel him pull both herself and Emon tighter to him. His eyes glowed like amber. Rose thought if he never stopped looking at her, she would begin to glow too, and that her body would fill with that glow until she shone bright enough to turn night to day.

She reached out and took Emon's hand in hers as the first rays of the returning dawn touched the Tarenr Sea with starlight.

And as the sun rose red over the pink city skyline, Rose turned, Beo's and Emon's silhouettes visible in her periphery. They would rebuild Sanmarian. Somehow, they would rebuild their families and themselves. As the sun touched them with molten gold, they were together, and they were love. They lived in the dawning day, the promise of thousands more in their eyes, and around them their world lay awash in colour.

AUTHOR'S NOTE

Dear Reader,

I wrote this book in the lead-up to the 2016 US presidential election when I was still living in the United States, just outside DC. When I was at university, I studied the rise of far-right politics in a post-WWII world alongside my studies of the Holocaust, much of which I did on-site in Kraków and Oświęcim, Poland on exchange with the Międzywidziałowe Indywidualne Studia Humanistyczne (MISH) program at the Jagiellonian University. In that context, I bore witness to the early stages of precisely one such rising.

I participated in counterprotests against far-right groups, including one where I happened upon a pair of Jewish students from Israel who were visiting the concentration camps in remembrance—and they happened to be in Kraków the day there was a march of the radical nationalists who performed Nazi salutes on the street as they marched.

That moment has never left me. It would take a soul without compassion to fail to see the danger there and the feelings those kids, whose elders died in the Holocaust, had at seeing Nazi salutes in 2007 Poland sixty years later. We say "never forget," but too many have already forgotten.

That day, the march was only about three hundred strong—the counterprotest was nearly as big—but just a few short years ago, that same group marched again in Warsaw with numbers in the tens of thousands.

Look to the Sun is a book that came out of a very particular experience of seeing and recognising a dangerous far-right populism emerge in the country of my birth. While I am not Jewish, I am queer, autistic, and non-binary. As I write this today in 2021, just three weeks ago, that far-right movement staged an insurrection in the US Capitol Building as elected officials were doing their oath-sworn duties to facilitate a peaceful and democratic transfer of power.

I watched from Scotland in real time, seeing tweets from journalists and lawmakers inside the Capitol Building reporting the sound of gunshots, of teargas deployed in the rotunda, and I saw pictures of insurrectionists wearing shirts that said "Six Million Wasn't Enough" and "Camp Auschwitz: Work Makes You Free" (the English translation of the infamous sign at the Auschwitz death camp that reads Arbeit Macht Frei in German).

I think much of America has not yet reckoned with just how close they came to watching the live execution of American-elected officials on Twitter. All that stood between Vice President Mike Pence and a crowd chanting "Hang Mike Pence" were sixty short seconds and one human being called Eugene Goodman, who, upon seeing that the door to the senate chamber was not secure, risked his life as a Black man to goad white supremacists into following him away from a room still filled with lawmakers.

I would like to also mention that for many members of Congress who regularly get death threats and worse (women like Alexandria Ocasio-Cortez and Nancy Pelosi and Ayanna Pressley and countless others), that day was one where they each thought, with every possible reason, that their lives were actively in danger. They were.

Imagine how it would feel to be a Jewish member of congress hiding from insurrectionists, seeing through social media that they are carrying symbols of your people's genocide, when your *children* came with you to work to see democracy in action and instead were greeted by an attempted coup. That is reality for Rep. Jamie Raskin of Maryland, who brought his family that day, made even more heartbreaking by the fact that barely a week before, they had lost a son and brother to suicide. Fascism has—and has always had—violent goals in mind, and those who know they are targets can never safely forget it.

It is a terrifying dichotomy to support healthcare and education and fair compensation for all and know that, in turn, there are people who want to put you before the firing squad. That is a fundamental incompatibility, and it is one that cannot be reconciled by "bothsidesism." There is no acceptable middle ground between "I want every human being to exist in peace and security" and "certain people deserve to die, and we decide who." Democratic institutions, as we have seen for the past five years, are only ever as strong as the people who make them up. What is happening in the US today in 2021 is not over. It is ongoing.

While it may seem strange to accompany a work of fiction with a long note about politics, *Look to the Sun* is inherently a book of political fiction. In my book, the fascists have already won. And here's the kicker: life goes on for a while…until it doesn't. Eventually, we all have to decide what to do with the time given to us and what violence we can tolerate being done to our neighbours. My book isn't about revolutionaries; it is about survivors.

There have been many think pieces that seek to "humanise" the people who invaded the US Capitol, and before that, did the same with the Nazis from Charlottesville and others. Each of those pieces misses the fundamental point while skirting very close to it: they are indeed human beings with lives and dogs and jobs you wouldn't blink at. But that is the entire point. There are no monsters; there are only human beings who choose to do monstrous things. That is the crux of the danger.

Ashli Babbitt may have been nominally polite to the white man who sat next to her on the plane on the way to an insurrection, but she also gleefully retweeted calls to reinstate the firing squad to execute "traitors"—and in a fascist mob, a traitor is anyone who gets in their way. Just ask Mike Pence, a staunch, far-right Republican. The world of Kael is not the United States. It's not Scotland or Poland or anywhere else. But when I wrote this book, it was out of a need to believe that it isn't too late. That ideals are important.

Though I emigrated from the United States with no plan or desire to return, I want to believe in the American ideal of liberty and justice for all. But "all" means every, and this ideal has yet to be realised anywhere, let alone in the country that enshrined it into its collective psyche. Justice is work. It is action and the continued movement away from injustice. It takes an enormous amount of collective will, and without justice, there is no liberty. America has spent a long time focusing on the individual—but no human since the dawn of time has ever survived purely on their own. We *need* each other. We need community and mutual aid, and we will not survive the coming tide of climate change without a shift in our collective consciousness toward that interdependence and reciprocal reliance.

My hope for you is that you leave Sanmarian feeling that change is possible, and like Beo and Rose and Emon, you are willing to work for it.

In hope,
Emmie Mears

ABOUT THE AUTHOR

Emmie Mears is the author of over ten adult fantasy novels, including *A Hall of Keys and No Doors*, the Ayala Storme series, and the Stonebreaker series.

Their bilingual work as M. Evan MacGriogair can be found on Tor.com, *Steall Magazine*, and *Uncanny Magazine* along with poetry in *The Poets' Republic* and elsewhere. Their novelette *Seonag and the Sea-wolves* was longlisted for a Hugo award in 2020.

An autistic queer author, singer, and artist who sings and writes in Gàidhlig and in English, they sing in two Gaelic choirs both in Scotland and internationally, and they are an award-winning Gaelic solo singer. They live in Partick with two cats and dreams gu leòr.